The RPG Apocalypse

Jeremy Chambless

Published by Level Up in the United Kingdom in 2021

Cover illustration by Sippakorn Upama
Cover by Claire Wood

ISBN: 978-1-83919-379-8

www.levelup.pub

Jeremy Chambless was born in Deerfield Beach, Florida and studied Psychology at Florida Atlantic University. Gaming has always been a part of his household: as far back as he can remember, he was holding a NES controller. His own gaming passion has been focused on MMOs and RPGs. Jeremy is an avid LitRPG reader turned writer. A love for RPGs sparked his desire to create *The RPG Apocalypse*.

Chapter 1: It Begins

A constant banging beat against the wall of my room and also my brain. The creaking of a bed continuously pierced my eardrums.

"Argh, will you keep it down?" My open palm slammed on the wall as I shouted to the two on the other side. Unsurprisingly, the noise continued unhindered as if I had said nothing at all. *Tch, just because you put a sock on your door handle doesn't give you the right to make such a ruckus!* The only way to get any peace and quiet was to bury my head in my pillow and squeeze my ears.

College life really wasn't at all how my family had portrayed it would be. I had been coerced into living in the dorms. "Joseph, just think about how much fun you'll have! All the new friends you'll make, the girls you'll meet. I'm sure it will be a blast. You're eighteen and this will be the most memorable year of your life!" Or so I was told.

The reality couldn't have been more different.

Having a roommate had turned out to be terrible. My roomie, the Slob, as I liked to call him, had zero respect: for me or himself. Not only did he not pickup after himself, he had no boundaries. He ate my food and invited his friends over without so much as a courtesy heads up. They always created one hell of a ruckus that kept me from studying. I was quite miserable.

I blindly reached for my nightstand and ran my hand along it. I grasped and grasped until I felt the cool plastic case and knew I'd found my phone. It was eleven-thirty. I had an hour and thirty minutes before class. I should probably have gotten up and showered and at least started getting ready, but I had no motivation to even get out of bed.

A question popped into my head that had been visiting me daily. What was the point of it all? College was a means to an end, but even that end wasn't exciting. Life was dull. Couldn't I have some excitement for just one day of my life?

The banging on my wall reached a crescendo and I couldn't help but groan in disgust. My neighbor's most private and intimate moment was broadcast through my wall quite clearly. The reality of it all reinforced just how miserable I really was.

As the banging and creaking stopped I let the pillow fall from my ears and stared up at the ceiling. I could hear the rustling as the two fumbled to get dressed.

"Don't catch feelings," the girl said.

"Not a problem."

How romantic. My attention shifted to my own room; the bed across from me was empty. I guessed the Slob had enjoyed another late-night. The one solace was that he avoided bringing girls over.

I squirreled out of bed and barely managed to catch myself before falling. I didn't even feel like moving but I knew if I stayed in bed any longer that would be the end result of my entire day. The showers were relatively empty and I snuck to the far end unnoticed. The warm water let me know I was alive, and I took my sweet time.

The towel I grabbed was already damp and I couldn't help but sigh. *Why couldn't people be considerate?* You could bring your own towel, but the University also provided them for you. I reached out until I managed to grab a clean towel and wipe myself down. I wrapped myself up and headed back to my room.

After getting fully dressed, I took a bit of time to do my hair so I didn't look as bedraggled as I felt inside. If there was anything I'd learned it was to always be presentable. Opportunity was always knocking: a phrase my father coined and which I liked to say to myself multiple times a week.

There were ten minutes to kill before I needed to leave. I opened my laptop and signed into my email. The due date for my term paper had been announced. I grabbed my red marker and flipped the page of my calendar before circling the date. The lid of my laptop closed with a snap and I slipped it into my backpack.

"Get to safety if you wish to survive."

Huh? A voice came over the intercom, or maybe it wasn't the intercom. I couldn't tell as it sounded as if it had been spoken directly into my ear. I opened the blinds behind my desk and peered out onto the breezeway. Everyone seemed to have stopped moving and I could see several people looking around in confusion.

Was someone playing a crude joke?

"Ten. Nine. Eight. Seven…"

This time I confirmed the noise wasn't coming from the intercom but was being transmitted to me directly. There was a commotion in the dorm-room.

"Did you hear that?"

"Six. Five. Four."

"What the hell is going on?"

"Three. Two. One."

By now I was thoroughly freaked out and people had started to run from the breezeway. The situation outside was becoming quite hectic.

"And so it begins."

I continued to look outside as a blinding light began to shine down all over the school grounds. People started running for cover. *Could this be a terrorist attack?* The light seemed to avoid buildings and simply touched down on concrete or grass.

Once the light faded, beings began materializing as if being warped or spawned in. At first the view was incredibly blurry. It took a few moments before the figures became clearer: almost as if they were originally translucent. My hand clenched the blinds tightly as I realized what they were.

Kobolds, goblins, ghouls and other creatures simply spawned out of thin air. Those were the names I assigned them from creatures I'd only seen in games and cartoons. They remained stationary as the people outside stared at them in utter shock. Once the monsters were fully material, they began charging at the humans around them.

The kobolds and goblins wielded small weapons such as hammers and axes; a few had daggers and swords. The kobolds looked like walking dogs. The fur of their body was light blue, except for their chest: their chest was white fur from neck to crotch. Their mouths let out little yips and barks as they rushed around.

The goblins were smaller than the kobolds. Their skin was green and sleek, almost as if the sun would reflect perfectly off their bald heads. They hobbled around and gruesome throaty noises came from their mouth.

The zombies and ghouls moved around slowly but relentlessly. The zombie's arms remained outstretched as they dragged their heels along the grass and concrete. Their bodies were patchy with flesh and white bone could be seen coming through their tattered clothing.

While the zombies looked remnants of a human, ghouls were another matter. Their arms and legs were irregularly elongated. Their mouth was filled with razor sharp teeth that grew out with almost no pattern. Despite that, their bodies didn't look fragile like the zombie did.

The air was thick with the sound of yelling and screaming. It was entirely possible to outrun these small and slow creatures. The only problem was the sheer amount of them. They had spawned in numerous places all around campus. Nowhere outside a building was safe and those who weren't fast enough to get inside were swarmed.

I watched with bated breath as those unlucky enough to trip or blindly run into a pack of monsters were tackled to the ground. The kobolds and goblins hacked and smashed any piece of flesh available to them. Even from a distance of a hundred feet it was possible to hear the sound of crunching bones and broken screams.

The goblins with daggers repeatedly stabbed their targets without stop. Even when the lifeless corpse ceased to move and make a noise they kept plunging their daggers as if in ecstasy. This impression was strengthened by their constant hobbling and cackling which made it appear as if they were dancing for joy.

It wasn't only this, though. People also materialized out as if being moved to another plane of existence. The incredibly busy Campus suddenly became eerily quiet as a huge amount of people vanished into thin air.

Those that were unlucky enough to remain found themselves running for their lives, trying to find any cover possible. I couldn't help but wonder just how many of us even remained here? Had I also been shifted to some other plane and not even realized it?

The dorm was not filled with commotion like I was expecting. I didn't hear the ruffling of my neighbors or the slamming and locking of doors. It was eerily peaceful. As if the scene outside was merely my own imagination.

I found my throat dry and my back drenched with sweat. My hand holding the curtain constantly trembled. My curiosity fought my urge to close the blinds and hide under my bed. *This is a dream…has to be a dream.*

I kept watching. An unlucky woman tripped and fell. Her head turned back to see her pursuers rush up as she crawled along the ground screaming. Her scream was soon choked with a wet sound. The nearby monsters simply swallowed her up. A pool of blood slowly seeped out from their enclosure.

Huh? As soon as the monsters separated, there was simply no body to be found. Only a red pool of blood signified that a human was once there. By now, there were very few people left out in the open.

Something moved in my peripheral vision and I turned my head. A lone student ran past the sidewalk and through the grass. He was sprinting with incredible speed towards the cafeteria. I couldn't help but find myself cheering for him. *Keep going! Almost there!* My cheers were cut short as goblins intercepted him before latching onto his legs.

The student fought hard to keep them off as he continued to move. He dragged one or two goblins along the grass before kicking them off. His speed slowed considerably and red blood drenched his legs. In the end, he collapsed and several goblins dogpiled him.

His blood curdling screams made my hair stand on edge. I could clearly see the hammers and axes being lifted and dropped over and over again. An eternity passed before the only thing that could be heard was wet thuds.

I resisted the urge to vomit and forced myself to pay careful attention. The goblins and kobolds obscured most of my vision, but his legs that were previously shaking and moving were still in view. As the crowd dispersed around him, his body simply disintegrated.

Disintegrated? Was that the right word? Maybe de-spawned would be a better term for what I saw? All I know is that his body ceased to exist.

A loud bang woke me from my stupor. *Shit!* I turned and rushed to my door to lock it. My back pressed against the door as I slid down to the floor.

I rested my head in my hands and couldn't help but look down. This was too much to take in at once. I needed to stay focused right now. Most people on campus would be in class, so the dorm was at its emptiest. The Slob passed through my head before I pushed the thought of unlocking the door out of my head. *Absolutely not!*

The dorm grew quiet once again. I stood and made my way back over to the window before opening the curtain a few inches. Sure enough, the monsters outside were still there. They simply walked around as if patrolling and showed no signs of leaving.

There was a scream on my floor. A girl down the hall began yelling, "HELP! PLEASE LET ME IN." She went from door to door banging. Her voice grew louder and louder as she approached. *Please, don't get this far, someone let her in!* I tiptoed back to my door and listened to her footsteps moving down the hall.

She was only a few doors down as she continued to rattle every door. *Fuck! Fuck Fuck!* My door started to shake as she pounded into it. My hand grasped the doorknob and caused the metal to jingle. My heart was in my throat as the pounding stopped.

"PLEASE, I KNOW YOU'RE IN THERE!"

My hand squeezed the metal so hard I felt as if it would break. *Arghhhhh! FUCK!* I unlocked the door and before I could even open it she barged through. Her charge knocked me on my ass she sprinted by me and jumped onto Slob's bed. I couldn't help but look back at her before her scream shook me and got an impression of long brown hair and bright pajamas.

"CLOSE THE DOOR, IT'S COMING!"

It's coming? There was no need to voice the question, as a ghoulish arm reached around the corner of the doorframe. I felt an electric shock surge through my body as the lethargy of the morning left me.

The ghoul's upper body and arm was already halfway through the doorway when I managed to smash the door against it. Its arm flailed through the air and disgusting mucus dripped from its mouth. A terrible stench wafted through the room.

I put all my weight against the door and kept it locked in place while my eyes scanned the room. "Help me!" I yelled at her. She remained huddled on the bed and tightly gripped a pillow to her chest.

Despite being undead, the ghoul had considerable strength and I found it hard to keep the door pushed up against it. The thought of sitting on my ass quickly passed. If I were to get on the floor now there would be zero chance of standing back up again.

"Under Slob's bed! Look!" I yelled at her. "Under the bed you're on right now!" I corrected myself. She rolled off the bed and then kneeled on the floor before digging under the bed. Her arm emerged with a metal bat. "Quick! Quick! Bring it here!" I was frantic.

She looked at the ghoul and hesitated for a second before crawling over and passing me the bat. "Help hold the door, please!" She looked on for a little longer and then crawled by my side. "I just need a few seconds." I pleaded. I spread my legs and allowed her to crawl between them. She put her back against the door and then pushed hard against the wall nearby to brace her as she kept the ghoul out. Her physique was sturdy and up to the task.

"Ready? Three, two, one." I counted down and then left the door. Her body flinched for a moment as she had to bear the pressure the ghoul was exerting solely on her own. My hands grasped the metal handle of the bat that was already slippery with sweat.

I raised the bat above my head and with all the force I could muster, swung down hard. The bat collided squarely with the head of the ghoul before sinking an inch into it. I nearly vomited as the skull caved in slightly and brain juices escaped from within. The smell was many times stronger than previous.

Despite my first swing, the ghoul continued to flail. I raised the bat again, and again, and again. After the third swing all that could be heard was a mushy wetness and none of the previous hardness. The top of the skull was nowhere to be seen.

The ghoul's arm fell to its side and the pressure it had been exerting on the door disappeared. A moment passed before the body simply disintegrated into nothingness. For the first time I felt I owed Slob an apology. A brown book floated where its body once was. If I hadn't seen it with my own eyes, I would have found it hard to believe.

With the ghoul gone any resistance to closing the door disappeared. The girl received quite a scare as the pressure on her back abated and her body tumbled. The door slammed shut and she frantically crawled across the ground before jumping on the bed and facing the door.

"It's dead," I said. She looked at me curiously. I ignored her gaze and looked at the book floating a foot in front of me. "Can you see this?" She nodded her head.

I reached out and grasped the book in my hand. Despite it floating there as if an imaginary object, I could feel it's weight beneath my fingers. The cover was coarse and well-worn. The moment I flipped the cover a message was transmitted directly to me.

BOOK OF *FIREBALL* LV. 1

What in the fuck is this? Fireball? Almost immediately after reading the details of the book another message popped into my head.

DO YOU WISH TO LEARN *FIREBALL* LV. 1?

I pondered for a moment. *Yes!*

CONGRATULATIONS! YOU HAVE LEARNED *FIREBALL* LV. 1. RE-PEATED USAGE OF THE SKILL WILL GRANT FURTHER MASTERY.

The book that was floating in my hand simply disappeared from between my fingers.

"Where did the book go?" she asked.

I had to consider for a moment if I should tell her what just happened. "It was a skill book." As of right now we were in this together.

"A skill book? Huh?" She was as confused as I was.

"I'm not sure yet what that means." The information floated in my head as I read over the skill description.

> **SUMMON A BALL OF FIRE TO INCINERATE ENEMIES IN YOUR PATH.**
> **CAST TIME: 1 SECONDS**
> **MP COST: 4**
> **DISTANCE: 6 METERS**

MP cost? Is this referring to mana? Like in video games?

"What are you doing?" she complained. "You're standing there staring into space, it's weird."

I came back to reality. For the first time I stopped and took a good look at her. She was the definition of nervousness. Her hands fidgeted around the clenched pillow while her green eyes shifted between me and the door. She was terrified, and rightfully so.

She was wearing a pair of pajamas made for children. I recognized the cartoon character plastered across the t-shirt. The whole outfit somehow still sagged on her lean frame. She gave me a nerdy vibe.

"I'm Joseph." I was the first to introduce myself.

"Veronica."

"This… sort of feels like the beginning of an RPG." I didn't know how to break it to her so I blurted it out.

She looked confused but didn't retort, "What should we do?"

I took my phone from my pocket and checked for a signal. There was nothing. "I think we sit tight for now." I walked over and sat on my bed. She remained on Slob's. I pushed as many useless thoughts to the back of my head as I could. Classes, my term paper, none of them were important any longer.

A picture of my mom floated through my head. I wondered how everyone was doing. My stomach started to gurgle. I tried my best

11

to ignore it until a rolling desire to eat spread through my insides. "Gah, I'm fucking starving." I spoke out of habit and forgot Veronica was sitting just a few feet from me.

I turned and scurried to the mini-fridge at the end of my bed. The inside was scoured clean. There was absolutely nothing of substance to eat. All that was left was a half-gallon of milk and an open soda can. The thought of apologizing to Slob faded immediately.

The hunger brought me back to our current situation, "Do you have food in your room?" I looked to Veronica.

"I live off campus."

I looked at her curiously, "Then what are you doing in the dorms?" She was even wearing pajama pants.

"I was visiting a friend. She rooms on the third floor. I slept over and she left for class early in the morning."

I stood and walked to the door before opening it just a crack. There had been no noise since our battle. I poked my head out and looked both ways.

"What are you doing? Close the door!" Veronica was spooked.

I looked back at her and put my finger over my mouth. She was being a bit too loud. She covered her mouth in embarrassment and nodded her head. I couldn't blame her for being over-excited but we needed to avoid unwanted attention.

"We can't stay cooped up in here forever. I'm starving and I need to use the bathroom." My gurgling stomach was addressing more than just hunger. We needed to do something.

She opted to stay in the room and I wanted to relieve myself. The hallway was empty all the way down to the staircase. I wanted to make sure there was still running water. My feet glided across the carpet and stopped before the water fountain.

I pushed the handle down and that faithful but shitty stream of water poured out. The stream was so small that you almost needed to wrap your mouth around it to get any water. I hated this stupid thing, but I couldn't be any more thankful than right now. I drank my fill and then rushed into the bathroom.

Veronica was still curled in a ball on the bed when I returned. Her hands hadn't stopped fidgeting. It looked like she was peeling the skin from her fingertips.

"There's running water at least."

She looked at me and forced out half a smile.

I shrugged it off and sat on my bed. The skill description for *Fireball* floated in my mind as I had a strong urge to use it. I pushed that thought to the back of my mind. I couldn't afford to burn down my only shelter as of right now. There would come a time when I could practice thoroughly.

Hours passed with nothing of note happening. If there were more of us locked in the dorm, they were doing a great job staying quiet. I noticed Veronica fiddling with her phone every couple minutes. "Have you heard anything back?" I looked down at my own phone that still had no signal.

"No…" She said dejectedly. "I haven't had signal all day." She buried her head in the pillow in frustration while grunting. "I was finally supposed to see my dad today." Her mood clearly dropped a level.

"You don't get to see him much?" I asked. I was in the same boat. I barely saw my parents after starting school. Between classes and their work it was hard enough even to get a phone call in.

"Maybe once a year…"

"So little?"

"My parents got divorced when I was young and my mom got custody. I didn't know back then but it wasn't an amicable divorce. My mom always told me he split but I found out that wasn't the case. She fought him tooth and nail to keep him from seeing us: me and my brother."

I didn't know how to respond and I couldn't relate. I nodded my head and just kept listening to her. "He lives in another state so he can't visit as often. He was making plans to move back and said he had a surprise for us today…" She eventually buried her face back in the pillow.

"Sorry…" I fumbled out while checking my phone.

Calls went straight to an automated system and every text was marked with 'unread' at the bottom. It didn't seem like there was any way to get in touch with my family. This thought didn't stop me from checking every few minutes. I hoped that 'unread' would turn to 'read'. It never did.

As night came around, the goblins outside became even more rowdy and loud. Their cackling mixed with the sound of crickets. My hunger stopped me from falling asleep. I laid there in silence fantasizing about enchiladas for whatever reason. I had a strong craving out of nowhere. I eventually dozed off.

***

It wasn't long after waking to the early dawn light that my hunger returned. There was also an itching on the back of my neck, an urgency to act. I needed to try using *Fireball*. I hopped up from my bed and walked to the door.

"I'm going out," I said to Veronica whose red eyes made it look like she had been awake the whole time.

She looked at me confused. "Outside? With those things?"

"Yes." The screams and sounds of fighting had long ago ceased. I felt it was now or never. I couldn't shake the bad feeling I had. There was something prickling the back of my neck. Things were only going to get worse from here on out.

"Will you come with me?" I asked.

Veronica looked incredibly conflicted with the situation she was being forced to make. "I'll stay here..." she mumbled out. I was conflicted as well. I didn't know if I should try and convince her further.

"Alright." Our relationship would turn sour if I forced her to go. There was no benefit for either of us in that situation. I decided to give her a bit more time before asking again.

The door clicked behind me and I made my way down the hallway towards the staircase. Looking down the dark stairwell, I started to bang on the staircase doorway just to make some noise. If there were any hostiles down there, then based on what I'd seen from their behavior, the noise would bring them towards me. I much preferred that than going down and being ambushed.

Chapter 2: First EXP

The staircase seemed empty and I grabbed the railings as I walked down. If I had a calm outer appearance, it was a facade. Inside, my body was screaming at me. Sweat covered my back and hands, my legs felt like mush. I reached the bottom at record pace: if they kept records for the longest taken to descend.

The exit was a single doorway that had a glass panel just above the door handle. Wire mesh zigzagged inside the glass. I pushed my face up against it and stared out. The area the doorway exited into was quite awkward. There was a large bush immediately to the left that completely obscured the view. My hand grasped the door handle and I browsed the fireball skill again.

I held out my other hand and stared at my palm. *Fireball!* That single word ran through my mind. A peculiar feeling flowed through my body and into my hand. After a second of time, a ball of fire the size of a tennis ball calmly floated there. *So it was real.*

There had been a doubt in the back of my mind up until that moment. Skills? Who could believe such bullshit? The reality in front of my face left me with no choice but to accept it. My hand grasping the door handle pulled down and the door opened with a click.

The sunlight caused me to squint as I poked my head out and around the door. I could easily see the varied monsters in the distance. They moved in packs around the school grounds and seemed to stay to certain regions. From the looks of it, only the ghouls and zombies roamed more widely. I looked back down at the fireball still sitting in my palm. Without much effort it stuck to my hand like glue. I was hesitant to walk past the bush in fear of what might be just around the corner.

A lone ghoul that was wandering aimlessly happened to venture very close to the dormitory. *This could be my chance!* I made a rough estimate of the distance. *I hope this is less than six meters...*I flung out my hand. The fireball left the grasp of my fingers and flew through the air.

Time slowed as I watched hopefully. The fireball soared through the air before landing directly on the ghoul's chest. Almost immediately, flame began to break out over its body. Its head jerked every which way before hungrily staring in my direction. The fire burned faster and hotter as it fumbled towards me.

It managed to move a dozen feet before falling to the ground. Smoke billowed out through its skin as its chest smoldered. The smell of burnt flesh filled the air and I couldn't help but gag.

CONGRATULATIONS! YOU HAVE REACHED LEVEL TWO. AS A REWARD FOR LEVELING UP, YOU HAVE BEEN GRANTED THREE STAT POINTS!

Level up? Stat points? As soon as I thought of stat points a window became available to me.

```
CURRENT EXP: 20/200     LEVEL: 2
HP: 90/90          MP: 16/20
            STR: 5
            AGI: 5
            DEX: 5
            VIT: 5
            INT: 5
```

```
                AVAILABLE: 3
```

I looked over the window briefly before making a general assumption of what each stat point did. Judging from my MP, I could only use fireball another four times today, after that I would have no real way to defend myself. *Should I put it into intelligence?* My experience with RPGs told me intelligence was for spell casters. It was a no brainer but I still found myself being hesitant. *I'll just use one point for now.* I put a single point into INT to test the waters.

The one point in INT gave me an immediate 3 MP boost: nearly the cost of a *Fireball*. I badly wanted to add the other two to INT as well. Being able to cast more fireballs would be incredibly beneficial. The only issue was how long I'd be using this skill. I decided to hold out on using the rest for now until I learned more.

I scanned the grounds for another ghoul before working up the courage to walk a few feet outside. My heart dropped when I walked past the bush that obscured my view and could see the reality of the situation. As far as the eye could see, even past the school parking lot and beyond, were monsters.

The bit of hope that the situation was isolated to only the school disappeared. The cars in the distance were back to back on the highway and showed no signs of moving. It took only a moment to shake off the shock, it really wasn't that unexpected. *Someone would have come to help if it was just the school.*

My next target was in clear view: a zombie just one-hundred feet away or so. I glanced around and confirmed the coast was clear. As long as I didn't walk away from this side-door, there shouldn't be adds. Since it was out of range of *Fireball*, I did my best to attract its attention by waving.

After what felt like dozens of minutes, the zombie noticed my presence and moved towards me. Its mouth opened and closed repeatedly while letting out moaning sounds. The stench hit me before it was even in range of throwing a fireball.

Just like before, it only took a thought to summon that burning ball of flame into my hand. I tossed it out in haste. *Shit!* My luck wasn't quite as good as last time. The blazing ball of fire sizzled past the zombie and missed it by a hair's breadth. The spent magical ball landed on the green grass and began to burn.

I was of a mind to run but decided against it. The zombie was moving quite slowly and I had a few seconds to summon another fireball. It would be problematic if it blocked the door and trapped me inside.

Luckily, the fireball I tossed out this time connected with it cleanly. Its dried and rotted flesh began to disintegrate within the flames. It fell much faster than the ghoul did. When its corpse disappeared, a shabby pair of shoes floated in the air. They constantly twirled in circles and nothing about them seemed extraordinary.

19

I did a double take of the area and after making sure nothing would latch onto me, I rushed over and grabbed the shoes. As soon as I had them in my hand I sprinted back and disappeared into the staircase. Once inside, I took a better look.

SWIFT SHOES: MOVEMENT SPEED +3%.
THEY'RE JUST A PAIR OF CRAPPY SHOES.

Well huh. It didn't seem like they were something I could actually wear. The size wouldn't quite fit on my feet. A prompt appeared immediately after thinking of equipping them.

WOULD YOU LIKE TO EQUIP SWIFT SHOES?

But of course I would! The shoes vanished into thin air and I immediately looked down at my feet. There was nothing there? I did a circle and looked around me.

Gear. Equips. Equipment. A window appeared and I could finally see where the shoes had gone. It was immediately obvious there were several more slots for equipment besides shoes. Just with a quick glance showed me that the basics were all there. Helmet, body armor, gloves, shield, weapon, there were even slots for what appeared to be rings and amulets.

There was no longer any doubt in my mind. I was playing an RPG. There were skills, levels, equipment and monsters. If it wasn't then what was it? Had God gotten bored and decided he needed some enjoyment at our expense?

I walked around the bottom of the staircase but really couldn't feel any difference. Three-percent really wasn't that much. I pushed it to the back of my mind and opened my stats window.

CURRENT EXP: 80/200   LEVEL: 2
HP: 90/90   MP: 8/23
STR: 5
AGI: 5
DEX: 5
VIT: 5
INT: 6
AVAILABLE: 2

From the looks of it, the zombie had given me 60 EXP. I had enough MP to cast two more fireballs and needed another 120 EXP to level. I thought back to when I obtained *Fireball*, mastery was mentioned.

Skills. Sure enough, another window appeared in front of me. Fireball was the only skill on the entire list.

FIREBALL LV. 1 30/100

I had cast fireball three times and gained 30 EXP. *Seven more times and I get to see what happens.* I didn't have enough MP remaining to cast that often, it would need to wait till my mana recharged, which would be when? Hopefully, not a whole day was needed.

I spotted a lone ghoul wandering aimlessly between packs of kobolds and goblins. Its pathing looked completely random, and yet it didn't stray far enough from the other mobs for me to pull it. I didn't know enough to feel confident walking farther out.

I was lacking critical information. If monsters had an aggro radius then I'd be in big trouble. Being cautious was my best course of action. I decided to wait.

After what felt like forty-five minutes, the ghoul moved away from the surrounding packs and more towards my direction. It was too far away for *Fireball* and I worried it would wander back and out of reach.

I glanced at the bushes to my side and towards their roots. The ground was a mix of dirt and stone. I scooped one up and tossed it towards the ghoul. It was a solid miss. The stone pebble didn't even land within a couple of feet. I hadn't thrown a ball or any object for a long time. I dug out a few more.

After the fifth throw I managed to pelt it directly in the back. There was a thud that told me the ghoul wasn't nearly as soft or fragile as the zombie was. There was some real substance under its decaying skin. It rushed in my direction.

Something else that was immediately apparent was the difference between zombies and ghouls. I had never pulled a ghoul from so far, and it built up quite a good amount of speed with the extra distance available to it. It was outside of my expectations.

A fireball surged into my hand and I found myself sweating. Not from the heat of my missile, but because I only had one shot. The ghoul would be upon me if I missed. I might not even be able to make it into the staircase at that point.

I tossed out the fireball and it flew a beautiful arc. My timing was nearly perfect. It hit directly into the ghouls chest right as he came into my casting range. The fire burned hotter than ever before as the ghoul rushed at me. Its added speed encouraged the fire to flare up and completely engulf it. It collapsed into a heap of char-coal just a few feet in front of me.

Unfortunately, there was no item or floating skill book above it. I looked down at my hand for a moment as the ghoul corpse des-pawned. The fireball I just cast didn't feel nearly as smooth as my earlier casts. I chalked it up to being low on MP.

> CONGRATULATIONS! YOU HAVE REACHED LEVEL THREE. AS A REWARD FOR LEVELING UP, YOU HAVE BEEN GRANTED THREE STAT POINTS!

That very welcome message greeted me once the ghoul's body disappeared. I quickly opened my stat window.

> CURRENT EXP: 0/400   LEVEL: 3
> HP: 120/120   MP: 4/27
> STR: 5
> AGI: 5
> DEX: 5
> VIT: 5
> INT: 6
> AVAILABLE: 5

I made a mental comparison with my previous stats. The level up provided me with 30 HP and 4 MP. None of my six stats gained any points at all. *God sure was stingy.* One level up had provided me with a lot less benefits than I expected. I checked my skill window and confirmed that *Fireball* was now 50/100 EXP.

I wondered how long it will take me to get my MP back? It surely couldn't be that I would need potions for that? I shivered just thinking about it.

My stomach grumbled but there was zero chance I could make it to the cafeteria. There was no guarantee the cafeteria was even safe. It was quite possible people had opened the doors and ghouls and goblins now lurked within. I turned and headed back up the stairs.

My hand grasped the doorknob of my room and gave it a turn. It stopped halfway and clicked, the door was locked.

I knocked. "Open up, it's me." I could hear the bed squeak and then shuffling footsteps. The lock clicked and the door opened.

"I didn't expect you to come back," she confessed.

"I still need a place to sleep."

She nodded her head and then hopped back onto the Slob's bed. I noticed she'd found some clothes: jeans and a grey jumper. I plopped backwards and fell onto my own sheets. I looked at the alarm on my head stand. It was surprisingly seven p.m. I didn't feel as if I spent that long outside.

I hadn't done any strenuous activity but I felt thoroughly exhausted. There was a pounding in my head that just wouldn't go away and my mind felt foggy. That, plus the lack of food, was overwhelming.

I turned to Veronica. She was still plastered to her phone screen, long brown hair forming a screen around it. "Anything new?" I asked. I had already stopped checking my phone. She was growing distant and reclusive. I had to push her now or she would never see the light.

"No…" Her voice was crestfallen.

"You know how I said it felt like we were playing a game?" I paused. "You looked at me like I was a bit crazy…"

"Mhmm," she admitted it.

"Can you think the word stats?" I asked.

"Huh?" Her green eyes went round as saucers. "What? What is this?"

"What's it say?" I was incredibly interested. All my stats were 5. Was I just average or did everyone start the same?

"It says I'm level One. All my stats are Five."

"Do you understand now? This isn't a joke. We have to act like we are in an RPG." I could see the turmoil on her face.

"What do you want me to do?"

"Come with me later and try to level up." She reluctantly nodded her head. "I need to rest just now though, casting spells wears you out."

When I opened my eyes again it was early morning. The red numbers of my alarm blurred as little dots floated in my vision. It was seven in the morning. I opened my stats and checked my MP. In twelve hours of sleep I had recovered all of my MP. That was good news.

Sun shone through the blinds of my window and illuminated the room in a low amber glow. I turned on my side and could see Veronica was fast asleep on Slob's bed.

My hands vigorously rubbed my face as I leaned over the side of my bed and stood. "Hey." I whispered. It was an odd thing to do because I was trying to wake her, but I didn't want to startle her. I reached out and pushed against her shoulder. She was startled anyway.

"We should start now," I urged.

Veronica rubbed her eyes before rolling over. Her feet dangled above the floor and her head drooped. She let out a huge yawn, "Alright." I was expecting some resistance but it seemed she understood the severity of our current situation.

I grasped the door handle tightly and carefully before opening the door to make as little noise as possible. I poked my head out and then looked back at Veronica. The coast was clear.

Old faithful provided us with a bit of water for the day. It was only a matter of time until running water and electricity would be a thing of the past.

There was a bubbling excitement growing inside of me that I couldn't quite understand. *Am I excited to go outside? To level?* We met in the hallway and headed down the staircase towards the side door. I double checked my MP and confirmed it was 27/27.

The difference between yesterday was immediately apparent at a glance. The size of the packs of goblins and kobolds was bigger than yesterday. There were even more ghouls and zombies roaming the school grounds.

I noticed something peculiar as well. The goblins were up to the same old, but the kobolds were working on something. I had pushed them both to the back of my mind, as they weren't something I could hunt yet.

There was a particularly interesting looking kobold. It didn't wield an axe or sword, or even a bow. It was holding a staff larger than its own body. The tip had the skulls of small rodents dangling around it. The wood was crooked and turned in odd shapes.

It looked like any other kobold except its fur. Its fur was a bit worn, as if time had taken a toll on it. I could tell it was more rugged, like an old dog. There were symbolic markings on its face that I couldn't make head nor tail of.

The positioning of this kobold was no coincidence. It was located dead center in the middle of many packs and well protected from any outside attacks. The kobold warriors, as I called them, paid careful attention to it.

The leader-type occasionally let out yelps and yips in response to which the kobolds around would turn and shift positions. I couldn't be sure what it was, but it was definitely out of the ordinary. It gave me a very ominous feeling.

"What should I do?" Veronica asked from behind. I must have been standing there for a dozen seconds without moving or saying a word. Her voice brought me back to reality.

"For now I just want you to pay attention. As soon as we can get a combat skill for you we can start working together. It's too risky for you to help with nothing."

She nodded her head in relief. Regardless of the situation I wouldn't ask her to throw her body at these things.

While the zombies and ghouls were a bit scarcer than the other monsters, I figured they were worth waiting for, as I knew I could handle them. They also roamed alone and didn't group up like the goblins or kobolds. It took just thirty seconds to find my first victim.

Summoning the fireball went smoothly. It seemed my thoughts flowed a bit better when I had full MP. The Ghoul caught the fireball like a football and continued running in my direction. The expected didn't happen, it didn't fall and smolder. *What?* I panicked and threw out a second fireball. The monster caught the second as well, but this time it burned for a brief moment and then collapsed on the sidewalk just in front of me.

Veronica was carefully watching from behind and I did my best to hide my surprise. I needed to look strong and confident. If I wavered, the confidence she had built up to come out and assist might crumble as well.

Phew! I wiped the sweat from my brow and leaned over. That was completely unexpected. Just yesterday fireball one-shot every monster I hit with it. The ghoul in front of me despawned and a beautiful book floated in its place.

A new skill? I didn't hesitate to grab it and flip the cover.

BOOK OF *INSPECTION* LV. 1
CAST TIME: INSTANT
MP COST: 2
DISTANCE: 4 METERS

I looked towards Veronica who was staring at me expectantly, "Take a look." I passed her the book. She took it in her hand and then flipped the front cover. "What do you think? It doesn't seem like a damaging ability," I said. *Inspection* sounded like it was meant to provide information.

"You're right." She paused. I could see there was a bit of disappointment in her voice. "You should learn it." She handed it back to me.

"Are you sure?"

"I don't want to be using it and wasting time passing on anything I learn to you. Assuming it allows you to learn something about gear, or even better, the monsters, wouldn't it be simpler if you had it?" She made a great point. I flipped the cover once again.

Yes! A new skill was added to my skill window, I looked at the skill description.

***INSPECT.* ALLOWS A PLAYER TO SEE THE STAT AND PROPERTIES OF CERTAIN MONSTERS. RESTRICTIONS APPLY.**

---

*Inspect huh…*It was a non-combat ability as we expected. The information it offered to provide sounded incredibly useful. It cost half a fireball to use which hurt me a little bit. Especially considering it might take two fireballs to kill a monster. I checked my own stat window and noticed that the ghoul today gave me 70 EXP instead of 60.

CURRENT EXP: 70/400   LEVEL: 3
HP: 120/120   MP: 19/27
STR: 5
AGI: 5
DEX: 5
VIT: 5
INT: 6
AVAILABLE: 5

If the monsters were going to be getting stronger every day, I needed to increase my power immediately. It was time to use the stat points I had received for leveling. If I didn't use them I'd be able to kill another two monsters today max.

Intelligence! Without a thought, I put all 5 available points into my intelligence.

```
      CURRENT EXP: 70/400      LEVEL: 3
         HP: 120/120      MP: 34/42
                  STR: 5
                  AGI: 5
                  DEX: 5
                  VIT: 5
                  INT: 11
              AVAILABLE: 0
```

The benefits were immediately obvious. The 5 extra points in intelligence added 15 MP to my maximum. I also felt a clarity that made my thinking just a bit smoother. I needed to cast another three fireballs before my mastery would improve. I was expectant of the benefits it would provide.

Despite there being more ghouls and zombies to hunt, isolating targets became even more difficult. The added movement from the kobold packs often had them intertwining and crossing each other's paths.

If this was an RPG, then mob training was a very real possibility. If I made a bad pull I could end up grabbing two or even three packs of kobolds and goblins. The only outcome from that would be death: definitely a painful one.

I knew for sure monsters had an aggro radius. The kobolds and goblins were in clear sight and it wasn't as if I was hiding myself. They could absolutely see me. They just didn't come to attack me.

I didn't know what dictated that distance, but for now, they were ignoring me.

The one benefit from all of this was that zombies and ghouls definitely didn't have any set pathing or zone they stayed in. They wandered randomly and freely. I just needed a way to get the attention of one and get it out of that mess.

I caught myself looking at Veronica and then shook my head. I wasn't going to have her do anything risky. There was suddenly a strong gust of wind that caused me to shiver. An idea popped into my head.

We were standing upwind from all of these mobs and if zombie movies had taught me anything, their sense of smell was impeccable.

"Wait for me in the staircase," I ushered Veronica back inside. "I need to grab something." I didn't wait for a response and rushed up the stairs. I moved like a phantom back to our room and then slithered across the floor.

My hand scraped and rummaged under Slob's bed until I felt the crusty fabric. It was a dirty sock that absolutely reeked... of something. I didn't even want to hold it in my hand but it was the best I could come up with. My own clothing wasn't this bad.

Veronica gave me a baffled look when I returned with the sock in my hand. I only shook my head. I really didn't want to go into detail about this sock.

Once outside I rummaged through the bushes once again and dug out a few stones before shoving them inside. I tossed it directly out in front of us and into the grass where it landed with a thud.

You might think this wouldn't be enough, but you would be underestimating the smell of this sock. The smell emanating from it at arm's length was enough to make my hair stand. It took everything I had to not dry heave.

It was a waiting game that I was fully expecting to win. I knew Veronica was itching to know what I was up to, but I kept her in suspense. For some reason I felt incredibly proud of my plan. Everything would be clear once the bait started to work.

As expected, it didn't take long before a target appeared. It was a zombie. It was the closest undead to us and I paid careful attention. At first it was moving without purpose, but that changed. It quickly picked up Slob's scent and moved towards the sock curiously.

Once it was near the sock it was easy pickings. It hobbled over the area and stuck around. It was drawn to that human stench and had no intention of leaving. I lit up a fireball and tossed it out. The zombie had no idea what was coming.

My fireball drew a beautiful arc before landing upon its shoulder. Before the zombie could even turn in our direction its upper body was already burning. Its mouth opened and the bottom half of its jaw fell to the floor.

I prepped another fireball and was ready to throw it out when the zombie collapsed. Relief washed over me. I didn't have to spend a second fireball and the threat was eliminated. Despite the ease, my adrenaline was pumping. I felt high.

I took a moment to consider the reasons for finishing it in one cast. First, it was a zombie and not a ghoul. They could have different stats. Second, I had just raised my INT stat significantly and maybe my spell was stronger. The answer was most likely one of those two.

I looked at the smoldering corpse in expectation and triggered my new skill.

Well shit. That complicated things quite a bit. The four-meter range on the spell was a very short distance and one I wasn't at all comfortable with yet. I couldn't exactly pull with *Fireball* from a safe distance and then cast *Inspect.*

A moment of brain storming brought a solution. I'd *Inspect* the next monster that I could isolate and Fireball it right after. I'd then hide in the safety of the stairwell until it burned up. The only issue was, I needed to inch forward until I could cast inspect.

"What was on that sock?" Veronica asked curiously.

"Uhh… let's not talk about it." I mumbled.

The sock continued to work wonders as any zombie or ghoul that wandered directly downwind was captivated by its stench. The pressure of making a risky pull was completely gone. We only needed to wait, that was the safest play.

I looked back at Veronica. "You should hold the doorway open for me. This might be dangerous."

"What are you going to do?" She didn't hesitate to retreat into the stairwell and hold the door open.

"The range on *Inspect* is too short." I complained. She understood what I was getting at. I started inching forward while trying to cast *Inspect.* My forehead was dripping with sweat. Twelve feet never felt so short before in my life. The worst outcome happened: the zombie aggroed me before I was in range.

I made a split-second decision and didn't turn to run immediately. I stood my ground and kept casting.

A wave of information was passed directly to me. That was my cue to run.

RAGGED ZOMBIE	LEVEL: 2	UNDEAD
HP: 210	MP: 1	

STR: 10
AGI: 1
DEX: 2
VIT: 8
INT: 0

A RAGGED ZOMBIE. ITS DRY AND ROTTED SKIN MAKES IT SUSCEPTIBLE TO FIRE.

I summoned a fireball into my hand while jetting towards the staircase. This feeling of being alive was impossible to describe. It made me feel bold. My body was telling me to run. I turned around anyway and tossed the fireball out.

The Ragged Zombie was definitely much slower than me. I made considerable distance in those few moments and managed to reach a respectable range. It didn't continue running at us much longer before collapsing.

The Ragged Zombie turned into a pile of ash before despawning. Similar to the ghoul before, it gave me another 70 EXP. A beautiful looking sword, or maybe it was a rapier, floated above where its corpse used to be. It was a thin and double edged sword with an incredibly pointed tip. There was a curved and intricate guard resting just above the handle.

I walked over and looked at it.

INFERIOR RAPIER.
A RAPIER MADE FROM UNREMARKABLE MATERIAL. IT SEEMS TO BE GOOD AT PIERCING.

I picked it up by the handle.

WOULD YOU LIKE TO EQUIP INFERIOR RAPIER?

No. It remained in my hand and I walked back to the staircase where Veronica was looking on curiously. "What do you think?" I asked her.

"This…you want me to use this?" she asked.

I handed her the Inferior Rapier. "It's your decision to make. I won't force you to fight close combat."

She took it in her hand and swung it around in the stairwell. She was swinging it so haphazardly the air started to howl from her whipping.

"Calm down, calm down." I panicked. She had almost lashed me with it.

"Sorry, I got a bit carried away." Veronica chuckled. "It's surprisingly fun to use."

"Read the description first."

"Oh… so I should stab?" She playfully jousted towards my direction "Like this?!" She started to poke here and there with it. "I'll think about it." I nodded my head in relief.

I finally had a moment to think about *Inspect*. I'd definitely gained useful information. If nothing at all, it let me know this new world at least followed logical conclusions. The zombie was weak to fire. It made sense.

My growling stomach echoed through the stairwell. My hunger gave me heartburn that was so strong I felt dizzy. The temptation to travel to the cafeteria grew stronger and stronger. *Not yet!* It was too soon.

I looked back at Veronica who was stabbing here and there. She had already worked up quite a sweat. "Can you hold the door for me again?" She nodded without a word and I walked back outside.

There was a lone ghoul bent over biting and gnawing at the now mostly destroyed sock. This was going to be the real test. The ghouls looked sturdier and of course were more agile than zombies. I had experienced firsthand just how fast they could get if given the chance.

I didn't want to move away from the staircase more than I had to. Throwing rocks was a better option. I also needed to modify my strategy. I'd delay throwing my fireball till a hit was sure. Hopefully, I could then cast Inspect before it burned up.

I managed to hit the ghoul on my first throw of a stone. My throw had definitely improved significantly. I let it reach about halfway before tossing out a fireball. Once I saw my missile land I moved back to the staircase.

INSPECT!

```
RAGGED GHOUL     LEVEL: 2         UNDEAD
            HP: 280            MP: 1
                  STR: 8
                  AGI: 1
                  DEX: 2
                  VIT: 10
                  INT: 0
  A RAGGED GHOUL. ITS SAW-LIKE TEETH AND LANKY LIMBS
              HOLD SURPRISING POWER.
```

I watched hopefully from safety as the ghoul burned. It felt like a dozen seconds passed before the flames went out. *Shit!* The ghoul remained outside the staircase door and didn't collapse into a heap of ash.

I was now locked inside as the monster battered against the door and rubbed its face into the glass pane. Green goop eventually obscured it from view. From the last two battles, I could calculate that my fireball must do somewhere between 211 and 279 damage.

I paused for a moment and considered getting the bat from upstairs. I checked my skills page.

```
           FIREBALL LV 1. 90/100
```

The temptation to see the result of my mastery increase trumped that idea as a fireball appeared in my palm once again. I pulled the handle of the door down. The door opened outward so no matter how hard the Ghoul pushed and shoved it could not get in

"Wai—" Veronica started to back away in a hurry.

I pressed my foot against the door and kicked out hard, sending it swinging open and the ghoul flying backwards and onto the ground. It shuffled to get back up.

A fireball soared out and landed on its body before setting it ablaze. Its struggle lasted only a brief second before it ceased moving.

CONGRATULATIONS! FIREBALL HAS REACHED LEVEL TWO!

Nice! I opened my skill window and selected Fireball before looking at the skill details.

FIREBALL LV. 2
CAST TIME: 2 SECONDS
MP COST: 5
DISTANCE: 7 METERS

The cast-time DOUBLED? I suddenly felt that I had made a mistake. The cast-time had increased from 1 second to 2 seconds. The chance that fireball did twice as much damage as before seemed slim. If that was the case, I had just lost DPS.

My gaze hovered on my DEX stat as I thought of previous games I had played. Not all games allowed you to allocate your stats… but for a good many that did, DEX affected cast speed.

If that was the case, DEX was just as important as INT. That wasn't as obvious while fighting one monster at a time, but once I needed to cast multiple times per fight? My attention turned towards the numerous packs in the distance and the problem was obvious. It wouldn't be long before I did need to cast multiple times.

What was also immediately obvious, the fireball in my palm was bigger and burned brighter than before. *It has to be stronger, right?* There was no way it wasn't. The first zombie I hit with the new fireball burned up in half the time it took for the level 1 version of the spell and confirmed my thoughts. Zombies and ghouls were now both one-shot targets again.

The body of a ghoul burned with incredible heat just a few feet in front of me. Despite it despawning, the putrid smell of burnt flesh still lingered in the air. A beautiful sight took its place. A bracelet that glowed brightly hovered in the air while spinning in circles.

BRACELET OF INTELLIGENCE: INT +2
A BRACELET OF FINE CRAFTSMANSHIP, YOU FEEL YOURSELF GETTING SMARTER BY JUST WEARING IT.

EQUIP!

The bracelet disappeared and I checked my equipment tab. Sure enough, it was there. Without realizing it I found myself addicted to killing monsters. The high I got from the possible skill book or equipment drop captivated me. I opened my stats page.

```
CURRENT EXP: 350/400    LEVEL: 3
HP: 120/120       MP: 15/48
STR: 5
AGI: 5
DEX: 5
VIT: 5
INT: 11 +2
AVAILABLE: 0
```

One more monster and I would level up. I checked the information on *Fireball* as well.

```
FIREBALL LV 2. 30/450
```

It would be a few more days before I could level it up again.

Veronica was still stabbing away in the stairwell. It seemed more and more likely she was going to accept the Inferior Rapier. I mentioned nothing about monsters or fighting and just let her practice. There was no reason to increase the pressure on her.

Chapter 3: Level Four

I turned my attention back to the outside. The majority of ghouls and zombies were now few and far between. The sock had been mostly torn to shreds and a good chunk of it was completely eaten.

There wasn't really anything left for me to hunt here. I refused to give up though. That next level was calling me and I desperately craved it. The good news was the immediate area outside the stairwell was clear of monsters.

I walked out a decent distance and found myself under the shade of a tree. I passed the sock on the way. It looked as if a lawnmower had run it over. There was nothing left to salvage of my bait.

My view from here was much clearer. I could see the parking lot behind the dorms and the subsequent roads coming into the school. As expected, the parking lot was still filled with cars. The roads were packed with abandoned vehicles. I didn't see any people.

My eyes darted between the staircase and parking lot. I was conflicted. It felt like there was an angel and a devil on my shoulder. Lately, the devil was winning. I at least had the sense to give Veronica a heads up.

Once I let her know my plan, I moved back out into the open field and kept as far away from the building as possible. My field of view was much better this way. I wouldn't turn the corner and be greeted by a pack of mobs or a lone ghoul.

I walked about fifty feet towards the parking lot when I noticed something peculiar. There wasn't a single monster in sight. No packs of kobolds or goblins, no ghouls or zombies. It looked clear.

I walked about another ten feet when I noticed something. It was a black garbed figure. I could only see the back of its upper body over the top of a vehicle. There was an ominous chill that raced up my spine and my sweat turned ice cold.

I needed to leave and my senses were telling me that. The figure in question turned around and looked in my direction before I could react. Its eyes were a deep blue and the fear crept up and engulfed me.

YOU HAVE BEEN AFFECTED BY *CONFUSION*

Huh? I immediately felt foggy. As if my mind was swimming. I wanted to run away but my feet moved in the wrong direction. I started to walk towards that blue eyed garbed figure. Its eyes continued to pulse.

I wanted to close my eyes but I couldn't even manage that. My feet kept moving steadily and my entire body was now caked in sweat. I couldn't scream or resist at all. I was nearly at the parking lot when I broke line of sight with those deadly eyes.

I dropped to my ass and inhaled like I hadn't taken a breath in a dozen minutes. The skin of my hands was pure white and my shirt was plastered to my back.

It was only when I got this close that I could make out what it was through the fogginess. It looked a lot like a lich from some of the games I'd played. Behind those blue eyes was a bleach white skull. One of its boney hands held a rickety looking staff. The top was adorned with an elongated skull. Atop the skull were two swirling horns.

I peered under the car and towards its direction. It wasn't touching the ground. I could barely see the bottom of its garb hovering there. It started to float around the car and into the open area of the lot.

My mind was racing a million miles per hour. Liches were all spell casters. The staff it held supported that theory as well. I needed to run, and fast. I peered over the hood of the car and did my best to not look at its eyes directly.

As expected, it was looking toward my direction as it hovered across the ground. The garb fluttered with the wind as if there was nothing underneath it. I sat back down and prepared myself to run.

I steadied my shaking legs and moved to make a sprint. I was just about to pick up speed when I heard an unfamiliar sound behind me. A cracking sound followed by displacing wind. There was a sharp pain in my leg and then numbness.

I looked down to see my entire right thigh covered in a layer of ice. I couldn't move it at all. I heard another cracking sound and instinctively rolled across the floor. The spot I had just moved from now sported a new layer of ice. *Holy shit.*

I started to drag myself across the ground and towards the cover of another vehicle. The palms of my hands were filled with little bits of gravel. My body was shaking from the extreme cold coming from my leg.

I didn't stop crawling until I put several cars in between me and the lich. Only then could I assess the current situation.

```
CURRENT EXP: 350/400    LEVEL: 3
    HP: 75/120        MP: 15/48
            STR: 5
            AGI: 5
            DEX: 5
            VIT: 5
            INT: 11 +2
         AVAILABLE: 0
```

I had taken forty-five damage from the attack. That kind of damage would end me in just two more hits. It also didn't seem like the lich had any issues casting multiple times. I had enough MP for three fireballs only. Would that be enough?

I lit a fireball in my hand and then placed the blazing ball near my leg. The ice cracked and then started to thaw. It took around fifteen seconds before I could move my leg enough to break the encasing ice.

I constantly peered around and under the vehicle to keep track of the lich. It was hovering around my original location and glancing in my direction. These vehicles were the only thing keeping me from turning into a Popsicle.

My leg was starting to warm up and the numbness was slowly fading. I reached my hand around and under my thigh to gauge the damage. There was no puncture, just a spot the size of a tennis ball that hurt like hell, even through the fading numbness.

The pain intensified several-fold as I attempted to stand. I did my best to put the pressure on my left leg instead and started to hobble to increase my distance from the lich. There was no way to run anymore.

The situation was now do or die. The lich was blocking my exit route and I couldn't run for shit at the moment. I peered over the top of the vehicle and then instantly ducked. A ball of ice flew directly over the top of the car and I felt the displacing wind above my head.

I peered over the vehicle again and watched carefully. The next shot didn't come for around four seconds. That gave me a four second window between attacks to make any moves. To be honest, that was pitifully short.

I still had the fireball burning in my hand and finally tossed it out and towards the lich. My practice paid off as the ball of fire landed on its pitch-black garb. The garb lit ablaze and an ethereal-sounding groan came from its maw.

My initial excitement faded quickly. The garb stopped burning as it used all of its power to extinguish the flame. The power of its ice caused even the moisture in the air to condensate. It started to snow in its immediate vicinity.

Wasn't that just shit luck? Could there be a worse matchup for me? The garb of the lich was sporting a few new holes but overall the damage was very minor. Fire and ice counter-acted each other. I just needed a bigger flame then.

I scurried between two crashed vehicles that were in the middle of the lot. They were my only cover to cross from one side to the other. An ice shard landed just behind me and shattered. Little pieces of ice tumbled across the concrete.

I crouched to catch my breath and put my hand on the concrete. I retracted my hand almost immediately as I placed it into what felt like an oily slimy liquid. I wiped it off and onto my shirt and realized I was standing in a spot of concrete much darker than the rest. It was moist with what looked like gasoline, or maybe oil.

I really tried to calm myself and listened to the dripping liquid. Little droplets fell from under the front of the car and splashed below before assimilating into this puddle. The liquid was thin along the ground but it covered a decent distance.

I now had a shred of hope. I peered over and watched the lich conjure a shard of ice and launch it in my direction. This one didn't fly over the vehicle but instead shot directly through the window.

The driver's side window shattered and glass sprinkled onto the interior. The shard of ice didn't stop there and continued outward through the passenger window. The explosion of glass rained down from above. Bits of glass were stuck in my hair and the rest covered the concrete around me.

I stood up and rushed to the opposite side of the parking lot. The glass below my feet crackled as I stood on it. My leg was burning like hell. I only had four seconds before the next attack and needed to move. I pushed the pain to the back of my mind.

I counted the seconds in my head. I jumped forward haphazardly and nearly belly flopped onto the hard ground. A shard of ice collided with the side of a vehicle and caused a loud metallic sound to echo through the parking lot. I had barely managed to avoid the missile.

My elbows were red and scraped. I could feel the beating of my heart through my pulsing thigh. My adrenaline was pumping so hard that I forgot to be afraid.

If this didn't work then I had no other options. The lich floated towards my direction. I carefully watched through the car windows. My timing needed to be perfect.

The lich hovered between the two crashed vehicles. I lit a fireball and chucked it out once it was above the most concentrated area of petrol. The ground lit ablaze instantly. The flame wasn't high but the area around the lich was on fire.

The two vehicles directly next to it had fire burning under them as well and very quickly they also lit ablaze. That ethereal voice that sounded like fading wind came out again. There was too much flame around it for it to extinguish it all.

A thin layer of blue covered the garment of the lich that seemed to be protecting it. A layer of ice that was thinning at an incredible pace. It didn't seem like it would hold up for very long. I watched as the undead caster started to hover out of the flames and realized I needed to do something.

The shield layer wouldn't last long, but it was definitely going to last long enough for it to get out of my trap. I lit another fireball and moved out from behind the car. This was such a bad idea, but I knew that if it got out of those flames I was done for.

The lich looked at me and then the fireball burning in my hand. Its hand started to glow blue at the cost of its shield disappearing that much faster. I was betting everything on this. There was no way it would do 75 damage and take me out, right?

As soon as it raised its hand to fire I jerked my body to the right. The jolt of pain from stepping hard on my right leg shocked me awake. I felt so incredibly alert. Pain exploded from my left shoulder followed by numbness.

I didn't even need to look to know that my upper left chest was caked with ice. There was no time to hesitate. I tossed out my last fireball. The shield on the lich was already dimly glowing and was showing signs of collapse.

My fireball collided with that dim shield and finally shattered it. The garb lit ablaze and the lich let out a wail like howling wind.

There was no resistance to put out the flames. Its glacial power was fully extinguished.

The lich hovered for a few brief seconds before the burning garb and bleached skeleton collapsed into the flames.

CONGRATULATIONS! YOU HAVE REACHED LEVEL FOUR. AS A RE-
WARD FOR LEVELING UP, YOU HAVE BEEN GRANTED THREE STAT
POINTS!

I could barely stay standing and collapsed to my knees. I crawled forward towards the flames and rested just a few feet away. My body was burning hot but my shoulder was still frozen solid.

I ended up lying flat on my back with my left shoulder closest to the flames. I didn't move for several minutes. A puddle of liquid was now mixing with the sweat of my back as my left shoulder thawed.

I leaned up and finally glanced at the place the corpse used to be. There was an item, a ring to be exact. The flames that originally covered the concrete were gone and only the cars were still burning now.

The burning interior billowed black smoke that charred my throat and caused me to cough. I hobbled forward and grabbed the ring.

```
┌─────────────────────────────────────────────┐
│                                               │
│            SKULL RING: INT +1                 │
│   THE RING OF A POWERFUL LICH. YOU CAN SENSE NEARBY UN-   │
│        DEAD MONSTERS WHILE WEARING IT.        │
│                                               │
└─────────────────────────────────────────────┘
```

Despite my injuries, despite my near-death experience. I felt like I was on cloud nine. I equipped the ring and barely managed to stand. I opened my stats.

```
┌─────────────────────────────────────────────┐
│                                               │
│    CURRENT EXP: 600/800    LEVEL: 4           │
│        HP: 60/150        MP: 4/55             │
│               STR: 5                          │
│               AGI: 5                          │
│               DEX: 5                          │
│               VIT: 5                          │
│              INT: 11 +3                       │
│             AVAILABLE: 3                      │
│                                               │
└─────────────────────────────────────────────┘
```

I didn't feel like I was in a good condition. I was thoroughly exhausted and my mind was foggy. I limped back towards the stairwell.

"Oh my god, what happened to you?" Veronica helped to support me.

"I ran into some trouble…" I started to explain the situation. Veronica listened to me talk while she supported me up the stairs and into the room. I barely managed to get my shirt off before falling onto my bed.

There was a huge bruise on my left shoulder that was past the point of being purple and was now turning green. I finally felt comfortable enough to consider my level up and stats. I felt weak. I felt vulnerable.

I looked at my three available stat points and realized just how heavy the decision was. Every stat was incredibly valuable. The last encounter was also the first time I took any damage, and the only information I could go by. The realization was harsh: my pitiful HP pool wouldn't keep me alive.

INT, DEX, VIT… the three of them were incredibly important. I badly wanted to put a point into DEX and test its effect. The throbbing in my shoulder told me I was being foolish. No amount of DEX or INT would keep me from dying. I ended up putting all three points into VIT.

I opened my stats.

```
         CURRENT EXP: 600/800    LEVEL: 4
           HP: 110/195      MP: 4/55
                     STR: 5
                     AGI: 5
                     DEX: 5
                     VIT: 8
                    INT: 11 +3
                  AVAILABLE: 0
```

The 3 points into VIT gave me 45 HP total. It was nearly a 25% increase in my health, which, for one level wasn't bad at all. The min-maxer in me felt regret, but future me would be thankful for this moment, I was sure of it.

I rolled over to get off my back, as I heard it helped with heart-burn. My stomach was burning. I was hungry as hell but also incredibly tired. There was still plenty of daylight, so I opted for a short nap.

I slept for around two hours. I felt so much better after waking but my hunger still pined at me. It was decided, desperate times called for desperate measures. I didn't consider myself a thief but figured if we should search all the nearby rooms: if they weren't there now, they had no need for it.

"We have to make a stop first." I looked at Veronica. Her expression was one of curiosity but she didn't ask what I was up to. We walked to the far end of the hall together and stopped at a room that looked no different from the others.

"What's in here?" she asked.

"This is… the RA's room."

"RA?"

"Resident Assistant." It was evident from her blank expression that Veronica still didn't understand. "This is Sean's room. I know for sure he has a key to every dorm room in the building."

That was enough for it to click. "Right! Most doors are locked."

I nodded in response before reaching out my hand. There was a moment of hesitation before I knocked on the door, "Sean?" Nothing but silence greeted me. My hand moved onto the knob. I grasped it tightly and suddenly felt incredibly nervous.

I didn't know Sean's schedule at all. It was entirely possible he had left for class. I hoped that wasn't the case… but the flipside wasn't great either. If the door was unlocked and he wasn't here… maybe he had disappeared to wherever the others were.

My hand clenched harder and I turned the knob slowly. There was a click and then the door simply pushed open. The room looked as if someone had just been here and rummaged through everyone… and most likely that was the case.

This wasn't my first time in the RA's room. I had come to him before to express concerns about the Slob. Relieved, I saw the key-sets were all still here. They were marked by the floor they belonged to. "We should stay on our floor for now."

Veronica nodded her head and we started to divide the keys among us. Immediately after that we each took a side of the corridor and began our scouring of each room for food.

My hands shook as they grasped a bag of potato chips I found in a room three doors down. The pressure I exerted to open the bag nearly ripped it in half. I was just that hungry. They were salt and vinegar, not my favorite, but food was food. It took me less than a minute to empty the contents. I tipped the bag and leaned my head back. Crumbs poured into my mouth as well as down my face and onto the floor.

I spent the next hour and a half searching. Most of what I found was junk, but I didn't complain. I pocketed everything edible and brought it back with me. In the time I spent searching I recovered 5 MP. It seemed my regeneration abilities had gone up since increasing my intelligence, to somewhere around 3 MP per hour. Unless the food I ate was a factor.

I arrived back first and sat on the bed, munching on a candy bar and waiting for Veronica's return.

She came in soon after me. Her hands were filled with similar items. Mostly little bags of snack food and sweets. I grabbed an extra candy bar from my side and tossed it to her. "Here." It was the one snack food she wasn't carrying.

She seemed startled and fumbled it in her hands before it fell to the floor. She picked it up and ripped open the plastic. "This is so good," she said with a mouthful. We hadn't found much but it was a start. The fogginess slowly faded as I put some food in my stomach.

I couldn't help but feel these days were the most productive I'd ever been. *Is this what it's like when you're forced to survive?* I thought back to something a history teacher once said: people in the old days didn't have the time to be depressed.

Chapter 4: Forming the Party

The following morning I groaned while rolling over in bed. *Fuck it's hot!* Every crevice of my body was thick with sweat. The power was gone and the AC no longer worked. That meant Ol' faithful wouldn't be running either. From scouring the dorms, I had enough water for at least another week. All the same, we would need to extend our search soon.

I knew without electricity there wouldn't be running water either but my curiosity got the best of me. I checked the showers anyway and left in disappointment. There was nothing but a little trickle that emptied the pipes.

The fear I had of these monsters had dwindled since day one. The biggest thing on my mind was establishing a new base camp and finding more teammates. Veronica and I could only accomplish so much together.

Veronica was still sleeping when I returned. I gently shook her awake. She didn't startle like she did before. Breakfast was a half melted candy bar for the each of us. We also took note that finding water was a top priority now.

"How do you feel?" I asked her. It was a vague question but one she understood immediately. Today she needed to make a decision. Was the Inferior Rapier enough for her to risk fighting with me?

"I think I'm ready." As she spoke she reached around to fasten her hair back with a hair tie. Her face was broader than I'd noticed and the expression on it was determined. I felt relieved to know I finally had a teammate.

The encounter with the lich yesterday highlighted my weakness quite well. There was only so much I could do alone. With Veronica at my side, I felt more confident coming out of this alive. We headed downstairs together.

The ghoul goop on the door's window pane made it impossible to peek outside. I took a quick look at my MP, **55/55**. A bit more than what I was expecting. *Sleeping might provide a slight boost to regeneration?*

I was ready to summon a fireball immediately as I cracked the door open. Veronica held the rapier just to my side. The coast was clear and we breathed a sigh of relief. The ghouls and zombies that we had dispatched had been freshly replaced. The kobolds were still up to their shenanigans around their leader and I was growing increasingly worried by their activity. Time was of the essence.

If it was an RPG then surely there was a way for Veronica and me to group up. I looked at her and then thought the word 'group'. Nothing. 'Party'.

WOULD YOU LIKE TO CREATE A PARTY WITH THIS PLAYER?
YES!

Veronica received my request and then accepted. I could see her level clearly above her head now. She was level 1 as she explained. She started to wave her hand above my head as if to touch my level display.

"You'll act as my backup, but take it slow." I didn't want her pulling and getting aggro. It was best if she supported me until she truly felt comfortable.

The first target was a ghoul and I was curious to see what *Inspect* would say. I walked closer as Veronica followed behind me. I primed a fireball in my hand and my heart ached. I badly wanted to add a few points of DEX. I threw the fireball out and towards the ghoul.

INSPECT!

RAGGED GHOUL   LEVEL: 3   UNDEAD

HP: 325   MP: 1

STR: 9

AGI: 1

DEX: 2

VIT: 11

INT: 0

A RAGGED GHOUL. ITS SAW-LIKE TEETH AND LANKY LIMBS HOLD SURPRISING POWER.

The information came to me immediately as the ghoul barreled towards us. The single fireball was burning it up but it was going to reach us before then.

"It's your turn!" I yelled out. My voice was excited, and understandably so. This was Veronica's first test. The ghoul was only feet away when she moved forward and stabbed out her rapier with a vigorous thrust.

I was impressed to say the least. The tip entered cleanly through the monster's eye socket and right out the other side. The momentum of its running body continued as its head nearly went all the way to the guard. The surprise caused her to drop the rapier on the floor and back away.

The body slowly despawned and left the rapier sitting there on the floor. There was also a skill book floating there as well. We walked over together and gave it a look.

BOOK OF *PIERCE* LV. 1
CAST TIME: 0 SECONDS
MP COST: 1
DISTANCE: 1 METER

This... this was too much to be a coincidence. It was the first monster she killed and it dropped a skill book. Let alone a skill book that specialized in the weapon she killed it with. I read the description.

PIERCE
PERFORM A THRUST WITH DEVASTATING PENETRATING POWER

"This looks like it's for you," I said. Veronica didn't hesitate to pick it up and hold it in her hands for a few moments. I watched it disappear and knew she had learned the skill. "Try it out." I urged her.

"Okay." She held out the rapier and then performed pierce. The thrusting motion was so clean and fast. It was levels above the attack she just performed.

"How does it feel?" There was definitely something different, and satisfying about performing a skill.

"It feels so natural."

"That was exactly how I would describe summoning a fireball. You would think it feels odd or weird, but it just feels so right. Like the pieces of a puzzle coming together perfectly."

I turned my attention back to the information *Inspect* provided. As expected, the ghoul was stronger today than yesterday. The ghoul gained a level and a total of 45 HP. The EXP I received for killing it was 45 today and yesterday it was 70.

"How much EXP did you receive?"

"Forty-five." So she got the same amount as me. Simple math said they were worth 90 EXP total or 20 more than yesterday. This dynamic created a sense of urgency. The mobs were getting stronger every day. Everyone that didn't immediately start leveling would be at a big disadvantage.

Pushing Veronica was the right decision. If I let her delay another one or two days things could have gotten out of control. We still needed to find more teammates before things reached an unsalvageable level. *A vicious system…*

We spent a few minutes talking about the encounter. It was a good idea to help myself and Veronica feel more comfortable about it. I had nothing to defend myself in close combat. She was my lifeline and I needed to make sure she was ready when the situation called for it.

We just finished talking and were ready to find the next target when I felt a droplet of water hit my head. Then it started to pitter patter. Within seconds it was pouring so hard I could barely see a dozen feet in front of me.

"Geez, what awful luck." We retreated to the stairwell and waited around five minutes hoping it would clear up fast. It didn't. We both got tired of waiting and returned to the dorm room.

I opened the blinds of my window and peered out. The rain was coming down so hard I could only barely make out the cafeteria across the walkway. I turned my attention towards where the kobolds were. The rain was coming down too hard to make anything out. My intuition told me they were up to no good.

Sitting around was a waste of both of our times. We split up again, carrying containers like cooking pans and filled them with rainwater. We stopped only after the rain started to let up. After bringing the pans back, there was enough food and water to last us an extra three days.

The rain was only drizzling now. I could finally make heads or tails out of my window. I peered in the direction of those kobolds. Visibility was still not the greatest, but my suspicions were confirmed.

The area around them was excavated in a circular fashion. Every pack of kobold was sitting on their own little platform with the staff-wielding kobold dead center. They were digging runes into the ground and a portion of the symbol was already completed.

The pack of kobolds that stood upon that completed symbol was faintly glowing, and so was the symbol on the ground. There were four more symbols located inside the circle in a star shape that were not yet lit.

They were performing a ritual of some kind. Whether it was for summoning, or powering up, or any number of things, I couldn't be sure. Whatever it was, it definitely wasn't good for us. The problem at hand was the sheer amount of monsters in the way. Veronica and I couldn't deal with it ourselves.

"What do you think of that?" I beckoned Veronica over to the window.

"Of what?" She looked out.

"That." I pointed with my finger and gauged her reaction. She looked on curiously.

"What are they doing?"

"That's what I'm asking you."

"I think… it looks sort of demonic." Her voice was filled with uncertainty.

"Yeah…" The kobolds were still moving to and fro around the ritual circle. They excavated the ground with their little axes and hammers and received orders from the 'leader' of their group.

We waited less than an hour before the rain fully came to a stop. The outside temperature dropped several degrees and the dorm room felt comfortable again. The sun was still being blocked by thick dark clouds.

"Let's try again."

"Right." It was time to level up.

We focused on the task at hand and started to clear around the dorm again. The Skull Ring I received from the lich was coming in handy as I was getting alerts about the presence of undead.

Veronica trailed just behind me as we maneuvered out the front of the dorm and along the building. There were packs of kobolds and goblins to our left that we weren't prepared to face yet.

"Wait here," I said. I snaked against the front wall as carefully as possible. If the kobolds or goblins showed any reaction I would dash back to Veronica and we would retreat inside. I made it halfway to the corner and confirmed we were out of their aggro range.

I looked back and beckoned Veronica with my hands. She nodded and then snaked along the wall until reaching me. Together we approached the building corner.

I could sense many undead wandering around just beside the dorm. Plenty for us to hunt and the area was relatively open. We wouldn't have to struggle as hard to find a target.

I turned back to Veronica. "I want to start killing the goblins and kobolds today," I whispered. We were moving at a snail's pace.

"Because of the circle?"

"Yes and no." They were more humanoid and had at least basic levels of intelligence. Realistically they should be a tougher opponent. Harder fights meant more EXP and more loot. I was expectant.

We both poked our head around the buildings corner and looked at the many zombies and ghouls wandering about. There were kobolds and goblins as well, but they were farther away and almost certainly out of aggro range.

"Do you think you can take one alone?" I asked. There was a zombie meandering about. It was close enough to pull as a single.

"Maybe."

"Do you want to try?"

"Okay." She seemed uneasy.

"Worst case you can run and we take care of it together." The zombies were relatively slow. On open ground they could never match the speed of a person running. Ghouls, however, were a different story.

I summoned a fireball into my hand and watched her closely as she walked towards danger. If something happened I could assist in a moment. Veronica took her time and held the rapier steady in her hand as she approached.

I did my best to make note of the aggro radius. The distance was easier to measure while watching someone else, instead of experiencing it yourself. To my surprise, the 'battle' lasted a mere moment.

The zombie turned in Veronica's direction and started rushing towards her. I say rush but the speed was actually pitiful. She readied the rapier in her hand and then like a flash of lightning, struck out.

It was just that fast. The tip pierced into the zombie's skull and blew out the back of its brains. It was impressively fast and destructive. I imagined a bullet would probably look about the same.

She downed the zombie in one hit. *Isn't that a little overpowered?* It was definitely a result I wasn't expecting. I guessed that melee had a slight advantage. They had to fight in close combat after all.

Veronica rushed back with peachy cheeks and a smile across her face.

"Good job."

Both of us received a solid 45 EXP. "You leveled?" The level above her head now read the number 2.

"Yes!" Her breathing was erratic despite not exerting herself too much. She was high on adrenaline. I knew that feeling all too well. "What do you think I should put my stat points into?"

It was a good question. The stats themselves seemed straight forward enough. STR should improve your physique. AGI would help with quick and fluid movement. VIT should increase your life and stamina. INT should increase your mana and spell casting ability.

DEX was the most curious of the bunch. Typically, it increased your hand movement and that translated into a lot of things. The most notable of those was cast speed and accuracy.

Based on the fighting style Veronica would be utilizing. She definitely wasn't suited for brute strength. She needed to be quick and precise. A mixture of STR, AGI and DEX would be best. I thought about it for a brief moment before voicing my opinion. "I think you should put one point in STR, one in AGI and one in DEX." Her attacks needed to be accurate, quick, and powerful.

"I think so too."

I had a sudden realization. "I never asked you if you were familiar with RPGs."

"Well, I'm a little familiar." She smiled. "I'm more into hockey but I've sat around with friends playing WoW."

"Are you feeling more confident?" My eyes gazed hungrily at a pack of goblins.

"Yes, but let me warm up a bit."

I nodded and then scanned the field in front of us, "Let's solo the zombies and we'll tag team the ghouls." Now that I'd seen Veronica in action, it felt like this was the most efficient plan.

"Sounds good."

We made our way off the wall and started to pull our own separate monsters.

I found out very quickly that her first kill wasn't a fluke. I watched her blow the brains out of another zombie just a dozen feet to my right. Her efficiency and speed were getting me fired up.

We each killed our own zombie and dispatched one ghoul together. She was on the cusp of level 3 and I was barely a breadth away from level 5.

"Shall we?" I turned my attention back to the pack of goblins. I knew the safest play we could make was to search for and kill another zombie and both level, but my inner devil was searching for that next burst of dopamine. Plus, we were on the clock.

It seemed Veronica had a taste of it as well. "We shall," she responded.

My eyes locked onto the pack of goblins just one-hundred feet away from the dorm. There were a total of three of them hopping and hobbling with each other in a circle. My adrenaline started pumping as I approached to make the pull.

A fireball blazed in my hand and I looked back at Veronica one last time. She gave me a nod.

I threw it out towards the nearest goblin. The air literally sizzled as it soared in the pack's direction. My repeated usage of the skill had increased my accuracy and sense of distance.

The fireball arched and then landed cleanly on the backside of my target. A screech came from its mouth as its eyes turned a blood-thirsty red. Its two allies cackled and growled before moving in my direction.

Despite their short and stumpy legs, they moved quite quickly towards me. I immediately turned back and sprinted to regroup with Veronica. I summoned another fireball into my hand as Veronica passed by me to intercept the chasing goblins.

By now, the first Goblin had collapsed in the grass as its green body scorched black. My fireball's damage was nothing to scoff at. Veronica was only now reaching the second axe-wielding goblin.

I watched as her arm retracted back like a striking snake. It sprung forth and pierced directly through the second goblins eye socket. I could see the metal tip come out the other side cleanly. She pulled it back just as quickly and let the goblin fall.

It flailed and twitched on the grass as if crazed. The third goblin was only a moment away from Veronica at this point. My second fireball was ready and I tossed it out. It was in the process of raising its club when its face was blasted by hot fire.

The little club made of stone and wood was dropped to the floor as it grasped its face with both hands, swatting and smacking every which way to put out the flames. Black smoke billowed off its charred body.

In the end, it collapsed just as had the other two. My only regret was that I didn't think to use *Inspect*. I was happy to find out that they died in one fireball each and it was only possible to accomplish such a feat with that being the case. A welcome message greeted me just after the battle concluded.

CONGRATULATIONS! YOU HAVE REACHED LEVEL 5. AS A REWARD FOR LEVELING UP, YOU HAVE BEEN GRANTED THREE STAT POINTS!
CONGRATULATIONS! YOU ARE THE FIRST PLAYER TO REACH LEVEL 5 IN YOUR DISTRICT. AS A REWARD YOU HAVE BEEN GIVEN THE SKILL *SPEEDY RECOVERY* LV. 1!

A new skill? I quickly opened my skill window and read the description.

SPEEDY RECOVERY LV. 1
PASSIVE: RECOVERY RATE OF HP AND MP INCREASED BY 50%

There was no progress bar, which indicated to me it couldn't be leveled up. A downer for sure, but I couldn't complain. *This... this is amazing. Thank you God!* I opened my stats page.

```
CURRENT EXP: 40/1200    LEVEL: 5
HP: 225/225    MP: 32/59
STR: 5
AGI: 5
DEX: 5
VIT: 8
INT: 11 +3
AVAILABLE: 3
```

I told myself I desperately needed DEX but still carefully considered my options. Every stat point was precious. STR didn't seem useful yet as I had no equipment to carry. AGI was definitely a no. If the situation called for me to be agile then it was already disastrously bad.

I put one point into DEX and then started to summon a fireball. The feeling was faint, but it was definitely smoother to cast. I was sure of it. DEX would increase my cast speed and perhaps my throwing accuracy too. The question was if I should put all three points into it now. There was also the issue of gaining more HP: my life was important after all.

Looking at Veronica, who had the distant expression of someone looking at their UI, I decided to trust her. My job right now was to deal damage. She would be there to keep any monsters off of me. I put two points into DEX and the final point into INT.

I gained another 3 MP putting my cap at 59. I had enough MP left to cast *Fireball* five more times.

There was an item there waiting for us We both were excited. A short-sword of unremarkable quality floated where the second Goblin perished.

```
┌─────────────────────────────────────────────┐
│                                               │
│         CRUDE SHORT SWORD: STR +1             │
│   A SWORD OF POOR CRAFTSMANSHIP, THE BLADE    │
│          HAS CRACKS AND THE TIP IS DULL.      │
│                                               │
└─────────────────────────────────────────────┘
```

My excitement faded as I realized it wasn't something I could take advantage of.

"Do you wanna swap?"

Veronica looked at the crude and honestly unattractive sword and then down at her own fancy rapier, "No… not particularly."

I picked it up.

```
┌─────────────────────────────────────────────┐
│                                               │
│    WOULD YOU LIKE TO EQUIP CRUDE SHORT SWORD? │
│                                               │
└─────────────────────────────────────────────┘
```

No!

The sword remained in my hand and I realized I didn't have anywhere to put it. If this was a game then I should have an inventory. I concentrated on the word 'inventory' and a window appeared. I thought about placing the short sword inside the window and it vanished from my hand.

I started to summon the item in and out of my hand as Veronica watched. "What are you doing? Huh? Let me see it!" She was interested.

"Here, think 'inventory'." I passed it to her and watched as she played with it as I had.

I checked our EXP gain and was pleasantly surprised that all three goblins gave me a total of 180 EXP. 60 EXP per was considerably more than what the zombies or ghouls provided, a bonus for the increased risk of fighting three enemies at once?

Veronica had reached level three. She put one point into STR, AGI and DEX. Veronica's killing efficiency dwarfed mine. I chalked it up as a feature of the early levels of a spell caster. The day was young and we could definitely grind a lot more EXP. I had just a bit less than half of my MP remaining.

My desire to reach the cafeteria was still strong. I looked over the field at the many packs of kobolds and goblins. There were also the zombies and ghouls constantly roaming to worry about. I wanted to make that push today, or at the latest, tomorrow.

The kobolds were still up to no good. They bustled around like an ant-hive. Their yips echoed around the entire courtyard. If it was just one or two packs we could make do. The issue was that it was really five or six. There was also that spell caster to worry about.

The good news was, for now, they wouldn't bother us. It was pretty much confirmed that each monster remained in their own spawn area. The only exception to this were the ghouls and zombies. I could sense them all around me and it made that fact even more clear. They roamed freely.

"Ready for more?" I asked Veronica. She passed the sword back to me and I stored it away.

"What's next?" There were kobold and goblin packs scattered all over, tons of targets for us to choose from.

I looked in the direction of the cafeteria and started to count.

"It's about five or six packs…" I paused. "Maybe more depending on how far their aggro radius is." While we knew there was a radius, until we pulled them we couldn't be sure just how far it was.

"You're really speeding up the plan." She complained. "Earlier you said you wanted to take care of some goblins by tomorrow…"

"Well I didn't know you'd be this strong." Her face had a proud look as her cheeks turned a lighter shade of pink. I really wasn't trying to flatter her.

She looked at the mobs. "We can try but I don't think we'll make it that far…"

I silently agreed. I had half MP and it would be foolish to make her do all the fighting. There was a big difference between fighting one waist high goblin and three of them.

"We'll stop when it's too much then. Does that work?"

"Alright."

While the kobold ceremony was prickling the back of my neck, I still felt we had time. I didn't know exactly when they had begun their little ritual, but judging from their progress on the symbols it didn't look like it would be complete in the next day at least. I fully believed that by tomorrow we could reach the cafeteria.

"I think we should body pull the next pack." I suggested. Veronica shrugged her shoulders as if having no opinion on the matter. She was fighting close range anyway so I doubt it mattered that much to her.

We chose a pack together, one that was isolated and out of the way. Defeating it wouldn't give us any progress towards reaching the cafeteria unfortunately. Those packs were too close together. If we body pulled two or three packs at once things could get bad very quickly.

Adopting a fighting stance, Veronica raised her rapier. I summoned a fireball in my hand and did the same. The movement was robotic and awkward, but still, it was the best way to get an accurate judgment of distance.

Our target was a pack of three goblins similar in makeup to the first. They were all melee with either an axe or club. There were other packs around that were more varied. I didn't notice them before but some had little crossbows and bows.

There were also packs that had goblins and kobolds that wielded small wands. They were a far cry from the majesty of the staff the kobold shaman was wielding, but they were definitely spell casters. My body reflexively revolted at the thought. I could still remember the pain from those lich ice attacks.

We managed to get within twenty feet before the goblins cackled and turned in our direction. I immediately threw out my fireball towards the nearest goblin. Veronica started rushing forward to meet the second. I didn't summon another fireball and instead opting to push forward with her to cast *Inspect*.

GOBLIN (AXE)   LEVEL: 4   HUMANOID
HP: 215   MP: 25
STR: 5
AGI: 3
DEX: 4
VIT: 5
INT: 2
A WEAK GRUNT OF THE GOBLIN RACE. A STONE PICKAXE OF UN-
REMARKABLE QUALITY DANGLES AT ITS SIDE

My decision was a mistake: a failure in communication. Veronica was fully expecting my second fireball to assist her with the third and final goblin. "Watch out!" I yelled.

Almost at the same time I said that, a club thwacked across her thigh. She recoiled back, pulling the rapier out of the brain of the second goblin as she did so. She managed to move halfway between me and the goblin before falling limp.

Two of the three goblins were dead. It was only this one remaining. I wanted to summon a fireball but realized it was too close. I would hit it, and it would die, but Veronica would be mauled, or worse, killed.

I made a split second decision and pulled the crude short sword from my inventory before equipping it. I rushed forward haphazardly to meet its charge. I don't know what I was thinking, but I didn't swing out the sword.

I opted instead to kick as hard as I could. My foot collided directly with the goblin's face. The club in its hand was swinging down at that moment and brushed by my pant leg. If I had not set it off balance at that moment my entire shin would be shattered like a twig.

The goblin flew several feet back and I chased after it. It began fumbling to stand up as I arrived just over top of it. I kicked down hard on its back before plunging the crude short sword into its exposed neck.

There was a horrible gurgle from its neck. Bloody bubbles of air came out through the wound as I ripped the sword from its throat. Placing the bloody blade back in my inventory, I rushed back to Veronica.

She was nearly hyperventilating while sitting down. She kept her damaged thigh off the ground by arching her leg.

"Calm down. Let me see it."

Her broad face was entirely red, showing a mix of panic and pain. She didn't speak but swallowed hard and then nodded her head. She groaned while pulling her pants off and allowed me to see her thigh.

There was a horrible bruise the size of two tennis balls. It was entirely purple and there were little speckles of blood mixed in under the skin. I put my hand on her thigh and gave it a slight nudge.

"Ahh, ahh. What are you doing?!! Don't touch it!" she barked.

"I'm sorry. Please bear with me." I looked all around and didn't see any deformities or abnormalities coming through her skin. "Can you try and move it please? It's important."

She looked at me angrily before extending her leg all the way out and then moving around her thigh. She winced in pain the entire time and kept a scowl on her face.

"I don't think it's broken," I comforted. It was truly fortunate the strike was on her thigh. Not only was the femur the most durable bone in the body, she had a lot of fat and muscle there to absorb the impact.

"This is good," I said. Veronica nodded and forced out half a smile. "Let's get you up." I put my arm under her shoulder and hoisted her up as best I could. Her frame was small so it wasn't that difficult.

She let out groans of pain the entire way back. I didn't voice a word of complaint despite today's hunting coming to an end. This was entirely my fault. I should have told her my intentions from the get go.

I helped her onto Slob's bed and then looked out the dorm room window. There was still only one lit circle in the kobolds rune. I hoped I wasn't wrong. Time needed to be on our side now.

I passed a granola bar and bottle of water to Veronica. "I'm gonna do some more scavenging. You should rest." She nodded her head while nibbling on the bar. Once I left the room I had a strong urge to go level.

I kept true to my word and finished completely scouring the dorm rooms on our floor. A small pile of water and food accumulated in the hallway over the course of two hours. When I finally returned Veronica was curled in a ball on Slob's bed.

I moved everything into the room as quietly as possible so as to not wake her. Once done I sat on the floor against the wall and ate my dinner. It was early but the stress from today left me feeling lethargic.

Inspect! I tried to cast in on Veronica out of curiosity.

NO TARGET FOUND

It didn't work on other people. A bit disappointing but the skill did say it had restrictions and only worked on 'monsters.'

I took note of my MP regeneration with my new passive skill: *Speedy Recovery.* The surprise it brought me couldn't be underestimated. I had recovered nearly 5 MP per hour while active. Unsure how strong the effect would be while I was sleeping. I checked my stats before heading to bed.

```
CURRENT EXP: 400/1200   LEVEL: 5
    HP: 225/225      MP: 36/62
             STR: 5
             AGI: 5
             DEX: 7
             VIT: 8
           INT: 12 +3
         AVAILABLE: 0
```

I woke the next morning to that same terrible sticky feeling. The weather felt hotter than it had been yesterday. I checked my MP and was pleasantly surprised to find it a full 60/60. My regeneration was now levels above what it had once been.

Today was supposed to be the day we made it to the cafeteria. I couldn't be sure that was still on the menu, to use an appropriate idiom. Veronica was still sleeping like a log and I didn't have the courage to wake her.

I pulled the blinds to the side an inch or two and peered out. I made it a habit to keep tabs on our kobold friends. A second circle had been lit and it looked like they were working diligently towards the third.

The clock was ticking. It wouldn't be long before we couldn't survive cooped up in this dorm room. We both wanted to know what had happened to our family members. There were too many questions still left unanswered. We needed to find more companions to survive and get those answers.

I left alone and went straight towards the front entrance. I was no longer interested in using the discreet side exit. The front exit was closer to the cafeteria and definitely more dangerous. The side area door was metal while the front doors to the dorm were glass with a metal frame.

My confidence in the glass holding up to the axes and hammers of the goblins and kobolds was next to nil. Moving forward from this direction was our only option, defense was out. Or we would need to clear more monsters than the two of us could deal with in a day.

I looked out over the breezeway and the grassy areas on either side while taking note of the amount of possible enemies we would have to contend with. There were six packs of goblins and kobolds strewn about. Not to mention the numerous ghouls and zombies that lurked around corners or took random paths.

After considering several possibilities, I decided that it was realistic to aim to avoid two or three of those packs. Thanks to yesterday's test we had a general idea of how close we could get before pulling. The issue was how far apart packs would need to be before they chain pulled each other. Trial and error: that was all we could depend on.

I didn't have any intention of going out alone. Right now, I was just information gathering. Veronica was in no condition to be running around. That didn't mean she couldn't fight though. There was a simple solution. I would bring the mobs to Veronica.

She could hide around the corner in the lobby and pick off a free goblin or kobold as they passed by her. It would be bringing the mobs directly to our doorstep, which was risky by itself, but we needed to stay active.

The zombies and ghouls were something I could comfortably dispatch alone and shouldn't be a problem outside of a massive mistake by me. I was determined to do things correctly.

Veronica was awake when I returned. She sat on the bed with her back against the wall. Her right pajama pants leg was rolled up all the way. The bruise was now a mix of purple and green. It covered the entire right side of her thigh.

"How are you doing?" I asked. I picked up a bottle of water from the floor and passed it to her.

She put the bag of gummy bears down and took the water, "It hurts, A LOT." I walked closer to get a better look. "Don't touch it." She warned.

"I won't." There was a bit of swelling but not nearly as much as you'd expect if it was broken. "Have you tried to walk?" If the circumstances were different I'd let her rest in bed as long as it took. That wasn't an option.

"Let me finish eating first."

I sat on my bed and leaned back. My mind started to wander, "What if we can't find anyone?"

"What do you mean?"

"What If we're the only two people left?"

"On campus?"

"You could say that, but what if it's not just the campus?"

"I… don't want to think about it." It was a depressing hole to climb down. She balled up the empty gummy bear bag and then tossed it into the trash. Her face contorted as she scuffled off the bed and carefully set both feet on the floor below.

"Do you want help?"

"No, it's okay." She managed to steady herself and looked to be okay once she was standing.

"How is it?"

"It only hurts when I first apply my weight onto it."

"So you're saying walking is gonna be uncomfortable."

"No, walking is gonna HURT," she corrected me.

"Are you up for it?"

"It's not like I have many choices." It wasn't a complaint. She was simply stating the facts. I nodded in agreement and held open the door. She did her best to hobble out without causing herself too much pain.

I went against her wishes and directly supported her down the stairs. "I'm sorry about yesterday." I finally worked up the courage and apologized for my mistake.

"It's alright." I felt a weight lift off my shoulders. "Do you have a plan for today?"

"I do." I started to explain my vision for the encounters. We were nearly to the first floor when I heard a metallic click. It was the sound of a door closing. It was incredibly quiet, as if someone was closing it with extreme care.

I came to a standstill. Veronica turned her attention away from the stairs and looked at me, "What is it?"

"I heard something." I whispered. We both went dead silent and continued to listen. There was no sound. I wasn't hearing things, I knew that. I helped Veronica to sit down as carefully as possible, "Wait here for me."

I couldn't be mistaken. It was definitely hard to hear over our conversation, but I wouldn't mistake that sound for anything else. I glided up the stairs and went one flight higher than my room's floor.

I stood in front of the doorway in complete silence for a dozen seconds. There was still absolutely no sound. I reached out with my left hand and grasped the metal handle. A fireball appeared in my right.

I pulled down the handle and then pushed with explosive force. The door flew open and I flew into the hallway.

"Wait, wait! Please don't hurt me!" A young man yelled out. He was sitting with his back against the wall just to the right of the doorway. He scurried into the corner.

I didn't recognize him. To be fair, I wasn't exactly the most social person. "Explain yourself." The fireball in my hand gave me total control of the situation. "Why were you stalking us?"

He glanced at the fireball, "Sorry, sorry! Really I'm sorry! I saw you and that woman outside yesterday fighting the monsters and I was curious."

"You saw us? From your dorm?"

"Yes, I'm in room three-one-seven. It's on the front side and it looks out over the breezeway. I swear! I can show you."

I didn't want to leave Veronica too long, "Do you have your school ID?"

"Yes, yes." He fumbled through his pocket and pulled it out of his wallet.

"Andrew?" I held it up and compared the two. They were identical. He had short dark hair and thick rimmed glasses in both photos. The only difference was his shirt color.

"Yes, that's me." He breathed a sigh of relief.

"It says you're a med student?" The fireball in my hand subsided.

"Yes, I'm a third year." He was finally calming down.

"Come with me." He nodded his head and then walked with me down towards the first floor. Veronica was still waiting on the staircase there. She wasn't that surprised to see a second person with me. While he had been quite loud and frantic when I confronted him, he was quiet now.

I introduced him. "I'm Joseph, this is Veronica."

"Andrew." We formally shook hands. He stretched his hand towards Veronica. She had to struggle to reach his grip and winced in pain, "Are you injured?" He asked.

"Her thigh is hurt. Will you look at it?" She glared at me for volunteering without her permission. I put my arm under her shoulder and helped her up, "He's a medical student. It will be fine." She glanced at Andrew for confirmation and he smiled and nodded his head.

I helped her to lie down on a couch in the front entrance and Andrew inspected her wound. "Sorry in advance," he said. "It might hurt a little bit."

Veronica braced herself as he started to probe at her thigh. She ended up biting on her shirt collar to avoid yelling too loudly.

"The good news is that it isn't broken. The bad news is it's gonna be a while before it will heal fully. You might have a mark here permanently." I let out a sigh of relief. "I have some aspirin in my room if you want. It should help reduce the swelling and pain."

"That would be nice."

"I'll be right back then." He rushed up the stairs and left Veronica and I alone.

"What do you think about him? I want to get him to join us." I asked.

"We don't know him that well yet."

"True, but we also didn't know each other that well." Veronica didn't refute me. "We need more companions, now more than ever."

"Alright, if you think it's the right decision then I'll trust you."

I warmed to her for that.

The two of us could hear the jingling of pills coming down the staircase just after our conversation finished. He passed the entire bottle to Veronica without a complaint. My opinion of him rose a few points.

"Do you know anything about what's going on?" I asked him.

"Not that much…"

"Here's what we know." I informed him on the system commands we currently knew and briefed him on skills, stats and levels. We spent about ten minutes talking about it. "Now that you've heard it all, will you join us?" I sent him a party invite.

There was absolutely no hesitation at all. He joined the party and his level appeared above his head. "Veronica can't move very well as you can see. So I'm going to be pulling to here." I pulled out the crude short sword from my inventory and passed it to Andrew.

"You… want me to fight?"

"No, that's just in case. I want you to watch for now." I didn't expect him to fight, nor could I trust him to have my and Veronica's back so quickly. "You'll be able to protect yourself at the very least."

He looked down at the sword with an uneasy expression. Unfortunately that's just how it was now. There was no more time for coddling. I would do my best to keep him safe until he was ready. Eventually the onus would be on him to perform.

Veronica started to get up from the couch, "Not yet. There's two zombies and a single ghoul I need to pull first." I could sense them through the Skull ring. I would handle them alone as agreed upon. Veronica would only assist when I started pulling packs.

Chapter 5: Level Six

I made my way out the front and waited for the most opportune timing. The zombies were no longer a worry but I still needed to be wary of the ghouls. I would make this as quick and clean as possible.

My first target was a zombie. I didn't put much thought into the engagement. I only needed to make sure it was far enough from anything else before pulling. There was no need for *Inspect* either. If things were progressing as normal it would be slightly stronger than yesterday.

I threw out a fireball as soon as the undead was within my range and far enough away from any surrounding monsters. The zombie only made it halfway to me before smoldering. I received 40 EXP for the kill and found that a bit higher than I had anticipated for a three-player party.

I pushed the thought to the back of my mind as the next zombie followed closely behind the first. I wasn't going to let anything slip through the cracks. My performance today needed to be perfect. Not only for myself but for Veronica and our newest recruit Andrew.

I didn't hold anything back when it came to a ghoul. By the time it reacted to my spell I had already summoned another fireball. I wasn't interested in finding out if one or two were required to down it. An item dropped.

> ***Dagger of Ghoul:*** **Poisons target.**
> **A dagger made from the humerus bone of a Ghoul. You can feel your life draining by just holding it. HP -1 for every 10 seconds it's equipped.**

This was another item that neither I nor Veronica could take advantage of. I stored it away and returned back inside. My repeated use of *Fireball* had bolstered my confidence quite a bit. My ability to kill the zombies and ghouls was at on another level. It took me around twenty minutes to dispatch the three and that was mostly time spent waiting.

"How much EXP did you get?" I asked Veronica.

"One hundred and twenty."

"What about you?" I looked at Andrew.

Andrew paused and blanked out while looking at his stats. "Sixty."

Veronica and I received forty per kill and he received half of that? Maybe there was a level penalty I didn't know about. If that was the case, I was the culprit. I delegated the party leader as Veronica and left the party.

"What are you doing?" she asked.

"It looks like I'm too high level at the moment. You should party with him until he's in EXP range." I pulled out the Dagger of Ghoul and showed it to Andrew. "Any interest in using this?"

"Uhh… I'd prefer to be a healer if possible," he replied. Basically, Veronica and I would have to carry him for now. If he really did become a healer, however that would be a more than acceptable situation for the outcome.

Veronica sat up from the couch and made her way over to her backstab position. It was a hallway just to the left of the main entrance. She would be unseen from outside and have plenty of time to react and pick off a target as they came towards me.

This was the first real challenge of the day. It was a pack of kobolds just one-hundred and fifty feet from the dorm exit. Two of them carried blunt weapons while the third seemed to be a caster of some type. It wore an odd, feathered mask and carried a wand in its hand.

I sensed the area with my skull ring and confirmed there would be no interruptions. My hands were clammy despite my new-found confidence. This was only my second encounter with a non-melee monster.

My mind flashed back to the lich and I shivered. There was no way this little kobold could bolster that amount of power, surely? There was also the added stress of its position in the pack. Both melees were in front of it and I had no real angle of attack. It couldn't be my first target.

I calmed myself as best I could. This was only the start of many hurdles ahead of us. I approached closer and closer. When I was around 7 meters away I threw out a fireball towards the nearest kobold.

My solution was simple. I could abuse line of sight. I'd eliminate the first kobold on pull and drag the second back to the dorm where Veronica lay in wait. I refused to believe the caster kobold could target me through walls.

The kobold pack began yelping as they turned and faced my direction. As expected, the caster didn't begin chasing but instead started to cast a spell.

I started to worry. The first kobold seemed to ignore its burning body and continued to rush at me madly. It was taking longer than expected to burn up. I summoned another fireball as I was moving backwards and threw it out as well.

Suddenly an odd feeling washed over me.

> ## You have been affected by *Lethargy*

My thoughts were flowing smoothly but my body wasn't. I found it hard to control my limbs as I rushed back. This was outside of my expectations. The only good news was the first kobold collapsed shortly after my second fireball hit him.

My movements had slowed considerably. I felt clumsy and somehow managed to trip on nothing and tumbled to the ground. I began to panic. The second kobold was nearly upon me. There was no time to summon another fireball.

Crude Short Sword! Nothing happened. How could I forget I had just given it to Andrew? My lack of experience in difficult situations was my biggest weakness. I looked at the kobold that was only feet away from me. I needed to evade the incoming attack before he smashed my skull open with a hammer but couldn't. Just moving my limbs around proved difficult.

I summoned a fireball and did my best to position my legs around to block, so the damage wouldn't kill me. I was struggling to raise my fireball when Andrew jumped over me. He held the crude short sword with both hands and plunged it directly into the kobold's chest. He was moving with such momentum that the kobold was literally lifted into the air.

Andrew and the sword didn't come to a stop until the tip pierced all the way through and skewered the kobold to the ground. The kobold let out a pain filled yelp. Its little paw like hands scratched at the sword blade impaling it. It couldn't break free at all.

Andrew didn't stop there and rushed back to me immediately. I felt his hands grab under my armpits. With superhuman strength, he dragged me inside the dorm and into the hallway where Veronica was waiting.

"What's wrong with him?" she asked.

"I don't know. He seemed fine and then he just fell." Neither of them could understand what went wrong. It didn't help that I found it hard to even speak.

"I... m... o... k... a... y." The words came out so incredibly slow.

"It's coming." Andrew was now side by side with Veronica. The wand-wielding kobold was rushing over now that no one was in sight for its spells. It crashed right through the glass doorway and was met with a *Pierce* directly to the head. It didn't even have time to yelp as its brains splattered over the tile.

Veronica dropped to her knees despite the pain from her thighs and started to shake me, "What's wrong with you? What happened?" I did my best to smile as it was much easier than speaking.

> *LETHARGY* HAS FADED! YOUR STATUS HAS RETURNED TO NOR-
> MAL.

"Ahh, my God!" I shouted in frustration. The feeling of being in slow motion was insufferable.

"You're okay." Veronica was relieved.

I looked at Andrew and held out my hand, "You sure were quick. You saved my ass." He grabbed it with a smile and hoisted me up off the floor.

"You looked like you were in trouble. I guess I forgot to mention I run track…" He scratched his head.

"Are you sure you wanna be a healer?" He was definitely athletic enough to fight in melee. Two horns poked through my skin as I imagined both Andrew and Veronica holding the frontline for me.

"Uhh… that's okay. I definitely want to be a healer."

"How was the EXP?" I asked them.

"One hundred and forty," they replied in unison.

"Me as well." It seemed I was spot on. I received 140 for my solo kill and they both received 70 for the remaining two kobolds. I turned my attention outside and spotted a skill book floating just above the Crude Short Sword.

I looked at Andrew with excitement, "That should be for you." I had a hunch that the first monster you killed would provide you with a skill book. It had happened to both me and Veronica. Andrew was no exception.

Veronica waited inside as we rushed over and took a look.

BOOK OF *HEALING* LV. 1
CAST TIME: 1 SECOND
MP COST: 4
DISTANCE: 5 METERS

There was no better confirmation to my theory than this.

"Take it," I said. I hadn't expected anything from him, but Andrew had ended up saving my ass. I knew Veronica would agree whole heartedly for him to have the *Heal* skill.

Andrew hesitated for a moment before picking up the skill book and flipping the page. It disappeared a moment later.

I turned my attention to the Crude Short Sword still embedded into the grass. I reached out and grabbed the handle before tugging. The blade snapped in half. A new description replaced its original.

BROKEN SHORT SWORD
A USELESS SCRAP OF METAL

I held the remainder of the sword in my hand. I was completely bewildered. *What do I do with this now then?* I left the tip buried in the ground and put the rest into my inventory.

"Let's go try out *Heal*. We fortunately have a member who could use some help," I said. Andrew nodded and we both returned to Veronica.

She took a seat on the couch in such a way to stay off her bruised thigh. "What was it?"

"You'll see in just a moment. Can you show us your bruise?" I asked.

"What are you being all mysterious for? What was it?" She complained. I didn't say a word and neither did Andrew. She hmmphed and then showed us the bruise. "It better be good."

"Give it a shot," I said. Andrew held out his hands and walked towards Veronica.

"Wait! What're you doing? I didn't agree to this!" she was fully misunderstanding the situation. Andrew's hands started to glow a white light. Veronica's thigh also started to glow a faint light. "Oooh, that feels kinda good…" Her attitude took a complete one-hundred-eighty.

A brief moment passed before the light faded and we all took a good look. The bruise was still there but the color was much healthier and the area it covered shrank considerably. Heal definitely helped.

"How does it feel now?" I asked. I couldn't help but go over and poke it.

"Ow, it still hurts you ass. Don't touch it." She swatted my hand away and then looked at Andrew with a completely different face, "Will you try healing me again pleaseee?" She looked like a puppy dog.

Andrew's face was glowing with pride and satisfaction. He nodded and then casted another *Heal*. We looked on in anticipation to see the result. Nothing happened this time. The bruise looked and felt the exact same as before.

"Guess there's a limit then. The skill is only level one after all," I said.

"True, it would be a bit broken if it could heal everything." Veronica agreed. Despite the minor setback Andrew was all smiles.

"You should allocate more points into INT now that you're level two. We need you to be able to keep those heals coming."

"Right!"

Veronica stood from the couch and stretched her legs. The pain seemed to be at a tolerable level now. As long as she wasn't sprinting or putting too much force on it then it would be fine.

"You're back in business," I said.

"Yep."

We all looked over the next pack of kobolds. It was three melee-type kobolds. I double and triple checked to make sure I wasn't seeing incorrectly. The only issue was how close to another pack it was.

The risk of chain pulling was very real. There was no way to test the aggro range without going for it. The pack just to its left also had a crossbow-wielding kobold. The weapon was nearly the size of its entire body. No doubt it packed quite a punch.

I expressed my fears to them. We were capable of fighting in the open but I didn't want anyone else outside. If things went badly we would rush up the stairs and hope for the best. We stuck to the original plan. I would pull to the dorm and Veronica would pick off what she could.

I made sure I was max range before throwing out my fireball. Time seemed to slow down as the nearest kobold was hit. They yipped as a group of three and started to move in my direction. There was a moment of relief before that turned into terror.

The pack to the left reacted a second or two after. The two melee kobolds in that group joined the first three. The archer started to load the crossbow before pointing in my direction. That wasn't all.

The pack to the left of that ALSO pulled. That pack had a caster in it. I didn't summon another fireball or even dare to look back. I was out of range of that caster for now, but if for some reason it got close enough and *Lethargy* was casted on me… I would die without a doubt.

My hair was standing on end, my adrenaline was pumping. Their yips coming from behind me were absolutely terrifying. I didn't dare look back and only ran in a straight line. There was now a wave of monsters chasing me.

I was five seconds away from the dorm entrance when I heard a whizzing past my right side. It was a bolt that barely missed me. The ground it struck exploded as if a miniature explosion went off. The black dirt and grass sprayed onto the concrete entrance.

I felt relief for the first time. That relief was short lived. I heard another whizz and then excruciating pain in my left arm. I didn't even look down. The pain vanished in a moment as my adrenaline was through the roof.

YOU ARE AFFECTED BY *BLEED.*
YOU ARE LOSING 10 HP PER 5 SECONDS. YOU WILL CONTINUE BLEEDING UNTIL RECOVERING ABOVE 75% HP OR USING A BANDAGE.

My vision was tunneled and all I could see was those two glass doors. One of them was completely shattered through. The glass crunched beneath my feet as I entered into the lobby.

"Your arm..." Veronica was covering her mouth with her hand.

"JUST RUN." I yelled at the both of them. We all turned towards the staircase and rushed inside. I couldn't bring myself to stop and we went up all the way to the second floor. There was a moment of silence before a loud bang.

The melee kobolds reached the staircase and started banging their weapons into the closed door. Every bang made my heart skip a beat. It showed no signs of stopping. The door also wasn't budging. It was made completely of metal.

"Joseph... your arm..." Veronica's voice was shaking. It was only then that I had the courage to look down. There was a bolt at least six inches long piercing through and all the way out the front of my left bicep.

The remainder of my forearm was drenched in blood. Somehow the sight made me dizzy and my vision started to fade. I felt Andrew put both of his hands under my armpits and the two of them dragged me into the hallway.

Their voices were muffled but I could pick out little bits and pieces of what they were saying. Andrew leaned in close and I heard him say the word "hurt." It was all I could make out.

Then I felt excruciating pain. The pain was at a threshold that made me almost completely lucid. Just below the point where I was going to pass out.

Andrew grasped the bolt and completely pulled it through my arm. There was a finger sized hole in its place that was bleeding profusely. Shortly after that was a tremendous amount of relief. I don't know how many *Heals* were casted on me.

YOU ARE NO LONGER BLEEDING

My vision finally focused and that distant and muffled feeling disappeared. Andrews's hands were covered in my blood. Veronica's face was tinged with worry. They both stood over me and looked down.

"How... was... it?" I managed to fumble out. I felt so damn tired.

"You're okay. It's okay," Andrew said. I managed to look at my arm and could see the wound was at least closed all the way through. My arm was still covered in blood that was now drying to my skin.

Once again, I could hear the banging and knocking from the kobolds below. They were still searching and kicking down doors. We probably had a little longer before having to face them. I looked at Andrew and then at my own arm, "We should clean up." There was too much damn blood.

Veronica insisted I stay where I was and came back with two bottles of water and a towel. The white towel was thoroughly pink when we finished using it. I could finally get a better look at my wound.

The entrance hole was completely sealed but it was a different color than my own skin. It was darker and looked like a bruise. I poked it and winced in pain.

"You were lucky," Andrew said.

"How was I lucky?" *Is that how you describe someone getting shot with a bolt?*

"You ever see an arm dangling off?" he asked.

"Uhh, no…"

"Well, if it went just an inch and half more to the right… your bone would have snapped in half," I gulped.

Guess I was lucky. I started to move my left arm and only felt a slight discomfort. As long as I didn't have to lift anything heavy I should be in fine fighting condition.

"What now?" Veronica asked.

"I guess we wait." The kobolds were still banging and smashing up the floor below us. The banging lasted for around five minutes and then came to an abrupt stop. I felt five minutes was a really long time to wait.

After another few minutes of silence, we looked at each other and seemed to have reached the same conclusion. That we should go down and see what the situation looked like. Quietly, we descended to the floor below us. There were no mobs. Then we moved on down towards the lobby and with no sounds from beyond it, I pushed open the staircase door. The other side was filled with scratches and dents. Their little weapons had done quite the number on the stairwell floor. There was also a bolt embedded two inches or so into the frame. It didn't go far enough to pass through the door.

Moving carefully forward, I reached the front glass doors, which were completely mangled. They both rested on the floor and glass was everywhere. Andrew and I did our best to drag them off to the side. I turned my attention outward.

The mobs had reset, with the pack of kobolds I had originally targeted down to two in size. My first fireball must have managed to remove one. There was no chance that I should pull that pair though. We either needed a solid plan or a way around them.

"Should we take a look around?" If we could go around them that was best case. Even with a single kobold down, eight at a time was not something we could deal with. Especially considering two were ranged and one was a spell caster. We had yet to see what spells it cast besides *Lethargy*.

Veronica and Andrew both agreed. We went out the front and hugged the building. The entire cafeteria and breezeway, was surrounded like a fortress. The situation wasn't very different on either side.

The pulls were all sketchy. It became apparent our original pull was in fact the safest one, as laughable as that sounded. When we had discovered their reset time was around five minutes, I thought that it was a pain in the ass. But now I reckoned this could be exploited. I could throw a fireball and then run until reset. If it was possible to kill them from out of range without their retaliation, that would be best. I said this aloud.

"Could we trap them in the stairwell?" Andrew asked.

"And then what? Just leave them in there?" Veronica didn't seem convinced.

"Well, if we could somehow trap them in the stairwell and deal with them from safety that would be ideal," I said. "But is there a safe way to fight them in the stairwell?"

First Veronica, then Andrew, shook their heads.

"What if we start a fire in the stairwell?" Veronica asked.

"Are you trying to burn down the building?" I retorted.

"No, no. Hear me out. What if we just smoked the entire stairwell up? Surely they breathe like you and I? If we trapped them and suffocated them inside the stairwell we could kill them that way."

"We would have to stuff towels under the doors to keep the smoke in," Andrew chimed in.

"Yeah, if we mess up the entire building is going to smell like hell, too," I said.

"We don't have to burn a lot… we just need a lot of smoke."

"Green wood smokes a lot," I said. It was all the extra moisture still inside. It caused a ton of excess smoke. "The problem is where do we get it?"

"The bushes at the side entrance…" Veronica said.

The plan was starting to seem possible, "this could work…" I started to delegate tasks. "Veronica can you get a bunch of towels from the shower? It's actually better if they're still moist. Andrew, you come with me."

Veronica split off from us and Andrew went out the side exit with me. My arm was still not in the best shape so I had him do all the tough work. He grabbed a thick branch and started rocking his entire body weight back and forth.

Once the branch started to rip and tear, he kicked out several times with his foot to snap it off. Directly under the bark was moist and still green. The branches were all bendy and malleable. It was going to smoke a hell of a lot when burnt.

There was a tree out in the open field, just past where my sock bait laid to rest. I went under it and started to pick up dead branches and leaves off the ground. My fireball burned hot, but we still needed something to get this wet wood burning.

Veronica joined us after about five minutes. We started using the excess towels as sacks and transported the leaves and branches to a pile beneath the staircase of the front stairwell. The entire process took around forty-five minutes. The base of our bonfire was a bunch of dry leaves, then small kindling, and finally a stack of freshly ripped bush branches.

"How do we want to do this?" Andrew asked. There was still the fact we needed to pull the mobs, get them into the stairwell, and then trap them there.

"I'll go out there, neither of you have any ranged abilities."

"Right," they both agreed.

"I want Veronica to remain hidden down here. Andrew will wait for me on the second floor. When everything enters the stairwell, you will shut them in."

"I can do it," Veronica said.

"Why am I waiting on the second floor?" Andrew asked.

"I'm gonna be running up to the second floor and entering the hallway from there. God forbid I get hurt... you need to be there to heal me." I really didn't want it to come to that.

"Oh..."

"Once we group up on the second floor, assuming I'm in one piece, we'll head down the opposite staircase and loop around to the front. We regroup with Veronica there and assess the situation." I turned towards Veronica. "You'll be down here alone, so I'll leave the timing up to you. If they don't all go into the stairwell and it's not possible to trap them… don't risk it."

She nodded her head in understanding. The side hallways had small offices she could sit inside. As long as she didn't make a move they would never know she was there.

"Let's seal off the first and third-floor doors with towels now. We also need to wedge open the stairway door. The wedge needs to be something you can remove easily and won't get knocked away as the kobolds rushed in. Once you seal them inside you need to stuff a towel under the door as well," I reminded her.

Everything was in order after another ten minutes of shuffling. We managed to find a rubber doorstopper and wedged it into the open door. All Veronica would need to do was pull it out and the door would close on its own.

"Are we all ready?" I looked at the two of them. I was putting on a confident facade. I was truly terrified of going out there and pulling them again. Every part of my body was drenched with sweat. I did my best to hide my fear.

"Ready." Veronica disappeared into the first office in the left hallway. Andrew rushed up the stairwell and to the second floor. I walked outside slowly, as if it to take the scenery in. This really could be the last time I did something like this.

Veronica was peeking at me through the office blinds. She could see the entire situation unfolding and that gave me a bit more confidence. I summoned a fireball and steadied my shaking hand.

I tossed it out like I had done so many times before. It didn't even fly halfway when I knew it was going to connect. My feet started moving before my brain even told me what to do. I ran like a bat out of hell.

My head start this time put me out of harm's way. It seemed that even the nearest crossbow-wielding kobold wasn't close enough to take a shot. My heart was beating out of my chest. I felt so incredibly alive.

I summoned another fireball into my hand immediately after passing the destroyed front entrance. My steps slowed ever so slightly. The only way things could go badly now was if I slipped on this broken glass and fell.

The stairway was in clear sight. I darted inside and looked back for the first time. The first of the kobolds was only now stepping onto the concrete just outside. It was another five seconds or so before they entered the building.

Veronica was to my right just barely poking her head out the office. Once she had counted eight kobolds passing through and into the staircase, she could make her move. I gave her a smile and then threw my fireball into the pile of kindling. It burned fiercely and I rushed up the stairwell.

The second floor door clicked open and Andrew pulled me inside. He gave me a look over and it was clear that he was relieved to find me uninjured.

"They're coming," I said.

The yips of the kobolds echoed through the stairwell and reverberated all the way back down. Andrew stuffed the towel under the doorway and we both dug our fingers in as hard as we could to seal any crack.

It wasn't going to stop all the smoke, but it was definitely going to help a lot. We started our sprint down the hallway towards the opposite staircase right as the first bang rang out. The kobolds were now pounding on the door.

A 'donging' sound ran through the building, made by metal being pounded each time with slightly different weapons. Their little axes, clubs and hammers made a different noise with every hit. I hoped everything was okay with Veronica down stairs. I confirmed there was no undead in the vicinity and Andrew and I rushed around the outside and to the front of the dorm.

We found Veronica standing in front of the stairwell door. There was a white towel jammed beneath it. "Things went smoothly," she said. The kobolds were still yipping and yapping in the stairwell.

Small amounts of smoke started to seep out of the door cracks and we could smell the burning and feel the heat. The metal clangs from the floor above faded slowly over several minutes. The hits sounded weaker, then they fully stopped. The yips and yaps were now few and far between.

I suddenly received 140 EXP, and then another. Two of the kobolds had died. The fire was a result of my spell. I guess that dictated I earned the EXP. There was no sound of movement, or yipping, or anything from within the stairwell.

All we could hear was the crackle of wood through the door. "I got EXP for two of them. Did you guys receive anything?"

"No."

"So that means only two have died, let's wait a bit longer." I suggested.

We stood in silence.

"What about now?" Veronica asked.

"Still just two." After five minutes the crackling sound was starting to fade out and still only two had died. Either I had only received EXP for two of several kills or six were really still alive in the stairwell.

"Shall we check it out?"

"It's possible they're unconscious and on the verge of death." Veronica said. I started to bang on the door hard to stir a reaction. There was nothing.

"Let's check." I opened the door a crack and smoke plumed out. It wasn't even possible to see a foot in front of our faces. "Cover your face." We pulled up our shirts and cracked the door wide.

Smoke continued to pour out for over twenty seconds before there was enough visibility. Veronica led the way with her rapier, Andrew was next and I followed behind. I lit a fireball in my hand for protection as well as a source of light.

Veronica was spot on. There were kobolds strewn about the floor and staircase. They were already on the verge of death and didn't even have the strength to open their eyes. "Take them," I said. This was free EXP for Veronica and Andrew. It would put her at level four and him at level three.

We could party together after that. There was also the fact that of the nine mobs, I had received EXP for three already. In terms of EXP it was a perfect split. The three solo kills put me close to level six.

Veronica went from kobold to kobold piercing through their heads. It only took her two minutes to dispatch five out of six. We found the sixth at the very top of the stairwell in a corner. It was more lucid than the rest but still put up no resistance. It yipped as Veronica approached.

Yes.

I rejoined the party and could see a level 3 above Andrew's head and a level 4 above Veronica's. That had to be close enough in range to share group XP.

We rushed out of the stairwell and kept the door jarred open. Without a doubt all of our clothing smelled of smoke. The stairwell probably wouldn't be usable for the better part of a day. The fire was already mostly extinguished. We tossed the half damp towel over the remaining embers to put it out.

"That… worked really well." I had to admit. That was truly the first time we orchestrated a plan as a party and executed it properly. It felt good to do things correctly and be rewarded.

"Agreed."

"There's three packs remaining between us and the cafeteria. It's possible we can pull just two of those, maybe even one." There were two goblin packs and one kobold pack remaining in our way. After that we could directly access the building from the side.

The tiredness I had suffered from earlier was gone. It was replaced with a hunger to continue hunting and to level. I only needed a single pack of goblins or kobolds to reach level six.

"Shall we go outside now?" These three packs were spread out considerably farther apart. I felt confident that we could pull them one pack at a time. That being the case, there was much more risk for me to pull solo than if we just stayed together.

We walked farther into the grass than I ever had since the beginning of the apocalypse. The pack in front of us was three goblins, all melee. Considering what we had just experienced and dealt with, it seemed like child's play.

Retying her long brown hair at the back, Veronica was aching to get some real action after Andrew healed her leg. I didn't see any discomfort in her movement. There was also the added fact we now had a healer. Things were looking up.

Although I had never inspected a kobold, my suspicion was that they were stronger than the goblins. I based that on their reactions to being attacked. The previous goblin had caught my fireball and been simply burnt up in agony.

The goblins simply clawed and patted away at the fire until they died, unable to ever put it out. The kobolds, however, they ignored their burning fur and flesh and rushed at me as if possessed. They didn't care about anything other than hacking me to pieces.

Even if their strength was similar, that determination made kobolds more dangerous.

"Everyone ready?" I asked.

"Ready," Veronica and Andrew replied in unison.

I tossed out my fireball to start the engagement. The first goblin writhed in agony while burning as expected. The remaining two hobbled in our direction while cackling. They didn't make it halfway when Veronica intercepted the both of them.

Over the course of going from level 1 to level 4, her movements had become completely different. She was like a deadly dancer. She pierced the second goblin instantly and evaded the third's strike at the same time. A line of blood flew through the air as her rapier was pulled from its skull.

The third could barely turn around before the rapier's tip inserted directly through its ear hole and out the other side. Blood started to pour out of both of its ears before it slid off and plopped to the floor.

CONGRATULATIONS! YOU HAVE REACHED LEVEL 6. AS A RE-
WARD FOR LEVELING UP, YOU HAVE BEEN GRANTED THREE STAT
POINTS!
CURRENT EXP: 120/1600   LEVEL: 6
HP: 255/255   MP: 32/66
STR: 5
AGI: 5
DEX: 7
VIT: 8
INT: 12 +3
AVAILABLE: 3

I opened my stats to take a look. With the speed at which we were killing, I felt my MP value was steadily falling behind. I couldn't ignore DEX either and put 2 points into INT and one point into DEX. We now had a healer and VIT could be pushed back as a priority temporarily.

```
CURRENT EXP: 120/1600    LEVEL: 6
    HP: 255/255     MP: 46/72
             STR: 5
             AGI: 5
             DEX: 8
             VIT: 8
            INT: 14 +3
         AVAILABLE: 0
```

There was something so incredibly annoying seeing my INT stat at 14. I had a hunch that 15, or even 20 would make a difference. The same could be said about my DEX and VIT stat. They looked so unappealing, and that fueled my desire to level even more.

There was a book floating above the first goblin I hit with fireball. We huddled around it.

```
        BOOK OF SHACKLING LV. 1
         CAST TIME: 3 SECOND
            MP COST: 7
        DISTANCE: 10 METERS
SHACKLE YOUR FOES WITH POWERFUL ARCANE MAGIC. RE-
STRAINS TARGET FOR UP TO 20 SECONDS. DURATION BASED ON
    TARGETS AGI. DAMAGE THRESHOLD: 500
```

Wow. While not a damaging ability, its utility was incredibly impressive.

"This should be for you Joseph," Veronica said.

I looked at Andrew. "Any objections?"

"Nope, learn it," he insisted.

> ## Do you wish to learn *Shackling* LV. 1?

I didn't hesitate. While the spell wasn't something I could take great advantage of this instant, its power couldn't be denied. I pondered over what the 500 damage threshold meant. *If the target took more than 500 damage the shackle will break?* It was the only logical explanation.

The cost of 7 MP was high but reasonable. It was a worthy price to essentially take an enemy out of battle. There was one more group we needed to eliminate. If our distances were right then we could reach the cafeteria just after.

The last pack was a group of kobolds. Two of them wielded axes while the last held a crossbow.

There was no doubt in my mind that if that bolt hit any of us in the heart or head… *critical hit.* We wouldn't last more than a minute from a wound like that. I refused to believe that *Heal* could bring anyone back from the dead.

"I can try it out right now." I told the two of them. They both seemed excited to find out exactly how the skill worked.

I held out my hand and focused on the crossbow-wielding kobold. *Shackle!* Three spikes immediately shot from the ground around it and golden-purplish chains wrapped it up over the next two seconds. It struggled in place but couldn't move.

Meanwhile, his friends were on the move. I summoned a fireball while Veronica moved forward to intercept. My fireball managed to blind one of the melee types as the fire engulfed its entire chest and head. It swung its axe around wildly as if crazed.

Veronica was given a one-on-one that I knew she would have no issues with. I suspected she could probably dispatch an entire pack of melee enemies on her own now. She easily evaded the kobold's attacks and stabbed out two or three times in a single second. The kobold was sporting three new finger sized holes, two in its chest and one directly through the throat.

The kobold archer yelped and screeched while it frantically struggled. Its two companions were dead just like that. Not even ten seconds had passed and it was the only remaining enemy in front of us.

I tossed out a fireball at the same time Veronica ran in to pierce the kobold before it thought to line up a shot. The kobold didn't have a chance to cry out before despawning. Its body disintegrated and only then did the golden-purplish chains shatter into a spray of glowing dust. The spikes receded into the ground as if never having been there.

There was now a clear path into the cafeteria and the timing couldn't be more perfect. I was running dangerous low on MP. At best I could participate in one more fight. But then I changed my mind. "Should we return to our room for now?"

"Return? The cafeteria is right there... isn't that what you wanted?" Veronica looked at me, more with curiosity than puzzlement.

"Hear me out." I paused. "The day is still young and we don't know exactly what's in the cafeteria waiting for us... if something goes wrong I won't be able to help you handle it."

"What did we do all this work for?"

"The monsters won't respawn until tomorrow. We will still have time to return later today." I promised.

"Alright, fine," Veronica agreed and then so did Andrew.

We used the side staircase to avoid letting anymore smoke into the dorm. Again, I was exhausted from having cast so many spells, I could barely keep my eyes open. A feeling of tiredness hit me like a ton of bricks. Within moments of getting to my bed, I was gone.

Chapter 6: The Cafeteria

When I woke it was somewhere around six. There was at least an hour and a half of solid sunlight left. Veronica was sleeping on Slob's bed and Andrew had dozed off against the wall. I stretched my arms and let out a yawn.

My yawn startled Andrew and he jerked awake. It seemed he wasn't used to having others around yet. Veronica gave a snore louder than my commotion. I shook her a few times before she sat up and rubbed her eyes.

I got up and separated the blinds. Our friendly kobolds were hard at work and the third circle was fully lit. As expected, the packs we cleared hadn't respawned yet. I couldn't be sure if each individual pack had its own respawn timer, or if everything respawned at a certain time, like dawn or midnight. I double checked and currently had 30 MP, enough to defend myself.

We rushed out and towards the cafeteria, making sure to give a large amount of distance to the third pack of goblins we skipped. They were on the opposite of the breezeway and I figured as long as we didn't step past the halfway mark, they would leave us alone.

It took us just thirty seconds to reach the side of the cafeteria. This area was docking and it had its own inner wall. Inside were two full-size dumpsters and a trash compactor. We disappeared inside and shuffled between the two dumpsters. We hugged the wall until reaching the back patio.

The wooden steps creaked as we walked up. There was still trash and food left on a few tables but a lot of debris - trays, plates and food - had been blown off and now littered the shrubbery just behind. The tinted windows made it hard to see inside. I grasped the handle and gave it a pull. It was locked.

I continued walking to the other side of the patio and down. There was a rock garden just up against the cafeteria. I grabbed a large piece of what appeared to be granite rock and carried it back up in both hands.

I took a look around out of habit. Something everyone does when they feel they are doing something wrong. The back door shattered with a smash and glass fell to the floor. I reached my hand under and turned the deadbolt. It clicked into place.

"Let's go," I whispered. The two nodded and followed closely behind me.

The door opened and swept some of the shattered glass onto the back patio. The rest crunched beneath our shoes. The inside was very dark, only near the windows was there a bit of light.

After all this time, there was no clean air or fresh-food smell to greet us; instead the smell of decay was everywhere. The whole cafeteria smelled like old fridge and my hopes to find edible food dropped just a bit. Backpacks littered the booths and table tops, but I didn't see any blood anywhere. I also didn't see any people.

I measured my steps as I moved from one side to the other, all the doors had been locked from the inside. My hopes were dropping as I moved from shop to shop. The industrial freezers had all thawed and anything that could spoil was well on its way.

Our first really useful discovery were several bags of uncooked rice. There was at least ten pounds of it. I found some bananas and oranges as well but the bananas were rotten. The skin of the oranges was hard and shriveled. They were completely inedible.

Our last stop was the 'general' store. I always questioned its existence, but now I was praising whoever thought of it.

Inside was a mini-fridge that contained several sodas. The counter had some bags of chips but most of it was unusable garbage, commonly needed items for class: erasers, pencils, stuff like that. The rest of it was school souvenirs: hoodies, lanyards, etc.

I opened the mini-fridge and reached in for a soda when I heard the sound of a pot smashing onto tile. It echoed through the cafeteria. I retracted my hand and closed the fridge slowly. I looked at Veronica and Andrew. We all turned our heads towards the direction of the sound. "Hello?" I called out in a low tone.

I heard repeated shuffling and a hushed whisper coming from the back of the pizza line. "Is someone in there?" I called out. They continued to speak with hushed voices. "I can hear you." I finally said flatly.

The shuffling continued and then I heard the sound of a lock being turned before the backdoor opened. A male head peeked out. "It's safe?" he asked while looking left and right. He was tall, that was the first thing I noticed. His chest clearly showed over the serving line. He had to be over 6'5 while standing.

The second thing I noticed was his reddish-orange hair. It was short and curly on the top of his head. It reminded me of Velcro for some reason. He wore a basketball jersey with the number 23 on it.

"It is," I responded.

The door opened wider and he crawled up off the floor and stood. "It's safe." He looked over his shoulder. He really was over 6'5.

Another young man crawled in view from behind him. He was Asian, with pitch black hair that shone even in this minimal lighting. He had a t-shirt that looked like something from the 80s and had Pac-man on it. The two looked odd standing next to each other. The redhead was just too tall.

They exited the back and appeared behind the counter. Their eyes constantly scanned the area around them.

"Where are the things?" the redhead asked.

Things? I guessed he meant the monsters. "Outside."

"They're still outside?" He became incredibly nervous.

"Were you both hiding back there the whole time?" Veronica asked.

"Yes, we've been eating pepperonis the entire time. The sink was plugged and full of water already. We've just been drinking that."

"How much left?"

"We ate the last of the pepperoni today, there's none left."

A message was transmitted just as I was about to speak.

"Attention all players. The city of Deerfield Beach has been designated as a safe-zone. Please head to the area marked on your map. It is suggested you reach there immediately if you wish to survive.

"You have two weeks."

A map was shown very clearly in my mind. The safe-zone wasn't the entire city but only a small portion of it. I had never been there but the route to get there was very clear, as if all the information I needed was given to me.

"Did you hear that?" They looked at each other while speaking simultaneously.

"Everyone heard it. I need you two to listen to me. First, what are your names?"

110

"Aaron," the giant redhead said.

"Richard."

"Alright, I'm Joseph, this is Veronica, and this is Andrew." I introduced them before continuing my questions. "Do you excel at anything?"

"Basketball," Aaron said.

"So you're athletic?"

"Yeah." He was a potential tank. My thorns were growing.

"And what about you?"

"Computers."

I favored Aaron already.

"Alright, here's how it is." I laid out the fairytale like situation with Veronica nodding to reinforce my points.

"Stats? Levels? It's kind of hard to believe," said Aaron.

I agreed with him wholeheartedly. "Think the word stats."

Aaron's eyes immediately changed and he became very quiet.

"You too," I said to Richard. His eyes also went wide. I invited the both of them to the party. As expected, they were both level 1.

"You're level six!" Richard was astonished.

"You've been out killing monsters?" Aaron asked. I hadn't mentioned EXP but he picked it up quite quickly. "So it's like an RPG?"

"Yeah." There was a bit of silence, "Would you two be willing to join us?" The more companions the better. The transmitted message was no joke. The monsters were already getting stronger by the day. The connotation was that something big would happen after two-weeks.

Aaron looked at me, "Have you figured out what the stats do yet?"

I had a general idea. "A little bit." I gave him my basic knowledge of each stat point.

"I'll come along," Aaron said.

Richard looked uneasy but eventually agreed, "Me as well."

"Tomorrow we'll start your leveling." It was getting late and I would have to reorganize the party. I would have to drop out and allow Veronica to level them up until they were ready to fight on their own.

Grabbing all the food we could as a group, we rushed across the field back to the dorms. Aaron had extensive game knowledge and offered his perspective the entire walk back. It was our first night as a team but we slept apart. Veronica stayed in my room and Andrew returned to his. Aaron and Richard took an open room they found nearby.

I woke the next morning to the sound of fumbling. Richard was digging around for food. "Sorry," he said. I stretched and stood before waking Veronica. It seemed Richard also started his days early, that or he has really hungry. We woke everyone and grouped. There was still a lot to figure out.

"I don't have any skills for you two unfortunately. All I have is this." I held out the Dagger of Ghoul. My health began depleting slowly.

"Where did you pull that from?" Aaron was astounded.

"My inventory."

"Can I see it?" I passed it to Aaron and he grasped it in his hand. He tossed and turned it in his hands for a few moments. "I feel kind of sick holding this." He passed it back to me.

Breakfast was a bag of chips and a soda, arguably better than most breakfasts I'd had these past few days. I went more into depth about our situation and then passed the party leader to Veronica before disbanding from their group.

I looked out the window of the dorm. Sure enough, the three packs of monsters we dispatched yesterday were respawned. The kobolds and goblins weren't exactly the same though. I didn't see any caster or crossbow-using kobold. All the goblins just looked the same to me and I couldn't tell if there were any non-melee classes.

The runic circle was now almost fully done. Whatever was happening would most likely kick in tomorrow. We would only have a day to get Aaron and Richard into fighting condition.

They didn't have any skills or weapons. The monsters were a few levels stronger than day one and I couldn't be sure how badly a single strike would injure them. It was best to let them leech EXP.

My confidence in Veronica was through the roof. They were in good hands and I'd be there to support them as well. We had the making of a great party. We exited out the side staircase as five. I wanted Veronica to fight only zombies and ghouls. I explained to Richard and Aaron that they should pick a class specialization and concentrate on it, as that was likely to affect the skill books that dropped.

"We could really use a proper tank, so Veronica can flank and backstab."

"I'm happy to be melee," Richard said. He looked nerdier, and while Aaron was more physically suited to be a tank, I would take what we could get.

Leading her group against a pack of zombies, Veronica was fully confident in dispatching them with ease. Her solid display of strength must have bolstered the confidence of our newcomers. While I preserved my MP in preparation for a long day of grinding, Veronica was like a grim reaper.

After the zombies came ghouls, who could get close but never touch a single hair on her head. Her rapier was like a piston pumped straight through their skulls. I couldn't even see the movement of her hand anymore. It was just a blur and then the monster would fall.

I felt a real sense of accomplishment. It hadn't even been a week since we considered these deadly foes. Now we looked at them as nothing more than walking EXP.

She was killing so fast that Aaron and Richard had reached level 2 and we're now halfway to level 3. An item dropped on the floor and we came together for a discussion.

CRUDE SHORT BOW: RANGE +1M.
A STICK AND SOME STRING, WILL IT EVEN FIRE?
SHODDY ARROW QUIVER
A QUIVER FOR HOLDING ARROWS. THE CONTENTS SEEM UNREMARKABLE.

"Who fancies being ranged?" I asked and maybe it was because I was already looking at him, but Aaron raised his hand. He now had a weapon. It was possible for him to kill a monster and get a skill.

"How many arrows do you have?" I looked to Aaron.

"Five hundred."

A pleasant surprise. There were plenty for him to work with. I had a plan.

"Stop killing for now Veronica." She wiped the sweat from her brow and returned her blade to her side.

The four of them followed me around the backside of the building. My skull ring was incredibly useful for finding isolated and easy targets. The parking lot I fought the lich was in this direction but I didn't see him floating about. It had only been two days but my outlook had changed.

I started off by pulling a zombie first. I knew from experience that they had low HP and should be relatively easier to dispatch. The two newcomers fidgeted and spooked as it ran towards us but I assured them it would be okay. "It's fine!"

I allowed it to get within thirty feet before making my move. *Shackle!* Those marvelous spikes and golden-purple chains extended from the ground and grasped it in place. It was only fifteen feet away after my three second cast.

"Go!" I shouted at Aaron. He seemed completely zoned out. His hands fumbled and shook as he did his best to nock an arrow. It took him a full five seconds before an arrow flew out with piss poor strength. It hit the zombie directly in the chest and didn't even enter inside its rotting flesh.

"Take your time!" I reassured him. He seemed much steadier as he nocked another arrow. The second arrow flew with a much better trajectory and inserted itself into the eye of the zombie. It continued flailing and biting the air as if unaffected. The shackles stayed strong.

"Again!" I hid my inner nervousness with a calm outer appearance. I was banking everything on being able to cast *Shackle* on the same target again. The zombies and ghouls were also a perfect target because of their low AGI. I was very sure the shackles would last the full twenty seconds.

17, 18, 19. I had been counting since the beginning. The shackles were going to break any second and I prepared myself to cast again. The zombie was close to the point of being frightening for Aaron and Richard. They could, in fact, be badly hurt if it got to them. An arrow was nocked.

The shackles shattered into dust and the zombie began its move toward us. Both Richard and Aaron were unaware of the time restriction on *Shackle*. They had both assumed they had unlimited time to act.

"Shoot it!" Richard yelled. His fear caused a sudden outburst. The nocked arrow was let loose and soared through the air. I still needed two more seconds before *Shackle* would land again. The five of us watched with bated breath as the arrow entered into the same eye-socket as before. Drawing her rapier once more, Veronica was preparing to intervene.

There was a cracking sound followed by a black and thick goop leaking out of the undead monster's eye. The zombie collapsed before I could finish my cast. "That was close..." Aaron muttered.

He let the final arrow fly without much thought. The body of the zombie despawned and a skill book floated there. The two looked at it with greed in their eyes. "Go see what it is." I urged Aaron.

It was guaranteed that your first kill granted a skill book. The world now was hectic but it hadn't come across as unfair. If you worked hard and took risks, you were given the necessary abilities to succeed. Shouldn't it be the same for everyone?

Aaron grasped the book between his hands, "Nice!"

"What is it?"

"Book of *Powershot* level one."

"It's ranged?"

"Yes!" Aaron had made it obvious he wanted to be an archer and he was up and running already. I looked at Veronica and wondered if she secretly wanted to be melee or was happy with DPS.

"You should learn it," Andrew urged him. I watched the book disappear from Aaron's hand and an incredible grin covered his face.

It was immediately obvious *Powershot* was a formidable ability. Aaron left golfball-sized holes in the faces of each zombie or ghoul. Veronica and Aaron were a two man wrecking crew. By the time they were finished, Veronica was an iota of EXP away from level 6, Andrew was just above halfway into level 5, and both Aaron and Richard were level 4.

Richard was instructed to save all of his stat points for now and Aaron went one-to-one on STR and DEX. The increase in his stats showed immediate improvement. He nocked arrows faster and the strength at which he shot was a level above previous.

"Let's keep going. Today will be a long day." The five of us headed towards the front. The kobold and goblin packs were now on the menu "Invite me to the party." I was level 6 and they were both level 4. The difference shouldn't be a problem anymore.

It seemed the max share range without penalty was four levels. Five and above taxed the lower levels fifty percent of their EXP. There was no issue after I rejoined the group. EXP was split evenly among the five of us.

Aaron had become proficient enough to deal with a single yard trash monster on his own as long as he used *Powershot*. Veronica, Aaron and I could dispatch a pack of kobolds or goblins in a matter of seconds. Andrew was prepared to heal us if anything untoward happened.

I glanced at the area where the runic circle was being constructed. There were still so many active kobolds moving about. It looked like the pull, at minimum, would be five packs of kobolds.

Then too, there was the problem that the composition of the classes of our enemies was well varied.

There were casters and ranged kobolds strewn about. Even if Richard had a decent weapon I questioned if we could take it on. The spell *Lethargy* was deadly and the bolts did devastating damage. And what if one of their casters had *Shackle*? I didn't think any of us had been pushing up AGI.

We surveyed the alternatives: there were at least fifteen or twenty packs of goblins and kobolds spread around the area. An amount I had never considered taking on before. Having Aaron with us increased our killing speed substantially. I looked forward to when Richard had the skills and gear to properly tank.

"I'll pull." Aaron stood just beside me as we both eyed a pack of goblins. He nocked an arrow and pulled the bow taut. An arrow that caused the air to whistle tore a hole directly through the heart of the nearest goblin. Almost immediately after, my fireball soared through the air before landing on another, burning it up in seconds. Veronica ripped through the throat of the third.

A familiar item dropped.

CRUDE SHORT SWORD: STR +1
A SWORD OF POOR CRAFTSMANSHIP, THE BLADE HAS CRACKS AND THE TIP IS DULL.
WOULD YOU LIKE TO EQUIP CRUDE SHORT SWORD?

I carried it back to Richard. "How about it?"

He had been watching Veronica plow through mobs with ease. "I do want to be melee...but why does this look so dreadful?"

Richard accepted the blade with a sour look. The sword looked absolutely poor, as if it would fall apart at any time.

"Put your points into STR and VIT for now," Aaron said from beside me.

"Okay, done."

"How much HP did you get per point of VIT?" I was incredibly curious.

"Uhhh, fifteen." It was the same amount I gained as well per point.

"And what's your total HP?"

"Two hundred and eighty-five."

If he kept putting points into VIT and STR, by the time he was my level he would have considerably more HP than me.

I looked over the packs and found the easiest one possible: a group of goblins that all carried blunt weapons. "There." I nodded. "I'll shackle one and Aaron can eliminate one immediately. Richard you will face off against the third on your own. Andrew can heal you if anything goes wrong." I didn't want Veronica to interfere, on the assumption that if Richard got the kill, he'd get a relevant skill book.

Then too, although the game helped us, Richard was level 4 but had never used a weapon nor fought an enemy in combat at all. Stats weren't everything here. You needed practice as well. If he was going to tank then he needed to be competent.

The excitement Richard felt earlier had clearly greatly diminished as came close to being time to put his money where his mouth was.

"Go!" I yelled out. A shackle appeared from the grass below restraining one of the goblins. At the same time, an arrow whizzed through the air and popped the head of another like an exploding melon.

The third cackled and rushed in Richard's direction. I watched as he hacked and slashed the goblin repeatedly before using his brute force to insert the sword directly through its chest.

The weapon was so dull that instead of cleanly entering, it broke the ribs of the goblin before plunging inside. Blood poured from its mouth as it struggled to breathe. Aaron shot a Powershot through the head of the remaining shackled goblin.

A skill book floated in front of Richard, spawning directly from the goblin he had killed. He snatched it up.

"What is it?" I called out.

He grinned. "Cleave!"

"Learn it." It was a sword skill no doubt.

We began moving towards the next pack. We were all getting fired up. Maybe a little bit too much.

"Guys! A little help back here?" We turned back to see a zombie chasing Andrew in the open field. We were all starting to tunnel a bit too hard. I blamed myself more than the others. There was no excuse when I had a ring that could sense undead. I casted *Shackle* to restrain the mob.

The golden-purple chains wrapped the zombie and enclosed it. Regardless of its struggle it couldn't escape the enclosure. Veronica started to walk forward when I stopped her, "Wait. Can you try to heal it Andrew?" It was something I was curious about. *Heal* was typically a holy spell and zombies and ghouls were sometimes vulnerable to holy. In theory healing undead might work as an attack spell.

He nodded his head and then his hands glowed a white light. I didn't mind the MP waste as we weren't taking any damage.

Andrew spent most of his time standing around trying to stay alert in case of mishap.

There was a pause and then a flash of light enveloped the zombie. It was the first time I heard one of them groan. Its body started to burn up in a pure-white light before the effect stopped.

"Again!" I said.

The second heal caused the zombie's dirty bones to become bleached white and all the rotted skin disappeared. It collapsed into a heap before despawning. A skill book floated in place.

BOOK OF *HOLY PROTECTION* LV. 1, DAMAGE TAKEN -5%
CAST TIME: 1 SECOND
MP COST: 3
DISTANCE: 2 METERS
DURATION: 1 HOUR

"Is it a buff?" Richard asked.

"It sounds like a buff to me."

"Made for Andrew, I'd say." No one had any objection. The book disappeared from his grasp.

"Cast it on me!" Richard was a touch over-eager. But that was understandable when one blow from a goblin hammer could break an arm or worse. A few moments passed before a translucent angel spawned behind Richard in the air, it sprinkled something on him before disappearing without a trace.

"Cast it on Veronica as well?" I suggested. They were the two people fighting in melee and most likely to take damage.

I received an unfamiliar message suddenly.

Huh?

Everyone paused at the same time. Their faces had a tinge of confusion. I wasn't the only one to receive it. After concentrating on various options, I eventually found out how to read it by focusing on the word 'mission'.

STOP THE KOBOLD MYSTIC

An interesting title that brought one monster to mind. I started to read the contents.

THE KOBOLD MYSTIC HAS DRAWN A SUMMONING CIRCLE NEARBY. THE RITUAL IS NEARLY COMPLETE. VERY SOON, A DREADFUL KOBOLD WARRIOR WILL DESCEND UPON THIS PLANE AND WREAK HAVOC UPON THIS LAND. YOU MUST PUT A STOP TO THE SUMMONING AT ALL COSTS.
CONDITION: KILL THE KOBOLD MYSTIC AND DESTROY THE RUNIC PILLARS. FAILURE TO COMPLETE THIS QUEST WILL TRIGGER ANOTHER QUEST EVENT.
REWARD: ???
DURATION: 6:00:00

To top it all off there was a six hour timer on the quest. "Did everyone read it?"

"Yeah..."

"Kobold Mystic? What's this a reference to?" Aaron asked.

"I think it's best if we go upstairs and I show everyone." We returned to my dorm room and grouped around the window. I pulled the blinds wide and pointed it out. There were so many kobolds bunched around the circle you would think they were defending a fortress.

"This… doesn't look like it will be easy," Aaron said. He wasn't wrong. It was probably fifteen or so kobolds at the minimum. Not to mention the ones rushing back and forth.

"Do we have to complete it?" Richard asked. It was a good question. The penalty was an unknown factor. How strong was this kobold warrior going to be? What if the follow up quest wasn't optional but mandatory?

I held back on my opinion and asked the group, "What does everyone think? We should consider this carefully."

In my view, it was difficult to judge the challenge. Was this a raid event, where we needed to find more survivors to work with? If so, a group, even a well-balanced one like ours, had no chance.

The immediate threat of all those kobolds felt much more real than the consequence of the unknown quest and monster if we chose to ignore it.

"Can we just leave?" Andrew asked.

"That's a possibility." We were on a timer to reach the designated safe-zone already. "Are we ready to leave?" I asked everyone. I had a feeling things weren't going to remain as they were once we left this area. Monsters would grow stronger and the types would definitely change as well.

"Erm… maybe." Andrew shrugged. No one could give a definite yes or no answer.

"I think we should give it a try shot first," Aaron said. "If there's a way we can escape if it proves too tough."

"I agree. This place is a treasure trove of EXP for us currently. We have a shelter above our head and food for now. We can't know what's waiting for us once we leave the campus," I said.

"Running doesn't guarantee we can even evade the follow up quest." Aaron added. I was already appreciating his logical way of thinking.

"If we plan to make an attempt then we can't waste the time we have. We need to keep leveling as fast as possible and get any new skills and gear we can," Veronica pointed out. "Then we can try it with around an hour of time remaining."

"There is one problem." I paused. "My MP is already running on the lower end. Supposing we try the quest, I need to sit out and regenerate my MP. That means leeching off all of you... is that fine with everyone?" I felt it only right for me to ask.

"There's nothing to it," Aaron said.

Veronica nodded. "Agreed. We need you in top condition if we want to have any chance at completing the quest."

I sighed in relief.

I ended up hovering in the back with Andrew. Any worry I had about sitting out quickly vanished. Aaron was a great leader. He had a keen eye for strategy and directed Veronica and Richard with ease.

I only needed to remind him once about chain pulling. He made the proper adjustments and avoided packs that were too close together. He was either a natural strategist or just very familiar with RPG games in general.

I watched hungrily as Veronica carried a staff back with Aaron and Richard in tow. She passed it to me and I got to see the stats. I was blown away.

STAFF OF RECHARGE: INT +1, RECOVER 2 MP EVERY 15 MINUTES.
A FAVORITE OF WIZARDS AND MAGES. THIS MAGICAL STAFF BOASTS OF REMARKABLE RECOVERY POWER!

"What dropped this?" I asked.

"One of the goblin casters. It looks nice doesn't it?"

"Yeah…" I looked to Andrew. We were the only two people who could make use of it currently.

He held up his hands, "All yours."

"Are you sure?"

"My MP is nearly full. Have you seen me casting heals?" He asked. I guess that was true. I equipped the staff.

My body was jittery with excitement. The special effect on this staff more than doubled my MP regeneration. My current MP regeneration was somewhere around 6 per hour, this staff provided me with an extra 8. *Should I complain more?*

I equipped it without hesitation and marveled at its appearance. The staff was as tall as me and contained golden rings at the top. A beautiful gem was implanted inside. My motivation to keep leveling doubled.

I was excited to see how much more powerful it was. I decided I would join them for the next pack. One cast of fireball wouldn't hurt…

Cold sweat ran down my back as I looked at the new MP cost and the ever-increasing cast time. *Thank God I found this staff...* The cast time and distance had increased slightly. The damage surely went up as well.

My new level of *Fireball* was at a power that at first I couldn't quite comprehend. I targeted a zombie while they were off dealing with a pack. The level 2 version of *Fireball* used to ignite them and they would burn up after some time. This time the zombie simply died on being hit. The difference was staggering.

I was also on the cusp of level 7. I checked my stats and my current EXP was 1570/1600. One more pack of kobolds or goblins would push me over the edge. Veronica and Andrew were both 6 while Richard and Aaron were level 5. The gaps in our levels were shrinking as the EXP required per level climbed higher.

CONGRATULATIONS! YOU HAVE REACHED LEVEL 7. AS A RE-
WARD FOR LEVELING UP, YOU HAVE BEEN GRANTED THREE STAT
POINTS!

It became clear that DEX was nearly as important as INT. My cast times would endlessly grow higher and my need for the DEX

126

stat would only grow as well. I ended up putting two points into DEX and one point into INT. It satiated my OCD just slightly.

```
CURRENT EXP: 140/2100          LEVEL: 7
        HP: 285/285    MP: 33/82
                  STR: 5
                  AGI: 5
                  DEX: 10
                  VIT: 8
                  INT: 15 +4
               AVAILABLE: 0
```

The only use I'd found for AGI was resisting *Shackle*, which was potentially very useful indeed, but very situational. Looking at my stats, I reckoned STR was coming up on the menu very soon. The staff in my hand felt like pure gold and had considerable weight to it. There was also the issue of our upcoming journey. I couldn't afford to be over encumbered.

Increasing my power for the upcoming quest battle outweighed everything else though. With so many targets I needed to ensure my casts came quickly and efficiently. My teammates depended on it.

The amount of EXP required for the next level was staggering. By the time I reached level 8 everyone would be level 7. I looked up at them.

"How's it going?" I asked.

"Well!" Veronica gave a thumbs up before wiping the sweat from her brow. Even Richard seemed a bit more cheerful than before.

"Did you find anything good?"

"No skill books but we did find a *Bow Thimble* for Aaron. It gives plus two DEX," Veronica said.

"That staff looks really good," Richard said. I was holding it majestically in my hand.

There were three hours remaining of the designated six. A large majority of the packs nearby had been wiped clean already and wouldn't be respawning anytime soon. We squeezed out all the benefits we could.

"We should decide how we're going to approach this," I said at last. It was going to be the most difficult pull yet.

"We should start by tallying up mob composition." Aaron said. "We need to know how many melee, ranged and casters there are. If we can eliminate the ranged and spell casters first and foremost, the battle should be much easier.

We spent around thirty minutes going around the summoning circle and tallying each mob type. There were two spell casters, four ranged, and a whopping eleven melee. This wasn't including the kobold Mystic.

"Eighteen mobs in total…" Hearing the number out loud made me doubt this was the right decision.

"How can we fight this head on? I don't agree to it," Richard said. I couldn't blame him. He was one of two melee classes, and the only person interested in tanking. It was too easy for me or Aaron to say go ahead. We were safely in the back.

"I don't agree either," I chimed in.

"What if we can split the mobs up?" Aaron asked. "Let's say we can make these eighteen monsters turn into nine instead. At the cost of one of us leading them away."

"Four versus nine seems a lot more manageable," said Andrew; Richard and Veronica both agreed.

"I can shackle one and eliminate one immediately as well."

"Four versus seven then," Aaron said.

"How do we split them up then?" I asked.

"You said mobs have a five minute reset timer? Well, as far as we know."

"Yeah."

"Why don't I go to the opposite side and pull. You pull just after me. We split the mobs in half that way."

"And what will you do?"

"Run like hell. My speed is enough to keep the kobolds off me for five minutes. It won't even be an issue."

"It could work."

"Also, the majority of ranged and spell casters are on the side I'd be pulling from. You shouldn't have many to deal with, two at most." He was right. I could shackle the caster on this side and fireball the remaining ranged monsters.

"And what about the Mystic? We have no idea what he is capable of casting."

"True."

"Regardless, I don't think we have any other option besides this," Aaron said. "It's clear to everyone here we can't engage eighteen kobolds at once."

"Then we decide as a group now. We either use Aaron's plan and split them up... or we abandon the quest," I said. There was silence as everyone thought carefully about the situation.

I wanted to give it a shot but waited for someone else to speak up before voicing my opinion. My influence as the highest level might pressure them to respond contrary to their feelings.

Surprisingly, Richard was the first to speak up, "I'll do it."

"Let's try," Veronica was next.

The two melees agreed and Andrew saw no reason to not go along. "I'm in."

Aaron was already decided, I was the only one left. "It's settled. Let's have a quick meal and then get into positions."

The meal was anything but luxurious. We each grabbed our preferred candy and finished off a bag of chips together. I felt like we were about to go to war. We were.

"If things don't go as planned then we call it off immediately. Don't worry about me and just get to safety. I'll be fine," Aaron said. "Rendezvous here when you can."

"Understood." I would be pulling just after him. It was my discretion that would determine if we fought or ran.

Chapter 7: Boss Fight

The deadline for completion was a bit under three hours after our meeting and meal. We had plenty of time to finish the quest. We could even attempt multiple pulls if they didn't go as planned. Aaron positioned himself on the opposite side of this gigantic pack. We remained on the dorm side.

He raised a hand high to indicate he was ready and we had no problem seeing it as he towered over the kobolds. They looked like baby dogs in his presence. "Ready?" I asked the three behind me.

"Now or never," muttered Veronica, her rapier raised.

I turned back towards Aaron and raised my hand high. I gave him a thumbs up. Whether he could see it or not wasn't important. The hand raise was the signal. My heart was beating in my chest.

He nocked his arrow, steadied his aim for several seconds, and fired. Before even seeing the result of his shot he had started to run. I could see it though. His arrow pierced directly through one of the ranged kobolds and dealt a grievous wound.

It yipped in agony and then began its chase. Its sudden movement caused a chain reaction. The kobolds all around it looked in Aaron's direction and started to make chase.

My timing was crucial. There was around a second of delay between the chain pulling of each pack. I needed to strike now and pull the remaining three packs in our direction. I threw out my fireball towards the only crossbow-wielding kobold on this side.

I targeted the spell caster with *Shackle* while my fireball was still in the air. If everything went as planned we would have only seven enemies to deal with. Seven melee mobs would be very manageable for Veronica and Richard. It would all come down to whether the boss in the middle, who was currently conducting the ritual, would get involved.

My fireball connected and *Shackle* latched a second later. I had successfully made the pull and the two biggest threats were at least occupied. Aaron was sprinting off with a train chasing behind him. The remaining three packs now faced in our direction. Everything looked like it was going clean when two monsters broke off from Aaron's train and returned.

There was a second of doubt in my mind, *should I call it here?* We had agreed on an even split or better. Eleven mobs were more than we bargained for. I turned around to give my verdict and Richard and Veronica were already passing me.

"It's not a problem!"

"We'll take care of it!"

They both rushed by me. If they were fine with the outcome of the pull I could only accept it. The brunt of danger fell upon them.

I shouldered the responsibility of dealing with that extra ranged kobold. I rushed forward with them to meet its approach. If I had anything to do about it, it wasn't taking more than one shot.

I summoned a fireball and realized my hand was shaking. The situation was much more stressful than I could have imagined. Veronica and Richard were now colliding with the eight melee kobold. They took four each.

I launched the fireball like a trebuchet. Only a second later was there an explosion of dirt and grass around Richard's feet and he skipped in pain. That was the result of the one and only shot I'd allow their caster to take. My fireball engulfed it in the middle of its reload. The strength of my new flame incinerated it in mere seconds.

That miniature explosion startled Richard enough to make him lose focus. His leg was sliced by the blade of an axe. My heart dropped. I turned towards Andrew only to find he was already casting heals. The wound was not as bad as it originally looked. It didn't hit bone and only cut an inch or so into his skin. It was a superficial wound that heal closed up immediately.

Despite that, Veronica and Richard both backed away at the same time to make some distance. "Gahhh, that fucking hurt," he cursed. It was the first real wound he received. Despite being a game, the pain was very real.

In that five second skirmish two melee kobolds were killed, and I dispatched the second ranged kobold. Despite the minor setback things were turning in our favor. The caster was still shackled neatly in the back and showed no signs of breaking free.

The smell of burnt hair wafted in our direction. The kobold Mystic was still stationary in the summoning circle without showing any signs of movement. This was the absolute best case scenario. It was too preoccupied to stop and assist. Was it really going to go this smoothly?

We had plenty of time left. Richard took a good look at his leg and found nothing wrong with it. The blood was still there but the wound was completely closed up. They rushed back into brawl.

The melee kobolds didn't chase but backed away slightly. They were tightening around the summoning circle, as if protecting the Mystic. It seemed like a reasonable action. Veronica and Richard pursued.

With the shackle still locking down the spell caster and the remaining six melees tied up. I turned my focus towards the Mystic. I summoned a fireball in my hand and prepared to throw it out. I saw it just a second too late.

"Look out!" I yelled. There was a black shadow crawling along the grass. It was moving at the speed a man could run towards Veronica and Richard. It extended out from the Mystic's feet. I was wrong that he was only watching: he was casting a spell.

Veronica wasn't fast enough to evade, nor did she know what she was looking for. The shadow connected with her feet. "RICHARD!" I yelled.

He realized something was wrong and pressed hard against the remaining few kobold warriors, pushing them back and away from Veronica. He swung out repeatedly with cleave and grazed against their furry bodies.

Veronica was still like a statue. I stopped what I was doing and rushed to her side immediately. I reached her in moments and could see the problem. The black shadow was ascending her body towards her neck.

"Can you move?" I asked. She didn't respond and shook her head slightly, brown ponytail swaying just enough to be an answer. Just that effort made her face completely red. She was battling with all her strength to keep the shadow at bay. I could only imagine what that black hand would do once it reached her neck.

My first thought was to move her. If I could just pull her away then it would be fine. I could break the shadow that way.

"Richard, protect us!" I didn't need to tell him but said it anyway. He was swinging out like a wild beast and keeping the kobolds from getting any closer.

I grasped Veronica and tried to move her. She absolutely wouldn't budge. Not only that, it seemed me trying to move her caused extreme pain. The shadow gained a couple inches on her upper chest. I didn't dare touch her again.

I summoned a fireball and looked towards the Mystic. He remained in the same spot as before but his eyes were watching us. He was the source of this shadow. I would have to kill him. My fireball looked like it was going to connect when it collided with a barrier.

The summoning circle flickered for a moment and even the shadow climbing to her neck receded an inch. It seemed like the Mystic needed to borrow the power of the runic pillars to defend him during this crucial moment.

I summoned another fireball and threw it out. "Richard! We need to kill the Mystic now!" Veronica's face was fully red and her veins were bulging on her neck. Even the vessels in her eyes looked like they were going to burst from the pressure she was fighting back with.

My fireball resulted in another barrier and a bit more time bought for Veronica. Richard heard my warning and started to act more aggressively. He took hits to his arms and legs while Andrew healed him up. There were now three melee kobolds remaining.

I forgot to count the seconds. My attention was so focused on Veronica and the Mystic that I didn't think about the spell caster waiting in shackle. It broke and my heart stopped. The little wand waved in Richard's direction before my fireball could connect.

Richard's limbs went stiff and his body slowed. I knew what it was. He was affected by *Lethargy*. "Andrew, I need you up here!" It was the last resort. He didn't hesitate and sprinted up to me. "Get Richard."

135

Richard was struggling to even walk backwards as his body moved in slow motion. If the kobolds hadn't decided that protecting the Mystic was their most important task they would have chopped his limbs clean off.

Andrew grabbed our tank under his arms and started to pull him back. It was then that the Mystic let out a yip. The three remaining kobolds grew bolder and started to move forward again, weapons raised. There was only me and my staff in the way.

No amount of fireballs could get me out of this situation. Richard was out of commission for at least thirty seconds. Andrew had no weapon. Aaron was busy kiting. I grasped the staff with both hands and poked and prodded at the incoming kobold.

The best I could do was simply push them backwards and hope Richard broke out of it faster than I did. I pushed into the belly of a kobold while another smashed his hammer into my hand. I cried out in pain. Andrew quickly healed me.

I managed to hold them off for around fifteen seconds and countless wounds to my arms and legs. "Joseph, I can't heal much longer… I only have mana for two more casts!" Andrew yelled from behind.

Richard was still on the ground struggling to move his limbs. He couldn't even speak. It was then that I noticed in my peripheral vision. The train of kobold Aaron dragged away was returning. They would be here in thirty seconds at most.

"Why…? Why is this happening?" Tears started to well up in my eyes. It hadn't even been two minutes yet.

I glanced back at Veronica in exchange for a wound to my hand. The shadow was nearly around her neck. Her face was sunburn red and her eyes were bulging.

Her eyes were pleading with me. They were filled with desperation. *Fuck it...* I summoned a fireball in my hand and kicked out with my foot. One of the kobolds went flying back and another burned to ash.

The third managed to slice my leg with his axe. The physical pain was far less than the emotional turmoil I was feeling right now. I summoned another fireball and incinerated him as well.

I was going crazy. I summoned a third fireball and threw it at the Mystic, and another. The shadow on Veronica's neck receded ever so slightly, but it wasn't enough. I wasn't strong enough.

"Joseph... I have nothing left!" Andrew yelled from behind me. My HP was below half already and his heals were out. The kobold were just moments away from returning. There was no way they wouldn't chase us on our retreat.

I could see the ranged and spell casters leading the charge. If we didn't retreat we would all die. I looked at Veronica one last time, "I'm so sorry...I tried my best." My voice cracked.

The desperation on her face vanished at my words. She knew it was over, her fight was over. Her face suddenly relaxed and a bit of the red faded. The shadowy hand jolted forward and wrapped its grip around her neck.

I couldn't bear to watch and rushed by her. "We have to go." I moved next to Andrew and assisted him in grabbing Richard.

"What about Veronica?"

"We have to go," I repeated.

"We can't leave her!"

"WE CAN'T!" I caught myself. "We can't... save her." My tears were already falling to the grass below.

My sudden outburst shook him awake. We both grabbed Richard and rushed back to the dorm. I wished so badly my hands were free to cover my ears. I guess it was my punishment, to be able to hear the final abuse Veronica took before death.

Richard was able to move when we reached the stairwell and we returned to my room. I was so afraid of what I would see when I looked out the window. I mustered the courage and looked out.

The kobolds had reformed and there was no sign of Veronica. She was really gone…just like that.

I couldn't even bring myself to speak. The words didn't want to come out. My mouth didn't want to open. I felt dead inside: utterly defeated.

I fell onto my bed and stared at the ceiling in a haze. I had known Veronica for less than a week. Why did it hurt so much? By any definition we were merely acquaintances. She was simply a passerby in this unfortunate circumstance. Who was I kidding? I knew the answer.

The trust and reliance we developed in these few short days was something you might never develop in a friendship. She was a comrade in arms, someone who had battled side by side with me in life or death.

Why was I so naïve? I had seen the people swallowed up by the horde of monsters on day one. I knew we were risking our lives. I knew death was a possible outcome every time we went out to fight. I had brushed all those warnings off. It could never happen to me: that's what I told myself.

This was a brutal wake up call. I wasn't special. None of us were special. *I'll die if I don't wake up.*

The door suddenly jolted open and Aaron entered inside. "Shit, we miscalculated." He was panting hard from just running back. "The reset timer isn't the only thing we should have worried about, they tethered after I ran a certain distance. It's good to see you all made it back tho... where's Veronica?" He cut himself off.

I put my arm over my head to cover my eyes. I couldn't bring myself to say the words. Andrew just shook his head. Aaron understood. He didn't keep talking and instead sat down and leaned against the wall.

The mood in the room was quiet. No one felt like speaking. Nearly thirty minutes passed before Aaron worked up the courage to speak. "I know this is hard to hear... but we need to think of the next plan."

He was right. I gave him the most honest answer I could come up with. "I know... but I need a little bit of time." That's all I could do. I needed to fix my head.

"I don't know if you checked, but the timer for the quest was pushed back twelve hours. Whatever you managed to do delayed their plan."

I didn't respond and simply delved into my own thoughts. My mental state wasn't in a position to lead, or to fight. Veronica swam through my head. I replayed our chance encounter when I was praying she'd leave me alone, our introduction, our first battles, and our shared joy of loot and skill books.

She would never fight by my side again. That was a hard realization to swallow. "You three should discuss our next course of action. I trust your decisions. Just give me a bit more time to come to grips," I said to Aaron.

They all nodded and disappeared into the hallway. The sadness left me feeling lethargic. I fell asleep.

Someone shook me awake early the next morning. I could barely see who it was in the darkness.

"We can't let you sleep anymore." It was Aaron's voice.

I rubbed my eyes and sat up. "What is it?"

"There's an hour left before the quest fails." I checked my info and read the timer. It read 58:47.

"What did you all decide?"

"We decided to fail it and take what comes. It's best if we're all awake and together when it happens."

"Alright, give me a few minutes." He turned and left back into the hallway. I sat in silence for thirty seconds before turning over and standing. The top of Slob's bed was empty, it felt so surreal. My body felt empty. It was more than just my hunger though. I didn't make them wait for me long.

I was sore all over as well. My HP had regenerated back to full while I slept but the discomfort from the bruising on my hands and legs was still there. I entered the hallway where they were all huddled together.

"We should gather what we can and prepare to leave. If we can't handle it then we get out of here immediately," Aaron suggested. It was an agreeable plan. I emptied my school bag and then put two clean sets of clothes. Any remaining space went towards food and water, which we were running low on.

Both Aaron and Richard lived off campus and resorted to raiding other rooms to pick up bags and clothing. We spent thirty minutes gathering and preparing. There was a little less than twenty-five minutes remaining when all was said and done.

Everyone sat around me in a circle in my dorm room. "From what I can tell, it's at least fifteen miles to the safe zone. If we make it to the highway and follow it down till the exit we can avoid any detours. From there it's just traveling through residential neighborhoods." I spoke as if I knew exactly how to get there.

The reality was that I did know exactly how. The information was implanted directly into my head: the same as for everyone. The distance, the direction, the routes and streets, all of it was very clear. Two miles a day is all we have to achieve and that will leave us several days to spare." No one disagreed.

The sun was only now rising over the distant horizon. The breezeway and surrounding area were lit in a low orange hue. Visibility was bad, but it didn't stop us from seeing the kobold ritual.

The runic circle was vibrantly glowing as all five pillars were fully lit. When five minutes remained, it started to pulse like a beating heart. A feeling of trepidation washed over me as I realized it was matching my own heartbeat.

It felt like an eternity before those five minutes were up. The pulsing suddenly stopped and the circle illuminated more brightly than ever before. The entire area around was being lit like a second sun was rising in the courtyard.

There was a strong pulse that thrummed. Then there was another. It wasn't constant but instead deep and powerful. Every thrum gripped at my heart.

A small circle suddenly appeared above the Mystic. The pillars surrounding the ritual lit one at a time as the kobolds in that little section died. Their deaths caused the pillar to fade into darkness. The circle above his head was a portal.

The portal started to grow wider as each pillar was extracted of its energy. It finally reached the last two pillars that had absolutely no kobold at them. We had killed them yesterday and they hadn't respawned yet.

The pillars went dim and the portal looked to be closing. Without the live sacrifices it couldn't sustain itself. It shrank by half the size, and then another half. Nothing had come out and the portal was shrinking rapidly.

"Is it going to close?" Richard asked.

"Nothing has co—" I didn't finish my sentence. A single dark and fur covered hand grasped the portal from inside. Then there was a second hand. A brief struggle ensued until the two hands literally stretched the portal wide.

The creature that walked out wasn't human. By comparison with the kobold Mystic beside it, the new arrival must have been eight or nine feet tall. Its entire body was dark brown. Its eyes were glowing blood red.

I couldn't tell if this was a type of kobold or not. All I knew was it was bestial. There were cuffs around both wrists that dangled broken chains. Its ankles were also cuffed with torn chains. A spiked collar went around its neck that also had a broken chain dangling from it.

The two hands were adorned by incredibly sharp claws. Despite that, two cleavers the size of my thigh rested in each hand. It looked like leaving was the best course of action.

The kobold Mystic got down on its knees and kowtowed towards the newly spawned beast. It bowed repeatedly while letting out barks of worship. The creature simply looked at it with disdain.

I thought that was the end, but it wasn't. The creature lifted its cleaver high and then cut the kobold Mystic directly in half. It picked up one half of the body and started to gnaw it. We could all hear the crunching of bones from here.

"I think this is one of those situations where we should leave."

"Agreed."

I opened my quest window to take a look.

Are you fucking kidding me? I nearly blurted the thought out loud but kept it in my head. "Looks like leaving isn't an option."

"What do we do?" For the first time I didn't have an answer. That thing was an absolute monstrosity. I wasn't confident we could defeat it now.

"The quest said 'Hunt'. Doesn't that worry any of you?" Andrew asked.

"We should be safe inside still though, right?" Richard was the most uneasy out of all of us. He was now the only melee remaining in the group. Those cleavers looked like they would easily chop him in half.

143

"All we can do is watch and hopefully gain some information," Aaron suggested. We continued to look out the window. Feroce remained in the runic circle gnawing on that kobold Mystic corpse.

It didn't seem like he was interested in doing any sort of hunting. He ate his meal for dozens of minutes before turning his attention elsewhere. The sun was high enough now that the area was clearly visible.

"Is he looking at the goblins?"

"Can't be sure." Feroce walked out of the circle and towards the dorm. There was conveniently a goblin pack in his path. I was expecting to see more carnage.

Instead, Feroce stopped and crouched down. His gigantic hand put down his cleaver and then tore out a large patch of grass. He raised it to his nose and started to sniff. Once he was finished he stood and walked past the goblin pack without so much as a second glance.

"Is he...?"

"He can't be."

"There's no way." He was walking towards the dorm entrance with intent. Nothing else around him caught his attention.

"Guys... I think he's coming here," I said. Everyone was in denial. That was until his feet touched the concrete and we could no longer see him. He walked directly into the lobby and out of our sight.

We rushed out the room and towards the stairwell. "He shouldn't know how to open doors right?"

"Right." Richard assured us all. He didn't seem that confident.

We could hear Feroce fumbling in the lobby below. His loud footsteps came to a stop at the stairwell door. Then there was prolonged silence.

The door budged slightly as his hand pushed against it. It started to shake and rattle more as he pushed into the door frame. "See, nothing to worry about," Richard said again. The silence came again.

"Did he give up?"

"He's too stupid to come up here." There was suddenly an incredibly loud bang from the door. It was the sound of metal striking metal. The sound made us all jump in fright. It echoed through the stairwell.

The bang came again, and then another. We could finally see what it was. His cleaver came through the door and out the other side. Feroce pulled it back and kept hacking away. His repeated strikes were slowly mutilating the door.

Our hearts were in our chests. "We can't stay here." I made the call. It wasn't going to be quick, but he would eventually break that door down. Then it would be this one, and finally my dorm room.

"Where do we go then?"

"Anywhere but here." We grabbed the things we had prepared and then rushed to the opposite stairwell and through that door. By the time he made it up the stairs and into the corridor we would be away. That was the idea at least.

We opened the side staircase and looked out. The packs of mobs were numerous and yet far from our minds. We needed to distance ourselves from Feroce as quickly as possible. The breezeway seemed like the best option.

It ran directly through the middle of the entire campus. Almost every building was connected to it. That would give us plenty of places to hide.

"We should go around the buildings. If he catches sight of us in the open we might be in trouble." That was surely the smart play.

We would lose some time but the longer we moved undetected by him the better. We started to rush through the open field towards the school's front office.

Richard led the way and downed any zombie or ghoul in his path. He was completely fearless with Andrew behind us. His trepidation from earlier seemed to have disappeared after our last battle. Taking damage was inevitable. He was already growing as our tank.

We ended up looping all the way around the school's front office and cut back into the breezeway. It was the opposite direction we needed to travel to make it to the safe-zone currently.

"We need a plan," I said. We couldn't just run forever. Time was not on our side.

"Leaving isn't an option," said Aaron.

"Well, fighting isn't an option either!" Richard complained. He looked at the shoddy-looking blade in his hand and his face soured. One swing from Feroce and he wouldn't have a weapon at all.

"Then we can only get stronger," I said. "As long as we remain on campus we will always have buildings to run to and doors to hide behind. Once we leave… there will be nothing between us."

"What do you suggest?"

"We lead him on a wild goose chase. We use that time to better equip ourselves, to level up."

"And if that isn't enough?"

"Then… we find another way." I refused to believe he was an undefeatable monster. There was no way to gauge his true strength until we exchanged blows. "The only thing we know for sure right now is that he won't stop chasing us. It doesn't seem he is that intelligent either. He chose to hack apart a door instead of turning a handle."

Aaron nodded. "That's true."

"We can use that to our advantage then. He follows our trail like a hunting dog. Then we just need to make the trail as difficult to follow as possible."

"Should we split up then?"

"I don't think that's a good idea. If we split up then we can't know for sure who he will follow. If we stay together at least we'll have an idea of where he is."

"We should see how long it takes him to find us," Aaron suggested.

"If we wait on the second floor we should be able to see him. We can find out if he follows our same route or if he comes directly to where we are now."

"Good idea."

Any information we could gather about Feroce was incredibly important. Only when we knew our enemy could we make an appropriate plan. I hadn't forgotten about *Inspect* either. There just hadn't been a safe moment to use it so far.

We waited looking out of the window for what felt like an hour before spotting Feroce moving towards the front office building. A journey that took us less than five minutes took him an hour. Mostly because he had to hack through four metal doors.

"We should leave now." We had seen enough. He was mimicking our route. We didn't go into the front office but around it. At the pace he was moving he would be upon us in less than five minutes.

We moved along the second floor and to the far end of the school campus before descending to the first floor. Once there we cut through the business administration building, walked all the way to the opposite end, took the stairwell to the third floor and then walked all the way back to the opposite side.

We were creating a maze with our pathing, one that would surely buy us a lot of time. After that we moved to the English and writing building and did the same. Only after all of that did we dare move back down towards the breezeway.

I didn't believe for a second he wouldn't chase us if he saw us. It was just that the campus was so big it was unlikely we would ever cross paths. Considering we knew the path he was going to take, we wouldn't make that mistake.

Together, we moved all the way to the opposite end of the campus and back towards the dorms. "That should give us an hour or two of breathing room," Andrew noted.

"We can't waste this time then." We needed to grow stronger, and fast.

My depressed mood was completely on the back burner. I still missed Veronica. It still hurt, but the looming shadow of Feroce caused all unnecessary thoughts to vanish. All my mind could think about right now was how to survive.

We looked over at an open field of kobold and goblins. The way I saw them now was completely different to that first hour after the warning. They used to terrify me completely. I was sure the others felt the same. Despite that, I gave the mobs the level of respect they deserved. Anything that had a weapon could kill you.

"That's a lot of EXP," Richard remarked. Even his uneasiness from before was fading away.

"Let's split into groups of two, it'll be faster that way," I said. "Richard you take Andrew and I'll take Aaron. Stay close." We weren't going to split up, but we could focus our attention on different group of enemies.

I told myself I wasn't strong, and that was true. Maybe to Feroce I was like an ant or fly waiting to be swatted. But to these kobold and goblin, I was still king. I summoned a fireball and Aaron charged up *Powershot*.

As we rampaged through the nearby packs, a different feeling came over me. It was something that I rarely felt. I was having fun again. After Veronica died I thought this feeling wouldn't come again for a long time. It was like the whole apocalypse. Was it wrong to relish the challenge? Maybe there would come a time when the massive loss of life would really hit me, but right now we had a fight to win.

I looked to my right after Aaron and I dispatched a pack of goblins. Richard wreaked havoc upon any monster unlucky enough to end up in his sight. He cleaved left and right, quickly dispatching any enemies.

Any time he took damage a bright light would envelope him that healed him back up. Richard and Andrew were an unstoppable force. I couldn't help but yearn for when I received my first AOE spell and could clear packs of monsters like that. Aaron was probably thinking the same thing.

Our killing speed was staggering and because of that my next level came fast. Andrew made it halfway through level 7 and Aaron and Richard were ninety percent of the way through level 6.

CONGRATULATIONS! YOU HAVE REACHED LEVEL 8. AS A REWARD FOR LEVELING UP, YOU HAVE BEEN GRANTED THREE STAT POINTS!

Carrying around this heavy staff was starting to weigh me down. It wasn't as obvious as before when the trip was just outside the dorm. With Feroce on our trail we needed to constantly be on the move. My low STR stat was holding me back. I put all three points into STR.

```
         CURRENT EXP: 260/4700   LEVEL: 8
            HP: 315/315      MP: 27/86
                    STR: 8
                    AGI: 5
                    DEX: 10
                    VIT: 8
                    INT: 15 +4
                 AVAILABLE: 0
```

We also picked up a decent amount of loot.

```
    STAFF OF HEALING: HEAL +40. HEAL COST -1 MP.
   A REMARKABLE STAFF IMBUED WITH HOLY POWERS. A BEAUTI-
              FUL RED GEM ADORNS ITS TIP
```

There was no one other than Andrew who could use it. He accepted it happily.

Richard received a new weapon that made his eyes pop out of their sockets. It was also aesthetically pleasing enough as I didn't hear a single complaint about how it looked.

```
POLISHED GREATSWORD: STR +5
A TOWERING SWORD WITH INCREDIBLE CRAFTSMANSHIP. YOU
FEEL YOURSELF BECOMING STRONGER JUST HOLDING IT.
```

Aaron received a shiny pair of boots.

```
QUICK-FOOTED BOOTS: MOVEMENT SPEED +5% AGI +1
YOU FEEL LIGHT ON YOUR FEET
```

Richard also learned a brand-new skill to go along with his two-handed sword. This was arguably the most important drop.

```
SWORD CRASH
SLAM THE FLAT SIDE OF YOUR SWORD INTO YOUR ENEMY. GEN-
ERATES A LARGE AMOUNT OF THREAT
```

Hopefully this would allow him to hold aggro in the longer fights, specifically against Feroce.

"My MP is running on the low-end," I said.

"Mine as well." Andrew had a sour look on his face. He was experiencing the exact opposite situation. Just a day ago he barely needed to heal, now he was healing too much.

"I'm fine," Richard boasted. There were bangs and bruises all over his arms. He didn't seem to mind at all with the new greatsword resting against his shoulder.

"Shall we rest for a bit and have a go at Feroce?"

Richard coughed, "Well… I don't know." The smile and his readiness for combat faded away at the name. He didn't have a shield, but the greatsword was so big it might as well double as a shield anyway. The question was how well he could use it.

"We can test the waters at the very least. Let's absolutely not meet him on open ground though. We need an easy escape route." The brainstorming began and the answer was simple enough.

"Let's just fight on the breezeway. There's plenty of places to retreat. As long as Richard doesn't get taken out in one hit we can gauge the situation and go from there." It was unlikely Feroce was so powerful that he could swat Richard like a fly. Our tank was pumping STR and VIT every level after all.

We all looked at Richard and waited for his response. He was going to be the only thing between us and Feroce. The final say was up to him.

"Can't we wait another day?" Richard asked.

"I'd like that as well… but there is one problem," I said.

"And that is?" Aaron asked.

"Is there any indication that Feroce will give us any breathing room at all? How will we even sleep?" This was the one issue tickling the back of my neck. We would only grow more tired as time went on. If that was the case, dealing with Feroce as soon as possible was our only hope.

It wasn't totally sure that our enemy would keep going…but I hadn't seen monsters sleep at any time. The goblins cackled through the night and the kobold barked. Once we fell into that hole it would be harder and harder to climb out of.

"It's still early in the afternoon. We have a good seven or eight hours of sunlight left. Consider it while we rest," I suggested.

Richard nodded his head and we entered into a nearby building.

Several hours passed without any sign of Feroce. Was it possible we lost his trail completely? I found it unlikely. It seemed that our confusing movements bought us more time than we had expected.

It was also possible that he wasn't currently hunting us. It didn't say we would be hunted every waking moment, but that he would never stop. I was beginning to question my own decision when Richard spoke up, "Alright, let's try him today on one condition!"

"Sure, what do you suggest?"

"We retreat if I find it necessary. No exceptions."

"Understood." None of us had a single complaint. The pressure would be on him. He was the only one who could know his own limit and the difficulty of the encounter.

"Shall we set up then? He can't be much longer…" With a look of determination that was encouraging, Richard led us out of our building and positioned himself on the open narrow breezeway. Feroce would inevitably come through here following our trail. We wouldn't miss him and he wouldn't miss us.

We fanned out on the breezeway but stayed close to a building's entrance. Richard was the only one who would have to spend some time to get inside. There weren't any metal doors between us but it wouldn't matter.

Just given the monster's size, it would take him a lot longer to squeeze through the doorways to reach us.

"There he is." We didn't have to wait too long after setting up. He appeared halfway down the breezeway. He didn't immediately notice us and instead crouched down to smell us out. Only after standing back up did he finally notice us.

There was an invisible pressure shrouding all of us. I noticed Richard constantly re-gripping the hilt of his greatsword. His hands were drenched with sweat from the nervousness. I even found my own staff slippery with sweat.

We were all expecting Feroce to rush at us recklessly and without regard, but instead he walked in our direction quite calmly. His demeanor made me worry even more than the fight with the Mystic. Was he more intelligent than we gave him credit for?

I summoned a fireball and Aaron charged *Powershot*.

Feroce continued to approach and then abruptly came to a stop around ten meters away. His mouth opened and a voice came out. "Humans… you… die." He struggled to get out the foreign words. It was bestial and deep, almost like he was growling while speaking.

He then pulled the two cleavers from his side and rushed directly towards Richard. "Guys!" Richard called back. He didn't have time to look and see if we were ready.

"We're here. Do it!" I shouted. We had his back.

Richard steadied his feet and then braced himself to meet Feroce, sword high in both hands. We let our spells fly and Andrew prepared to heal.

Feroce seemed completely unfazed by our attacks. He raised the cleaver of his right hand and deflected *Powershot* cleanly. The arrow glided up and into the breezeway ceiling before exploding.

My fireball looked like it was going to connect when he swatted it like a tennis ball with his other cleaver. It launched into the side of a building and extinguished with a poof.

Richard took a few steps and swung the greatsword down. Feroce didn't even use his two cleavers and instead parried with the metal cuff of his wrist. The greatsword collided directly with it and caused sparks to fly.

Feroce's arm lowered just a few inches from the impact until he pushed out hard and sent Richard stumbling back and nearly onto his ass. *Isn't this a bit much?*

I was already preparing to retreat when Richard yelled out, "AGAIN!" He steadied his feet and then rushed back at Feroce. This was against my expectations. I summoned another fireball and Aaron charged *Powershot* once more.

This time went slightly better. Feroce managed to swat away my fireball but Aarons Powershot connected cleanly with his left arm. Blood started to drip through the dark fur and caused it to mat up.

Feroce was thoroughly enraged and finally swung out with his cleaver. Richard held the greatsword flat in front of him to block the attack. There was an incredibly loud clang and Richard was sent hurdling several feet back. He barely managed to get to his feet. Andrew tossed him a heal.

Feroce was getting dangerously close to us and the plan was entering a phase where retreating was going to be considerably more difficult. *Shackle!*

> **SKILL HAS FAILED. YOU CANNOT SHACKLE ELITE MONSTERS**

Welp. That was terrible news.

Richard was only just managing to steady himself. The last attack shook him quite badly and I was almost worried he'd forgotten to call for a retreat. Aaron continued to shoot out *Powershots* and I summoned another fireball.

"Richard!" I yelled at him. We had given him the authority to call it off. It was time for his decision.

Feroce continued to walk forward while deflecting our attacks. He was finally in range for me to cast inspect. *Inspect!*

INVALID TARGET

It was a response I'd never received before and I didn't know what it meant.

"Retreat!" Richard managed to yell out after steadying himself on his sword. Andrew and I ran right while Aaron and Richard bolted left. Feroce chose to chase Aaron over anyone else and broke through the door frame.

Chapter 8: Hunted

The door frame aided in slowing Feroce's speed considerably. Aaron and Richard disappeared inside. They traveled up to the second floor and above the breezeway where we regrouped. From there we ran like hell and did some retracing of our previous steps.

"How was it?" I asked Richard. I knew the answer was going to be bad.

"Unstoppable." His response was outside of my range of reactions. "I lost thirty percent of my HP just from blocking his attack." He held out his arms, "Look… my arms are still shaking." They were red and jittery. "I felt like my bones were going to break."

We were all speechless. Just how strong were you expected to be at this point? I thought we were doing incredibly well. "*Shackle* doesn't work. Neither did *Inspect*."

"So we've gathered very little info," Aaron said.

Richard was just above the level of 'swatted like a fly' in front of Feroce. None of us would fare any better. I said, "fighting him in a fair battle seems to be out of the question."

"The difference in power didn't feel like something one or two levels could fix," Richard said.

"We know he isn't impenetrable. My *Powershot* made contact and drew blood. It wasn't much but… if we could accumulate damage overtime…"

Aaron seemed to be venturing into the same territory I was. "Hit and run," I said. Could we become the hunters instead of the hunted? It was possible. We were the ones hiding away. We had the advantage of stealth.

"We can take away his biggest asset in finding us: our scent," Aaron continued.

"How can we do that?" Richard asked.

"He's following our trail based on our scent, our previous movements, right?" Aaron said.

"True," I answered.

"We can fix that by going everywhere. Put our scent everywhere. We won't leave him a trail at all. He'll be engulfed in a swamp of our scents and smells."

"With no trail he'll be wandering blindly then," Andrew said.

"Right, and that's when we'll strike. We might not succeed every time… but overtime…"

"The damage will accumulate until we can face him." Richard said.

"Guerilla warfare," I said. It was a good plan. We couldn't face Feroce head on. Our only option was to chip away at him slowly. He would eventually become a problem we could solve.

"Let's get started then." We needed to move through every building on the breezeway and visit the majority of rooms, hallways, and stairwells. "It's gonna take a while." There was a lot of ground to cover.

We managed to clear one building when I caught Richard pissing on a wall.

"What are you doing?"

"What? I'm spreading my 'scent' like you all wanted."

I didn't reprimand him. It didn't really matter. He also wasn't wrong. I thought that would be it but somehow I found Andrew doing it as well. Turns out Richard somehow convinced him to do the same. They started to 'spread' their scent on the walls and class-rooms.

"That'll teach you to give me a D plus…" Richard mumbled.

We managed to work our way through one side of the breezeway in around an hour. It wasn't too slow at all considering we went through every floor and entered classrooms when possible. There was still several hours of sunlight left. Feroce was currently missing.

Richard and Andrew made sure to give extra care to open areas, particularly the pathing on the breezeway. They spread their 'scent' all over the pillars and stairways. I caught them both snickering on occasion. It didn't seem like it was about fooling Feroce anymore. They were enjoying themselves.

We crossed to the opposite side and started on the first building when Aaron stopped us. "He's outside."

We sneaked a look and could see Feroce walking the breezeway slowly. He occasionally stopped at a pillar and gave it a sniff before moving on. Richard's smile grew so bright I almost wanted to slap him.

Feroce was completely oblivious to our location. "Should we try it out?"

"Let me," Aaron said. I didn't disagree. He was more suited to sneak attack anyway. His arrow was much faster than my fireball.

Aaron stepped quietly out the back of the building and worked his way around the outside. He was now behind Feroce. He hugged the building corner and watched carefully. The timing needed to be perfect.

Feroce came to a stop near a pillar and leaned down again. *This is it…* I knew it already. This was the best opportunity for Aaron to strike. I watched Feroce with great intensity. He seemed oblivi-ous to Aaron's ambush.

I heard the faintest rush of wind and realized Aaron had taken his shot. I was expectant. Feroce was none the wiser. His body still hunched over sniffing us out. Suddenly, his entire body jerked and his hand flew back.

Aaron's arrow that had been heading for the back of his head, entered cleanly into Feroce's palm. There wasn't enough strength for it to pierce through and into his face. Feroce let out a low growl and snapped the arrow in half before pulling it from his palm.

Aaron took off before there was any chance for the monster to give chase. My jaw nearly dropped. There couldn't have been more than a second of time from the moment of firing to impact. Feroce had reacted in that time frame and blocked the arrow with his palm?

He did end up hurt… but still. Everything about him was superhuman.

Now we had to wait for Aaron to find a new chance to shoot. Two or three minutes passed with Feroce reaching the corner where Aaron had previously been hiding and the scene repeated itself.

This time there was an arrow lodged in the back shoulder of Feroce, coming from near where he had just been injured. I watched as he grabbed it and jerked it out in one pull. There was a short spurt of blood and then the fur of his shoulder darkened with fresh blood.

"It's working…"

Feroce turned back again and I was expecting Aaron to launch another attack when the backdoor creaked and Aaron sneaked inside.

"You're back?" I asked.

"Yeah, I had a bad feeling on my last shot. It felt like… if I took the next shot I'd be in trouble. I can't explain it well."

"You did some damage at least."

"There's something peculiar about it though. On my first shot, I can swear Feroce reacted too fast. It was like he was prepared the second I fired that arrow."

"It did seem too fast," I agreed.

"So I tried something on the second. I didn't put any intent in my second arrow. I wasn't trying to kill him, or even hurt him. I just imagined him as any other object and shot it out."

"And?"

"He didn't react, at all. It hit him square in the shoulder." I was having trouble following and it seemed the others were as well.

"So what does that mean?" Richard took the words out of my mouth.

"It means that... he can sense our thoughts when we are about to attack him. That's how he stopped the first arrow."

Richard shook his head. "That shouldn't really be possible though, right? That's basically movie-level shit."

"Do you remember that feeling we had when he first glared at us down the breezeway?"

"I remember," I answered. It was a suffocating and invisible pressure.

"That was his bloodlust: strong enough to be tangible. I think that even if we hadn't seen him and he was secretly watching us, we would have still felt that."

"So you're saying the moment you fire your arrow he can sense it?"

"Right. That's why I shot the second arrow the way I did. I was going to do the third the same way but my gut feeling told me something bad would happen if I did."

"Then what now? Only you and I can use ranged attacks. I'm not suited to sneaking around."

"We move and setup the next attack." We let Aaron lead us from here on out. He had the best idea as to what was happening out of all of us.

It took a good fifteen minutes to relocate without alerting Feroce. Eventually, Aaron was ready to try again and managed to catch the boss mob coming out of one of the buildings. The arrow connected cleanly with his furry thigh. Feroce let out another angry low growl while ripping it out.

Aaron made it a habit to shoot and run without even checking the damage he did. By the time Feroce managed to reach where Aaron shot from he had already fled at least a building away.

This wasn't fast by any means, but it felt like our only choice. And it was working. We regrouped with Aaron and patiently made our way from building to building to line up the next shot.

As Aaron prepared his next attempt, I watched carefully as Feroce turned his back to us. Something felt off.

Aaron hesitated for a moment with his bow and I knew he felt the same. Feroce turning his back seemed intentional. I was of a mind to relocate and try again in a few minutes.

"It's no rush." I whispered to our archer.

"I want to try. I need to know what it is. Why do I feel anxious on some shots but not others?"

The bow creaked slightly as Aaron pulled it as far back as possible. His muscles were straining and sweat dripped down his brow. I turned my attention away from Aaron and to Feroce.

I heard the rush of Aaron's release, my eyes locked on our target. The same second, no, the exact same moment as Aaron fired,

Feroce's shoulder tensed and his muscles bulged. He whipped around and threw out a cleaver like a boomerang.

Aaron managed to dip behind the wall in retreat when the cleaver connected. The entire corner of the building was blasted clean off. The cleaver didn't stop there and inserted itself several inches into the wall of the building next to us.

If Aaron didn't make it a habit to leave without looking at his shot, he would have been cut clean in two. None of us needed any word of encouragement. We ran like hell and didn't look back.

We ran for what felt like fifteen seconds before we heard a loud and vicious roar. Feroce was angry as hell. We now had an answer as to what that bad feeling was. Impending death.

"Are you okay?"

"Not really..." Aaron was shivering. His hands were trembling. Only by tightening his grip around his bow could he make it stop. "I saw death for a second."

"Your arm... it's bleeding."

Aaron looked down at the small cut in his arm. There was hair thin gash. A bead of blood dripped down and towards his elbow. "It's nothing serious."

"Run!" cried Andrew.

"Why the fuck won't he stop chasing us!" Feroce was now hunting us more ferociously than ever. No amount of zigzagging and stair climbing could get him off our trail. It was like he knew exactly where we were at all times.

"I don't know how much more I can run..." Richard said. He was carrying the most weight out of all of us. The greatsword's size was nothing to scoff at. I was incredibly happy I put three points into STR, it clearly had a bearing on whatever calculation of weight and speed allowed you to keep running.

"What changed?" I panted. Ever since our last sneak attack, we were unable to lose Feroce, no matter what we tried.

Aaron looked down at his arm. There was some dried blood still there on his arm and shirt. "This is new?"

"Get your shirt off!" Andrew commanded. He cast *Heal* to make sure the wound was fully closed.

"I have some water." I pulled a water bottle from my bag and poured it over his arm. We used Aaron's shirt to wipe the dried blood off and tossed it. There was no more wound nor any blood on his body. If Feroce was drawn by blood, this should stop him from tracking us.

We took off running again, only taking a break two buildings away. I wiped the sweat from my brow. It was a hot day to be running around like this. "Will this be enough?" I wondered aloud.

Almost immediately after I asked that question was there a crash. Feroce was still right behind us.

There weren't many more buildings to run through on this side of college. The doorways that were originally acting as a restraint were now mangled and destroyed. Feroce had slowly carved out pathways with his body to chase us through the buildings.

I bumped into one of the bent metal frames on my way out and scratched my arm. I looked down and saw the scrape and resulting blood. Feroce who was relentlessly chasing us suddenly stopped behind us.

I had the nerve to look back. He bent down at that metal framing and stuck out his tongue before licking the metal framing clean. *Why would he stop just to lick my blood?* It wasn't making any sense at all... unless.

I had an epiphany. It wasn't that our scent, or our wounds or even our blood he was tracking. Was it a special power he had?

Ingesting the blood of his victims allowed him to track or sense them?

"We need to split up," I said. "Aaron you come with me. Richard and Andrew wait for us in the library." It was a good way to test my theory and also allow Richard some time to rest. There was no hesitation as the two broke off.

Only after Aaron and I separated did I begin my explanation, "He's been able to track us because of your blood, but not in the way we originally thought." Aaron just listened. "He ingests it. Something about him eating it lets him know where we are."

"How can you be sure?"

I showed him the wound on my arm, "He was just a dozen feet back and yet he still stopped. He licked the hint of blood I left on the doorframe."

"If you're right then he can track both of us."

"Right, but that also means Richard and Andrew are both invisible to him now." This was both bad and good news. It meant we could set up a trap.

After a few twists and turns confirmed my idea, we led him around for a solid five minutes before reuniting with Richard and Andrew in the library.

"Richard you need to go to the science building and open a first floor window on the east side. If there's any screening there, remove it. It needs to be done within ten minutes. Wait outside with your sword drawn after. Andrew, I have special instructions for you." I explained my idea to our healer in the short moment of time we had and he nodded approvingly.

I trusted when the time came Andrew and Richard would both perform marvelously.

"If this isn't enough to kill him then I don't know what else to do." I confessed to Aaron as we took off running. We were growing more tired, while Feroce seemed unfazed with this constant moving.

There was a little less than an hour of sunlight left. If Feroce continued to hunt us through the night, there was no doubt we would all be cut apart by those sharp claws. The entire breezeway and every building would be pitch dark. Running and evading would be impossible.

We did a loop and kept Feroce at tail's length. A cleaver suddenly jolted past my shoulder as I turned a corner. I felt the wind displace and a cool brush of my neck. The cleaver buried itself several inches in the drywall. "Fucking hell!" I yelled. Just two inches to the left and I'd have been buried halfway into the wall with a cleaver through my neck.

"I can't keep this up for much longer…" I wasn't athletic by any means. My legs were burning and my voice was raspy. Running around this much was already a miracle.

"Let's hope it's been long enough," Aaron said. My sense of time was skewed. I felt like I had been running for an eternity. We bolted out onto the breezeway and darted towards the science building.

Feroce busted out just behind us and we were finally both on open ground. The ten second head start we had slowly shrunk until he was breathing down our necks. Head down, concentrating on the ground in front of me, I rushed inside.

The winding hallway assisted in giving us some breathing room as Feroce bumped and collided as we turned corners. It was much harder for his burly body to make these quick direction changes.

"There, Just ahead!" It was the east side science classrooms located directly on the building's corner. Richard had left the doorway open, and that let us know if we went inside we weren't going to be trapped.

I could feel Feroce stomping behind us. Ducking through the opening we slammed the door shut and a moment later his cleaver smashed into it. Bits of wood chunks flew into the left side of my face. The monster's weapon had passed eighty percent of the way through and dangled there.

One of us would have been killed if it had just a bit more force behind it. I closed the door and rushed over to the open window. I leaned over and started to climb the sill. Aaron did the same.

My body was halfway through when I heard splintering wood. Feroce had just pulled his cleaver from the door and then kicked the entire frame in. I tipped forward and fell onto the ground below.

Richard was just outside and out of vision when I landed. He was about to come and assist me when I yelled at him, "Don't!" He needed to stay out of sight. Aaron and I both scurried off the floor and pretended to be running away.

Feroce approached the window and while it was tight, he could still fit through. He took the bait. He shoved his head and then upper body through the narrow window and started to squeeze himself out of the room.

The drywall around the framing started to chip and looked as if it was going to burst. His head and one arm and shoulder was now sticking out. He needed another foot or two before his other arm would unlock from the side of his body and be free.

That was when Aaron and I turned around. Richard was also waiting to the side. He held the greatsword high and rushed over to slice down at Feroce's exposed neck. The greatsword dropped like a guillotine and yet Feroce had the foresight to tilt his head.

The blade of the greatsword connected with a part of the monster's neck and was then stopped by that metal collar. It was incredibly ironic. A collar put on by humans to enslave him had saved his life in this very moment.

Still, Richard had made a gash at least five inches long and one inch deep that ran from Feroce's shoulder blade to the base of his neck. It wasn't a fatal wound, but that wasn't the end. I threw out my fireball and Aaron used *Powershot*.

The fireball landed on the nape of Feroce's neck and scorched his fur. Aaron's *Powershot* entered in his left eye and caused blood to spurt from his face. Feroce growled in agony and anger. His body started to squirm even more vigorously. He was no longer trying to get out but pull himself back in.

Where was Andrew this entire time? He was on the third floor classroom, two stories above Feroce. On the windowsill was a basketball-sized granite rock that he was tipping over the edge.

There was a satisfying crunch when the rock smacked into the back of Feroce's head. The force was so strong that Feroce's head bobbed downward like a spring when the rock bounced off him. The granite rock hit the ground and rolled a dozen feet away.

It still wasn't enough. "DO IT AGAIN!" I yelled up at Andrew. I had instructed them to get as many rocks as they could up there. That was their mission. Feroce was already struggling a lot less. His mind was surely swimming after such a blow.

None of us let up. The second rock came down and smacked into his head again. I thought back to the first ghoul I ever killed. The wet mushy sound when I smashed his skull with a baseball bat. It reminded me of that.

Immediately after the second rock Richard came in for a second attack. Feroce didn't react at all and this time our tank managed to bury his greatsword several inches into the monster's neck. My fire-ball hit the top of his head and Aaron's *Powershot* tore into his jugular.

Only after all that did Feroce's head dangle there lifelessly. It was finally over. The fatigue hit me so hard I fell to my ass.

YOU HAVE COMPLETED THE QUEST: DEFEAT FEROCE!

I checked my stats to see the EXP gain.

CURRENT EXP: 2360/4700 LEVEL: 8
HP: 315/315   MP: 27/86
STR: 8
AGI: 5
DEX: 10
VIT: 8
INT: 15 +4
AVAILABLE: 0

I wasn't sure if completing the quest had given me 2100 EXP or killing Feroce had done it. The quest had said our only reward was survival. For the sake of my own morale, I decided that the decent chunk of EXP was a reward for killing Feroce.

The monster's body faded into particles before completely disappearing. I looked at the two items hovering there. The first was a skill book and the second looked to be an accessory of some kind.

BOOK OF *TAUNT* LV. 1
CAST TIME: INSTANT
MP COST: 5
DISTANCE: TWO METERS
COOLDOWN : 15 SECONDS

There was no doubt the book was for Richard. Discussing it was pointless. He scooped it up and learned it immediately. The second item was a rather peculiar. It looked like a dog collar with some spikes around it.

MARTYR'S LEASH: VIT +3, PHYSICAL DAMAGE TAKEN -7%.
A SYMBOL OF YOUR UNWAVERING BELIEFS. NOTHING CAN SHAKE
YOU

I couldn't lie. The item sounded fucking awesome. Richard was already eyeing it greedily.

"Richard again?" I asked, just to make sure. VIT was a useful stat for everyone, but the damage reduction on it indicated it was meant for a tank to wear.

"That's fine with me," Andrew agreed and Aaron gave a nod.

"Congratulations." It was the first time I said that after someone received an item. It felt so satisfying in this situation. This had been a truly torturous encounter. That we'd triumphed was a cause for celebration.

We had needed to use our teamwork, our skills, and our brains to defeat Feroce. If any single one of those facets was lacking then we wouldn't have made it out alive.

The others felt the same and we went over the battle as we walked as a group back to the dorms, each of us admitted to moments when we felt we were doomed.

Richard was the only one who had received any items, but none of us felt jealous about this. If we were going to survive, it would be as a group. I felt out of everyone, he had grown the most in the last day. He now had two separate threat-generating abilities. Now that he had *Taunt* I felt he was a real tank.

The kobold and goblin packs from earlier in the day were still all dead. Reaching the dorm went without a hitch. When we got there, we could see the destruction Feroce had inflicted upon the stairwell doors. They were torn and mangled, and hanging off the hinges. His power was truly frightening.

The next morning started bright and early. Each of us carried an empty backpack over our shoulders and working as a group we quickly cleared our way to the cafeteria.

Once inside the cafeteria I returned to those bags of rice and we split them in proportion to our STR. After an hour, the cafeteria had been cleared of everything useful. We took some silverware and two pots for cooking with, then exited the opposite side of the cafeteria and looked down the breezeway.

There were two more fast food restaurants we could check. The first was a staple of college life: a coffee shop just a couple hundred feet down. Aaron and I didn't mind as Richard continued to charge into each intervening pack. We saved our MP and allowed him to hone his skills.

"Phew, I'm beat." Richard hunched over and rested his hands on his knees. He had cleared five goblin and kobold packs before we reached the coffee shop.

"Take a break." He nodded and sat at an outside table while the rest of us entered inside. Aaron insisted on taking some filters and ground coffee.

"Even without a machine we can still make coffee." Or so he said. I wasn't in the mood to argue, he would have to carry it anyway. We took all the beverages that were still sealed and left everything else.

By the time we finished, our bags were full of junk food. Richard tipped over a vending machine and insisted I burn off the front with a fireball. We managed to get a ton of high-calorie foods for our trip.

"Let's do some scouting," I suggested. I refused to believe that the only monsters were goblins, ghouls, kobolds and zombies. We made our way up the stairs and onto the second floor of the breezeway. There were no monsters up here. We walked down towards an open area and stared in the direction we would need to walk.

Sure enough, there was a clear divide and change in monsters. I could immediately see wolf-like creatures roaming about. There looked to be trolls and orcs in packs as well. They didn't remain stationary but patrolled around.

Besides that, there was a particularly big creature that walked on all fours. I couldn't be sure what it was but it had to be over ten feet tall. It circled an area of a hundred feet or so just near the exit to the main road.

What we would be facing in the upcoming days was completely unknown. Regardless, the mood among us was nowhere near as tense as previous days.

"I can't believe that I am looking at those mobs and thinking about EXP, instead of hiding in terror," Aaron even made a joke out of our situation.

That made me feel almost nostalgic though, "Yeah." I couldn't help but think about Veronica. It was impossible to escape that melancholy just yet.

We watched as Richard tore into packs of kobolds and goblins completely solo.

He didn't even need Andrew to heal him anymore. One cleave was enough to slice the entire group in half.

"It doesn't seem quite as exciting as before," I said to Aaron as we watched. There had been a certain thrill with the early battles. From the moment after Feroce had died, that had been lost.

Nothing here could pose a threat to us anymore. Well, as long as we weren't completely careless.

"That means it's time we move on then," Aaron said.

"Agreed." Richard returned with his greatsword hoisted over his shoulder. Andrew followed closely behind him. Our tank didn't need the heals this time but it was now a habit. Andrew had become Richard's keeper. Or maybe it was the other way around.

"Are you two ready to go?"

"Yeah." There was nothing left for us here. Our packs were filled with the food we gathered and the few items of clean clothes we had remaining. It was time to move on.

"Do we have everything we need?" We took a quick count. We had food, water, the rice, some silverware and two pots. We had no idea where we would be sleeping but we didn't have any camping equipment anyway. "Let's go."

We didn't waste any time at all and travelled right towards the school parking lot. We needed to cross it and then make our way to the highway. It was only a mile or so from where we currently were. Aaron and I stood back while Richard led the front.

His new greatsword was a formidable weapon. He didn't need our help at all to dispatch the packs of goblins and kobolds. Besides a few heals from Andrew every now and then, he was carrying us as a team.

It took us an hour to cross the parking lot and make it to the highway. On the other side just a few meters away was that obvious divide in spawns. An imaginary line perhaps, where no mobs of monsters spawned. It wasn't easy to notice from up close but looking from the breezeway earlier made it clear.

After we stepped through this twenty-foot section, we would be entering a completely new zone. While completely devoid of any monsters, the open area exerted an invisible pressure on all of us. "Shall we go?"

Everyone nodded their head in unison before we trekked forward.

CONGRATULATIONS! YOU HAVE SUCCESSFULLY LEFT THE NOVICE TRAINING GROUND. AS A REWARD, YOU WILL BE GRANTED +1 TO ALL ATTRIBUTES.
PLEASE BE ADVISED, MONSTERS OUTSIDE THE TRAINING GROUND ARE CONSIDERABLY MORE DIFFICULT BUT PROVIDE MANY MORE BENEFITS. DO YOUR BEST!

We walked towards the on ramp and then followed it into a circle. The highway was filled with cars. So many were crashed and smashed together, it was absolute destruction. It was hard to see monsters in all the debris but we knew they were there. I moved to the nearest vehicle and climbed up on top before peering into the distance.

Chapter 9: Orcs

The highway was littered with monsters. Some of them were animals but others were creatures that had never existed in this world before. The most noticeable were the orcs and trolls moving in packs. The orcs had bone helmets and carried incredibly large great axes. The trolls had feathered face masks of varying colors and spears as long as they were tall.

Boars, wolves, and large cats wandered around on their own. Our environment was completely changed. We had no idea just how strong were monsters outside the Novice area. We grouped together and moved along the highway shoulder. It was the clearest path we could possibly take.

"Get ready." There was a large dire-wolf moving in our direction.

As soon as it noticed our presence it made a mad dash. *Shackle!* In the three seconds of my cast it had closed within a dozen feet. *Inspect!*

```
RABID WOLF        LEVEL: 9 BEAST
    HP: 1375           MP: 10
              STR: 17
              AGI: 10
              DEX: 7
              VIT: 12
              INT: 1
A LONE WOLF WITH NOTHING TO LOSE, ITS PACK HAS ABAN-
                 DONED IT.
```

Holy shit! The difference between a goblin or ghoul and this was night and day. I couldn't be sure how long the shackle would even last. "Richard!"

"Got it!" Richard moved forward and swung out. I sent a fireball hurdling in its direction as Aaron used *Powershot*. The shackle immediately broke upon our three spells landing as the 500 damage threshold was reached.

"Don't be stingy with heals!" I was already in the process of throwing out another fireball when its paw connected with Richards' upper arm. Blood flew through the air and he flew to the side.

"Heal him!" Aaron yelled out. Immediately after that my *Fireball* connected once again and the wolf let out a yelp before burning up. Its body disappeared and we each received 200 EXP. This one wolf was worth more EXP than an entire pack in the Novice Grounds.

The slash on Richard's arm disappeared after receiving a heal. "Ouch! That fucking hurt a lot."

"How much damage did it do to you?"

"Somewhere between a hundred-and-forty and a hundred-and-seventy damage. I lost around thirty percent of my health from a single attack."

Being level 7 and distributing his stats evenly between STR and VIT, he couldn't have much more than 450 health. I was only at 285 HP. A single hit would nearly KO me. An item appeared as the corpse faded.

WOLVERINE'S RING: STR +3 VIT +3
A RING MADE FROM THE FANG OF A WOLVERINE. IT LOOKS INCREDIBLY VICIOUS

The decision was unanimous as Richard gladly accepted the ring. He was taking on the most risk leading the front lines and we needed him to tank up as fast as possible. We took a short break and tried to find the safest route.

The next monster in our path was a furry looking boar, maybe a warthog? I couldn't tell. We found the most open area before pulling it. It snorted and squealed as it rushed in our direction. *Shackle!*

CONGRATULATIONS! SHACKLE HAS REACHED LEVEL 2!

I ignored the message and cast *Inspect*.

```
WARTHOG  LEVEL: 8 BEAST
HP: 1805            MP: 10
          STR: 20
          AGI: 5
          DEX: 3
          VIT: 17
          INT: 1
A WANNABE PIG WITH A FACE ONLY ITS MOTHER COULD LOVE
```

The monster was tankier than the Wolf from before but was considerably less agile. *Shackle* locked it in place as we bombarded the target with our abilities. Richard was prepared for when *Shackle* broke and promptly cast *Taunt*. The warthog despawned shortly after.

It wasn't entirely clear to me how aggro worked yet. Some monsters seemed to attack the closest target and exchanged blows with Richard, while Aaron and I did the most damage. Even while we bombarded Feroce with abilities in our first exchange he focused solely on Richard. Well, he did chase Aaron during our retreat after his successful arrow hit.

We had yet to encounter any monster that tried to avoid Richard and attack Aaron or me. Despite that, I felt fortunate Richard had *Sword Crash* and *Taunt*. They were eventually going to come in handy.

A total of 180 EXP went to the each of us when the Warthog despawned. While the EXP was better, there was considerably more risk. We couldn't one-shot any of these monsters and the possibility of injury was very high. We were also burning a lot of MP. The situation was worrying.

Every monster we fought I needed to *Shackle*, *Inspect*, and then throw two fireballs. That was a total of 23 MP. I had already used 46 and we only just started moving. I recalled that *Shackle* had leveled up and pulled up the new skill description.

SHACKLE LV. 2
CAST TIME: 3.5 SECOND
MP COST: 9
DISTANCE: 11 METERS
SHACKLE YOUR FOES WITH POWERFUL ARCANE MAGIC. RESTRAINS TARGET FOR UP TO 22 SECONDS. DURATION BASED ON TARGETS AGI. DAMAGE THRESHOLD: 900

The cast time increased slightly as did the MP cost. An extra 2 seconds were added on the duration and 400 damage on the threshold. A balanced increase in strength for the new cost.

"We should have stayed at the dorm for a few days more," Richard complained, "we are hardly making any headway here."

"I see you've maxed Hindsight," Aaron said.

I didn't disagree with Richard though, if only we had known how tough and how frequent the mobs were beyond the campus, we might well have tried to level up some more first.

"Should we go back?" I asked.

Richard shrugged. "It may not help anyway. Everything is growing stronger every day. They'll just be stronger in the days to come as well."

"Then we keep moving." All we could do was move forward and get to the safe-zone as fast as possible.

But it wasn't long before we encountered our first pack.

"How should we go about this?" A pack of 3 orcs were just 20 meters in front of us. It was impossible to get around them without aggroing them.

"Can you *Shackle* more than one monster at a time?" Aaron asked.

"I've never tried."

"Let's go with that then, pull with *Shackle* and then *Shackle* again on a different one as they come towards us. If it doesn't work then we try our best. Worst case we run."

I jumped atop a ruined Honda and then started to cast. My heart hurt having to expend so much MP. I had a little over 60 remaining but after this fight I would be running incredibly low. *Shackle!* The spikes rose and the golden-purple chains wrapped up the target. The two other orcs let out a vicious roar while sprinting in my direction. *Shackle!* I silently prayed.

The first Shackle didn't break as the second restricted another orc. The only enemy unrestrained continued to move at us. As it closed in it was easier to tell that it was female. It had long hair in a ponytail and big red lips. Its fat body made it hideous to look at. *Inspect!*

```
ORC MISTRESS      LEVEL: 8 HUMANOID
    HP: 2310             MP: 20
               STR: 20
               AGI: 8
               DEX: 10
               VIT: 20
               INT: 8
THE BEAUTIFUL MISTRESS OF AN ORC WARRIOR
```

She carried a cleaver in her hand that looked as if it came straight from the kitchen. Richard sprinted forward to meet her approach as Aaron and I channeled our spells. A clang rang out as the cleaver smashed against Richard's greatsword. His arms buckled under the weight and he was pushed back.

At the same time, a *Powershot* and a fireball flew past him and directly collided into her body. Her screams sounded human but with a thick, throaty sound too. Almost as if someone was trying to clear their throat. The two attacks put her off balance as Richard thrust the greatsword forward and directly into her gut. My second fireball followed up right after.

"Next!" Richard said while moving towards the nearest shackled target. He didn't wait for either of us as he slashed down in a horizontal arc. His one swing alone broke the *Shackle* with an incredible display of strength. I ignored his hasty decision and casted *Inspect* again. It was incredibly important to know what we were dealing with.

```
ORC WARRIOR        LEVEL: 9HUMANOID
       HP: 2710            MP: 20
                  STR: 20
                  AGI: 5
                  DEX: 5
                  VIT: 22
                  INT: 5
       AN AVERAGE GRUNT OF THE ORC RACE
```

The warrior carried a battle axe. His frame was much more toned and muscular compared to the female Orc. I contemplated re-shackling the third orc but cast a Fireball instead. Richard's huge attack at the start the fight meant we should be able to finish it off quickly. And indeed, one *Fireball* and a *Powershot* directly to the head dispatched it.

The third and final orc was also another Warrior. The *Shackle* timed out, allowing the orc to rush in Richard's direction. My MP was dangerously low but I had enough to finish this foe. The orc grunted as it swung out the huge axe. Aaron had completely used up his MP and nocked normal arrows, they barraged the sturdy body.

Richard haphazardly rushed forward to meet its charge. The Warrior and Richard both swung out with all their strength. There was a loud clang as the axe pushed the greatsword away and then continued unhindered towards Richard's chest.

At the same time, my fireball had just connected with the Warrior's side. There was a spurt of blood as the great axe landed on Richard's chest and left a deep gash from top to bottom.

"Get BACK!" Aaron yelled. Shock allowed Richard to move only a few feet before he collapsed to the ground.

"Heal him fast!" I yelled at Andrew. He was already casting a heal of course, but I was fired up. I contemplated casting another *Shackle* to stop the fight but a second fireball would come much more quickly. I tossed it out and directly into the face of the Warrior. It fell to its knees as its hands clawed at its burning face. Five seconds passed before it plopped face first onto the concrete. The fight was over.

I rushed over to Richard who was supporting himself with one arm and barely leaning up. Andrew had to cast *Heal* three times before the gash on his chest closed. Blood could still be seen on the edges of his tattered shirt. His eyes were wide as saucers and he was caked in a thick layer of sweat.

"My life flashed before my eyes." He tried to force out a laugh. "A critical hit for three-hundred-and-eighty damage. The next attack would have ended me."

"Let's take a break. My MP is nearly exhausted."

"Mine as well," Aaron chimed in. I checked our EXP gain for that fight and was pleasantly surprised. Each orc gave 300 EXP, a total of 900 for the fight. I opened my stats.

```
CURRENT EXP: 3640/4700  LEVEL: 8
HP: 330/330      MP: 17/89
STR: 9
AGI: 6
DEX: 11
VIT: 9
INT: 16 +4
AVAILABLE: 0
```

It had been a little over an hour and I had gained 1280 EXP. Not bad considering the circumstances. The only issue was that we hadn't made it very far, not even half a mile. I pulled a candy bar and bottle of water from my pack. In just a few seconds the candy bar was gone. I sipped on the water over a few minutes before putting the remainder back.

"How is your MP Andrew?" I asked.

"It's still okay, more than half." I nodded my head and closed my eyes to rest. We waited a full hour and a half before moving again. My MP managed to regenerate to a bit less than half. The staff did wonders.

We walked for what felt like twenty minutes before coming across the next monster, another orc. There was something peculiar about this one, however. It wasn't green like a typical orc but instead fully silver. On its head was a brown skull helmet that had three spikes coming out of it. Its body was a foot or two larger than a regular orc as well.

"What do you guys think?" Just from appearance alone, it was obvious this wasn't a normal monster. That and the fact there was absolutely nothing else around it for nearly a mile.

"Let's repeat *Shackle* it, 'till it dies?" Aaron suggested.

I thought about this and it seemed like a good solution. If I timed my recasting correctly, we could burn down the orc from a distance even if *Shackle* only lasted 4 or 5 seconds.

"So pull with *Shackle*?"

"Yeah." Both Aaron and Richard agreed aloud, Andrew caught my eye and nodded. I moved forward slowly, all the while constantly trying to cast *Shackle*. This was something Aaron suggested to me. I could get an exact distance by knowing my cast distance. The moment it let me cast would be 11 Meters away. A solution so simple I felt stupid for not thinking about it myself.

Shackle! I watched as the spikes shot from the ground. The golden-purple chains started to wrap around before shattering into dust.

SKILL HAS FAILED. YOU CANNOT SHACKLE ELITE MONSTERS

The Orc recognized my aggression and turned in our direction. A soul-shattering grunt pierced my ear drums and made my hair stand on end.

"I can't shackle it! It's an Elite monster" I yelled in panic. "Fight or run?" We had about a second to decide our course of action. Both Aaron and I looked at Richard. He would have to fight in melee range, the final decision was his.

His face looked uneasy, but he braced himself: "Fight!"

Anxious, with a feeling we might be about to lose another comrade, I followed close enough behind him to cast *Inspect*.

```
┌──────────────────────────────────────────────────────┐
│                                                        │
│   HIGH ORC*        LEVEL: 12        HUMANOID           │
│          HP: 5715              MP: 55                  │
│                    STR: 30                             │
│                    AGI: 10                             │
│                    DEX: 7                              │
│                    VIT: 35                             │
│                    INT: 15                             │
│   A ROYAL OF THE ORC RACE. SUPERIOR IN INTELLECT AND BAT-│
│                       TLE.                             │
│   CONGRATULATIONS! INSPECT HAS REACHED LEVEL 2!        │
│                                                        │
└──────────────────────────────────────────────────────┘
```

It had more than twice the HP of a Warrior and considerably more STR. I worried for Richard. The axe it wielded had a menacing skull directly in the center. Richard knew better than to compare strength with it.

An arrow of Aaron's landed cleanly on its body, as did a fireball from me: the High Orc seemed unfazed. Its axe connected with the trunk of a car and sunk inside before appearing through the other side. If Richard were hit by that, there would be nothing left of him.

The High Orc's chest and shoulder had been scorched black by my second fireball. Up until this point Richard had simply retreated and never attacked. The High Orc gave a grunt and then switched directions. It looked directly at me.

I felt as if I had entered a marsh pond and recalled its high INT stat. This was a mob with enough intelligence to know it was being kited. Sweat dripped down my back and I didn't hesitate to immediately start running. Its injuries allowed me to get a bit of a head start. Its burly body bumped into cars as it pushed in my direction. The cars it touched trembled.

Aaron held nothing back as he launched *Powershot* after *Powershot* into its back. I looked back and could see Richard rushing after it. He raised an arm into the position to cast taunt.

"Watch out!" I yelled at him. Richard's eyes showed surprise as he positioned his sword. The High Orc swung out blindly as it did a complete hundred-and-eight degree turn.

Richard raised the sword against his shoulder and leaned into block the incoming mighty blow. The axe connected with his sword and sent him flying several feet away and into the door of a car. I didn't hesitate anymore and casted a fireball. Richard had bought me a second of time, I needed to use it. My fireball connected with the orc's chest and caused it to let out a roar.

It didn't go down though and there was nowhere else for me to run. The monster was only a few feet away and I was surrounded on all sides by vehicles. I didn't have time to try and climb up and over. It raised its axe as it rushed in my direction. I could see the menacing skull on the axe with great clarity. It was seconds away from cleaving me in two.

Just before the High Orc brought the axe down, an arrow pierced through the back of its neck and through its mouth. It coughed a mouthful of blood and the axe fell backwards and behind it. It fell to its knees before face planting just a foot in front of me. I fell on my ass in shock. It wouldn't even have taken a critical strike from the High Orc to have killed me. That axe was at least the size of me.

Andrew healed Richard, who still struggled to stand. There was a large chip in the side of his greatsword where the axe had connected. They all moved over to me.

"Thanks for the save. I thought I was going to be cleaved in two and no amount of heals would be able to save me."

Aaron reached down and helped me to stand. My legs were still trembling.

CONGRATULATIONS! YOU HAVE SLAIN AN ELITE MONSTER. AS A REWARD, YOU HAVE BEEN GIVEN THE TITLE 'FORMIDABLE'. EQUIPPING THE TITLE GRANTS +20 HP AND +10MP. CONGRATULATIONS! YOU HAVE REACHED LEVEL 9. AS A REWARD FOR LEVELING UP, YOU HAVE BEEN GRANTED THREE STAT POINTS!

I was bombarded with system messages. The High Orc had given 1200 EXP, a total of 4800 for the group. *Inspect* had reached level 2 but I hadn't had the time during the fight to look at its new effects.

INSPECT LV. 2
CAST TIME: INSTANT
MP COST: 3
DISTANCE: 5 METERS

A two meter distance increase would prove incredibly useful. Crucially, I needed the range on *Inspect* to be sufficient to use it without drawing aggro. Five meters was close to the kind of distance that might work: for some mobs it might already be there.

The exp required to reach level ten was more than double the exp I had gained so far. I hesitated with my three stat points. I needed both damage and survivability. My new title sat neatly next to my level.

The thought of dying as a result of just one attack put me under a lot of pressure. A gain of 15 HP per attribute point didn't seem like much, would 45 HP be the difference between life and death? I couldn't be sure. There was also the growing issue of my lacking MP for sustained activity.

Yet, beside that last Elite fight, I never ended up in melee range and Richard's potential as a tank was getting better every fight. So I ended up putting one point in DEX and then two points into INT. I still hadn't found another use for AGI just yet, beyond resisting *Shackle*.

CURRENT EXP: 140/10100 LEVEL: 9   FORMIDABLE
HP: 360/360   MP: 32/109
STR: 9
AGI: 6
DEX: 12
VIT: 9
INT: 18 +4
AVAILABLE: 0

I felt better after putting those two stat points into INT. Everything so far but AGI seemed incredibly important, and yet I couldn't fall behind on my main role: shackling and killing. It was clear now that DEX and INT were my two main stats. Slightly favoring INT over DEX would probably prove the most efficient spending going forward.

I turned my attention back towards the front where everyone was gathering. The High Orc corpse had fully despawned and more than one item had dropped.

A Maiden's Veil*: Int +2, Physical Damage Taken -10%. The Beautiful Fabric of a Maiden. It's a wonder how an orc managed to obtain such a fine piece of clothing.

Sturdy Longbow*: DEX +5, Ranged Damage +10%. A Bow made from the finest Oak wood. Its length allows for explosive firing power.

There was also a skill book.

Book of *Meteor Storm*** LV. 1
Cast time: 7 Seconds
MP Cost: 22
Distance: 10 Meters

We looked over the items as a group. The longbow went to Aaron without question. It was majestic and lordly compared to his previous crude weapon. I eyed the Maiden's Fabric and shared a glance with Richard. Despite it giving +2 INT, the -10% physical damage couldn't be ignored. He was our tank and front liner.

"Go ahead and take it. It looks ridiculous," Richard said.

He wasn't wrong. The veil was a thin and see-through fabric. I was unsure how it would make me take -10% physical damage but I didn't question the system.

"Are you sure? I really think it would be best on you." I insisted.

I had never seen Richard so serious, "I would rather die than wear it," he said flatly.

"Suit yourself…" I mumbled out before scooping it up. It definitely wasn't appealing at all, but I wasn't about to complain. Two more INT and -10% physical damage taken? *Hell yes.*

The final item was a skill book that everyone stepped back from so that I could get it. *Meteor Storm* was obviously a spell caster's ability.

DO YOU WISH TO LEARN *METEOR STORM* LV. 1?**

Abso-fucking-lutely! The book vanished from my hand as a new skill appeared in my skill window. I recognized the 2 stars near its name but couldn't be sure what it signified just yet. I was so incredibly excited. The MP cost and cast time was enormous, but the distance made it so I could cast it safely from range. I was eager to try it. After what felt like an eternity, I had now received a new skill.

"Let's take a break." We had covered a lot of ground because of the Elite. The area it inhabited was at least a mile long and had given us a lot of free travel time. I couldn't help but check my stats again.

```
CURRENT EXP: 140/10100  LEVEL: 9        FORMIDABLE
        HP: 360/360     MP: 34/115
                   STR: 9
                   AGI: 6
                  DEX: 12
                   VIT: 9
                 INT: 18 +6
               AVAILABLE: 0
```

I looked at the map provided by the system. We had already reached our two-mile quota for the day. It would be completely acceptable if we setup camp now and called it. I asked the others, "Should we keep moving? We've made good progress today."

"I say we keep moving," Aaron echoed my thoughts exactly.

"We should take advantage while we can. There's no point in stopping if we can make easy progress," Andrew said.

I didn't want to be the one to decide. This was a party and while I felt a responsibility – based on my insight into the game so far – to offer leadership, we made decisions as a group. Aaron had also proven himself as a voice of reason. He wasn't always right, but he put careful thought into his words.

Despite having 24 total points of INT, I couldn't be sure if it made me any smarter, or if it was just a measure for stats like MP. Perhaps my thoughts flowed more smoothly, especially when casting. Then too, since this had all kicked off, I hadn't had one of those moments where you feel like things are on the tip of your tongue and you can't get them out. I wasn't sure if I was smarter or just more focused given the life-or-death challenge.

"And you?" I looked at Richard

"Uhh, keep moving I guess," Richard said.

We rested for two hours. I had started to keep track of the time by my MP regeneration. My INT plus the staff were somewhere around 15 or 16 MP regen per hour. I had recovered 30 MP since we stopped. "Are we ready?"

"Ready!" We all got up and started to make our way down the crowded highway again. I had recovered enough MP to cast *Meteor Storm* three times. I was looking forward to it.

It was less than five minutes before we came across the next pack.

A group of trolls were huddled around a campfire speaking in an unknown language. They constantly gestured with their hands, their spears rested on their lap.

"I'd like to try *Meteor Storm*." No one voiced any opposition.

I approached within 11 meters and started my chant. A peculiar ring spawned around my feet that flashed vibrant colors. I was counting in my head the entire time. Just as the cast finished, the ring became fully lit and shined brightly, engulfing me in light. Meteors spawned in the sky hundreds of feet above the trolls.

At first they appeared small, but as they fell they grew in size and clarity. The balls of white light were about six feet in diameter, or as tall as a person. They burned as they crashed down. The trolls looked up into the sky but it was too late.

Bang! Bang! Bang! Three meteors crashed down in succession. Each one caused a fiery explosion at least a dozen feet wide. When the smoke cleared there were no trolls. The fight had ended just like that. I didn't even have the chance to inspect them.

Everyone was shocked, but also excited. 22 MP and 7 seconds was all it took to clear an entire pack of trolls.

"From now on you should save your MP for packs, we'll deal with single monsters," Aaron suggested. I nodded. I felt like a badass at the moment and another 900 EXP was added. Richard and Aaron were both level 8 and Andrew was almost there. They would all be level 9 before I reached level 10.

I opened my skill page and looked at *Meteor Storm*.

METEOR STORM LV 1. 10/250

So I needed to cast the spell another twenty-four times before it reached level two. That seemed reasonable considering the level of power it had just displayed.

We were also walking along one side of car-strewn highway. Every pack of monsters we encountered was forced into tight little areas that made a skill like *Meteor Storm* king. There would be no escape once the meteors started falling.

Beyond the highway was a sandy dirty area and then a fence. The other side of the fence was mostly businesses. Occasionally we crossed over a regular street and could see the destruction below. It didn't seem like anywhere was faring better than what we'd seen so far.

We made a group decision that I would save my MP for dispatching packs of monsters. Aaron and Richard would two-man any solo mobs and I'd assist if absolutely necessary. I was definitely excited to focus more on my AOE ability.

"Hey Richard." I called out as we walked on towards our quest goal.

"Yeah?"

"What was your major?" I asked. He always came off as a goofy, non-serious person. The only thing I knew was he liked computers.

"Computer Science," he said.

"Is that like programming or what?"

"Yeah."

"What about you Aaron?"

"Business Administration."

"And you just happen to like basketball?"

"Yeah," Aaron replied seriously. He was the type of person that switched gears very easily. When things needed to get done he was all work. Once it was free time he was carefree and relaxed. There really hadn't been much time for play lately though.

"Did anyone manage to get into contact with their families?" I glanced at Andrew to make sure he was included in my question this time.

"After the event? Nope," he answered. The other two shook their heads.

"I even tried to call from one of the payphones on campus." Richard said. "Didn't even hear a dial-tone on the other end."

The chat didn't last long as we encountered an enemy.

```
┌─────────────────────────────────────────────────────┐
│                                                       │
│   BLOOD-THIRSTY CHEETAH      LEVEL: 10       BEAST     │
│             HP: 1825              MP: 10              │
│                    STR: 10                            │
│                    AGI: 25                            │
│                    DEX: 7                             │
│                    VIT: 10                            │
│                    INT: 5                             │
│     AN EXTREMELY AGILE AND BLOOD-THIRSTY FELINE.       │
│                                                       │
└─────────────────────────────────────────────────────┘
```

It was the first cat we encountered. I had to intervene because it was too agile for either Aaron or Richard to hit it. I cast *Shackle* and managed to lock it in place. I knew my spell wouldn't last long because of the creature's impressive AGI stat, but it proved long enough for Richard to land a crucial blow: the shackles grasped the cheetah and stripped it of its mobility. Richard rushed forward and used *Cleave*. There was a loud snap as the front leg of the cheetah broke. The shackle disintegrated and the cheetah hopped backwards awkwardly. It no longer sprinted around but instead limped. Aaron made quick work of it. A *Powershot* entered cleanly through its side and eviscerated its organs.

We managed to move another mile, taking out another group of trolls and two of orcs, before my MP were fully exhausted. We decided as a group that we wouldn't take on fighting any more packs. If I didn't have the MP to cast *Meteor Storm* then we would wait. We had killed three packs and 5 or 6 solo monsters. *Stats!*

```
CURRENT EXP: 3840/10100        LEVEL: 9
                FORMIDABLE
        HP: 360/360     MP: 3/115
                  STR: 9
                  AGI: 6
                  DEX: 12
                  VIT: 9
                INT: 18 +6
              AVAILABLE: 0
```

A little more than a third of the way to level 10: I was expectant. When I reached level 5 I had received a reward, I was hoping level 10 would be the same. Aaron and Richard had reached level 9 on the last pack and Andrew was more than halfway through level 8. It felt like we were making incredible progress, but were we matching the expectations of whoever had imposed the game?

The sun was falling from the sky and my low MP made me incredibly tired. It seemed everyone felt the same after such a long day. Richard was barely able to keep his eyes open as he weaved like a drunk. While *Heal* could recover HP, it didn't remove fatigue. When we called it, we pulled back from our most advanced position and I looked around before finding a relatively intact car and disappearing inside. I slept in the back seat with Aaron tipped back in the passenger seat and Richard and Andrew in the car next to ours. We planned watches and Aaron was to wake me for the final two hours of darkness.

In fact, I woke to the sound of howling. It must have been sometime around 4 or 5 A.M. The sky was still dark and the moon shone brightly. I peered out the tinted windows but really couldn't make out a thing. My MP had fully recovered and I felt wide awake. I struggled in the backseat and just couldn't force myself to get a few extra hours of sleep.

The side-door cracked open as I slithered out. I stretched and hopped once or twice to get the blood flowing before climbing on top of my hotel and looking out. Richard was sat on top of his car looking up the road, towards the howling, but nothing wandered close to our camp.

Chapter 10: Everything Wants to Kill Us

I couldn't make out anything in the distance despite the moon shining so brightly. Excitement bubbled inside me as leveling up was all I could think about. I dreamed about my new skill *Meteor Storm*. It was no longer, 'how much MP had I?' but instead 'how many *Meteor Storms* could I cast?' With my current max of 100 MP, however, that number was barely 4.

"I'm going to check it out." I crossed to Richard's car and kept my voice to a whisper.

Richard frowned but said nothing as I moved forward to a point not far from where we had left off. The ground began to quake. Vibrations traveled from down the road in front of me and just past my feet. Far in the distance was a massive shadow, a creature I could barely make out. It towered the size of a building, walked across the highway and disappeared. A red skull floated above its head like an imaginary light in the sky. It was at least 5 or 6 miles away.

I held my breath. The monster's size was staggering. *A raid boss?* That was the only explanation. I was sure that the red skull signified one thing, and that was death. I ran back to my vehicle and slipped inside. I waited for the others to wake.

The sound of a door opening roused me from my drowsing. I no longer hesitated and stepped out as well. The sun was barely peeking over the horizon yet that small amount of sunlight hitting my shoulders felt incredible. I chose to say nothing about the monster I saw earlier. There was really no point to it besides causing panic.

"Morning." Aaron was the first to wake. We discussed strategy over breakfast and about thirty minutes later Richard emerged. When he did, Richard was impatient to set off and eventually went to wake Andrew. I no longer carried a phone to check the time, but I estimated it to be around 7:30 when all four of us were ready.

Yesterday we had made about 3 miles of progress, if we could keep that up or even surpass it, we would be at the safe-zone in less than a week. The strategy was the same as on the previous day: Aaron and Richard would deal with the single mobs and I'd *Meteor Storm* whenever we came across enemy groups.

"What in the hell is that?" exclaimed Andrew.

There was a goliath-sized beast walking slowly down the opposite side of the highway. It was larger than a minivan and covered in completely slick black skin. Little wings poked out of its back that were definitely too small to lift its body from the ground.

It reminded me of a gargoyle, except the body was so incredibly disproportionate. It looked more like a giant gorilla with wings.

"Let's not fight it." Richard spoke frantically. The monster towered over Feroce in size. It could probably grab our tank in one of its hands and squeeze him to a pulp. It continued to walk on all fours and it was getting closer.

"Get off the road," Aaron yelled. We bolted to the barrier wall and jumped over. Our feet hit the mix of sand and dirt before nearly tumbling down a hill. Behind us, the ground shook as the creature approached.

It wasn't the boss that I had seen last night but it was no doubt a formidable elite. I wanted nothing to do with it, and neither did the others. No one even had the courage, or stupidity, to peer over and watch it pass.

My legs were covered in a thin layer of dirt and sand, but so long as I could hear the slow movements of the creature above, I didn't even dare brush it off. No one moved until the shaking had stopped for at least several minutes. Only then did we scurry up and enter back onto the highway.

"Coast is clear," I said. We all hopped the barrier wall and started moving. Tensions were a bit higher than before. If for some reason another one of those creatures, or even a different one, was blocking our route, we wouldn't really have anywhere to go.

"Let's focus on what's ahead of us," Aaron reminded everyone. That was most important. We all buried the 'what-if's' and pushed forward, attacking singles and occasionally needing *Meteor Storm*. Our killing speed increased even further as we worked with quiet efficiency: none of us wanted to remain out in this dangerous region any longer than necessary.

At the rate we were killing monsters and moving. I would hit level 10 by tomorrow. I was incredibly excited about the possible rewards if I was first in the district to achieve that level. *Speedy Recovery*, which I'd gained from being first to 5, was, in my opinion, a completely imbalanced skill. A 50% recovery rate was nothing to gawk at, especially for a passive.

Yet despite my delight in the fact I was mastering this new challenge, become someone significant. I couldn't help but find myself slipping into lapses of unhappiness. I missed my parents, I missed my brother.

All the messages I had tried to send remained unread. I didn't know if they were safe inside when the event happened or if they died moments after, but if I was being honest with myself, I had to admit they were probably dead. I might never see them again and that thought hurt. The only time this miserable line of thought went away was when I had nothing else to think about but getting on top of the game and surviving.

Two hours into our grind and a valuable item dropped.

> ### Robe of Casting: Int +3 MP +15.
> ### A robe made with Enchanted threads. Its mixture of white and red embroidery is breath-taking.

I wanted it, but I had received a skill book and the fabric from yesterday. I put it up for public discussion. "What does everyone think?"

"That's a lot of MP..." Richard said. I agreed with him.

"Andrew, how often are you having to heal?" Aaron asked.

"Well... not a ton."

"Does your MP ever really dip below half?"

"Not since the High Orc fight."

"I think it should go to Joseph then," Aaron declared.

Ever since getting *Meteor Storm* the dynamics of our battles had changed. The threat we were under dropped drastically and the amount of MP he needed to expend was very little. He was in no threat of running out of MP, whereas I was nearly always low.

I would be happy to accept but still looked at Andrew, "Are you okay with that?"

"It's fine. I agree with Aaron anyway. It's definitely better on you right now. I'm not expending nearly as much MP as you are." He was a lot more careless about this than I expected. Almost as if he didn't care about improving his powers and chances. It made me slightly worried.

From my perspective, the extra INT and MP would allow me to cast another *Meteor Storm* without having to rest up and it also increased my over-all regen. I equipped the drop. A beautiful scholar's robe replaced my tattered clothing. It fell perfectly to my legs and obscured my feet from view. The collar had beautiful red patch with intricate patterns. The rest was a flawless white. I had to check my stats.

```
CURRENT EXP: 5140/10100        LEVEL: 9
                FORMIDABLE
HP: 360/360     MP: 110/139
              STR: 9
              AGI: 6
              DEX: 12
              VIT: 9
              INT: 18 +9
          AVAILABLE: 0
```

"Fuck, it's so hot!" Richard complained at the front. As the sun beat down on us, I was sweating and constantly wiping my brow. It was the hottest day I could recall since gaining the system. 'The System' was what we had decided to call it. That was Aaron's suggestion and no one disagreed.

From time to time, Richard enjoyed rambling about the situation we were in. He'd say things like "maybe we've been living in a simulation all along and they just changed the settings." His guess was as good as any other so I didn't bother trying to refute his claims. Despite all the deaths, a part of me felt grateful for the system, but I didn't voice this aloud, I felt too guilty about it. For the first time in my life, I felt as if I had a purpose, even if it was just to survive.

Both Richard and Aaron's skills had gone up a notch. I also noted over the past few days that both their bodies had become more toned and muscular. STR provided an actual increase in one's physique. I was curious what a person with 150 STR might look like, or if it simply capped at a certain point. My guess was that it capped and you would look normal, with just super-human strength.

The morning grind was dull; there weren't many packs along the highway. If I was alone I'd perhaps search out groups of mobs in order to level, but the others seemed content with the relatively easy gains. So far my original estimate of 2 miles a day had proven incredibly conservative. We had only been walking for 2 hours and had covered that distance already.

"Hyah!" Richard yelled out as he slashed diagonally across a Warthog. About thirty-minutes earlier he had started randomly making noises with every slash and strike.

"Are we in an anime?" I whispered to Andrew, who couldn't help but cover his mouth and chuckle. Richard seemed to enjoy putting on a performance. I shook my head but didn't say anything.

If that was what he needed to do to relieve some of the stress of constantly fighting in melee, I was all for it. A piece of jewelry floated above the despawning corpse.

```
ROSARY: INT +1 HEAL +5%
A BEAUTIFUL ROSARY MADE OF PURE SILVER. ITS VERY PRES-
ENCE WARDS OFF EVIL.
```

"Everyone in favor of Andrew?" I asked. This was a no brainer.

"Definitely." The decision was unanimous. I felt less guilty about having hogged every INT and MP item.

The silver beads appeared around his neck moments later. They shined in the sunlight and nearly blinded me. The magic items looked really good. He occasionally held it in his hand to take repeated looks at it, a proud expression on his face. *Maybe I was wrong about him not caring?*

The day dragged on. The surrounding area was just more of the same. Regardless of what street we looked down, what vehicle we climbed on, nothing changed. The world was in ruins and monsters were at every turn.

Part of the problem was also us. We encountered several larger and burlier monsters during our journey. Our decision was to avoid them completely. The alluring name of our goal, the 'safe-zone', made us extra cautious.

There was a light at the end of the tunnel, a hope we didn't have while on campus. We were on our way to a place of safety and would do anything to see the end of our journey. That in turn made our days boring but safe.

We spotted a payphone connected to the back of a business just over a fence. We all looked at it without even saying anything. It seemed like we were thinking the same thing.

"Should we try?" Richard wondered.

Aaron shrugged, "does anyone have any quarters?"

"I have a few in my bag," I said. The top compartment had a zipper that I could chuck loose change in. There was probably five or six dollars in coins in it.

We stepped over the barrier wall and onto the sandy roadside. The ground was a mix of dirt and gravel and white sand. Little blotches of weeds and greenery sprouted up here and there. Our feet sank just a bit as we walked down.

Occasionally our steps would slide as if we were descending a sandy hill. Eventually we were all gathered by the fence. I grasped it and was prepared to climb over when Richard called out. "What are you doing? Step back." I moved away.

He held up the greatsword and then sliced down with tremendous force. He managed to cut a single line through the chain link fence that he then pried open. He held it spread for us, "Let's go."

It felt odd standing in the parking lot behind a convenience store. At least it was something different from that grey, concrete highway. I pulled out a few quarters and approached the payphone. I told myself it wasn't possible, nothing was going to happen when I picked up the phone.

Despite that, my hand was slightly trembling. You couldn't out reason your emotions. Telling yourself there's no reason to be sad, or scared, or angry: it didn't work. My brain was a mess of emotions.

I picked up the payphone and hesitated to put it to my ear. I was afraid there would be nothing on the other side. No sound, nothing.

Andrew noticed my hesitation, "It'll be fine regardless. We've made it this far without any answers. What's a bit more?" He was right. My hand gripped the warm black plastic and pulled the phone to my ear.

There was nothing. I started to crunch buttons and even pulled on the hook several times. Nothing happened. Despite having known this was the most likely outcome my head drooped a little lower. I dropped the phone and it swung on its cord before smacking into the booth.

I turned around and faced everyone and no doubt there was a sour expression on my face. "Let's go." We started to walk towards the hole we'd made in the fence when I noticed something out of the corner of my eye. There was a flickering movement in my peripheral. It was the tree at the edge of the lot, just against the fence a ways down.

I paused and looked in that direction. Nothing was happening but I was sure I saw something. Everyone stopped and realized something wasn't quite right with me.

"What's up?" asked Aaron, who then turned and looked at the tree I was staring at.

"It's nothi…" I broke off when I realized what it was I originally saw. The flickering movement was that of eyes opening and closing. It wasn't just any pair of eyes though. The tree had a pair of eyes.

To be exact, it wasn't a tree, but a monster of some sort. The ground started to quake as the asphalt in that area trembled and cracked. Eventually the tree completely uprooted itself and stood up.

The branches that were originally messy and scattered morphed into two arms. It even plucked a branch out of its head and then held it like a club of some sort.

"What the hell…"

"Is that?" Everyone was thinking the same thing. We had seen our fair share of odd and surreal creatures. But a living tree? That took the cake so far.

"Can we avoid it?" I asked. We had a good system in place that was getting us reliable EXP and items. This tree was a big unknown, and when I said big, I meant BIG. Just the branch making up its arm was so thick it would take two of us locking arms to wrap around it.

"It won't hurt to try," Aaron said.

Richard was already at the fence prying apart the opening, "Hurry up!" He said. Andrew was just about to move through when an old and ancient groan came from the tree. It tossed the club made of its own body into the fence.

Everyone, including Andrew was left with no choice but to fall back towards the building. It was more like the trunk of a tree instead of a branch, but that was just how big this monster was.

The fence couldn't withstand the weight and smashed down in that section. The concrete supports buried beneath the sand and asphalt immediately ripped up and the fence bobbed up and down like a trampoline.

We were blocked off from getting back to our route. The street just in front of the business went under the highway. Either we crossed to the opposite lot and climbed over there or somehow made it past this behemoth.

If the street wasn't filled with monsters, the decision would have been a no brainer. The problem was that to rush under the highway was a death sentence. We would aggro multiple packs of other mobs while contending with this tree giant.

It seemed the most dangerous decision was the only right one. "We have to fight," I said.

The giant tree pulled another branch from its head and then held it like a club. It lifted one of its 'feet' and then stepped onto the asphalt. My entire world was quaking.

"Spread out while we can! Richard you take the front, go with it for now," Aaron barked. The alley behind the building was big enough for us to get some distance from each other. At least in that way we wouldn't all take a tree to the face.

I rushed to the far left and Aaron stayed on the far right. Andrew positioned himself a dozen feet behind Richard, directly in the center of all three of us.

"Do your best to defend Richard!" I cried. There was really no chance Richard could contend in strength. The trunk of the monster was thicker than several of his bodies stacked together. I casted *Inspect* once we got in position.

```
ANCIENT ONE*      LEVEL: 15       PLANT
           HP: 7311              MP: 15
                   STR: 50
                   AGI: 5
                   DEX: 5
                   VIT: 40
                   INT: 15
A LONG DETACHED DESCENDENT OF YGGDRASIL, THE WORLD
                    TREE.
```

"Richard you can't take it head on! But it should be incredibly slow, just try and dodge!" 5 AGI with a body of that size was basically nothing.

Richard kept his eyes locked on the Ancient One while nodding his head. "Got it!"

I said the monster was slow, but it didn't seem to matter that much. It extended its arm with the tree club and swiped in Richard's direction. The branch was so thick that there wasn't really anywhere to dodge. Richard barely managed to jump up and over the trunk as it came towards him.

The tree club connected with a dumpster just behind him. The impact caused it to ring out like a struck bell. The crumpled dumpster rolled all the way into the concrete building before coming to a stop with a smash. The clang echoed all the way through the back alley.

The good news was the tree took an incredibly long time to wind up its next attack. Richard managed to rush towards its bulky legs and slash out. The greatsword didn't do much damage but every little bit counted. A foot-long gash started to drip bright green sap.

This had to be my battle. I lit a fireball and tossed it out into the mess of green leaves on the Ancient One's head. A small fire started and I was buoyant.

Aaron was also ready with a *Powershot*. I didn't imagine he could do much damage with an arrow, but he proved me wrong. His target choice was excellent. An arrow flew through the air and smashed directly into one of the monster's eyes.

The Ancient One let out a prehistoric groan. Its free hand reached up and ripped the burning branches from its head before tossing them in my direction. The creature's entire body whined like a tree battling hurricane winds.

It wasn't agile but its strength was tremendous. Those burning branches rocketed towards me at an incredible speed. I only just managed to avoid them by flinging myself flat. The burning leaves on top scraped by my arm and upper body.

It didn't hurt as bad as I was expecting. I wasn't in contact for long enough to get burned but I did have some ragged scratches on my upper arm.

Richard was still slashing out repeatedly. The sap was pooling below the Ancient One at an incredible pace. He was only forced back when the hand holding the club managed to retract back.

It swung out again at Richard and he was ready to do the same trick as last time. It seemed the high INT stat that the mob had wasn't just for show. Right as Richard jumped the Ancient One swerved upwards to smack into Richard's belly, where he found himself stuck.

The trunk was building speed with Richard on it. "Help!" He yelled. He was going to be smashed into a pulp against the dumpster. I wasn't sure if he would survive an impact that strong. I had to try to stop it.

I tossed my lit fireball at the extended arm. It caught fire but the Ancient One didn't seem to care. He was intent on dispatching Richard regardless. Richard was moments away from being crushed.

"Get ready to heal him!" I yelled at Andrew. As long as he didn't die in one hit Andrew could save Richard and we could get him out of here. If that meant running into more monsters and risking it all then so be it.

Moving forward, I got ready to grab Richard after the impact when I heard the rush of Aaron's *Powershot*. His second arrow connected cleanly with the remaining open eye and fully blinded the Ancient One.

Now the Ancient One couldn't see where he was swinging Richard and misjudged. There was a gap between the wall and the dumpster, big enough for about two people to fit in.

The Ancient One extended his club just a bit too far and managed to smash Richard into that little gap. The trunk below him hit the dumpster and forced it to a full stop. He was still flung off the

212

trunk and struck against the concrete, but he wasn't completely smashed to a pulp.

I could hear Richard let out a huge groan of pain and the resulting collision. The dumpster rang out once again and then recoiled off the wall from the impact. Richard was left there in the corner of the two connecting buildings.

I waited for the Ancient One to retract his arm, then ran over and got a grip under Richard's armpits, then began dragging him towards Andrew. Our tank was promptly healed but the damage wasn't something he could completely ignore. His ribs had probably been broken in the initial impact and he still needed time to recover from the fatigue loss.

The Ancient One was fully blind, or so we thought. Aaron came over to us as well, "How is he?"

"He'll live, but he can't fight right now," Andrew said.

"Joseph and I can probably finish this."

With the Ancient One blind and unable to lash into the alley, we were safe enough to continue fighting.

There was no reason to spread out, and so we didn't. We started to bombard the Ancient One with fireballs and arrows aimed repeatedly at the eye area. The damage was slowly accumulating, with sap pouring from the eyes like tears, and we thought the battle was in the bag.

There was no way for the Ancient One to even retaliate, and he was no longer trying to. It looked like the battle was coming to a close. Suddenly, the Ancient One began to glow with a green light. He wasn't taking those hits for nothing. He was casting a spell.

The Ancient One radiated so brightly that the walls of every building were coated in a green hue. I originally thought it was heal, but it wasn't. Little sprites came out from all over the Ancient One and perched on his branches.

They were now acting as his eyes and ears. With their assistance, he was no longer blind. "Get Richard inside!" That was my decision. Andrew and Richard were easy targets. Richard couldn't even move.

"There's five sprites. I can maybe take them out," Aaron said.

"Alright, I'll try and buy you time." I started throwing out fireballs like a crazed madman. I wasn't even trying to be efficient. I was just throwing them in the most annoying places possible.

Every time the Ancient One caught fire he needed to use one of his arms to snuff it out or pull the burning area from his body. I targeted between his legs, under his arms, on top of his head.

It didn't seem like he was happy with my arrangements. He tossed a burning log bigger than me directly towards me. Although I was ready for the throw, I barely managed to dodge. It smashed into the building behind me and burst into a mess of splinters. I would have been turned into meat paste had it hit.

Still, the Ancient One's attack was too predictable and his windup was too slow. I wasn't restrained like Richard, I didn't have anyone to protect. Richard and Andrew were already safely inside, Aaron could fend for himself. I only needed to dodge.

There was a twang and then one of the spirits was blasted to bits. Aaron's accuracy was leagues above that first day when fighting zombies. I couldn't remember the last time he missed a shot. It also didn't seem like the little spirits were moving much either. I tried my luck at dispatching one as well.

On my second fireball I managed to kill a spirit. Aaron had already dispatched two on his own. The Ancient One was slowing considerably. The time it took to put out one of my fires was much longer than it took me to start one.

The entire right side of the tree was already starting to burn. There were also no sprites there. It was a complete blind spot for the Ancient One. I decided we should put the nail in the coffin.

I rushed over to Aaron and held out my palm. A fireball was burning brightly in it. I didn't even need to instruct him as Aaron pulled another arrow from his back. He nocked it and then placed the tip in my fireball.

It ignited with a poof in under a second and he fired it out in one smooth action. Aaron continued to light and fire arrows into every nook and cranny of the tree. These were much harder to extinguish than my own. If there was a hollow point in the tree then Aaron managed to shoot a flaming arrow into it.

The Ancient One didn't last even thirty seconds. His entire body was caked in fire and there was no putting it out anymore. His legs collapsed under him and caused the earth to quake. "Watch out!" I yelled. We darted to the side as he fell forward and smashed into the roof of a building.

CONGRATULATIONS! YOU HAVE REACHED LEVEL 10. AS A RE-WARD FOR LEVELING UP, YOU HAVE BEEN GRANTED THREE STAT POINTS!

HEAD TO THE SAFE-ZONE TO ACQUIRE YOUR NEW CLASS.

I pushed the welcome message to the back of my mind. The building the Ancient One had collapsed on was the same that Andrew and Richard had gone into. Aaron and I rushed around and opened the front door.

"Andrew! Richard!" I yelled.

The back part of the building's roof had collapsed and dust and debris were rich in the air. "We're okay! Back here!" A voice yelled through the cloud of smoke.

"We're coming!" Aaron and I started wade through the isle. Many shelves had tipped and their contents spewed along the floor. We eventually found the two of them under a shelf that had tipped and fallen into the opposite wall. It didn't collapse and kept the falling ceiling from crushing them.

"Get Richard out first," Andrew said. We managed to grab him by his feet and drag him out. Andrew crawled out moments after. Richard was still unconscious. Despite Andrew healing him to full health, he still hadn't woken up.

While *Heal* could keep you from dying, it wasn't a cure all. It could assist in healing wounds and repairing broken bones, but those things still took time.

"Let's get him outside. We can't stay in here." The buildings structure was severely compromised. It wouldn't be surprising if the entire thing came crashing down.

The back alley was once again safe. Something peculiar was that the Ancient One didn't despawn. Maybe it did despawn, but the original appearance of the tree was all that remained. It looked like a tree was blown over in a storm and fell atop this building.

It was possible that the tree was simply a host for the Ancient One and the sprites were its true form. I was only guessing as it was impossible to know. However, the tree remained and there were two items floating below the debris.

```
┌─────────────────────────────────────────────┐
│                                               │
│              YGDRASSIL BERRY                  │
│  A FRUIT OF THE WORLD TREE, YGGDRASIL. ITS    │
│  DELICIOUS TASTE IS FULL OF LIFE. RENOWNED    │
│  FOR ITS MIRACULOUS HEALING EFFECTS.          │
│                                               │
└─────────────────────────────────────────────┘
```

It was a one-time consumable drop.

"We should use this on Richard. What does everyone think?" He still hadn't woken up and we couldn't move without him. It might be days before he would be up and about again. The clock was ticking.

"Agreed." Andrew picked up the Yggdrasil Berry and walked over to Richard. I held his head while Andrew did his best to open his mouth, then stuck the berry in one side of his jaw and moved his chin up and down.

I could see the berry explode with juice that coated the entire inside of Richard's mouth. It didn't even go down his throat but instead disappeared into his gums as if being absorbed.

It didn't take more than three seconds before his mouth was chewing on its own. His eyes started to flutter and his face scrunched before jerking up. "What did you just feed me? I've never tasted anything so good before."

Only after several pats on the back and a reassurance that Richard seemed okay did we turn back to the remaining item. It was an arrow quiver.

```
EMPOWERING QUIVER: DEX +1
ARROWS HELD INSIDE THIS QUIVER ARE NURTURED AS IF ALIVE
```

It was an interesting item to say the least. How did it nurture arrows? We would only be able to see after Aaron figured it out himself.

There were no more items under the tree and Richard was finally able to move again. It looked like we were about ready to get back on the highway. I turned my attention back towards the level message from earlier.

I couldn't be sure if someone else had beaten me to level 10 or if there was just no reward. I had received *Speedy Recovery* for being the first level five in my district and I was disappointed not to get something for being level 10. Still, apparently there were new classes available to me, which I was excited about. Regardless of what they were, I would play some form of a caster. *Stats!*

```
CURRENT EXP: 1370/13200 LEVEL: 10     FORMIDABLE
              HP: 390/390    MP: 84/143
                    STR: 9
                    AGI: 6
                    DEX: 12
                    VIT: 9
                    INT: 18 +9
                 AVAILABLE: 3
```

I ended up putting two points into INT and then another point into VIT. Not only did it look nice on my stat sheet, it pushed me closer to being able to cast an extra *Meteor Storm*. I was slowly learning to strike a balance with my stats.

Another exciting discovery was that my EXP required to level had evened off. I was incredibly worried it would keep doubling and doubling. Andrew, Richard, and Aaron were all level 9. Hopefully, they would reach level 10 by day's end.

Regaining the road, we proceeded even more cautiously, but never encountered anything we couldn't fight safely. Progress was steady all afternoon. When we reached within 2 miles of the safe-zone we could see a marvelous phenomenon. A square of light shone up into the sky as far as I could tilt my head. *We were almost there!*

The number of monsters we encountered tapered off until there was nothing between us and the light. As when we had left the training ground, there was a zone of several hundred feet with absolutely nothing in it. It lay just outside the wall of light.

Only when we had entered a hundred feet or so into that dead-zone could we see the appearance of a wall. It was like staring into a mirage, as the image beyond the wall (of a suburb) seemed to ripple in waves.

We rushed towards the wall with no fear. If the System wanted to harm us with a trick, it didn't need to lie about this. Touching it, my hand disappeared, so I kept on going. I didn't feel anything particular or unusual as I passed through the wall but the view on the other side was anything but that of a residential neighborhood.

In the very center of the safe-zone was a clock tower that nearly touched the clouds. The floor was cobblestone and neatly paved. A map of the entire city appeared in my mind. There were four entrances that led inside.

We had entered in the east side. The map displayed an Inn, General Store, Guild Hall, Bank, Weapon shop, Repair shop and a few other miscellaneous buildings. There were also symbols all over the map I didn't recognize. We passed under an arch and then across a bridge. A moat completely encircled the inner part of the city.

A woman in old-style clothing greeted us just after passing the bridge. Her head was adorned with a bonnet. "Welcome to safe-zone Three-Seven-Three! As this is your first visit, you need to be aware of the rules." She passed a booklet to each of us. It floated in the air before dissolving in our hands. The information was instantly available in my head. "Please read over them carefully." She walked away.

I looked at the others before focusing my attention inward.

No PVP in the safe-zone.
Assaulting NPCs in any way is not allowed.
No stealing.

The rules seemed simple enough. There was no listed penalty, though. I sprinted ahead to catch up to the woman whom I assumed was an NPC. "Excuse me!" She turned around to face me. "There's no listed punishment here, what happens if you break the rules?"

She turned and faced me with a smile, "Execution, of course!"

My next words were caught in my throat.

The others all could hear what I had asked and the response. "Let's walk around?" I asked. Everyone nodded without a word. We headed towards the clock-tower in the center. It was probably a mile away from our current location.

Chapter 11: Safe Zone 373

At first, we didn't see any people, but as we approached more towards the city-square we started to see them. In fact, there were hundreds of people, maybe even thousands. I had grown accustomed to seeing no one but this was a breath of fresh air.

The center was bustling as people ran to and fro. A part of me had half-expected us to be the first group in the safe-zone. Naive thinking: there had to be people closer by than us who made it here first.

"What should we do?" Richard wondered aloud.

"Why is everyone crowded around that specific spot?" Aaron asked. One particular section of the center square was filled with several times more people than the others. We moved in that direction.

I squeezed through the crowd and found myself in front of a large wooden board. I did my best to see what was so special about it. I looked to a person standing on my left, "What's so special about the board?"

"First day here? It's a mission board. First come, first serve. Great rewards."

"Like a quest?"

"Sort of, you either kill some monster or collect some item. Bring it back and you get your reward. Sometimes its exp and sometimes it's an item."

"Can only one person accept a mission?"

"Nope, anyone can accept a mission on the board, but only the person who returns first gets the reward. If you complete it as a party then the reward is just split. You don't get more."

"Thanks." I turned back to the others and explained what I'd been told.

"Should we take a mission?" Aaron asked.

"We just got here." Richard complained.

For once I agreed with Richard, but I still decided to take a gander at the rewards. Besides items there was a reward called Zeny, and it was given out in the hundreds for a successful mission. It sounded like a currency but I couldn't be sure.

We continued to wander the city and made a stop at all of the major buildings. All of the merchants and street stalls required Zeny.

I went up to an NPC food vendor to explain the question of currency to me.

"At the moment, missions are the only way to acquire Zeny," he said. "Fortunately, the basic necessities are free while the two-week deadline approaches."

"Missions are the only way?"

"Once the two-week deadline is up every monster will have a chance to drop Zeny. For now though, it's only the mission board," he confirmed.

It seemed there was going to be a lot to do once the deadline came around. We had managed to make it to the safe-zone on the sixth day after the event. There were still another eight to wait before we could reliably earn Zeny.

All of us were eager to explore and so we went our own ways; the zone was not so big, I assumed I'd find my friends again when

I needed to. So I went to browse the shops alone and was amazed at what I found.

One vendor sold potions, both HP and MP pots. There were lower tier potions that cost just 50 Zeny each, all the way up to more powerful potions at 600 Zeny each. They healed more HP and MP than I had total. There were potions that removed poison and other status affects I had not seen or heard of: Bleeding, Stun, Chill, Silence.

The armor smith and weapon smith sold low quality weapons and armor. These didn't provide any attribute increases but any bit of protection helped. Once I had the ability to do so I would pick up pieces for any slot I didn't have equipped.

Shit, I knew I was forgetting something! I needed to find the NPC for my class upgrade. The hustle and bustle had excited me to distraction. I found another NPC and asked for instruction.

"Where do I go to class change?"

"To class change you need to meet the mayor inside the top floor of the clock-tower." I didn't hesitate and made my way there immediately. Once in front, I spotted two guards holding large halberds. They remained crossed as to block any entry. I walked forward and waited for them to lift them so I could enter.

I waited for what felt like five minutes. I coughed, "Ahem, I've come to class change." There was a moment of silence before the halberds raised and allowed me entry. Once inside, I hurried up the stairs. I don't know exactly how many steps I climbed before I reached the top, but my lungs and thighs burned.

"Welcome adventurer!" A man wearing a suit and monocle sat behind a desk. There was an ink pen in his hand. He just finished writing something down in a document.

"I've come to class change."

He adjusted the monocle and took a better look at me. "Let's have a look at your stats."

Without me having to do anything my stats appeared.

CURRENT EXP: 1370/13200 LEVEL: 10   FORMIDABLE
HP: 420/420   MP: 116/149
STR: 9
AGI: 6
DEX: 12
VIT: 10
INT: 20 +9

AVAILABLE: 0

"I see, you do qualify." The mayor opened a drawer on his desk and began fumbling inside before pulling out a sheet. "Take a look at this." He slid it across the desk and in front of me. It was a list of possible classes. First Classes to be exact.

I took a better glance at the listed First Classes.

Swordsman
Mage
Thief
Acolyte
Merchant

Archer

Exorcist

Enchanter

The first six choices were mostly self-explanatory, option 7 and 8 were more obscure. "What's an Exorcist and what's an Enchanter?"

"An Exorcist specializes in curses and the undead." His response was incredibly vague.

"And Enchanter?"

"Enchanters use powers of coercion to gain powerful allies, usually with nature."

"Like a druid?"

The mayor paused for a minute, unsure if he was allowed to answer. "A druid would be a more advanced version."

"This says First Class. Does that mean there are further classes?" Another pause.

"There are further classes that stem from these classes."

"I'd like to be a Mage." There was no other option for me to choose from. My stats were focused heavily on INT. I was a spell caster through and through.

"Are you sure? Once you choose your class you can't choose another."

"I'm sure!"

"Alright, please sign here." He pushed another paper in front of me and passed me the feather ink pen. I did my best to sign without tearing into the paper. It was surprisingly hard to write with. Once I finished, he took out a stamp and stamped it.

The air in the room suddenly became turbulent and an odd feeling welled inside of me. A blinding light flashed from my body and I was prompted with a message.

CONGRATULATIONS! YOU HAVE BECOME A MAGE. YOUR HP AND MP VALUES HAVE BEEN ADJUSTED ACCORDINGLY. YOU HAVE LEARNED THE SKILL *ENERGY COAT* LV. 1
YOUR AFFINITY WITH MAGIC HAS INCREASED. AS A RESULT, YOUR MP REGENERATION HAS INCREASED. THE AMOUNT OF MP YOU GAIN PER INT AND LEVEL HAS DOUBLED.
THE AMOUNT OF HP YOU GAIN PER VIT HAS DOUBLED.
THE EFFECT OF DEX ON YOUR CAST-TIME HAS SUBSTANTIALLY INCREASED.

I checked my stats.

CURRENT EXP: 1370/13200 LEVEL: 10
MAGE   FORMIDABLE
HP: 715/715   MP: 270/270
STR: 9
AGI: 6
DEX: 12
VIT: 10
INT: 20 +9
AVAILABLE: 0

This…I had gained over 200 HP and nearly doubled my MP value from changing class. Let alone the benefit to my MP regen. I looked at my new skill *Energy Coat*.

> **ENERGY COAT** LV. 1 SUMMON A COAT OF ENERGY TO SURROUND YOU. WHILE ACTIVE, 30% OF DAMAGE TAKEN IS TAKEN FROM MP BEFORE HP. EXCHANGE IS 1 MP: 1 HP.

Energy Coat was broken. There was no other way to describe it. This was the effect at just level 1? I needed to figure out how to level it immediately. All in all, my defense doubled. I wanted to level so badly.

I wished we'd arranged to contact each other. Tempting as it was to go outside solo, the sun was coming down and I needed to find a place to sleep, and soon. I made my way to the inn on the map. Unsurprisingly, there were no available rooms. The lodging was free until Zeny was introduced. I slept on the street.

I woke the next morning with a killer back ache. Sleeping on solid cobblestone rock was not advisable. Many others slept on the street just like me. A nice touch was the clock-tower. I didn't need to guess what time it was, 6:30 A.M.

Despite being completely safe here, I wanted to level. It was a constant process. Being complacent now would just hurt you in the long run. I wanted to stay ahead of the curve. I wandered around the center-square for a while but didn't manage to find Aaron, Richard, or Andrew. Today, I would level alone.

After double checking with an NPC that I could come and go as I pleased I headed out the eastern entrance and into familiar territory. I knew there were packs I could prey on there, as long as I was careful I could take on the solo mobs too. If I factored in the burning damage from fireball then most of them should only take two casts. I walked for about an hour before returning to the highway.

As expected, all the mobs had respawned and there were plenty for me to hunt. I decided to test the waters and started off with a Rabid Wolf. Their HP was the lowest of any of the solo-monsters we had encountered.

My idea was simple: start the fight with a fireball, immediately *Shackle*, and then fireball again for the kill.

After my opening shot, the wolf yelped then barked viciously while running towards me. The smell of burning hair filled my nostril. Its side had been singed down to raw skin. *Shackle!* The wolf ended up restrained just two or three feet away from me. I wiped the sweat from my brow and backed away to the max range I could cast *Fireball* from. The second cast landed cleanly in the face of the wolf. It yelped in agony as its face melted.

The wolf died before the *Shackle* broke. Its body despawned and the spikes disappeared into the ground with it. I checked my EXP. The wolf had given a total of 800 EXP at the cost of two *Fireballs* and one *Shackle*: 25 MP. This was not particularly efficient and the lesson was to avoid solo monsters as much as possible.

One *Meteor Storm* was only 22 MP and would dispatch 3 monsters of the same level or even a little higher. I continued forward in search of a suitable pack. I came upon an open area like a former basketball court. The only monsters in it were three packs of orcs and a single pack of trolls. *Is this what heaven looked like?*

After waiting to confirm there were no roaming singles, I skirted around the edge towards my first set of victims. *Meteor Storm!* Those beautiful burning rocks fell from the sky and crashed into the asphalt. The three orcs directly below the explosions disappeared. As a four-person group we had received 300 EXP per kill. Now 3600 EXP was given solely to me.

The possibility that I could level in these remaining three packs was an unbelievable prospect to me. I made my way around the area clockwise, wiping out the remaining three packs one after the other.

CONGRATULATIONS! YOU HAVE REACHED LEVEL 11. AS A RE-WARD FOR LEVELING UP, YOU HAVE BEEN GRANTED THREE STAT POINTS!

I felt like my cast speed was severely lacking while hunting alone. A particularly fast monster like the blood-thirsty cheetah would be on me before I could even cast *Shackle*. I decided pushing my DEX closer to my INT was the most beneficial move.

CURRENT EXP: 2570/16200   **LEVEL: 11**

MAGE   **FORMIDABLE**

HP: 745/745   **MP: 260/278**

STR: 9

AGI: 6

DEX: 15

VIT: 10

INT: 20 +9

AVAILABLE: 0

I gained the same amount of HP as before, 30 per level. My status as a mage granted me 8 MP for my level and then another 18 for the three INT. I had been using *Energy Coat* the entire time.

I had also obtained two items from the four packs, quite a nice haul.

> **WOODEN STOUT SHIELD: PHYSICAL DAMAGE TAKEN -20**
> **A WOODEN SHIELD AS THICK AS A DOOR, IT SHOULD PROVIDE**
> **GOOD PROTECTION.**

I didn't know of anyone that could use the shield so I stored it away. The second item was also not one that I could use.

> **SKULL WAND: INT +2, CAN SUMMON ONE ADDITIONAL UNDEAD**
> **AT A TIME.**
> **THE SKULL OF A POWERFUL NECROMANCER, YOU FEEL CLOSER TO**
> **DEATH WEARING IT.**

It was an interesting item. Something an Exorcist would badly want. I would trade it once Zeny became more available. I'm sure I could make a pretty penny.

> **ENERGY COAT LV. 1 0/300**

Despite using it full time, I had gained zero experience towards the second level of *Energy Coat. Did I need to take damage?* I shivered at the prospect but didn't rule it out as a possibility. There was only one way to confirm.

I found another wolf and pulled it into a secluded area. I started my pull off normally with a fireball, but decided against shackling. Smoking as it rushed me, my second fireball connected cleanly, in the few moments before it melted, the wolf managed to leap out and swipe its paw at me.

The air around me seemed to deform as I was hit. A stinging sensation spread across my shoulder. Luckily, the wolf died before it could attack again. I checked my HP and MP. The attack did a total of 200 DMG. 140 subtracted from my HP and 60 from my MP. It was a very costly but worthwhile test.

I pulled up my skill window and looked at *Energy Coat* again.

ENERGY COAT LV. 1 10/300

That pretty much confirmed it. The only way to level *Energy Coat* was to take damage. Something else came to me that I hadn't considered. I could use my staff to assist in blocking attacks. The thought had never crossed my mind until watching that wolf leap at me. I had resisted the urge to raise my staff and hold it in front of me just for the test.

Although I wanted to stay out for as long as possible, that wouldn't be much longer. I had already used 173 MP. I thought I might be able to squeeze out another level, if that.

I managed to kill another two packs before deciding it was best to be careful. I couldn't afford to head back with no MP in case of a random encounter. Without my spells, I would be helpless.

```
CURRENT EXP: 9770/16200        LEVEL: 11
          MAGE            FORMIDABLE
       HP: 745/745      MP: 87/278
              STR: 9
              AGI: 6
              DEX: 15
              VIT: 10
              INT: 20 +9
            AVAILABLE: 0
```

I returned to find Andrew waiting at the bridge.

"There you are. I didn't know how else to find you, so I've been here off and on for hours." His tone was disheartened.

I scratched my head. "Yeah, sorry. I shouldn't have gone out to level alone but I just got so excited."

"It's not about that."

"Spill it, you can tell me straight." His tone was more-so like we weren't friends. It was starting to make me feel uncomfortable.

Andrew let out a long sigh, "I won't be going out to level anymore. I'm sorry but you'll need to find a new healer." The news hit me like a ton of bricks.

"...Why? Aren't things going well? Don't we get along okay?" I couldn't understand.

"It's not about you, or anyone in the party."

"Then what is it? I don't get it Andrew." I really couldn't understand.

"I told you before my dream has always been to help people. I can finally do that. I'm a real healer now. I can stay in the safe zone and help people. I can't do that if I'm following you."

"How will you sustain yourself? Things won't always be free. Time won't wait for you," I said.

"It WILL work. I can charge just enough to pay my fees. There are others like me who don't want to fight. I will make it work."

"How long have you been thinking about this?"

"Since the day the message came through."

"So the entire time you chose to say nothing? You could have told us differently. Aaron and Richard both deserve to hear it from you."

"I was afraid to tell you then. People are fickle. Their hearts change too easily. I needed you all to reach here." I felt a chill run up my back.

"Weren't we friends?" I asked.

"We were, and that's why I can't bear to face Aaron and Richard, too. It took me everything to give you a heads up. I wanted to just disappear until it blew over."

"So that's it? Did all that time spent together mean nothing?"

"It meant a lot, but I can't give up my dream. I'm sorry." He didn't wait for my response and turned away before disappearing into the nearest crowd.

I was still like a statue. It wasn't something I was expecting at all. The pieces started to come together slowly as I thought more about it. He was always quiet and didn't contribute as much to our discussions.

My hunch that he didn't care about getting magic items was also spot on. I had ignored the signs that Andrew was keeping a certain distance from us as a group. Maybe only Richard had managed to break that wall slightly.

My harvest for today didn't seem all that impressive anymore. I found my spot near the city center and lay on the hard cobblestone. The night ahead was going to be a sleepless one.

I woke the following morning and did my best to find both Aaron and Richard. It took an hour and a half of diligent searching to find them. There were just that many people around.

"Guys, I have some news." They both seemed excited. The news lately had been on the good side. "Let's go somewhere quieter." There was too much bustling going on around us. I didn't want to have to shout. It would just make me angrier at the situation.

We found a bench by a well. "Andrew isn't going to heal for us anymore."

"Wait, what? I just talked to him yesterday and everything seemed fine." Richard said.

"I ran into him last night. He said he's done with the party."

"Did he give a reason?" Aaron asked.

"He doesn't think he can help people if he sticks with us. He wants to stay in the safe-zone and support people that way."

"How does he plan to survive once the deadline is up?" Aaron asked. It was the same objection I had raised.

"I asked him the same question. He seemed convinced he had it all figured out."

"Guys, let's find him and persuade him! I'm sure that if I can talk to him he'll change his mind."

I was debating whether I should say the next sentence, but I decided they needed to hear it. "Andrew said he doesn't want to see either of you. He barely worked up the courage to see me, and that was only to give us a heads up. He doesn't want to see any of us again."

"What…" Richard mumbled out. It seemed my last comment hit him like a bag of bricks. "That can't be true…"

"He said it. I'm sorry. It's best we try to forget Andrew and find a new healer." I finished. "We can't get complacent now. We all read the rules and know things won't stay the same. It's best we keep our current progress."

"How can we level without a healer? I won't do it…" Richard mumbled. He was level 9 and so was Aaron. They were both just one level from their class change.

"At level ten you can change classes," I said.

"Did you get to see the class choices?" Aaron asked.

"You would be an Archer and Richard would be a Swordsman," I said. That was the most realistic choices for their stat allocation and weapon usage.

My comment managed to perk Richard up for a moment before he resumed his depressed attitude.

"You're level eleven now? Did you go outside the safe-zone?" Aaron asked.

"Yeah, yesterday I did a bit of leveling alone. I couldn't find anyone and just got too excited after my class change."

"I'll go with you next time," Aaron said.

"What about you Richard?" I asked.

"…No, I won't," he denied it flatly.

"Alright, take some time to get your head straight then. It will be good to get a break." I figured he would change his mind with a day or two of boredom.

Aaron and I spent the next week grinding monsters throughout the day. Richard was still acting distant. We asked him every day to come level and he gave a resounding no. Despite the repeated rejection we kept at it.

Aaron and I could instantly deal with any solo monsters. I dealt with the packs. Despite having to split the EXP 50/50 it was still faster leveling. I could stay out longer with his assistance and there was less risk. Every day we stayed out as long as we could. After five days I had ground out five more levels. I looked at my stats.

```
CURRENT EXP: 2750/27350          LEVEL: 16
            MAGE            FORMIDABLE
        HP: 1015/1015    MP: 381/381
                  STR: 10
                  AGI: 6
                  DEX: 20
                  VIT: 14
                  INT: 25 +12
              AVAILABLE: 0
```

I had ended up putting 1 point in STR, 4 points in VIT and the remaining ten points went evenly into DEX and INT. The increase in DEX made my casting feel so much smoother. I wasn't sure if it was a flat reduction or each point was a percentage. The difference between 5 and 20 was night and day, though.

More good news was that half way through the grind, my *Meteor Storm* hit level two. Something I had been eagerly waiting for. I was not let down in the slightest.

```
METEOR STORM** LV. 2
CAST TIME: 6.5 SECONDS
MP COST: 28
DISTANCE: 10 METERS
```

When I first saw the description, I was disappointed. Six more MP for 0.5 seconds off the cast time, it felt incredibly lackluster. My first cast, however, blew me away. Originally, the skill would summon three Meteors, now it summoned four. An extra Meteor was essentially a 25% increase in damage on the skill. It was just a shame that the next level was very far away.

Besides receiving a level in *Meteor Storm*, I had also leveled *Inspect* to 3. A new tidbit of information was added to the monster description: their elemental affinity. For example, Orc Warriors and Orc Lady's were both Earth property monsters. They took increased damage from fire. The Bloody-Thirsty Cheetah on the other hand, was Wind property. It took increased damage from Earth. I had learned quite a bit, specifically what each element was vulnerable to. It went like this:

Fire > Earth

Wind/Lightning > Water/Ice

Water/Ice > Fire

Earth > Wind/Lightning

This created an interesting dynamic. I wasn't sure how many more elemental properties there were. I knew of Holy, Undead and also Neutral properties. Neutral property monsters had no weakness. Holy and Undead were the nemesis of each other.

Inspect also had an 8-meter range now.

Over the five days, Aaron and I had found numerous items and I had acquired two new skills.

GLACIAL SPIKE
CAST TIME: 2 SECONDS
MP COST: 7
DISTANCE: 7 METERS
SUMMON A SHARD OF ICE TO PIERCE YOUR ENEMIES FROM BELOW

Besides my new ice skill, I had obtained a channeled spell as well

---

*ARCANE MISSILE**
CAST TIME: CHANNELED — 5 SECONDS
MP COST: 14
DISTANCE 6 METERS
SUMMON BOLTS OF ARCANE FROM THE VOID TO ASSAULT YOUR ENEMY. SHOOTS 1 BOLT PER SECOND

Of the two, I much preferred *Arcane Missile*. From what I'd seen so far, it could completely replace *Fireball* for single target. Something else Aaron and I deduced was that the * next to items or skills corresponds to their rarity. Apparently, my *Meteor Storm* was an incredibly rare skill.

Of all the items we found I could only equip one. The rest were shared and stored away for trading.

> ## Seer's Circlet*: Int +3, MP +15, MP regeneration +10%
> ### A Circlet worn by a once great Prophet.

Besides rings and amulets, which seemed to be incredibly rare, I had an item equipped in every slot.

We came up to the twelfth day, just two to go. Aaron and I agreed ahead of time to make the thirteenth a light day of grinding. That night I sought out Richard.

"Richard," I said.

He sat up but didn't say anything. I felt like I was nagging him but I didn't want to let him disappear without fighting for it.

"It's almost day fourteen. We need you."

"Do you though? You and Aaron seem fine. You're level fifteen and sixteen." There was a bit of sarcasm in his voice.

"We asked you to come with us every day. We even offered to leech you." I paused. "Besides, the levels aren't important. You can catch back up to us in just a few days." I pleaded. I couldn't figure out why he was resenting us. What did we do wrong?

"You just want someone to stand in front and take a beating for you. A beating that is incredibly painful. It's always been that way."

"Richard, you're the tank! You wanted to be the tank from DAY ONE. That was your decision!" I said. Somehow we were now the bad guys. I couldn't understand it.

"And? That doesn't change the fact that I get my ass kicked every fight. Do you know how many times I nearly died?"

"Too many times," I said. "I know it's unacceptable. We're learning and growing stronger, though. We need you." I pleaded. He didn't respond. "I have plans Richard. I want to form a guild, with you and Aaron."

I waited there in silence for thirty seconds before he finally spoke, "Leave me out of your plans." He curled back into a ball and turned away from me.

"If it's about not having a healer we can find a new healer!" I said. "We can all look for one together." He didn't even turn back to respond. I waited for a minute before walking away.

I was hurt and confused. Was he truly mad at us or was he mad at himself? If he was regretting his decision to be melee and tank then I could understand his frustration. Those were things we could work on. He didn't want to do it, though.

Andrew was right. Human hearts were fickle. I still couldn't understand where we had went wrong. Maybe we didn't do wrong in the first place at all? I had my truth and Richard had his. Mine was to level up and get on top of this challenge. Richard's were something else. I just needed to accept it. Regardless, time would wait for no one.

The following morning, I had to break the news to Aaron. It wasn't the most exciting prospect. Losing Veronica was bad enough. Now we had lost both Andrew and Richard in just a short week. Everything was falling apart.

"Morning," I said.

"Morning. How did it go?"

"It didn't go well. Richard's also out," I said.

"I honestly wasn't expecting things to go south so quickly. If I knew it was that bad I'd have come with you."

"He wasn't in a great mood."

"What did you say to him?"

"He was in a bad mood before we started talking. I told him what he needed to hear and he didn't want anything to do with it."

"You mentioned the guild?"

"Yep, told me to keep him out of it."

"We made our intention clear. We can only hope he changes his mind before tomorrow."

"Right."

We turned our attention towards the bustling city center. Today was the last day before the fourteenth. No one knew if this was good news or bad news. Some people sat around leisurely while others bustled to and fro.

The general consensus was that most people were racing to increase their strength. In fact, we saw plenty of groups leaving everyday to hunt. Some of them simply went on a grind and others accepted quests from the mission boards. None of them exited our side of the safe-zone and I couldn't be sure of their strength.

Aaron and I had also taken two quests from the mission board just a day prior. They were EXP-based quests. One was to obtain six orcish vouchers. The other was to gather three animal claws. The drop rate seemed to be one hundred percent.

We gathered the orcish vouchers after two packs of orcs. It was a sort of insignia that symbolized what tribe they were a part of. They were carved out of wood and had shoddy designs on them. The quest didn't give incredible EXP since we were splitting it two ways.

The animal claws were even more simple. Two rabid wolves and one blood-thirsty cheetah was all it took to finish it. The EXP for that quest was even more pitiful. They were a supplement to grinding only. Aaron and I would need to put in the time and grind monsters to level up.

Aaron reminded me to be incredibly wary of non-party members. The first rule of the safe-zone was no PVP. Obviously then Player vs. Player existed within the system. Could players kill each other or was it limited to just duels and skirmishes? I didn't really want to find out.

The only thing I paid attention to outside of grinding was the guild hall. It was something I was incredibly interested in. I probed the NPC inside but the most information he would give me was that you needed to be first class, and present an item to the guild hall to create a guild. What the item was, he wouldn't tell me no matter how hard I asked.

My experience in RPGs told me that guilds were mandatory. Mandatory in a sense that not being a part of one was a humungous mistake. They provided too many benefits to count. Just the information fellow guild mates could give you was incredibly important.

It wouldn't have surprised me to discover that Aaron and I were two of the highest-level characters in the safe-zone. We killed effectively and efficiently. If so, then becoming a respected guild leader and increasing our scope was possible. People rallied to the top level players.

Finding a new healer, new tank, new third DPS. All of those things would be much easier with a guild. I couldn't help but think back to the enormous beast walking along the highway that I'd seen during the night.

If there were raids then having a guild was going to be a requirement. I didn't feel comfortable allowing someone else to make decisions for me, especially when my life was at stake. If I was going to take orders, they had to come from someone I trusted. That was my main reason for wanting to create a guild with Aaron.

We headed outside the safe-zone for a little less than an hour before returning. I wasn't feeling up to it at all, and neither was Aaron. That feeling of impending doom we had originally escaped was creeping back up.

We were nearly at the deadline and we were a two-man party. No healer, no tank: things weren't looking good.

"We should scout to see who is available," Aaron suggested. The best place for that was the mission board. We setup camp nearby and carefully watched.

Occasionally a small group would visit the board to pick out missions. I approached a group of three players. "Excuse me, what classes are you three?"

"Classes? What's he talking about?" They looked to each other with confused expressions.

"Oh, never mind. Sorry."

If they didn't know what classes were then they must have been level 9 or lower. Being level 16 and 15 allowed us to be a little picky. There was also the level penalty we needed to worry about.

The majority of parties passing through were more than three, unfortunately. Our idea shifted from the mission board to random people along the street. It was even more of a needle in a haystack.

Most people waiting along the street didn't have the same intentions as us. They simply refused to level or had given up entirely. They weren't people we wanted in our party anyway. We hadn't managed to recruit a single person by nightfall.

I admired my inventory one more time before heading to sleep. *I was rich!* That feeling of impending doom couldn't fully extinguish my excitement for the coming day. Whatever was about to happen would dictate our futures.

Chapter 12: Valkyrie Geirdriful

My eyes opened and looked up at the giant clock: it was 6:30 A.M. Over the past week I had grown accustomed to sleeping on the hard cobblestone, it now only caused me a bit of discomfort. I was nervous with excitement. Today was the fourteenth day.

As the sun continued to rise, more and more people gathered in the center-square. The amount of people that had shown up after my group had arrived was several thousand, at least. Even finding a place to sleep at night was hard to do. When the clock ticked over to 12:00 P.M. it did something it hadn't done before.

The clock rang out repeatedly for 10 minutes. The clapping shook the air and caused it to vibrate. I couldn't be sure if the safe-zone walls had a dampening effect on sound, but if they didn't, it was sure that anything within a dozen miles could hear the noise.

The ringing stopped abruptly as it started. There was absolute silence in the square as everyone held their breath.

CONGRATULATIONS TO EVERYONE WHO HAS MANAGED TO SUR-
VIVE UP TO THIS POINT. A LOT OF PEOPLE ARE WONDERING TO
THEMSELVES, 'IS THIS A GAME?' NO, THIS IS REAL LIFE.
YOU HAVE RECEIVED THE TITLE 'PERSISTENT'.
YOU HAVE RECEIVED 10,000 ZENY.
TODAY I'LL BE HOSTING A LAUNCH PARTY TO CELEBRATE ALL
OF YOU. BUT DON'T WORRY, JUST THIS ONCE, IF YOU DIE TO-
DAY, YOU'LL RESPAWN TOMORROW AT 12:00 P.M—SO EN-
JOY YOURSELVES. CONSIDER THIS A REWARD FOR YOUR EF-
FORTS.

Launch party? Aaron pulled me to the side, "We need to get back! Monsters are going to spawn." Many people started retreating in a hurry while others stared in confusion. A dozen seconds passed before creatures spawned randomly around the city.

A centaur over twelve feet tall spawned just a hundred-foot away from us. It twirled its axe around while galloping out. At least fifty people instantly turned to particles. Monsters like this spawned all over the city at the same time. I was in a stupor until the sound of Aaron's Longbow twanging woke me.

A *Powershot* flew out and hit the chest of the centaur, it left a small red blotch but didn't sink deep. "What are you doing? Kill it!"

Today I could fight without fear. I rushed forward and cast *Fireball* followed by *Arcane Missiles*. The initial confusion faded almost immediately. The centaur had been surrounded by over one-hundred people and was in bad shape as soon as they started to fight back. Spells, arrows, spears and other weapons bombarded it from all sides.

Inspect!

```
CENTAUR**        LEVEL: ??              BEAST
     HP: 36725                   MP: 300
              STR: 60
              AGI: 15
              DEX: 25
              VIT: 80
              INT: 15
A MYTHICAL CENTAUR. IT IS MORE BEAST THAN MAN.
```

The Centaur remained trapped within the crowd and held out for a dozen breaths before it let out a sorrowful wail and collapsed. Three items dropped beneath its feet as the crowd rushed forward to grab them.

Aaron and I pushed forward as well and noticed that no one else could pick up the loot. We forced our way through the crowd and scooped up everything in a hurry.

"We did the most damage," he said. I nodded my head in understanding.

We didn't stop to check the loot but moved quickly to the next monster. Time was of the essence. This was an incredibly lucky opportunity. I couldn't help but check the EXP I had gained. 3,200 EXP. An enormous amount considering how many people were wailing upon the mob.

The next monster was a Yeti. I literally felt a chill run down my back. The air around it seemed frozen for dozens of feet. It remained in an enclosure and blood seeped from dozens of spots around its fur. Occasionally it would summon a shard of ice in its palm and throw it out. The shard would kill three or four people instantly.

Aaron and I managed to cast one spell each when it despawned. The loot was swallowed up immediately and the EXP we gained was pitiful. Not even 300 EXP. We looked around and decided moving around wasn't the best option. Everything that had spawned by now was most likely tagged, we wouldn't get anything for it.

The clock tower rang out again as the last monster fell. When the air stopped vibrating another wave of monsters spawned. Instead of just being single creatures, hundreds and hundreds of monsters spawned along with them.

All the players were gathered in the inner part of the city. There were four bridges and a moat that separated us from the outer city. The waves of monsters spawned in the outer city. Aaron and I positioned ourselves accordingly on a bridge.

The non-elite monsters were mostly undead.

I recognized ragged zombie's and ghouls immediately. There were also other undead monsters, Orcs and trolls as well as numerous other creatures. Well past the army of the undead, just near the exit, was a grayish humanoid figure. His hair was a solid white and his body was covered in bones. He looked like a necromancer. There was a red skull floating above his head.

A single Elite spawned in the inner portion near us. It was a gigantic rock golem that had no legs and simply floated off the ground. Its attack pattern consisted of tossing a boulder and slamming the ground with both its hands. It moved back and forth slapping and clapping noobs.

Its defense was incredibly impressive. Arrows and anything physical simply bounced off it and left almost no marks. *It was my time to shine!* I began to cast *Meteor Storm* as runes lit up around me. I was bathed in a golden light as the four meteors spawned in the sky above. They started to rain down.

People in the area started to panic as they didn't know where the attack was coming from. Everyone assumed it was the Stone Golem. The first Meteor collided with its back and shattered into a billion pieces. Sparks, fire and rock flew through the air. Some of the rock was from the golems back and others were bits of Meteor. The impact caused it to fall two or three feet towards the ground.

The second Meteor landed just a breath after and hit the same spot. The Golem was forced even closer to the ground. More of its back had been chipped off. There was now a light cloud of dust in the air. The third Meteor slammed it into the ground as it lost all resistance. A large smoke cloud obscured it from view. Only the burning debris could be seen through the murky air.

The fourth Meteor caused the ground below our feet to shake. The Golem had been hammered into the cobblestone at least five feet deep. There were cracks all over its body as it hoisted itself up. Its body was full of vulnerabilities. It was bombarded by attacks and spells. The attacks seemed to deal damage now as the thick armor was mostly destroyed. When it died it simply crumbled into stones that eventually despawned. I gained 10,320 EXP

Aaron and I knew the drill, we rushed to the pile of loot and scooped it up before disappearing into the crowd. We made our way back towards the bridge. There was already a large amount of people shooting arrows and casting spells. Undead did their best to cross the bridge towards us.

I had begun casting *Meteor Storm* again when the area I was aiming at suddenly lit up. A bright light rose from the ground that caused every undead in the area to groan in agony. Their bodies quickly bleached white as the light purified them. Only two seconds or so passed before the entire area was devoid of any undead. I had to cancel my cast.

I moved forward a bit more and cast into the crowd of undead just behind the bridge. The four meteors rained down as undead were blasted into smithereens. Those that weren't directly in the blast zone caught on fire as burning undead bits fell from the sky.

CONGRATULATIONS! YOU HAVE REACHED LEVEL 17. AS A REWARD FOR LEVELING UP, YOU HAVE BEEN GRANTED THREE STAT POINTS!

CURRENT EXP: 11245/32000   LEVEL: 17

MAGE   FORMIDABLE

HP: 1045/1045   MP: 340/389

STR: 10

AGI: 6

DEX: 20

VIT: 14

INT: 25 +12

AVAILABLE: 3

A single cast had given me over 20,000 EXP and that was while sharing it with Aaron. His face seemed excited as he immediately gained a level. He was now level 15. There was another bright light that wiped out another large portion of undead. I was jealous that I was slow to the party. *So much EXP gone...*

There were no longer any large clumps of undead and people rushed across the bridge. I didn't bother to cast any spells and simply got in a good position. Something I hadn't previously noticed besides the red skull was the name above the necromancer's head.

Necromancer Sezhul, The Blightcaller.

It only took a few brief moments before the remaining undead were dispatched from the area. There was nothing but the boss and us in this little area.

"So? Are you all ready to die?" His voice had a spectral quality that made my hair stand on end. Almost immediately after speaking a gas spread out from his body and covered the entire area.

> YOU HAVE BEEN AFFECTED BY WEAKEN. ALL STATS -10

My world seemed to slow down from this effect. I opened my stats.

> CURRENT EXP: 11245/32000   LEVEL: 17
> MAGE   FORMIDABLE
> HP: 745/745   MP: 246/329
> STR: 10 -10
> AGI: 6 -10
> DEX: 20-10
> VIT: 14 -10
> INT: 25 +2
> AVAILABLE: 3

My stats took a nose dive. I had lost 300 HP and 60 MP immediately. Despite that, the changes to my physique were the most noticeable, and deadly.

I could barely move from the position I was already standing in. The staff in my hand felt dozens of times heavier than before.

I rested the staff on the ground and used it to help support my body. Even gripping the staff was hard enough. The weight of my body nearly made me lose my grip. I wanted to move away but found my movements nearly impossible.

I did not have the strength required to lift my leg. My legs just wouldn't move. I could spend hours just trying to walk a few feet like this. I was stuck in place. This was a mixture of having 0 STR and -4 AGI.

I made a split-second decision and put all three points into AGI. The effects were immediately noticeable. It was hard but my limbs were actually maneuverable again. Being able to move at a snail's pace was better than not being able to move at all, no matter how I looked at it.

CURRENT EXP: 11245/32000   LEVEL: 17

MAGE   FORMIDABLE

HP: 745/745   MP: 246/329

STR: 10 -10

AGI: 9 -10

DEX: 20 -10

VIT: 14 -10

INT: 25 +2

AVAILABLE: 0

I wasn't the only one negatively affected. There were thousands of people in this east quadrant and just one boss. I figured the three other quadrants were also dealing with something similar. Those that could move forward did so slowly. I didn't hesitate to cast *Inspect!*

INVALID TARGET

My inspect wasn't able to see the details of boss monsters. It was disappointing, but something I half expected.

"Die!"

Sezhul pointed out a hand and a bone spear at least two-feet wide pierced through the crowd and into the distance. No matter how many people were impaled it continued unhindered before despawning. There was a gap in the crowd as if a beam had been fired through it. He raised his hands in the sky and skeletons appeared all around him.

I was so incredibly thankful my first reaction was to find a spot off to the side. Those who simply rushed directly at the boss and were weakened found themselves trapped in place. All they could do was wait in terror for his next bone spear.

The melee classes had no choice but to contend with the numerous skeletons around him. I did my best to cast from my flanking position. Raising my arm was tiring enough as it was. There was also a clear problem with my casting.

My casts were slow, at least twice as long. I originally started with fireball but found it much too slow. It seemed the five-second channel for *Arcane Missile* was unaffected by my increased cast time. I only casted *Arcane Missiles*.

I looked around as that bright light spawned under Sezhul's feet and started to incinerate him. For the first time since the fight began he let out a groan in discomfort. I wanted to know who was casting it.

It had to be a holy spell. I recognized that bleaching effect it had on the undead and I was in need of a priest. I looked and looked but couldn't find the player. Sezhul raised his hands again as if he was summoning more skeletons. The ground began to quake, something that hadn't happened before.

There was a peculiar feeling below my feet but I realized it too late. Bone spikes immediately shot out in a dozen locations as hundreds of people were killed. I couldn't even move. In fact, the best way to move currently was allow gravity to take me.

I stopped supporting myself and tipped over before rolling away. In the short moment of attack I took a total of 600 damage, 420 to my HP and 180 to my MP. No one else that I saw hit managed to survive.

I leaned against the side of a building in agony. Blood dripped down my thighs as large chunks of my flesh had been gouged out. Sezhul continued to roar. I didn't have the ability to cast another spell. Not because I was out of MP, but because I was in so much pain.

YOU ARE AFFECTED BY WEAKEN.
YOU ARE AFFECTED BY BLEED.

I looked at the bleed status.

> YOU ARE LOSING 10 HP PER 5 SECONDS. YOU WILL CONTINUE BLEEDING UNTIL RECOVERING ABOVE 75% HP OR USING A BANDAGE.

I quickly opened my stats.

> CURRENT EXP: 11245/32000   LEVEL: 17
> MAGE   FORMIDABLE
> HP: 325/745   MP: 66/329
> STR: 10 -10
> AGI: 9 -10
> DEX: 20-10
> VIT: 14 -10
> INT: 25 +2
> AVAILABLE: 0

I needed to have at least 589 HP to stop the bleeding effect. I had no potions and no healer so things weren't looking good. I closed my eyes and laid there for what seemed like thirty seconds before a warm feeling washed over me. I immediately felt better but the bleeding status was still in effect.

There was another warm feeling, followed by another. I realized that I had been healed.

Just as I opened my eyes I witnessed Sezhul cry out in agony. His body was constantly bombarded by holy fire as priests in the area spam healed him, which caused him damage. His entire body began to convulse before disappearing into a puff of smoke. Loot poured out and to the ground below.

The weakening effect disappeared and my mobility had returned.

I didn't bother to try and rush for the loot, I knew that I hadn't done the most damage, nor had Aaron. The owner of that peculiar spell absolutely had done the most. "Aaron, we need to see who grabs the loot!" I yelled. The biggest priority right now was to identify that person.

There was no doubt it was a holy ability, one on par with my Meteor Storm. They were a high-level acolyte at the bare minimum, someone we desperately needed.

Aaron rushed over to me and helped me off the ground before we ran towards the despawning corpse. The area around Sezhul was like a feeding frenzy. We couldn't even make it within twenty feet before hitting a solid wall of people.

"It's no use," Aaron said.

"Shit!" I felt like this was a good chance to find out who it was and at least open communication. There was also the person who healed me. It was impossible to pick anyone out in this crowd.

Despite the hundreds upon hundreds of deaths, there were still a thousand people or more here. It was like finding a needle in a haystack. We watched but couldn't see who managed to grab it all in the end, there was just too many people swarming his corpse.

"Let's go," Aaron said. We were far enough apart that only I was hit with those bone spikes. Even though I had been healed, I still felt incredibly lethargic. I staggered a little and then managed to stay on my feet. The entire group crossed the bridge together and walked inward.

I estimated that at least a thousand people died, maybe more. The number we walked in was much larger than what we walked out with. I had gained another 2500 EXP from Sezhul being defeated.

I curiously checked my stats after the weakening effect was gone and I had a moment of air to breathe.

CURRENT EXP: 11245/32000   LEVEL: 17
MAGE   FORMIDABLE
HP: 1045/1045   MP: 126/389
STR: 10
AGI: 9
DEX: 20
VIT: 14
INT: 25 +12
AVAILABLE: 0

The mystery healer had fully healed me, but my MP was dangerously low. Luckily, I had a decent amount of MP regeneration compared to before. It was workable as long as I didn't need to cast *Meteor Storm* and focused solely on single-targets.

When we reached the center we found the other areas were still battling their bosses, three more necromancers.

No one was excited to go assist as there was nothing to be gained at all. The people who did the most damage were already decided. I continued to look around for anyone that stood out. A high level acolyte would make our party whole again.

Ten minutes passed before the groups started to return and the extent of the damage could be clearly seen. Our group had fared much better than everyone else. More than half of the original people in the safe-zone were dead. At least they would respawn tomorrow.

Everyone believed that to be the end, but it wasn't. There was a blinding light as the sun eclipsed in the sky. A figure clad in pure gold descended from above. Beautiful white wings adorned her back and a spear larger than her was grasped firmly in her hand.

She floated near the top of the Clock tower, a red skull above her head.

Valkyrie Geirdriful

She looked down at us as if we were ants before raising her spear. I didn't wait to start running for my life. The spear rocketed down towards the center-square and implanted itself into the cobblestone. An explosion of unprecedented magnitude shook the entire city.

The people that hadn't managed to back up simply disappeared in the shockwave, gone without a trace. Her feet touched the cobblestone with grace. She plucked the spear before wreaking havoc on anyone in the area. Even if she could kill one person per second, there were thousands of us.

Arrows and spells started to fly as she was bombarded constantly. Her figure was hard to make out under all of the attacks.

She moved like a phantom through the area, constantly stabbing and slashing out with her spear. Every attack marked another dead.

Aaron and I did our best to constantly be on the move. We never stayed in one spot too long, and I never stayed in place for more than 5 seconds, the duration of my *Arcane Missiles* channel. Every melee player simply ran for their lives and didn't bother to try and fight. Her 11-foot Spear simply killed anyone within that range.

I couldn't help but think that she would look better adorned by a black cloak and scythe. Despite her impressive killing speed, there was just too many of us and the spells continued hammering into her unimpeded. She spoke for the first time. There was something incredibly alluring about her voice.

"Heavens, Help me!"

The clouds in the sky parted before several beams of light touched down onto the cobblestone. They were entirely solid and impossible to see through. They started to twirl around her and anyone touched by that maelstrom was engulfed by holy fire. They swiftly burned to death.

Valkyrie Geirdriful has become enraged.

Her attacks became more fervent. She glided across the cobblestone in a blur. Her figure charged back and forth. Her speed of killing doubled or even tripled as the amount of people started to dwindle.

We continued to swarm her like ants. Her golden armor developed cracks and one of the wings on her back was drooping at an odd angle. There was panic on her frenzied face. The amount of abilities being thrown at her were staggering.

Fireballs, arcane missiles, frost bolts, you name it. The sheer amount of arrows flying in her direction blotted out parts of the sky. People were even throwing their spears and swords at her. Anything to deal some sort of damage and stay alive.

Suddenly, Geirdriful stopped moving. She stabbed the spear tip down into the cobblestone and started to float. Her body curled into a ball as her wings covered her body. There was electricity arching across her wings as they shook violently.

Her beautiful body was being bombarded the entire time, even more so than before. Every spell and arrow now hit its mark with her movement coming to a complete standstill. Her biggest asset was her speed. That was now gone with this new development.

Suddenly her wings opened as a blinding light radiated outward accompanied by a beautiful shout. The very air itself began to shake. Every attack currently coming at her disintegrated into nothingness.

Wave after wave of damage hit every single person in the area. Each wave did 200 damage and people fell like dominoes. By the third wave, over 90% of people had perished. Each wave did 160 to my HP and 40 to my MP. I was completely exhausted of my MP by the second wave and took the brunt of it to my health. It did 720 Damage to me in total and left me completely exhausted of my MP.

Luckily, there was no fifth or even sixth wave of damage. It seemed like the attack was made on her deathbed: a final attack to drag as many to hell as possible. Geirdriful let out a mournful cry and collapsed to the ground. Her golden body armor was covered in cracks. Her pure white skin was revealed beneath it before she disappeared.

I looked around. There was maybe twenty people still standing in the square from the thousands we started with from the days beginning.

CONGRATULATIONS! YOU ARE THE MVP. AS A REWARD, YOU
HAVE BEEN GIVEN 50,000 EXP.
CONGRATULATIONS! YOU HAVE REACHED LEVEL 18. AS A RE-
WARD FOR LEVELING UP, YOU HAVE BEEN GRANTED THREE STAT
POINTS!
CONGRATULATIONS! YOU HAVE REACHED LEVEL 19. AS A RE-
WARD FOR LEVELING UP, YOU HAVE BEEN GRANTED THREE STAT
POINTS!

Besides the EXP for the MVP reward, I had received another 15,000 EXP from the boss kill for a total of 65,000. I opened my stats in excitement.

CURRENT EXP: 3245/46000   LEVEL: 19
MAGE   FORMIDABLE
HP: 385/1105   MP: 16/405
STR: 10
AGI: 9
DEX: 20
VIT: 14
INT: 25 +12
AVAILABLE: 6

I looked at my current available points and wondered just how rare an ability like *Weaken* would be. Sezhul was a boss, most likely something I wouldn't encounter again for quite some time.

The decision was a tough one to make. I was looking for a reason to put points into AGI and this seemed to the best one. I should at least aim to have +1 of every stat in such a scenario. I put 2 points into AGI, 1 pt into STR, 1 point into VIT and then added the remaining two points into INT.

```
CURRENT EXP: 3245/46000      LEVEL: 19
           MAGE          FORMIDABLE
      HP: 415/1135      MP: 28/417
               STR: 11
               AGI: 11
               DEX: 20
               VIT: 15
             INT: 27 +12
            AVAILABLE: 0
```

At least if I encountered a skill similar to *Weaken* in the future none of my stats would go below 0. I should at least have the agency to move around and escape if need be.

This was a 'better safe than sorry' moment, and there was a lingering fear I was spreading my stats a bit too thin. My next goal was to get an even 30 into INT. Not because I liked the way even numbers looked or anything.

Aaron had survived Geirdriful's dying attack but only received the 15k EXP from the boss kill. Only I received the 50k for the MVP reward. Still, all our long days of grinding had paid off for us both.

I hobbled over to the despawning corpse and grabbed all of the loot. I got plenty of ugly stares but did my best to ignore them. Only Aaron followed me as we made our way to the inn. I felt absolutely terrible but couldn't hold out on looking at the loot any longer.

There was loot from the Centaur, Stone Golem and Valkyrie Geirdriful in my inventory. I started to look through it.

STONE BUCKLER**: MAX HP + 250, PHYSICAL DAMAGE TAKEN -15%
A BUCKLER MADE OF STONE. IT'S INCREDIBLY STURDY BUT ALSO HEAVY.
BLOODIED DOUBLE-AXE**: STR +10, MOVEMENT SPEED +10%
AN AXE COVERED IN THE BLOOD OF A CENTAUR. A PECULIAR STRENGTH MAKES YOU MOVE FASTER.

HEART-STONE LOOP**: INT +2 VIT +2.
A RING OF STONE SHAPED LIKE A HEART.

VALKYRIAN SHOES***: MAX HP +10%, MAX MP +10%
A BEAUTIFUL PAIR OF SHOES ONCE WORN BY A VALKYRIE. THE BACK HAS A SMALL PAIR OF WINGS.

I didn't hesitate to equip the Heart-Stone Loop. Before I put on the Valkyrian Shoes I talked it over with Aaron, but he was fine with me having them. I couldn't help but check my stats again.

```
CURRENT EXP: 3245/46000          LEVEL: 19
            MAGE              FORMIDABLE
        HP: 490/1282     MP: 44/472
                  STR: 11
                  AGI: 11
                  DEX: 20
                  VIT: 15 +2
                  INT: 27 +14
              AVAILABLE: 0
```

I was proud of my own stats but the fatigue of the days battles was finally getting to me. I managed to rent a room for the night. Probably because almost everyone had perished and wouldn't respawn till tomorrow.

I checked my inventory a final time as well as my skill page, particularly Arcane Missiles. I had spammed it endlessly during the final fights.

```
        ARCANE MISSILE* LV. 1 300/500
```

It was considerably harder to level up, most likely a consequence of being a stronger ability. There was also now a spot for my Zeny in the bottom left of my inventory. Besides the 10,000 I received as a reward. There was at least another 25,000 I got from today for battling. After I had agreed to take a bedroom from the NPC, 500 was subtracted. Explaining my exhaustion to Aaron, who felt the same, I made my way up to the room. I fell asleep almost instantly.

I ended up sleeping for at least 15 hours and woke up at 5:00 A.M. I made way down to the first floor of the inn and sat at a table. A waiter walked over and handed me a menu. I wasn't expecting anything but I guessed now that Zeny were available business was open as normal. I ended up getting a typical breakfast. Eggs, bacon, sausage and some toast, it cost me 200 Zeny.

Aaron didn't come down and I didn't bother to wait for him. I wanted to visit all of the shops again and see what I could acquire. I had 34,200 Zeny to spend.

My first trip was to the armor smith. I took a look at his wares, he wasn't selling anything remarkable and all of my slots now had a piece of equipment, besides the amulet slot, which he didn't sell items for.

I pulled out some of the worst pieces of gear I had, like the Swift Shoes. I had only just replaced them today. He looked them over, "These are junk." He didn't even offer me a price for them. I put them back into my inventory to rot. I took them to the weapon smith after and he had the same thing to say about them.

I visited the guild hall and was surprised to find that the NPC inside would give me more information. I needed a piece of Orichalcum and 50,000 Zeny. Only then could I make a guild. I took a mental note of the material before making my way to the potions NPC.

This was the NPC I was most excited to see. I opened the menu and began to browse.

Red Potion – 100Z
Orange Potion – 200Z
Yellow Potion – 400Z

White Potion –800Z
Green Potion – 250Z
Small Blue Potion – 250z
Medium Blue Potion – 500z
Blue Potion – 1000z
Bandage – 500Z
Panacea – 2000Z

I studied the effects of each. Red through white potions instantly restored HP. They had a cool down of 10 seconds between uses. It went 70 HP, 120 HP, 230 HP, 420 HP in order from red to white.

A Green Potion removed poison effects and silence and had no cool down at all. Small, Medium and regular Blue potions restored MP. Small restored 60 MP, Medium restored 110 MP, and Blue Potion restored 200 MP. They had a much longer cool down, thirty seconds.

Bandages removed the bleeding effect with no cool down and *Panacea* removed all effects. *Panacea* had a five minute cool down.

This is good stuff! I started to do some mental math before realizing someone was watching me in my peripheral vision. I looked to the side and a breathtakingly beautiful girl was standing there staring at me: long, brown hair; vivid blue eyes and a lithe, compact figure. I almost mistook her as an NPC.

I looked in her direction and wasn't mistaken. Completely self-assured, she was staring directly at me but wasn't saying anything. Was there something on my face? I turned back to the potion seller and made my purchase "I want ten White potions, four Green potions, two Bandages and ten Medium Blue potions"

"That will be 16,000 Zeny. Do you accept?"

"I accept" I didn't have to do anything as the Zeny disappeared and the items were added to my inventory.

A voice came from my side, "You're the guy who got the loot from Valkyrie Geirdriful!" I felt a headache coming on.

"Do I know you?" It was obvious she was one of the dozen who had survived. It was still early and the remaining players had yet to be respawned.

"I also healed you on Necromancer Sezhul! Hey, what level are you huh? How did you survive both bosses? You clearly don't have a healer."

There was a bit of fire in her words that was a little more than playful. She was the one who healed me. *Could it be? Could she be the healer that I was looking for?* I suddenly felt restless.

"Hey, show me what you got off the Valkyrie and I'll show you what dropped off Sezhul, how about that?" She proposed. I froze for a second. "C'mon, let's see it!"

She also got the loot from Sezhul? Was the person using that miraculous AOE ability her as well? Was there such a coincidence?

"Absolutely." I wanted to be accommodating as possible. I unequipped Valkyrian Shoes and showed them to her. She pulled out a Grimoire and bone wand.

"Wow! That's really good. It's three stars too," she said. By now I understood that the stars were the rarity. "So what class are you?"

"A Mage."

"Really?"

"Really really." I wasn't sure how else to respond to that question.

"Do you have a party?" she asked.

"Just me and one other." Richard wasn't in his regular spot on the morning of the fourteenth day. I hadn't seen him around at all after our last talk. It was just me and Aaron now.

"What class is he?"

"Archer."

"That's great, I have a three-man party, and we can use two more people. We already have a tank and another DPS. Of course, I'm the healer."

I paused for a minute to think and then she started talking again. "Oh, wait, are you over level fifteen? If you aren't then forget what I said."

"We're both over level fifteen."

"Okay great! Meet me under the clock-tower at midday. The other two party members died fighting Geirdriful."

I stood there in a stupor for a moment before realizing what happened. *Had she just decided for me? Yep, that's exactly what had happened.*

I had already done all the tasks I wanted to accomplish today. I headed back to the inn and found Aaron. He was still asleep. There was drool hanging down his face when he answered the door.

"Hwat?" His voice almost slurred a bit.

"We have a party interview at twelve."

"A what?"

"There's a party that wants to recruit us."

"Do they have a healer?"

"Yeah, a good one too."

"Alright, let's meet up at eleven forty-five and go together." He closed the door. I went back to my room and lay on my back. I browsed my inventory repeatedly out of boredom. There were so many items waiting to be traded away. I would hold out for a few days to get an idea of what price people were expecting. I dozed off for what felt like hours.

A knock on my door woke me up, "Let's go! Its eleven forty-five." I jerked up and rubbed my eyes before rushing to the door. Aaron and I made our way to the square. The inn was only thirty seconds away. I walked with him to the two guards below the guard tower and we patiently waited.

"There she is." I nodded towards the incoming healer.

Only now did I really take in her entire appearance. She was average height for a girl, with chestnut colored hair that barely reached her shoulders. It looked a bit worn from a lack of mainte-nance. Her dress was a pure white gown that flowed over her curves and reached her ankles. Her hand held a religious book, most likely a healing item.

I wanted to call out to her but realized we hadn't exchanged any names. Luckily, she spotted us on the steps as we were a few heads taller than the crowd. It also helped Aaron was so tall and had a head of red hair. She rushed over.

"Is this the Archer?" she asked.

"Aaron." He held out his hand like a true gentleman.

"Isabelle."

"I'm Joseph." I chimed in.

Isabelle looked up at the clock, "Just a few more minutes." It was 11:57. According to the system announcement they would res-pawn at 12:00. As soon as the clock hit 12 there was a loud chime.

Once the area returned to silence, beams of light shot down from the sky. Inside the beams people began respawning. At first they were translucent but then their bodies fully materialized. It was almost identical to the moment mobs first began spawning, and people began disappearing from the campus.

"I'm alive!" a woman said while staring at her hands. She started to touch their face and all over their body. Similar scenes appeared all over the city. Several minutes passed before the lights disappeared. The area was once again crowded with thousands of people.

"Once again, congratulations to everyone who has passed the tutorial! I'd like to welcome you all to the planet Yetera, your new starting point."

I looked around and realized the city had changed somewhat. We were no longer standing below a clock tower but instead a bell tower. I tried to open my map but realized I couldn't. The ability to access my storage and stats was still there, though.

The mirage-like barrier that had previously surrounded the safe-zone had disappeared. Our view was no longer obstructed as we peered out. There were no houses. There were no cars. There were no highways and traffic lights.

We were in the middle of a foreign city. I spun around and realized thousands of us had been transported here. I turned and looked each way. The only thing I could see past the old style buildings was forest.

Chapter 13: Yetera

"Welcome to the continent of Eastrath. Your new starting point is called Elesham. Good luck!"

The voice continued to echo in my head. *We weren't on Earth anymore? And my parents?* My knees felt weak. Disbelief was in the air as everyone took in this new information. A few people in the crowd began to sob. Any hope of returning to a normal life was gone.

"Disperse! Everyone disperse!" Guards on horses rode into the center and started to break up the crowd. People were knocked over without care. "Who is in charge here? Who is allowing you to riot like this?" The guard yelled.

Just looking at the surrounding forest I could tell Elesham was not a big city. The amount of people currently gathered in the square was a formidable force. If we had ill intentions then over-throwing whoever was in charge would be very easy. The guards pulled swords from their side and held them out. Their hostile gazes scanned the crowd.

Once swords were drawn, people started to back away and disperse among the alleys and houses. I looked at the guards and couldn't be sure if they were NPCs or actual people in this foreign world. I couldn't be sure if there were ever any NPCs in safe-zone 373.They had been called NPCs, but was that just for convenience sake? I turned to Isabelle, "We should leave."

"Mark and Justin are just over there, let's find somewhere quiet." She signaled to her friends and we moved as a group through the streets. We stood in an alleyway in the corner of the city. Isabelle grabbed Mark and Justin and walked a dozen feet away. They whispered quietly in a group together.

"What do you think?" Aaron asked me.

I was still in a daze. "I don't know."

He could tell what I was thinking, "if we were transported here, then it's very likely everyone else on Earth who survived was transported to this world, Maybe not Elesham or Eastrath, but somewhere."

"Maybe," I fumbled out. I turned my attention to Mark and Justin.

Justin was on the younger side, probably around our age. He had a lean body that wasn't exactly muscular. His hair was brown, short, and messy. A dagger rested on each side of his waist. Just from looking at him I could tell he was a melee fighter specializing in AGI.

Mark was a head taller and looked overly serious. His body was muscular but in an oddly rectangular kind of way. His square hair was short and meticulously perfect. A shield and sword were strapped to his back. Something else I noticed was his posture. His posture was perfect. He stood straight as a statue without the slightest bit of slouching.

They didn't discuss long before walking over to us, "Alright, they're fine with it. What do you two think?" Isabelle asked us.

I turned to Aaron and he nodded his head, "We're fine with it."

I checked the party window and could see their classes and levels. Isabelle was a level 17 Acolyte, Mark was a level 17 Swordsman and Justin was a level 16 Thief.

"Oh wow, you're level nineteen?" Justin asked.

Isabelle gave me a dirty look. "Just how much EXP did you get from Geirdriful?"

I scratched my head, "A good amount…"

Aaron coughed, "We should figure out what we need to do from here on out. We're now in a foreign land and we don't have any idea of the dynamics."

"Right," Mark said. Just looking at him reminded me of someone in the military. His facial expression was stern. His body remained taut as an arrow. He didn't say anything more than was needed.

"We need information, and fast. Where are we? How big is Eastrath? What's the system of government like? Is it peaceful?"

Isabelle cut off Aaron, "Why fast?"

"Elesham is not a big city. We most likely doubled or tripled the population in just a single morning. Do you think there will be enough food for all of us here? Can we be sure the ruler of this little city will tolerate our existence?"

"It's safer to leave," I agreed. Neither Justin nor Isabelle had any issues with this.

"Let's gather as much information as we can first though," said Aaron. "We can divide the city into five areas and each talk to all the people we can."

This was met by nods.

"Meet back here by sunset?" I suggested, everyone agreed and went towards the sector assigned them by Aaron.

I wandered my part of the city and spoke to any merchants and shop owners I could, picking up as much information as I could.

"Are you going to buy something?"

"Erm…"

"If you're going to buy something I'll answer your question, else don't waste my time." It was typical of the responses I received besides the weird stares. My questions were things that people living in Eastrath should know.

One thing I did find out was that Zeny was the main form of currency in Elesham and also Eastrath. That and that Elesham was a relatively small and unremarkable city on the bottom right of Eastrath.

I gave up very quickly and killed time till sunset. Information gathering wasn't something I was cut out for, or comfortable doing. My people skills were anything but stellar. I was the first to return to the alley-way. Everyone arrived after I had been waiting for about an hour.

It became obvious who was more suited for information gathering. I, Mark and Isabelle had relatively little to share while Justin and Aaron came back with the majority of our information. In fact, Aaron came back with a map.

He pulled the map open and put it against the wall of a nearby house, "This is Eastrath." It was a large island. There was no measurement for distance or any scale. "And…" He dragged his finger along the map towards the bottom right corner, "We are here."

There was a miniscule dot on the map located in the very bottom right corner. It was so small and insignificant that the word

Elesham wasn't even there. The person he bought it from had to show him that it was Elesham. "Judging from the size, Eastrath is bigger than all the continents on Earth combined." He paused for a moment, "And that's not all. There are two more continents similar in size."

"I heard the same thing," Justin chimed in.

"Eastrath is the eastern most continent. North Maledith is the central most continent, and West Abithos is the far western continent. The good news is that Eastrath is relatively peaceful, at least for the past fifty years." He continued to bombard us with facts.

"Government is a Monarchy, but the continent is too big to be united under one banner. It's essentially been split into three countries. Elesham is the equivalent of a thousand-person town back in our world. It's out of the way and insignificant. We need to travel five hundred miles North-East to the kingdom of Egester." He showed us on the map. It was the largest dot for what appeared to be thousands of miles.

Looking at its position made it obvious why. It had the ocean at its back: which provided tremendous protection but also amazing prosperity.

"Five hundred miles?" Isabelle seemed unhappy.

"Everything goes through Egester—Information, trade, doesn't matter. It's the place to be."

Mark seemed to not mind, "When should we go?"

"About that, I tried to get us a carriage or some horses, but they aren't for sale. Only traveling merchants can bring horses through here. The ones that are born and raised here are only for guards."

"I may have a solution." Justin had been waiting to speak. "I spoke with a merchant. He is leaving for Egester in two days and in need of protection. There's been an increase in bandit activity as well as monster attacks. He says the trip is a bit over a weeklong and more than half of it takes place in the forest."

"Any catch?" Aaron asked.

"None, he'll provide food for the week. All we do is ride along and provide protection."

"Sounds reasonable," Aaron said.

I was of the mind that he should provide all of that and pay us, but decided to keep my mouth shut. After all, I had utterly failed at gathering any useful information.

"So we leave in two days then?" Isabelle asked.

"Two days it is. Let's do our best to find out anything useful in the meantime."

"Where are you three staying?" I asked. I had stopped by the inn earlier and tried to get a room for myself but it was completely booked.

"We're gonna head over to the inn and get a room." Their response was exactly what I already tried.

I broke the bad news. "Uhh, there's no rooms." Isabelle looked ashen. I sat down against the building and waited till I was tired enough. I was already used to sleeping on the cobble-stone. Everyone ended up crashing right on the spot. It turned out we spent the next two days sleeping in that alley.

***

"Don't drop anything or you'll lose your pay!" The merchant yelled. His goods for this trade were slowly being loaded one at a time into one of two wagons. Each wagon had a place for two horses at the front.

Everything being loaded was packed away in crates filled with hay. I did hear the occasional jingle of glass but didn't know the specific contents. The crew consisted of him, his driver and two close guards. Everyone else was hired protection: either from Elesham or Egester.

From the looks of it, we would have to follow beside the wagon on foot. Only the merchant and his driver would have a place to sit during the journey. It was quite the shitty set up, but either way we would be walking. At least like this we wouldn't get lost and our food and water situation was handled.

Once the last crate was loaded the merchant whistled through his fingers before climbing on the front seat. His driver climbed up with him and the two guards headed to the front. They smacked the ass of each horse as they walked by before taking their position about a hundred feet in front of the caravan.

Besides the five of us, there were another three people who stood out like sore thumbs. It was immediately obvious they were also fellow world-travelers looking to make it to Egester. They minded their business and we minded ours.

We were met by a beautiful sight on our departure. There was thick forest behind us and marvelous farm land as far as the eye could see. The sky was ocean blue with very little clouds. Visibility was great and the temperature was moderate. Overall, it was a beautiful day.

Our pace was steady, neither fast nor slow. We had been walking for more than half the day with farmlands on both sides of us and a forest in front, to which we were drawing near. The scenery had grown tiring, "How did you three meet?" I asked Isabelle.

"We're all coworkers. Well, we were coworkers." Justin and Isabelle both looked around our age but Mark was at least ten to fifteen years older. "It was only a part-time gig," she added.

"Doing what?"

"Working retail."

"My condolences." I worked customer service for two years. It wasn't an experience I'd wish on anyone. Customers would treat you as less than human on occasion. Not often but once was enough to put a bad taste in my mouth.

"Yeah. Now that I've stepped away from it I realize just how toxic and draining it was. No need to have a job anymore, though," she said. "What about you?"

"I took a year off from school after high school graduation to see what I wanted to do. Worked for my parents that whole time, then continued one more year into college. I was a waiter at their restaurant," I said. "What about Justin and Mark? Known them long?"

"Mark longer than Justin. Justin's only been with us a few months. Mark for the past two years. Justin keeps to himself mostly so I don't know a lot but Mark is ex-military."

"I figured." It wasn't hard to see that from his demeanor.

"We set up camp here!" The merchant cut our conversation short. The sun was starting to fall when we were just a few miles out from the forest. "The next few days we'll be sleeping in the forest so at least tonight will be a little bit safer."

He whispered to his driver and the guards returned. Just fifteen minutes later there were three campfires.

The driver secured two pots and began cooking dinner. We were given water while the merchant drank something that smelt strongly of alcohol from a skin. It didn't bother me because I was never a drinker, but Mark seemed a bit annoyed over it.

It only took about thirty minutes before a stew was cooked. There was a meaty, earthy smell that wafted through the camp. The driver began to pass out bowls and scooped each of us a bit of stew. I sat back down with everyone else before running my spoon through my meal. There were chunks of meat as well as what looked to be potatoes and carrots floating around inside.

My first bite was too hot to really taste anything and I nearly scorched my tongue. I furiously blew on my next spoonful before taking a bite. The chunks of carrots and potatoes were a bit under-done with a bit of a crunch to them. The meat was chewy and a bit gamey; it was nothing I'd ever tasted before.

"Hey you, where you from?" One of the guards asked a young-man in the other group. The kid still had on a t-shirt and some jeans. It just didn't match up with the attire of this world. My entire party had already acquired new clothing. We looked like regular residents of Eastrath.

"M-me?" He stammered out. He froze for a second and didn't really have a great response. None of us would. "Tampa." He managed to fumble out.

"Tampa? Never heard of it." The guard said curiously.

"Yeah… its way up north."

The other guard ignored his partner's conversation and stole glances at Isabelle. She didn't seem to notice but I could see the hungry stares he gave her. In fact, I think the only one who didn't notice was Isabelle herself.

Even worse was his blatant disregard for hiding it. Anger boiled up inside me and I contemplated saying something. I looked at Isabelle who was completely unaware and decided against it.

I told myself I shouldn't get offended on her behalf, especially if she was unaware. He was now on my shit list, though. There would be no opportunity for him to do anything untoward. I planned to keep a close eye on him the remainder of the trip.

The other guard didn't have any follow up question. He was familiar with most places on Eastrath and was obviously stumped as to how to continue the conversation. He became disinterested and turned his attention to the mouthful from the skin of alcohol the merchant allowed him.

The merchant, driver and two guards huddled together and drank with each other. They no longer bothered paying us any attention. The sun slowly fell while they drank. My mind was blown away by what I saw. There was not one, but four moons in the sky.

They provided just enough light to see a few feet in front of my face. The reality sunk in. *We're in a different world.* Despite being a few miles away, the howling of wolves and the hooting of owls traveled. The night was filled with the crackling of campfires and distant animals.

I looked at the other four, "I'm going to sleep." I curled up next to the campfire and closed my eyes. They were all still chatting when I fell asleep. I don't know how long that was though.

The next morning a foot nudged me awake, "Hey, time to get up." One of the guards was moving about rousing everyone. The sun was now in the sky and I didn't feel refreshed at all. I started to question whether night lasted as long as on Earth.

It seemed that everyone was experiencing the same fatigue. Even Aaron, who typically had an easy time waking up looked like a slug. I stood and stretched, then kicked some dirt onto the smoldering charcoal of our campfire.

"We're leaving in ten minutes!" One of the guards shouted. The driver was already sitting behind the front two horses.

The merchant was nowhere to be seen but I assumed that he was still sleeping. He had drunk quite a lot from that skin last night.

I looked at the forest in the distance. It extended all the way from the coastline and as far left as I could possibly see. It gave off an imposing feeling as the trees towered into the sky. They were much larger than the trees of Earth.

I trudged along as we moved towards the distant tree-line. The day didn't seem quite as beautiful with how tired I felt. There was a mushiness to my legs that made walking uncomfortable.

"Keep your eyes open!" One of the guards in the front yelled back. We were now entering the forest. The trees towered above and the temperature dropped several degrees. The dense canopy above obscured a large portion of the sun. It felt as if we were travelling through another climate.

It was humid as hell and my clothes quickly plastered themselves to my back. "This is awful." Everyone constantly pulled on their damp clothing.

"Yeah…" My robe went from my neck to my toes and provided almost no air flow. Every crevice of my body was drenched with sweat.

We saw the first 'monster' after an hour of walking. A lone wolf waited on the path and growled at the two approaching guards. I moved forward and cast *Inspect*.

```
WOLF     LEVEL: 7 BEAST  EARTH
    HP: 919              MP: 10
              STR: 10
              AGI: 10
              DEX: 5
              VIT: 7
              INT: 2
```

I was pleased to see that *Inspect* still worked. It was our first encounter with anything that could possibly be considered a monster and would give EXP.

The guards showed a bit of their ability and dispatched the wolf with ease. Maybe we were only here to help in case of bandits? I couldn't be sure what kind of monsters were around Elesham. I just wanted to make it to Egestor as quick as possible.

Aaron moved up to my side, "I've been looking at the map more closely, take a look." He pulled the map out and started to point. "The more I studied it the more I realized there are areas that have almost no humans." The map had locations for mountain ranges and mines. There were drawings depicting open fields and forests.

Despite this, there were two glaring areas that looked to have amazing landscapes, yet they contained no cities at all. "What do you think it could be?"

"I'd imagine monsters of some kind? Civilized possibly?"

I immediately imagined talking orcs and trolls, other humanoid creatures with levels of intelligence. This new world was very foreign. The possibilities escaped even my wildest imagination. "Did you ask the others what they thought?"

"They didn't have any opinion on it."

The area on the map he was referring to was just several hundred miles west of Egestor. There were even two mines in the area. Yet no human construction, it was very peculiar. Aaron slipped back into his position around the caravan and the rest of the day remained peaceful.

There were no other brave wolves or any animals dumb enough to attack. We did run into several bears, but they curiously looked onward and showed no hostility. As the sun began to fall the howling of wolves became more ominous.

The dense foliage overhead completely obscured the moonlight. The night was going to be much darker than the previous one had been. When visibility reached its lowest, the caravan came to an abrupt stop and dinner was prepared. There was only a single campfire tonight. The merchant wanted everyone to remain close and avoid danger.

"So what's it like in Tampa?" the guard asked.

"Oh, uhm… it's very hot."

"It's hot? I thought it was much colder up north."

"It's hot and uhh, and also cold too!" I couldn't help but shake my head and hold back my laughter. The guard wasn't wrong. It was cold up north. The top of the map of Eastrath was filled with mountain ranges depicted with snow.

"That's interesting." The guard didn't question him at all and simply went along with the conversation. Dinner ended up being the exact same thing as the previous night.

"What kind of meat is this?" I worked up the courage to ask.

"It's bear meat."

The merchant noticed Mark stealing glances at his skin of alcohol. "You want to try a bit?"

Mark nodded his head like an excited child before taking a few gulps. He ended up coughing a few times from the burn. "It's strong, right?" The merchant laughed. "This is some of the finest poitín Egestor has to offer."

Mark immediately seemed a bit more excited and his energy removed some of the darkness shrouding the camp. I was already incredibly tired from my lack of sleep but stayed up a bit longer. I started up a talk with Aaron.

"What do you think happened to our families?"

"I don't have any family anymore." It was the first time I heard him make any comment on the subject. His facial expression was mixed. As if it wasn't a happy or sad realization.

"Why do you say that? You can't know if they survived or not."

"I'm an only child and my father died when I was very young. My mom worked herself to the brink of destruction to put me through college." Only now did that mixed expression turn sad. "She hasn't left the hospital for the past two years. I can't imagine that day was any different…"

I wasn't sure what to say; he wasn't so foolish to be blindly motivated by a bit of false encouragement. The chance that someone managed to rescue his mom and also bring her to a safe-zone was next to none. "I'm sorry." I mumbled out.

"What about you?"

"My Mom, Dad and brother lived just three hours south of our school. My brother was a senior in high school and my mom and dad both ran a restaurant together."

"Did you get to talk to them?"

"I got to speak to my brother about a week before… we were making plans for his graduation party. He was going to be living off campus with me the following semester." I thought about how happy he was when we talked. He had worked hard to get a scholarship and to be accepted. "My parents are workaholics. I didn't get to hear from them."

"Your brother sounds like he would do what it takes to survive. He might be out there somewhere, maybe not on Eastrath but one of the other two continents."

"There's a chance." The thought that I maybe wouldn't get to hear from my mother or father anymore really cut deep. I just wanted to sleep this depressing feeling away. "I'm gonna call it a night. I didn't get much sleep last night." I admitted.

"Me as well." Aaron and I both checked out for the night. I ended up crawling under the carriage. I fell asleep to the soothing sound of crickets.

My eyes opened at an unknown time during the night. A smell of blood was in the air as I scurried out from under the carriage. The fire had already smoldered and visibility was near zero.

I could hear movement but it didn't sound human at all. I casted *Energy Coat* immediately and summoned a fireball. An area several feet around me immediately lit up as I rushed to find Aaron and the others. It took me only thirty seconds to find the four of them. Aaron was sleeping on his own and Isabelle, Mark, and Justin had huddled together.

"Get up!" I shook them awake.

"Hwatiz it?" Isabelle managed to fumble out. Aaron could already see the expression on my face and knew something was wrong.

"I smell blood. Something is moving around the camp." The tired looks on their faces was replaced with a serious expression as everyone climbed to their feet.

"I hear something." Mark said. He moved to the front. I followed just behind him and let my fireball illuminate some of the path. "A mushy crunching noise…"

"I don't hear it yet." We walked forward a few more feet towards the front of the caravan. Only then could everyone hear the noise. For some reason, it made the hair on the nape of my neck stand. There was something primal and bestial about the sound.

As soon as Mark turned the front of the Caravan the creator of the noise was in plain view. I could see his muscles tense as he took a step backward. We reached his side. There in front of us was a demonic looking creature. It resembled a wolf but was a deep red. Its coat appeared to be made of red needles. Its eyes were a deep red. I didn't hesitate to use *Inspect*.

DEMONIC WOLF**	LEVEL: 15	DEMON
	SHADOW	
	HP: 8923 MP: 10	
	STR: 15	
	AGI: 20	
	DEX: 10	
	VIT: 15	
	INT: 5	

"It's a level 15 demon," I warned them. Mark remained in front, two levels higher than our enemy.

"Does that mean it's weak to Holy?" Isabelle said from behind. "Maybe."

The Demonic Wolf turned to face us. It moved to our left and what it was chewing on became clear. One of the guards was lying face up. The majority of his neck was gone and only red gore remained there.

We moved forward a little closer and the bodies of everyone else became apparent. The two guards, the merchant and the driver were scattered in various pieces towards the front of the carriage. The three other players that were travelling to Elesham with us were half-way dragged into the forest. The grass had dark red blood that trailed into the darkness.

Justin couldn't hold his stomach anymore and immediately curled over and threw up. I fought the urge as best as I could. I needed to keep this fireball in my hand as it was our only source of light.

The Demonic Wolf lowered its head and then bolted towards Mark. Our tank's left hand held a short sword and the right had a shabby looking wooden shield. Deep grooves were carved in it as he was forced a foot back. He didn't take any damage.

Aaron lined up a *Powershot* and Isabelle began casting an unknown skill. Fairies floated in the air around her as she glowed with magic. There was a runic circle around her feet that flashed holy light, very similar to when I casted *Meteor Storm*.

The Demonic Wolf let out a yelp as the *Powershot* connected cleanly with its front leg. Black blood seeped out from the wound and added a dark sheen to its needle like coat. Justin was still recovering himself and hadn't approached. He wielded two daggers and I worried for his safety.

Mark remained like a statue at the front, he constantly deflected every attack. His ability to defend with such a shoddy looking shield was impressive. There were now claw marks all across it and shreds of wood rested on the dirt road below.

Suddenly, a holy chant sounded in my ears. It sounded like angels began to sing all around us. The sound gave me goose bumps as the area a dozen feet under the Demonic Wolf lit up. The earth shined with a light brighter than the sun and I immediately recognized the spell. *Of course she was the one...*

The Demonic Wolf growled and yelped before being swallowed up by that light. Its entire body became engulfed in flames that it couldn't extinguish no matter what. After six or seven breaths, the light faded and the ground returned to normal. The Demonic Wolf was bleached white and smoking.

It had hopped up off the ground effect almost immediately, but the fire on its fur didn't extinguish. Instead, it continued to burn furiously. The needle-like coat was mostly gone. Black blood seeped out from its white skin and dripped to the ground below. It was on its deathbed.

Its head looked up at us as it attempted to stand. Every movement it made was clearly accompanied by excruciating pain. Its yelps turned to whimpers. Aaron nocked another *Powershot* as he moved forward. He was only two or three feet in front of it. His hand was steady as he aimed directly at its skull and let the bow twang.

There was no sound but the impact of his arrow. The wolf convulsed on the ground for a few moments before becoming completely still. However, items did drop. Mark moved forward without hesitation and scooped them up before showing us. We each received a little less than 3000 EXP.

> **DEMONIC PEARL NECKLACE****: VIT +5, STR +5, INT -3
> YOU FEEL YOURSELF BECOMING A LITTLE LESS HUMAN.

"You should take it Mark," said Isabelle. We all unanimously agreed.

> **WOLF'S HIDE***: AGI +3 DEX +3
> THE HIDE OF A FORMIDABLE WOLF. ITS LIGHT-WEIGHT AND FLEXIBILITY ASSIST IN GREAT MANEUVERABILITY.

"I have something similar already, you take it Aaron," Justin said from the side. Aaron nodded his head and accepted without restraint. Besides these two items, nothing else dropped.

I took a look at Mark's shield, "Here, you should take this." I held out the Stone Buckler.

> **STONE BUCKLER****: MAX HP + 250, PHYSICAL DAMAGE TAKEN -15%.
> A BUCKLER MADE OF STONE. IT'S INCREDIBLY STURDY BUT ALSO HEAVY.

His eyes went wide as saucers as he looked at the shield and then back at me several times. He didn't have any words to say. "Just take it," Isabelle said. He nodded his head and then snatched it up.

Originally, I had wanted to trade it away, but he was now the only thing separating me from potential threats. I wanted him to be as strong of a tank as possible. He stored away the nearly destroyed wooden shield and wielded Stone Buckler.

The new shield was the size of his entire chest. Unusually, it wasn't smooth but was incredibly rugged, as if someone had chiseled it out of a boulder. There was a smile plastered across Mark's face that clearly displayed his appreciation.

Once the loot was settled, we slowly walked around the carriage and accounted for everyone. There were no other survivors. We chalked our luck up to being on the back left of the caravan. The two guards, driver and Merchant all slept towards the front, while the three other players slept just to the right.

The Demonic Wolf must have come from the front right and infiltrated silently. We looked over every body and could see that each one had their throats cleanly ripped out: an instant death without a moment to make any noise. Even the horses had been killed without a sound.

It was a grueling sight to behold. Justin hurled again but no food came out. Just stomach acid. It was still too dark to leave so the rest of us curled together in the second carriage and having agreed a rotation for guard duty, I fell asleep.

I woke the following morning from Isabelle shaking me for my turn on guard. The sun was high enough in the sky to give a grey illumination to the forest through its canopy. I could see clouds of insects and flies on the bodies the dead.

When everyone was awake, as I asked, "What should we do?" The carriages no longer had horses to pull them. Bringing these carts along wasn't a possibility.

"Eat and drink what we can now, carry as much food and water on us as possible," Aaron instructed. Despite us joining their party, he had become their decision maker. I crawled in the back of the first carriage and looked through the crates.

The goods being transported were beautiful glass pieces. Some of it seemed to be for holding candles and others were dining ware with intricate designs, something only royalty would use. Besides that, there was nothing else. I went to store as much of the glass as I could in my inventory and was disappointed. It had shrunk considerably, there was only one page and on that I only had three empty slots, which I obviously needed to keep free for more important items than glassware.

"Food here!" Justin yelled from the back. Three crates contained potatoes and carrots. Another had the salted bear meat used in the stew. We didn't hesitate to haul it out and make our own stew with it, at least enough for breakfast. The rest we stored back in the crates. We used the rope and tarp of the carriage to create a sack for each of us. We wanted to divide the weight as much as possible and limit the load on any one of us. As we were all suffering from near full inventories, anything extra we wanted to bring would have to be carried physically.

We spent about an hour after waking up scavenging and collecting all we could. It seemed that getting to Egestor only required us to follow this dirt road all the way there. We still had several days remaining, depending on how hard we pushed.

"We shouldn't leave them like this," Mark said. The sun was still low and the temperature was cool in the morning. Once the day became humid, however, the bodies would rot fast.

"I think so too. I wouldn't want to end up like this," Aaron said. "Eaten by insects. The thought makes my skin crawl."

"We can't bury them." Justin said. Not only did we have no tools it would take way too long.

Everyone suddenly turned to me and I knew what they were implying. "We can burn them then." I covered my nose with part of my shirt and helped gather up the bodies.

We spent about ten minutes stacking them all into the front cart where they filled up every open crevice of the back. Mark stood behind the cart and did a silent prayer. I watched as he crossed his hand over his chest and bowed his head in silence.

Once he finished I lit a fireball and tossed it in. It took a short thirty seconds for the cart to begin burning. Leaving the improvised pyre, we started walking into the distance and it didn't take long before the carriages couldn't be seen looking back. The smell of death was replaced by the fresh smell of the forest.

It took us a full three days to make our way out of the forest, without any sign of more Demon Wolves, though we were careful to mount guards during the night. We once again returned to the open prairie. There was a bit of salt in the air as the ocean was visible from our exit location. The coast was only a mile or two to our east.

There was more farmland for as far as the eye could see. There was no city in view yet, but cabins and little lodges dotted the distance, most likely the homes of farmers responsible for these crops. There were docks that led out in the ocean; fishing boats could be seen tied to them. Seagulls flew high into the sky and rested on a cliff-face that towered over the ocean. Just below the white waves pounded into its rocky bottom.

I found myself captivated by the beauty. *A life like this wouldn't be so bad...* There was something so simple and peaceful about it: something so carefree and pure. Our feet marched on as we passed by the miles and miles of crops. There were children as young as ten moving through the field doing maintenance and watering rows of plants.

The crops were incredibly varied. On one side there were carrots, potatoes, cabbage, and lettuce. On the other was corn and tomatoes, there were even orchards full of grapes and watermelons. Everything they needed to survive was right here. They had the ocean for fishing and the land for harvesting.

"Are you travelers from Elesham?" An old gentleman that walked with a cane stopped us. His face was covered in a smile from ear to ear.

"We are," Aaron spoke up.

"Let me treat you to dinner!" This wasn't a hospitality we were used to, any of us. We had spent the last three days eating nothing but bear meat stew, Isabelle looked at the man hopefully.

"If you insist." We followed behind him. He walked in front while chatting about the weather and how great the harvest was this year. He led us to his small cabin just a mile up the road. Once inside he filled the table with plates.

"Dear! We have guests." He called back and a lovely lady poked her head in.

"I'll make extras then." Her head disappeared followed by the sound of banging pots and pans. We squeezed around the small dinner table.

"Sir, what's your name?"

"I'm Donivan," he said. We introduced ourselves one at a time. "What brings you through these parts?"

"We're traveling to Egestor and simply following the road. We're not familiar with this area."

"I see. Where are you all originally from?"

Isabelle didn't miss a beat. "We're from Tampa."

"Tampa? I've never heard of it."

"It's up north."

"Ah, it must be cold."

"Yes, it's both hot and cold." I fought the urge to laugh.

Donivan chuckled. "I can't say I'd wish to see it then. Life is simpler down here. The weather is nice. Not too hot, not too cold." No one could disagree with him. It was beautiful outside. Well, at least outside of the forest it was.

"Dear! How's it coming?"

A voice called from the back, "Just a minute." We watched as she carried out two plates of food like a professional waitress. It was a simple meal. Each plate had a piece of white fish; some steamed carrots and broccoli as well as a baked potato. There was no butter to be found.

Not a single one of us complained as we scarfed it down. I let out a light burp and covered my mouth in embarrassment. "It's already late, we should get going," Aaron suggested. I knew what he was feeling: that we had imposed enough.

The little old lady shook her hand. "Nonsense! You can stay here tonight. It's dangerous outside!"

"Dear…"

"What? It's important they know!"

"Fine, fine. As of late there have been several attacks. Little children playing at night were snatched up and disappeared."

"Snatched up? By what?"

"We don't know. The children playing with them never saw anything. They only heard cackling and the screams as their friends were being taken."

I suddenly felt like this would have been the start of a quest back on Earth. I couldn't help but think that maybe the system didn't exist anymore. Was Yetera a planet where leveling and monsters were normal?

My map didn't work anymore but I could still access my character sheet and inventory.

I looked at Aaron. "Cackling? Like our first goblins?" I whispered to him.

"Could be."

"Where did this happen?" I asked.

"Just two miles north of here, our neighbor lost his only daughter."

"We appreciate the hospitality, but we have the means to protect ourselves. In fact, if possible we would like to help you. I don't suppose there are any goblins nearby?"

"Goblins? The nearest encampment of goblins is almost three hundred miles west of here."

Aaron pulled the map from his pocket and unraveled it. His fingers pointed at the two barren areas. "Here?"

"Yes! Those mines were over-run by goblins twenty years ago. Since then no one has bothered to try to take them back. The goblin leader is very formidable. Egester makes enough profit from these crops and their ocean monopoly that they've allowed the mines to remain in goblin hands."

"It's possible some strays have setup camp somewhere nearby."

"If that's true, then, it's very troubling…" Donivan scratched his chin. "I don't have anything to pay you with…"

"Its fine, we'll make no guarantees but do what we can. It is the least we can do from the kindness you have showed us." Each of us stood and made our way out of the little cabin and out into the twilight.

"What was that about?" Isabelle asked. "Goblins? How can you be so sure?"

"When Aaron and I first met, we spent many days fighting against them. Their cackling is a distinct signature. Did you not have to face goblins and kobolds in your starting zone?"

"No…" All three of them shook their heads. "The three of us were in the store together and were all on shift that day. Most of the monsters we encountered were insects and the occasional beast. We never ran into a single goblin."

I couldn't help but wonder what the point of all of that was. *Was it to train us to come to this world?* I put it out of my mind as we walked the two miles to the next shack. Then we took a left and cut through a small pathway between the crops before entering into tall grassland. The shrubs were tall enough to cover anything shorter than five feet.

*No wonder they never saw what it was…*I looked at Aaron, "Is there anything on the map?" He took a look and didn't see any landmark. "Nothing." We continued to walk for at least a mile before we exited that dense field.

Just several hundred meters out were five or six primitive looking huts. Beside them was a small cave formation in a group of boulders. Goblins were roaming about. A few sat around a campfire and cackled.

"Are those goblins? Disgusting!" Isabelle said.

"Wipe them all out," I muttered.

Goblins weren't particularly strong. The biggest asset they had was their unending numbers. This camp seemed to be relatively small, maybe fifty or sixty total. I used the cover of night to approach incredibly close. "Wait for my cast."

I started to cast *Meteor Storm*.

The runic circle shined around me before the sky lit up for a moment. The burning Meteors started to fall with the dark sky as a backdrop. It was breathtaking. The moment my casting finished the goblins noticed our presence and their mucus-filled cackles filled the night air. The four Meteors landed shortly after and wiped out nearly half of their numbers. Their huts burned but the smoke disappeared into the darkness.

Mark and Justin immediately rushed forward like specters as Aaron and I followed from behind. It only took a total of three minutes from the start to eliminate our enemies. Aaron shot arrow after arrow as I tossed out fireballs. We managed to kill every single goblin that was fleeing.

The EXP we received was almost non-existent and any item that dropped was basically useless. Those who still had a bit of room stored everything away before I scorched the remainder of the encampment. I didn't want any more goblins to take up home here after the fact. We found a relatively quiet area in the shrubbery and having arranged guard duty slept for the night.

With nothing to wake us and no strict timeline to follow, we got the first real night of sleep in several days.

"Why didn't you say you were the Mage that could use *Meteor Storm*?" Isabelle pestered.

"No one ever asked and I didn't feel the need to share." We were currently making our way through the dense shrubs and back to the dirt road. We sent Justin back to Donivan's little cabin and informed him of the goblin situation.

Chapter 14: Egestor

The remainder of our trip to Egestor was peaceful but tiring. There was nothing around but farmland and the sea. What was beyond the farmland remained unknown. It stretched an unknown distance. These were the crops that fed the hundreds of thousands of people living in Egestor.

Three days later we could finally see Egestor in the distance. It wasn't until we were just a mile away could we see just how impressive the architecture was. It was a solid stone city with walls towering well over forty-feet tall. The tips of the crenellations poked over the walls and extended towards the blue sky.

A solid metal portcullis welcomed us that had two guards on either side. Heads peeked over the walls above and stared daggers down at us. "Halt!" We came to a stop. "State your business!"

"We're travelers from Elesham."

"Pay the toll! Five hundred Zeny per person." None of us hesitated. The metal gate behind the guards was raised slowly and we were allowed through. Winding roads and cobblestone houses filled our vision.

Most people shuffled about on foot but there were several carriages, each being towed by single horse. The entire city was bustling. There wasn't an empty street in sight. We had no idea the layout of Egestor at all.

Luckily, there was a little shop right near the city entrance. It specialized in selling information to foreign travelers. The owner was on to a good idea as we purchased a map of Egestor without hesitation.

We made our way to the most open area on the map. Our fancy equipment attracted the attention of nearby merchants. They constantly tried to sell us goods, none of which we needed. Besides the re-appearance of the guild hall, another building none of us had seen before showed up on the map: the mission hall.

The mission hall was conveniently located in the open area we were headed to. Most likely the plaza was a core part of Egestor. We wound our way through a back-alley and a great open square was revealed. There was a towering building in the center: the mission hall.

Besides that, there were hundreds upon hundreds of people rushing through the city center. Various buildings sat on the outside of this inner ring; the guild hall was one of them. All of us stared at the mission hall before making our way over to it.

There were guards on either side of the entrance, but people poured in unobstructed. Their only role seemed to be to deter people from causing a ruckus. Inside, there were three different reception desks. Each one was backed up to nearly the door with people. I couldn't make out what they were saying to the first person in line. There was just too much noise.

"Looks like a sign up," Isabelle said, "let's find out what the fuss is about."

We got into line together and waited patiently. Luckily, the lines moved quickly and we didn't have to wait for long. We all approached the reception desk together.

"New adventurer or returning?" The man barely glanced up from his book. His eye glasses dangled at the edge of his nose, seeming like they would fall off at any moment.

"New, five of us," Isabelle answered.

He passed a paper to each of us.

"Fill that out and bring it back there." He pointed to a desk that was off to the side and gestured for us to stop holding up the line. The five of us moved to the single desk and started to fill out the form.

The form was quite simple. It asked for our age, name, if we had a profession, and what type of missions we were interested in: whether we preferred solo missions or planned on completing them in a group. We all filled out the questions and all answered 'group', then handed them over in a bunch. The man at the desk gestured us off to the side while he continued to deal with the person currently in the front of the line.

Only when he had finished with the person he was dealing with did the clerk wave us over again. "Alright. Since you guys are new adventurers the missions you can take are limited." He grabbed a book and flipped it open. He licked his finger before turning every page. "Take a look here." He pointed. "These are what you can do now. Once you build up a reputation the mission hall will give you more difficult missions." He passed us the book and allowed us to take it to the side and look over it.

The excitement we were feeling sizzled out as soon as we could see the entries. The majority of them were non-combat and simply asked us to transport goods or run errands. This wasn't what we were planning on doing. *What a disappointment.*

Aaron grabbed the book and headed back to the desk on his own. I could barely hear the conversation. "There has to be something else we can do. We are new to Egestor but we're not weak by any means." The eyes of the man behind the desk moved back and forth while he contemplated us. Eventually, he pulled out a slip of paper.

"Fine. This is something that's just come in and hasn't received a ranking yet. The king needs men to fight off Naga that have been terrorizing our largest port. It will become a large-scale battle and will be open entry by tomorrow."

"That works!" Aaron was excited.

"Fine, I'll assign you to it and give you a slip." He handed Aaron five pieces of paper that each had our name and an official stamp from the mission hall. "Be at the eastern exit tomorrow morning and give them this slip. You'll be transported along with the guards."

"Thank you!" Aaron was jubilant. He rushed back over and handed us our slips. "Make sure we prepare for tomorrow. You four need to buy the supplies we need as well as get potions. I'm going to get us lodging and find out more information. Meet out front in three hours."

We spent the next three hours browsing the nearby shops. I already had potions from when I purchased them in safe-zone 373. Besides that, we picked up some dried food that wouldn't go off too quickly: mostly jerky but we included some fruits and nuts as well. We visited the smithies nearby and found that most items being sold were of average quality.

There was nothing of value to be gained from the smithies. We did find, however, that some merchants were selling goods that had stats. When we asked where they obtained it, almost all of them were obtained from killing monsters. Judging from their stats, they would have come from low level ones.

When the three hours had passed, Aaron arrived to join us outside the mission hall, "Did you get everything?"

"Yep." We flashed the sacks of food for our trip.

"Good. I managed to get us a few rooms and find some information. According to the guards, Naga started appearing about a week ago. They were seen about a mile out and didn't bother the fishing or trading ships. However, two days ago a fishing ship and trading ship were both sunk by Naga attacks. A Naga army have started to make their way inland and they expect them to make landfall by tomorrow afternoon. Because of that, Egestor is taking a huge economic hit."

"Do they know how many Naga there are?"

"No, no one has any idea how big of a battle it could be. The mission hall receptionist is correct. Tomorrow they'll be opening the mission up to the public, no requirement. We managed to get a head start at least." Night fall was fast approaching and Aaron led us back to our lodging. It was an unremarkable inn at least a dozen blocks from the central area. The only perk was that it was incredibly close to the east exit.

Since Aaron could only get three rooms, he and I would share a room, Justin and Mark would share a room, and Isabelle insisted she got her own. It was only for one night and nobody complained.

We woke at the crack of dawn and received a small breakfast from the innkeeper: a single egg and some toast with jelly on it. We ended up sneaking a few pieces of jerky as well to satiate our hunger. It was only a five minute walk to the gate.

We could hear the commotion of soldiers from about two blocks away. They talked loudly and their armor clanked and jingled when they moved. When we arrived, there were forty or fifty soldiers moving into line against the wall, waiting to depart.

Aaron took all of our slips and found the person who appeared to be in charge.

"Get to the back of the line. We're leaving in another ten minutes."

We walked along the wall and separated ourselves from the guards. Their armor looked heavy and clumsy. Each had a spear in hand and a sword dangled from their belts. A few had bows strapped across their back.

"This doesn't seem like many people," I said.

"Eastrath hasn't seen true battle for the past fifty years. There are no large standing armies anymore. These are a militia mostly, and they can only spare so many men before the safety of the city is compromised," Aaron explained.

His explanation made sense. Armies were expensive to maintain and feed. If they weren't being used for fighting then they were costing money. It was more efficient to recruit citizens and pay them only for the time they were used. The downside was that they didn't look like they'd undertaken too much training.

"Hyuthyut! We're moving" The guard captain yelled out as the gate started to rise. I could hear the clanging of chains as the gate rose. The city of Egestor was only about two miles from the coast and the ocean docks could be seen immediately after leaving the gate. There were at least a dozen large ships docked. None could be seen out on the ocean.

It was obvious which ships were used for trading and which were fishing ships. The ships used for trading were fitted for maximum capacity. The top of the decks were relatively open and empty. The boats themselves were slightly larger.

The fishing ships had bundles of rope connected to metal cages. They were stacked neatly towards the back of the ship. There were nets spread around the edge that dangled just above the water. The deck wasn't as high up off the water as on the trading ships, most likely to make lifting their hauls from the ocean easier.

The salty air was pleasant and unfamiliar: I hadn't been to the beach in many years. As we approached closer and closer the sounds of seagulls chirping and the ocean waves battering into the shoreline became more distinct. We walked down a pair of steps and officially exited the prairie.

Our feet sunk into the sand as the docks came closer. Near the docks were clumps of people huddled together. They wore short-shorts and light clothing that exposed their forearms and shoulders. It was apparent they were dressed for comfort as well as flexibility. A few workers remained atop the boats as they untied ropes and unloaded boxes of cargo.

The captain started to break apart the group of soldiers. They were separated into three groups of 15 and each assigned a boat. "You will be going on the fishing boats with the crews. You will protect them with your life!"

"HYAAA!" The guards responded back.

I noticed that the guard captain had given us a look of disdain. He didn't bother to give us any task at all. "You five just wait here for further orders." He didn't hold us in high regard. We watched as each group of militia boarded the three ships. The fisherman joined shortly after.

"What should we do?"

"I guess anything we want. He doesn't seem to care much for us." I continued to watch as the boats were untied and drifted out onto the open sea. The waves constantly battered into them as they rocked up and down. Just thinking of the motion made me feel sea sick. I moved back towards the prairie edge and plopped down.

My feet dangled and barely touched the sand. I leaned backward and rested my head on the cool grass before staring up into the sky. I fell asleep without realizing it.

I woke an unknown time later to Isabelle's astonished voice. "Something is happening!" I came up slowly and looked out onto the ocean. The three ships were still floating there several hundred feet apart. The guards moved across the deck frantically.

My eyes focused on a guard who was leaning over the edge of the deck. He had a bow in his hand as he constantly nocked arrows. Something flew out of the ocean, a spear? Maybe a trident? It was hard to tell from such a distance. It shot from the ocean and pierced his chest before tugging him below.

In a matter of moments several other soldiers were speared and pulled overboard. The commotion on the ships was loud enough to travel to shore. The guard captain looked on from the quay with worry in his face. Two of the ships immediately started to sail back, but the third was in bad shape.

Creatures climbed up from the side of the third ship and it was quickly swarmed. The screams lasted for several minutes until the only things moving across the deck were Naga. The ship sunk lower and lower into the water before it completely disappeared. The sea swallowed it as if it never existed.

The guards on the remaining two ships could barely wait to touch land. They frantically pushed the fisherman out of the way and jumped onto the dock before rushing to the sandy beach. The guard captain's face was ugly. "What happened?" he asked.

The remaining twenty or so guards stood in front of him, the only thing greater than their shame was their fear of the ocean's abyss.

"Sir! Naga surrounded the ship and completely stopped us from fishing. When we demonstrated against them they retaliated! They threw tridents attached to vines and pulled men hit into the ocean." The soldier shivered as he recalled the scene.

The captain pointed to the guard that just spoke, "Take a message back. We need more men, and for the time being, fishing or trading is not possible. Let them know this is of the highest priority."

The soldier nodded his head before running up the beach. He disappeared into the distance. The rest of the militia looked at the shoreline in fear.

"Everyone else! Setup camp!" The remaining twenty or so guards moved to the prairie edge and began setting up large tents. I felt bitter as I realized those tents were only large enough for the remaining militia.

"I guess we sleep outside again?" It had become somewhat normal for us. I made a mental note to purchase a pack with camping equipment inside when we returned to Egestor. Aaron ended up getting some fire wood from the captain. We sat around a campfire and ate some jerky.

We just managed to fill our bellies when the scream of a dock worker attracted our attention. I turned back just in time to see a spear pierce his chest and pull him into the ocean. "They're here." We all stood from the campfire and pulled out our weapons.

"Prepare for battle!" The militia seemed extremely hesitant to leave their tents but they did so anyway. Everyone's eyes remained locked on the shoreline as all the dock workers ran for their lives. They left everything, as no cargo was as important as their life.

A minute or two passed before Naga began to exit the water. Their heads popped above the waves as they moved effortlessly. It was almost as if the movements of the sea had no effect on them. They had heads like a snake but with fins on them. The muscles on their blue and yellow bodies were toned and filled with strength.

The males had humungous whiskers that protruded from the side of their face and downwards. Their forearms had additional fins that came to a sharp point several inches long. The females had sleek bodies and their breasts remained exposed.

As they fully gained the shoreline their legless bodies came into full view. They had the tail of a snake as they slithered across the ground. The male Naga wielded tridents even taller than themselves. The female Naga dual wielded short-swords that were thin and elongated.

They approached close enough for me to inspect them. I made sure to do it for both males and females.

```
NAGA MALE        LEVEL: 15      FISH    WATER
                 HP: 4312 MP: 10
                      STR: 25
                      AGI: 6
                      DEX: 10
                      VIT: 12
                      INT: 15
```

```
NAGA FEMALE      LEVEL: 18        FISH    WATER
                 HP: 3312  MP: 10
                      STR: 15
                      AGI: 20
                      DEX: 15
                      VIT: 8
                      INT: 15
```

The males were stronger physically than the females, but were over-all less agile.

The two sides engaged in a staring contest as more and more Naga pierced the white waves and stood atop the beach. By the time they stopped appearing, there was at least a hundred.

They were bad news for me. The only spell I had that wouldn't be negatively affected by their element was *Arcane Missiles*. Up until now, I hadn't found a single lightning element skill and my strongest skills were of the fire element.

Mark was usually quiet, but right now he was deadly serious. "Stay behind me, we remain on the defensive." There were just too many to fight head on. They weren't like goblins that were incredibly weak. Each Naga was a considerable enemy. It felt like it had been an eternity since I opened my stats.

```
CURRENT EXP: 6545/46000        LEVEL: 19
           MAGE              FORMIDABLE
        HP: 1282/1282    MP: 472/472
                    STR: 11
                    AGI: 11
                    DEX: 20
                    VIT: 15 +2
                    INT: 27 +14
                  AVAILABLE: 0
```

Besides killing the Demonic Wolf, there had been almost zero progress towards my next level. We just hadn't run into any monsters besides the goblins, and they were too low level to really give much EXP.

"They're coming." The Naga slithered across the sand and in our direction. Their tails left a deep groove as they moved. We were in the front, and because of that, the main focus of their attention.

A trident flew through the air at amazing speed before colliding directly with Mark's stone buckler. It sent him back half a step before deflecting off and landing in the sand. A male Naga with bulging muscles rushed forward and stabbed out.

Mark pushed his sword into the prongs of the trident and held it in place, his arm trembled in exhaustion. Justin didn't waste any time as he appeared behind the Naga like a ghost. His two daggers immediately pierced the back of its neck, he pulled down hard.

I began to channel *Arcane Missiles* while Aaron nocked arrows. The combination of our three attacks swiftly ended the Naga as it collapsed into a heap on the sand. Red blood seeped from its back and pooled into a crater. I checked my EXP and was surprised to see that it had given 1500 EXP total or 300 EXP for each of us.

The Naga continued their assault. Justin supported Mark and repeatedly backstabbed any Naga that approached him. I channeled *Arcane Missile* after *Arcane Missile* while Isabelle kept us all properly healed. Aaron started to channel an ability I hadn't seen before. Arrows began to rain from the sky.

The Naga that were unfortunate enough to be in the area of his spell had hundreds of arrows fall upon their heads. The female Naga in the area died in a single cast while the male Naga survived with very little remaining HP. He began targeting them with individual shots and finishing them off.

The guards that were previously putting up tents had made it to the beach and set up just a dozen feet to our left. It took three of them just to contend with a single male Naga and even that was only a stalemate. In the time they dispatched one Naga we could deal with five or six.

Despite our swift killing speed, we had to continuously retreat. For every five we killed another ten or fifteen would come from the ocean depths and slither onto shore. The crowd of one hundred was constantly growing to something unmanageable.

"We need to get back!" Mark was currently using his sword to hold off one trident while his shield deflected a pair of short swords. He was already nearing the limit of his defensive ability. The Naga continued to push into us like a wave as we were given no other choice but to retreat.

We stepped backwards all the way up to the prairie wall and then leaped up. The Naga closest to us didn't continue to chase but simply slithered there on the beach before becoming disinterested.

The guards didn't dare stay once we left and retreated as quickly as possible. The pressure was too much without us.

"Phew." I wiped the sweat from my brow and plopped on my ass. The battle was only a short twenty minutes or so but it was exhausting. We had killed somewhere around 50 Naga in that time frame and netted around 15,000 EXP for the each of us. I checked my stats.

```
CURRENT EXP: 21945/46000      LEVEL: 19
        MAGE           FORMIDABLE
    HP: 1282/1282    MP: 300/472
              STR: 11
              AGI: 11
              DEX: 20
              VIT: 15 +2
              INT: 27 +14
           AVAILABLE: 0
```

I had used a considerable amount of MP in that short time frame. "What was that new skill you were using?" I asked Aaron.

"*Arrow Shower*—it does exactly what it sounds like," he said while chugging an MP potion. I imagined it took quite a bit of MP to launch that AoE.

I watched as the Naga on the beach slowly slithered back into the ocean waves. They weren't retreating but instead waiting where they were most comfortable. It seemed likely that if we returned to the beach they would appear again.

The guards huddled into their tent and didn't dare step foot back on the beach. We all ended up waiting for reinforcements.

Whether they would come today or tomorrow, we couldn't know for sure.

Three or four hours passed before more guards started to show up. Most peculiar were the two people leading them who did not wear armor. The stood out by the clothing they wore.

One was a man and the other a woman. The man carried a bow with intricate carvings along it. The points at which the strings attached each had a dragon's face. His clothes were tight fitting and covered everything but his forearms. His face seemed stuck in a snarl.

The woman wore a beautiful white dress that wasn't tarnished in anyway. It reminded me of a mage's robe. There was a veil covering her face and a circlet on her head. A gem rested directly in the center of it. On her back was a staff, the tip had little particles of light swirling around it.

I couldn't help but compare the similarities with player characters. Not everyone could use skills and levels but my intuition was that these two did. I'd gained the impression that the guards were NPCs. *Were the guards NPC's and those two 'PCs'?* I didn't know.

It was possible I was completely off and everyone on Yetera could level. Maybe the guards never took that jump? You still needed to make an effort to level up for the first time.

The guard captain seemed incredibly relieved as he rushed towards the two. Given the distance I couldn't hear what was being said, but he nodded his head like a puppy. I could tell immediately that they noticed our presence and were asking about us. The captain shook his head and they turned their attention back to the beach. The two disappeared into the tent.

"Who do you think those two were?" I asked Aaron.

"No idea. They look pretty serious though. The captain treated them like royalty."

The reinforcements consisted of at least fifty more guards and thirty or forty crudely equipped civilians. They appeared to be holding second-hand shields as well as poor quality spears. A few of them were even missing metal points.

The Naga were currently in the ocean so none of them knew exactly what they were getting into. There wasn't any sign of nervousness on their faces. Thirty minutes passed, then the two leaders left the tent.

Almost immediately after they left the tent, the captain started to put the newly arrived guards into position. They were broken into groups of six and then tightly packed together. Close enough to assist each other but not so close as to hinder each other's movements. They stepped back on the beach.

The guards that had seen and fought the Naga previously were behaving differently to the newcomers. Their hands trembled and their feet fidgeted. Despite the beautiful weather, their clothing was drenched through with sweat. Their breathing was ragged and their faces were tinged pink.

I prepared to step up when Aaron stopped all of us, "Let's just watch for now. There's no need to involve ourselves yet. We were assigned to the guard captain, yet he has ignored our existence."

I agreed. Doing nothing until we were made part of the army seemed right.

The Naga fins pierced the ocean waves as they approached once again. The captain had a smug look on his face while the new arrivals looked on in disbelief. Hearing stories and seeing something personally were two different things. The guards held position as those with spears held them out and planted their feet as firmly in the sand as possible.

Arrows were nocked and shields were held upright. The Naga slid efficiently across the sandy threshold and were upon the guards in seconds, crashing into the guards like a wave as the sound of metal battering into metal filled the air. More and more Naga continued to pour out from the ocean.

I kept my eye on the two leading figures. They sat atop the prairie just twenty or thirty feet back. There was no worry or surprise on their face, only arrogance. When it seemed like the guards were going to be pushed back, the human male wielding the bow nocked a single arrow. The twang caused the air to vibrate and even I, from this distance, could hear it clearly.

I couldn't follow the arrow with my eyes, but I noticed the impact on the sand, several feet past the front row of our guards. A second passed and then there was an explosion. It instantly wiped out ten or fifteen Naga. He nocked another.

The woman held her staff firmly in both hands and began to twirl it in the air. There were flashes on her body as lightning crawled over her dress. My hair began to stand on edge and my skin tingled. A ball of lighting appeared between her two hands. Electric snakes slithered and raced along it.

She tossed it out and ball simply floated through the air as if defying gravity. It passed over the guards and then began sending out bolts of lightning. The bolts jumped out endlessly as it hovered in the air above the battle. Naga were constantly being scorched and charred black. The two of these characters together had several times our killing power.

"I guess we aren't needed?" I suggested. "May as well pick off a few Naga then."

The anxiety I had felt vanished and we stepped onto the beach to flank the Naga. We carefully pulled a few Naga in our direction and started dispatching them.

CONGRATULATIONS! ARCANE MISSILE HAS REACHED LEVEL TWO!

I opened the skill page to take a look.

ARCANE MISSILE*
CAST TIME: CHANNELED — 5 SECONDS
MP COST: 10
DISTANCE 7 METERS
SUMMON BOLTS OF ARCANE FROM THE VOID TO ASSAULT YOUR ENEMY. SHOOTS 1 BOLT PER SECOND.

Arcane Missiles cost four less MP and gained 1 Meter on its cast range. I could only hope the damage went up significantly as well.

Their numbers began to dwindle until a Naga larger than the rest slithered from the sea. He had a crown on his head and a trident made entirely of gold. We were itching to fight but the two mysterious people became serious and worked together to defeat the king of the Naga. There was a fascinating array of spells and missiles flying through the sky over the course of two or three minutes, following which the leader of the Naga was dead.

My eyes constantly stole glances at the veiled women, not because of her attractive figure but because she was a true wizard: she was at a level I aspired to reach. She always knew I was watching, I could feel it. After the king Naga was defeated, she stared back at me for the first time.

There came a peculiar feeling as if something had penetrated my mind. She spoke to me through telepathy. *If you and your party wish to grow, then Eastrath is not the place to be. This continent is filled with regular humans and those who have retired. The Continent of North Maledith should be your destination, and there you can reach your full potential.*

As soon as she looked away that peculiar feeling instantly broke off. I was shocked yet excited. *So even magic like this exists?* It felt as if I was dreaming when she was speaking with me. I couldn't quite explain how it felt. Like a passing thought maybe?

The guards followed behind their champions while I continued to feel dazed.

"We should head back," Aaron suggested. He woke me from my stupor. The guards had already marched off about a mile away.

"Let's go!" I was in a hurry. There were so many questions I wanted to ask the female wizard. I jogged after the two powerful figures, but they disappeared behind the gate before I could reach them. I rushed to the captain, "Where did they go?"

"Where did who go?" I looked at him without an answer. I didn't know who they were. My confusion seemed to have sparked a realization. "You can't meet them. Take your slips and turn them into the mission hall for your reward." I felt crushed.

The others caught up to me.

"What was that about? Why were you in such a rush?" asked Isabelle.

"That woman... she spoke to me."

"How? You never left our side." They knew immediately who I was speaking about. The only women on the battlefield besides Isabelle.

"Telepathy. She said that Eastrath is a normal continent, for normal civilians or those who choose to retire."

"Adventurers? Us?"

"I guess. She said that if we want to progress and reach our potential we should go to North Maledith."

This was significant information. It essentially meant that the struggle to survive was over. It was possible to live out a carefree and peaceful life on Eastrath. I was about to voice my opinion when Aaron cut me off.

"Everyone should know what that means. We should spend the next few days deciding what we want to do from here on out. Whether you live the rest of your life in Egestor or you go somewhere beyond that."

The weight on my shoulders was more tremendous than I imagined. Logic suggested it was an easy decision. If I wanted to stay here, I could live as a king with the powers I'd already gained.

My heart told me otherwise. The truth was that I had never been happier. Despite my missing family, I had never felt more alive than I had in this past month—from the adrenaline rush and the desire to continue growing stronger—to gathering more skills and better items. Abandoning my progression for a quiet life was a decision that I couldn't take lightly.

We all walked to the mission hall in silence. The reward was 5,000 Zeny for each of us. Not exactly an amazing amount. Oddly enough, I didn't feel happy. This mission had led me to an undesired truth about myself. I returned to the inn we had stayed in the previous night and booked a room for the entire week.

We ended up staying in the inn as a group, but despite that had little contact with each other. It was obvious everyone was having difficulty making their decisions, and if anyone had come to an immediate decision, they didn't voice it.

I didn't know what I was expecting from my party, but I myself came to grips with my desire to see more of this marvelous new world. At a gut level, I had a hunger to master more magic. I would continue traveling and leveling: the question was whether I would go it alone or have companions to accompany me.

Chapter 15: Decisions

On the fourth day after the battle on the beach, there was a knock at my door; it was Aaron.

"Come in." I held the door wide for him.

He didn't beat around the bush, "I want to continue on," he said. The oxygen caught in my lungs escaped freely as a massive weight left my shoulders. If I had Aaron with me, even if the other three decided to stay, I would be okay.

After all, we were a two-man team before this world shift, and we could be one after. My biggest fear was being alone in this unknown world. It was an exciting yet scary prospect, but definitely easier with a companion.

I walked over to him and gripped his shoulders. "That's good to hear. Me too."

His face relaxed as a smile bloomed. "Jesus. It was so gloomy in here I was sure you were gonna' say stay." He wiped his sweaty brow. "What about the others?"

"I'm not sure. I've been cooped up in here." Aaron nodded in understanding. He was the same.

"Let's have a meeting and discuss it officially." He suggested. We walked to each of their doors and knocked with a heavy hand, suggesting to each that we assemble that night.

Mark and Justin called from inside their room to let us know they heard. Isabelle, however, opened her door. "Let's go out, I'm bored stuck inside all day," she pleaded. It was still early in the afternoon. There were four or five hours of good sunlight left, plenty of time before our dinner meeting. I glanced across at Aaron.

He noticed my stare, "What? I have plans already," he said.

"What? You didn't tell me about any plans."

"I'm gonna be gathering information for a while, if we are planning to keep moving we will need it." I couldn't argue with him. He was always the more logical one of the two of us.

As a result of Aaron's statement, Isabelle completely focused her puppy dog eyes towards me, "Yes? Yes? Yes? Yes?" she said repeatedly. I couldn't find any way to refuse her.

"…Alright," I mumbled.

"Great! Give me five minutes." The door slammed hard in both of our faces. Aaron looked at me with a mischievous smile while walking away. The smug look on his face made me want to bombard him with spells, and, as if he sensed it, caused him to turn tail and dart around the corner. His feet galloped down the wooden stairs.

I heard a scuffle below me and the voice of an old lady, "Ah, slow down young man."

"Sorry, sorry!" Aaron's voice was distant. I shook my head.

Isabelle didn't keep me waiting long. It hadn't even been five minutes when the door cracked open and she popped out. I took a good look at her but couldn't tell what she spent those couple minutes doing. She looked exactly the same.

"Okay! let's go!" She was enthusiastic as could be. I followed her down the stairs and out the front of the inn. The day was not bright and sunny as I had expected. The sky was a muggy grey and the cobblestone beneath our feet was damp and slippery.

"Where should we go?" I looked at her. It was her idea to come out and I fully expected to be the one tagging along.

Isabelle thought for a moment before looking at me with a smile.

"What is it?" I asked.

"Weeeeeelllllllll…" She kept that stupid smile on her face. "I dunno."

"You don't know what?" I felt confused.

"I don't know what we should do." She lowered her head.

I guessed I wouldn't be tagging along after all, but it was okay. "Well, I want to visit the guild hall and the mission hall," I said.

"Okay!" Isabelle nodded in agreement. I opened my map and started maneuvering the winding streets. Both the guild hall and mission hall were in the same center square.

I couldn't help but look at all the merchants and specific craftsman on the streets as we moved. A part of me was still treating this as a game. The thought had passed my mind many times before, but were these NPCs or actual living people? I couldn't exactly ask them.

I put the question away as the center square came into view. Despite the light drizzle, the city center was as bustling as before. I grabbed Isabelle's wrist and dragged her through the raging crowds that were bustling to and fro.

We made our way through the groups of people and stood just in front of the guild hall. "Uhm, Joseph…" Isabelle said meekly.

I looked back at her. "Yeah?"

"Your hand…"

I looked down at my hand that was still firmly grasping her wrist, dragging her like a child. "Ah, sorry." I coughed while jerking my hand away. "Let's go inside." I turned away and avoided making eye contact with her.

The inside was grand. It was so much more open and spacious than it appeared from the outside. The ceiling had a marvelous painting of the four moons, I found myself getting dizzy while looking at it, and very soon it was all I could remember about the inside.

"Excuse me," a voice called out to me and shocked me from my stupor.

"Ah, what was I doing?" I looked at him confused. "Is there something—"

He looked up at the painting on the ceiling and then back to me, "Yes. It was painted by an elite magician and some of her magic is still imbued into the picture today." I glanced back up at it for a brief moment and quickly looked away. *What powerful magic...*

"How can I help you today?" the man asked.

"Uhm, I'm looking for information on guilds," I said.

"Do you have any guilds in mind you're interested in knowing about?"

"Oh, I just need general information."

The man seemed a bit disheartened when I said that, but did his best to hide it. "Come with me." He brought us to a desk in the corner and walked behind it before sitting. His eyes glanced from our faces to the chairs in front of his desk. Isabelle and I both sat down.

"Alright, what would you like to know specifically?"

"What does it take to start a guild?"

He passed a book across the table and allowed me to read it directly. It was the same as before, Orichalcum and 50,000 Zeny.

"Just this?" I asked.

The man across the table guffawed, "Just this?" He tapped the table with a stern look a few times, "Do you know how much Orichalcum costs?"

I quickly realized my mistake, "Uhh… no."

"The fifty thousand Zeny is a drop in the bucket. A single Orichalcum costs at least three hundred and fifty thousand Zeny." I was about to speak out and apologize for my mistake when he continued, "ANNNNNND, that's the starting price. You will never find this for sale outside of an auction house."

"Ah, okay." I rubbed my head like a toddler being scolded. "Does being in a guild give you a lot of benefits then?"

"Absolutely!" He smacked the desk, he was getting fired up. "The benefits are well worth such a valuable material." Both Isabelle and I stared at him in a haze for a moment… he was getting a bit too animated.

He coughed twice to hide his embarrassment, "Sorry, ahem. If you're part of a guild, you receive numerous benefits." I listened attentively. "First, any missions that go up on the mission board are offered to guilds first. That means if a valuable mission shows up with a limited amount of entries, a guild will always get the first pick!"

"Second. Guilds get discounts from official merchants. If it's officially sold by a city or government entity, you can expect to receive varying levels of discounts depending on the items cost and your own merit. Some of the best guilds get up to fifty-percent off." He was getting warmed up again but neither Isabelle or I showed any enthusiasm in response.

"Third. Only guilds are allowed to purchase land and develop a territory. If you're not a guild leader then the most you will ever own is a small shop. Local territories will never allow you to create an organization near them."

"Fourth. Guilds receive preferential treatment wherever they go. You will be respected and fawned over if you're a part of a successful guild. I don't need to tell you how much easier that makes building connections and opening channels for trading." He was going on and on as if this was something he rehearsed in the mirror many times.

By now he was standing up from his seat and nearly shouting. "Fifth. Guilds have access to specific information that non-guilded citizens do not. Depending on the sensitivity and the danger, if you're not part of a guild you will not be able to get information, regardless of what you offer. Not only that, the price for information will be cheaper for guild members." He inhaled deeply to catch his breath while staring with intent at both of us. "Do you see how great guilds are now?"

I felt as if he was a man defending the love of his life from being insulted. "Yes, guilds are amazing," I said.

"It's good you know!" He patted his chest then sat back down.

"So as long as I have an Orichalcum and fifty thousand Zeny I can create a guild then?"

"Right." He nodded.

"Thank you." I stood to shake his hand.

"Wait, shouldn't you take a look at the current guilds recruiting?" He seemed confused. *Is this young man really trying to make his own guild?*

"Thank you, but I'm not interested."

"Ahh, right." He coughed. "Where are my manners?" He grasped my hand that was dangling in the air and shook it firmly. Both Isabelle and I turned and walked out of the building.

"What a weird old man…," she mumbled.

Next, Isabelle and I scrambled through the crowd of the mission hall. It was a struggle just to make it the hundred-feet to the stairs of the building. Once inside we patiently waited in line until we reached the mission counter.

The man took our identification without even looking at us. He was wearing glasses that seemed to defy gravity, floating as they did on his face, despite his looking straight down. He licked the thumb of his finger while flipping pages, but he did this so swiftly it seemed inhuman.

We both waited patiently until the clerk had an 'ah-ha' moment and looked up at us. "Alright, these are the missions available to you." They were the same crappy missions before, introductory missions that even regular humans could complete.

The man started digging back into his notes and books before we even had a chance to respond. "Is it possible that I can see all the missions? I know I can't accept them…" I asked.

He didn't respond for a few moments before he looked back up. "Well, there's no official rule against it." He reached to the side and grabbed a few pamphlets and handed them to us. "Next!" He didn't give us a chance to talk anymore.

"It's better than rejection." Isabelle said what was on my mind. We moved off to the side and started reading through the pamphlets. Not only was I curious about the contents of missions that were considered hard or difficult, but also because I wanted to know what kind of compensation we would receive.

There were missions of varying levels, and I quickly learned to distinguish them. Each mission had a grade, from A to F. This value determined its difficulty, and the compensation received for completing it.

After looking through every mission in each pamphlet, I suddenly realized why the clerk at the Guild hall had become so fired up: 350,000 Zeny was not a small number. Many missions did not even offer monetary compensation, and the ones that did were not impressive in the slightest.

The 5,000 we received for helping to dispatch the Naga harassing their fishing boats was actually considered above average as a reward. You didn't start seeing more than that until you really got up into the B tier missions and higher.

The biggest problem was that we couldn't even accept the well-paying missions. The pamphlet we could choose missions from were all F-ranked missions, also known as the non-combat missions. These were typically requests for manual labor. The mission hall was basically a job board, and F-rank missions were meant for regular citizens.

"Will we really have to work our way up like this?" Isabelle asked. She was reading over the jobs available to us. Most of them were straightforward, but some of them were downright disgusting. Isabelle pretended to gag as she read out a mission, "My horse is in labor and I need someone to help me deliver. Seriously?" Neither of us was accustomed to this new life yet.

I couldn't help but find her mockery a bit cute. I watched as she continued to flip through the pamphlet until she slammed it down in disgust. "This is a waste of time."

"Alright, let's go and check the shops." I suggested. We took a trip around the city that lasted around two hours and came back empty handed. Most of the items we found were too poor quality to be of interest to us.

It was starting to seem more and more likely that the mysterious woman wasn't lying. This place wasn't for us, we were meant to go somewhere farther, further beyond.

Lights started to flicker on as we headed towards the inn. It was getting dark and lamps with large candles inside were being lit around the street. I wasn't exactly sure how long we had been out. But it couldn't quite be dinner time yet.

The inn had customers sitting around waiting for meals, but it wasn't yet busy enough to be dinnertime rush. I looked around but didn't see Aaron waiting for us.

The stairs creaked and groaned as we went back to our rooms. Isabelle returned to hers and I went to find Aaron. I knocked on his door to confirm he was here. He opened the door a crack like he was hiding from someone and then pulled me inside.

"How was it?" I asked. I was very interested in what he found out for the day.

"Ahh." He yawned. "Let's talk over dinner. I don't want to have to repeat myself, y'kno?"

"Then what did you pull me in for?"

"Dunno, I just felt it was the right thing to do at the moment. You can leave now." He shrugged.

I stood there like a deer in headlights before turning around and leaving the room. I lay in bed for what felt an hour before there was a knock on my door. I opened it to see my four party members outside.

"Let's have dinner?" Isabelle asked. I nodded in response and we went down stairs. The heavy traffic had died down as most people were settling in for the night. The only patrons left in the dining area were those residing in the inn.

There was a table off in the corner away from any other occupants, big enough to fit all of us. Aaron led the way and we all found a seat. "Waiter!" He raised his arm while yelling out. I couldn't help but feel he was adjusting quickly to this world.

"Just a moment!" The frail voice of an elderly woman called from behind the bar counter, she was on the floor and her appearance was hidden. We watched for a moment before an older woman stood from behind the counter. She must have been sixty or seventy years old.

"EEP," Aaron shrieked. We all gave him a funny look. He tilted his head down and to the left and sort of tried to hide his face as she approached.

"Alright, what'll yo—" She paused and then looked for a moment. "You're that boy who ran me over today."

Aaron looked up nervously, "Sorry... I was in a hurry," he apologized.

"I'll forgive you cause you are cute," she humphed. "Alright, what'll you have?" Before I could even ask what was on the menu she started speaking again. "All I got tonight is beef stew and goats cheese on bread."

"That... works for me." I didn't bother trying to go against the flow, and everyone else felt the same.

"Any drink?" she asked.

Marks eyes lit up. "A beer."

"Alright, give me a few minutes." She disappeared into the kitchen.

Once she left, the atmosphere grew more cheerful. Aaron was feeling particularly relieved after dodging a bullet. He wiped his brow and then addressed the table. "Alright, it's been four days since our last mission. It's time everyone decides, here and now."

He paused and gave everyone a stern look. "I will continue advancing my character and leveling up," he said.

I was about to open my mouth when Isabelle spoke, "Me as well." I felt surprisingly uplifted by this. The entire day I hadn't asked what her decision was, only because I was afraid of the answer. We were in a new world and I didn't have the slightest hope finding a healer to replace Isabelle.

"I'm also going," I said. The only two people left to speak were Mark and Jason. There was an eerie quiet as neither of them seemed keen on speaking up.

Aaron looked at the two of them with a sad expression, even one of disappointment. "Does that mean...?"

Mark spoke first. "I'm sorry." He paused before trying to explain himself, "Things have changed... before... we didn't have a choice but to go out every week. Zeny was only obtained from monsters, but now..." He struggled to get the words out. "I don't want to fight anymore, I've fought enough..." He finished and then hung his head.

Isabelle had confirmed to me that Mark was ex-military. From the moment I saw him I could see he had formal training. I didn't know if he had ever seen action, but he was definitely old enough. I honestly couldn't blame him for his decision. He could use his levels to live out a peaceful life with a decent income and without ever experiencing the pain of being cut open.

We all turned our attention to Jason. He was just about to respond when the innkeeper walked over, tableware clanking as she walked. She skillfully pulled each of our stews from a tray before giving us each a spoon. She finished off her service by passing the beer to Mark.

Mark didn't hesitate and simply downed the entire beer in three gulps. The innkeeper didn't have time to even turn away when he gestured, "Another."

"Got it." She headed back over to the bar.

Our attention turned back to Jason who seemed to have lost his courage to speak. In the end, he gave a generic response. He just didn't want to risk dying in battles we were planning on facing. Isabelle was the most disappointed of the three of us, and for good reason. She knew them personally before all of this happened.

The mood around the table was grim. This wasn't an outcome I was expecting, or wanted to see. Losing Isabelle would have been worse though. I glanced at her and felt glad that at least we had her with us.

Isabelle's face was downcast and she couldn't even bear to look up from her stew. I wanted to break this silence that was destroying our meeting. "Should we talk about what you found out today?" I asked Aaron.

Everyone looked up, including Isabelle. "I don't think it's a good idea," Aaron said. He seemed to be the most unaffected of the group. I caught him stealing a glance at Mark and Jason. He didn't say it out loud, but I knew what that look meant, and so did they. They were now outsiders. My question had only further deteriorated the mood.

The innkeeper returned just at that moment and passed another beer to Mark. She looked at everyone, "Does anyone want dessert?"

"I think we're okay," I responded.

She suddenly leaned down next to Aaron, "I have free 'dessert' for you after dinner young man…" She licked her wrinkly and old lips seductively.

Aaron turned white as a ghost. His pupils dilated with shock and fear. I wasn't even the one who received the invitation and I had chills running down my spine. "No. That's okay." He forced the words out of his throat.

"Well… if you change your mind…." She turned away and made sure to shake her ass once towards him before walking away.

"Look at you, what a ladies' man," I joked. Aaron looked at me and simply made a cutthroat motion with his hand.

Even Isabelle let out a little laugh. "I didn't know grandmas were that bold," she said. A bit of comic relief brought out a few smiles.

Mark picked up his new beer and downed it in several gulps again. The mug came down heavily on the table and brought us all back to the current station. "I let you all down, I'm sorry." He stood up, then made his way out from behind Aaron and paused at the end of the table. He pulled out the Stone Buckler I gifted him earlier and handed it back to me. "I won't need this."

I accepted the shield and returned it to my inventory with a heavy heart. I didn't care about never getting the buckler back again. If only Mark would remain as our tank. I couldn't bring myself to say the words. I could be selfish, but not that selfish.

"Thank you all." He bowed and gave us one last, long look before retreating back to his room.

Jason must have felt like the black sheep at the table and stood up as well. "I'm sorry everyone." He also disappeared up the stairs and into his room.

"Shall we get down to business?" Aaron asked. Both Isabelle and I focused all of our attention on him. "I managed to confirm a few things today." He looked at me. "As far as what that woman said, she was telling the truth.

"People who can level up and use skills are called Adventurers, and while it isn't entirely true that this continent has no place for us, the majority of Adventurers embark to North Maledith."

"Why specifically there?"

"I talked to three different people, and while none of them said the exact same thing the general idea is it's the most suitable place for progression. The best guilds are all stationed there, and the biodiversity of the continent is much better."

"Biodiversity?" Both Isabelle and I were confused.

"To put it simply… If Eastrath had a 'level range' then it would be levels one to twenty-five. The majority of dungeons and monsters in this area are relatively low level. It's also the reason why citizens and retired Adventurers prefer to live here."

I nodded in understanding. It made sense from an outside perspective. The danger level was relatively low here. Regular citizens could live a normal life, and Adventurers were not required to perform any particularly dangerous tasks.

Even a small militia could have wiped out the goblins we exterminated on the way. As far as the Naga invasion went, it would've definitely taken longer and there would have been many more local casualties, but it could have been ended without a single Adventurer intervening.

"So our growth is destined to stop very soon if we don't move on," Aaron added.

"What about North Maledith?" I asked.

"If I were to give it a level range based on the information I gathered: fifteen to seventy-five. It's also much easier to gather parties, receive missions, and explore dungeons. Eastrath is considered a ghost continent in this regard."

I was sincerely impressed with the information Aaron brought. I couldn't help but feel guilty in comparison. His information gathering was so impressive that I felt like a freeloader.

Aaron continued, "Also, there are two methods to get there. The first is we travel to the west coast of Eastrath and take a boat. The trip on land is about two months and the ocean trip is another two months depending on weather."

"What's the second?"

"The second is we take a Zeppelin and fly there."

I knew what a Zeppelin was and was immediately interested. "I don't do well on water."

"Then we need to gather two-hundred and twenty-five thousand Zeny within six months," Aaron said.

"Why so much?" I was caught off guard. "How long does the Zeppelin take to travel there?"

"Fifteen days," Aaron responded.

"Fif-fifteen? How is it so different?" Isabelle sounded surprised.

"Magicians. The company which runs the Zeppelin is based in North Maledith. They employ several magicians powerful in Wind magic."

"Okay, so why six months?"

"Because the Zeppelin comes every six months and the last one departed a little less than a week ago." Everything was starting to make sense. "So we need to make a decision," Aaron continued. "We can get there in approximately four months via boat, or we can wait six months and take a Zeppelin for fifteen days."

"Are we confident we can make seventy-five thousand Zeny each?" Isabelle asked.

I checked my inventory and felt a tinge of regret for spending 25k Zeny on potions just before the world shift. "I have a little over thirty thousand Zeny right now," I told them.

"I have forty-five," Isabelle said.

"Forty here," Aaron said. "I think it's easily accomplished within sixth months."

"About that… we visited the mission hall today and got a look at all the missions available, even the ones we don't qualify for, and the payment isn't very good," I said.

"How bad is not very good?"

"The five thousand we received for the Naga recruitment is about what you receive for a B plus tier mission. The F tier missions give around five hundred Zeny only, some even less." From the look on Aaron's face, I had dropped a bombshell.

Aaron started to rub his head in frustration, "No choice. We take what we can get. Anything else?"

"I want to start a guild." I stood up. "The goal is incredibly far away, and not worth going into right now, but as my companions I wanted you both to know." Aaron already knew about it but it was Isabelle's first time hearing it.

"Alright, let's call it a night. We have a lot of time but we should be efficient," Aaron said. We all got up as a group and started to head upstairs. The innkeeper was behind the bar watching us as we left.

She watched Aaron and started to lick her wrinkly lips seductively while giving him the stink eye. I felt his hands grab me as he forcefully positioned himself behind me. "Keep walking." I felt like a human shield protecting him from unexpected gun shots.

Only after reaching the second floor did Aaron release me from his death grip. He took one glance back at the staircase before sprinting to his room and slamming the door shut. I could hear him fiddling with both locks before clicking them into place. I couldn't help but chuckle to myself.

I reached my door and turned to Isabelle, "Goodnight."

"Night."

The night was long and I found myself lying in bed with a sour feeling. *Why don't the good things ever last?* Veronica crossed my mind. Somehow I felt I'd never forget the first companion I ever had on this journey. No matter how far I would go...

I opened my stats out of sheer boredom, even though I know they hadn't changed for quite some time.

```
CURRENT EXP: 21945/46000      LEVEL: 19
            MAGE          FORMIDABLE
        HP: 1282/1282   MP: 472/472
                  STR: 11
                  AGI: 11
                  DEX: 20
                  VIT: 15 +2
                  INT: 27 +14
              AVAILABLE: 0
```

That itching desire to level was still there. I had been forced to bury that feeling until we got a solid footing in this new world and despite losing two members, we now had that footing. There was finally a goal, a direction to work towards. I longed to begin pushing on.

The excitement I fell asleep with woke me early. The humidity on Eastrath was often unbearably high, and this morning it was particularly bad. I made my downstairs to an empty dining room.

The innkeeper was wiping down the tables and chairs with a moist rag. She noticed me staring at her out of the corner of her eye. "Do you need something?"

"Is there somewhere I can wash?" I asked.

"You can use that." I followed her eyes to a bucket of water with a rag draped over the side.

Really? She was being completely serious.

"Take it outside, don't wet my clean floor."

I reluctantly picked it up before heading out the back. The visibility was low as the sun was only just peeking over the horizon. I cleaned myself in sections and walked back in feeling a bit damp in my crevices, at least I wasn't sticking together anymore though.

"If you're looking for breakfast, you're gonna need to wait about two hours," the innkeeper said.

"Ah, thank you." Surprisingly, I was not hungry and decided to make my way to the mission hall. The city center looked foreign this early in the morning. While a few people still rushed about, the area was mostly vacant.

Was this what they meant when they said 'the early bird gets the worm'? I could actually see the floor and path towards the mission hall. There wasn't even a line when I got inside. I walked up to a booth and checked the F missions available.

Around ninety percent of the missions were the same as yesterday, with a few new ones sprinkled in. Unfortunately, all of them were junk. I wasn't quite desperate enough to serve patrons or scrub down toilets yet. I left the pamphlet behind with a heavy hand.

A week passed by slowly as everyday was the same. The new missions were never more than menial tasks and chores. Most of them were even something your average person wouldn't want to do.

I had begged the mission hall clerk for something more challenging on numerous occasions and was rejected every time. There was no way to boost your rank, no shortcut, at least not for a few unknown adventurers. You simply had to complete missions and climb the ladder. "Just like everyone else." I could hear his voice and see his finger wagging in my thoughts.

Despite that, I returned to the mission hall every day. Is this what it felt like being crazy? Doing the same thing every day and expecting a different result? I shook my head and turned the street corner and went towards the city center.

It was mid morning and the traffic had already picked up considerably. The center was packed as expected, and yet something was off. I noticed the flow of people wasn't quite smooth as normal. My eyes scanned the crowd and discovered the problem.

A group of people remained stationary near the bottom of the mission hall stairs. Their hands held signs as they chanted, "We want answers! We want compensation!" I looked on curiously.

They showed no signs of moving despite the flow of people bumping into them repeatedly. They were the rocky shoreline being battered by the heavy waves. I snaked my way forward and stood just a dozen feet away from them. I ended up next to a man that was also just watching them from a distance.

"Excuse me." I did my best to catch his attention.

He turned to me. "Yeah?"

"What's going on here? What are they protesting for?"

He leaned a bit closer so I could easily hear him, "Apparently their family members haven't returned from a mission for the past three days."

"Is that abnormal?"

"Do you know the sewer cleaning mission?" he asked.

In fact, I did know it. It was one of the better-paying F class missions, though the pay was not good enough to wade through sewage. "I know it."

"Well, apparently the last group left four days ago and never returned. They sent in guards to determine the situation and they also didn't come back."

"Do they know why?"

"That mission is only supposed to take one day: start in the morning and done before dinner. The city has yet to explain the situation."

That was troubling. All the F class missions had one thing in common, and that was non-combat. One of the guarantees the city made was that F class missions were not dangerous to complete.

"Thank you." It was valuable information, and possibly a situation I could take advantage of. We parted ways and I shuffled up the stairs and into the mission hall. It was the glasses-wearing, finger-wagging gentleman behind the counter. By now, he recognized my face.

"What is it today?" he asked.

"I'd like to apply to the sewer cleaning mission."

"Not possible," he denied me flatly.

"I know about the disappearances, I still want to go." The information presented to me made it clear monsters were involved. Monsters meant Zeny and exp, something I desperately wanted and needed.

His face was conflicted as he read over my information. He could see that I originally signed up with a party of five, and that we had participated in the Naga invasion. He removed his glasses and rubbed the bridge of his nose for a few moments. It was something I'd not seen him do even once before.

"Can you come back after dark?" he asked me. "Bring your party members."

"Of course," I said it with a stern face and calm voice, but inside I was bubbling with excitement. I left it at that and rushed back to the inn.

When night came around I grabbed Aaron and Isabelle and there was no difficulty persuading them out onto the dark streets. The city center was dimly lit by candles and mostly empty. Even the protestors had been forced out by the city guards, else they would have protested all night.

I rushed up the stairs with both my comrades in tow before bursting through the door. Glasses was sitting off in a corner behind a desk. Papers were stacked so high I could only just make out his head from behind them.

My entrance attracted the attention of everyone in the hall. They all looked up with a confused expression. "Over here." Glasses called out to me. We walked over as a group and stood before his desk. "Where's the other two? You signed up as five."

"Well… they left our party." I scratched my head.

"Ahhhhhh, whatever! Sit down." He didn't seem very happy. We all took a seat and waited patiently for him to talk. "The situation is this: we sent guards to figure out what went wrong with the F class sewer mission, HOWEVER, they never returned."

Aaron and Isabelle looked at the clerk attentively.

"Because they didn't return, we don't know the situation in the sewers. Since we don't know the situation, we can't give the mission an accurate grade to list it, and we also can't send more guards to their death. This has put the mission hall in a very rough spot."

His frustration was understandable. Their reputation was on the line, and the only thing they had was their credibility. If taking an

F class mission meant potential death, how could anyone trust their judgment? "We are now in a position of limbo. We have personally reached out to many Adventurers, but all of them refused."

Aaron finally broke his silence, "Why did they refuse?"

"For two reasons." He paused slightly. "First, none of them wish to travel into the sewers. They feel it is beneath them to do so. Secondly, the city refuses to apply a monetary value to the mission. There is no guarantee they will even be compensated for their time." Even I felt a bit discouraged hearing his second reason.

"If there's no compensation, why should we bother?" Aaron asked.

"I cannot allocate funds, but the mission hall is in charge of something that even the city has no say over."

"What's that?"

"We are the sole authority in awarding ranks." He turned from Aaron and looked at me, "haven't you been trying to find a way to raise your rank quickly?"

"What is your offer?" Aaron cut right to the chase.

"I am not expecting you to solve the problem, but if you can instead bring back any valuable information, I will raise your ranks to E."

"Not enough." Aaron didn't bat an eye.

"Ahem, I will raise your rank to D."

"Still not enough," Aaron refuted him.

"Why do you say it's still not enough?" Glasses asked. I was just as confused as he was. Two ranks might seem like very little, but it would put us in a bracket with combat missions.

"Don't you think it's weird that no one returned?" Aaron asked. "You would think that at least one guard would have made it back to tell the tale, no?" Glasses couldn't deny that. Even missions to kill goblins and lesser monsters were D rank. If the danger level was only D, at least one or two guards could have escaped with their lives.

"Not only that, what if it isn't monsters at all?"

"What are you suggesting?"

"What if it's poison, or a disease? Who is to say we don't enter the sewers and swiftly die? We could very well be walking to our deaths. In that scenario, would earning the D rank be worth the risk?"

Glasses actually seemed embarrassed now that he put more thought into it. It was a very real possibility. "Ahem, what would you suggest then?"

"A rank."

His ahem turned into a full on cough. He was utterly surprised by Aaron's boldness. "A? Do you know just how long it takes to get A rank?" His voice was raspy and agitated.

"Do I take that as a refusal?" Glasses was stunned to silence. "Let's go," Aaron said. He looked at us and stood while beckoning us to leave.

"Wait, wait!" Glasses grabbed his wrist as he pleaded for him to say. "Okay, listen."

Aaron turned to him but didn't sit back down. It was clear by his demeanor that he would leave if the next few words didn't satisfy him.

"B rank! How about B rank?" He was pleading now. "I can't give you an A rank, it's outside my authority."

"Didn't you say the mission hall could grant ranks as they please?" I asked.

He looked at me like an idiot, "Do you think we give out A ranks like candy? I don't represent the entire mission hall. In fact, even granting you all the B rank is sticking my neck too far out."

Aaron beckoned for us to sit down. Glasses released his wrist once we were seated. He closed his eyes and breathed in deeply. It took him a few moments before he regained his previous calm demeanor.

"So you'll grant us the B rank?"

Glasses sighed heavily. "I can do it."

"Put it in writing."

"Alright." Glasses grabbed a fresh piece of paper and started scribbling with his ink pen. It took him a little over two minutes before the contract was fully drafted. "Sign here, each of you." We took turns doing our best to sign with a type of pen we'd never used before. Our signatures all looked terribly childish.

"Is there anything else we should know?"

"Meet here tomorrow at sunrise. Five guards will guide you through the sewers." He passed the contract to Aaron, who in turn folded it and slipped it away into his pocket.

I took another look at Glasses and couldn't help but think he aged several years during this negotiation. It was obvious these past four days had been a stressful nightmare for him.

"If there's nothing else, we'll take our leave."

"I won't see you out." Glasses was massaging his temples while completely avoiding eye contact with us. We turned and walked out calmly.

We made it half a block away before Aaron couldn't hold it in anymore, "HAHAHAHA. GOTTEM." He cackled like a madman.

I couldn't hold myself back either as I nearly jumped up on his shoulders, "Good shit." I would have sold us short in that position.

"So uhh, what if we just go down there and die?" Isabelle asked. It seemed like she was the only one who wasn't considering this a free mission.

Both Aaron and I coughed at the same moment. "It'll be fine... I think."

Chapter 16: Sewers

The sun had set some time ago; it was getting quite late and time was of the essence. Shops would be closing soon and we needed to gather supplies on short notice. Particularly, food and water was of extreme importance. This might not be a short in-and-out mission.

Aaron made the call to split up and we each disappeared down our own pathways. It wasn't until several hours later that we regrouped on the second floor of the inn.

"How'd it go?" I asked.

"I got the food." Aaron opened a sack with both hands, revealing the items inside. There was cured meat and chunks of cheese, as well as some fruits and veggies. All of it was food that would last at least two days.

Isabelle brought out pouches and handed two to each of us. They were water pouches made of sheepskin. Each one held enough water for a single day of drinking. A cork was pushed into the drinking hole to keep the contents within.

I pulled out what I was tasked to gather: protective gear! I passed out gloves made of sheepskin as well as booties to go over our footwear. There were also masks to cover our face and nose so we weren't breathing in sewage. It wasn't required, but it gave us each a bit of peace of mind.

I also made a special request of the innkeeper, to wake us up early and also prepare us breakfast. It was going to cost me two-hundred-and-fifty Zeny but the coming day was going to be a big one. I closed my eyes to sleep.

Unfortunately, some of that Zeny went to waste as I was wide awake come breakfast. I was like a kid the night before Christmas, too excited for my brain to shut off. I got maybe three or four hours of sleep: it was enough to get through the day.

The three of us arrived at the mission hall with full bellies. Glasses was relieved to see us and he personally escorted us inside. Once at his desk he went over the details of what we should accomplish. At the bare minimum we needed to at least discover remnants of the guards, and also discover the source of the problem.

If the problem wasn't something we could solve on our own, retreat. If it was something within our capabilities, take care of it. He then introduced us to the five guards waiting in a backroom, and made sure they fully understood they were to follow our orders, specifically Aaron's.

In the eyes of the guards we were a bunch of children, but they reluctantly agreed to Glasses's demands and we departed as a group of eight. The city streets were mostly vacant at this time and we left the city walls without delay.

Egestor was elevated several stories above sea level, and because of that, the sewer entrance was located a floor down from the city's base level. According to the guard leading us, the sewer had a total of four levels.

The sewage and ground water entered through designated openings along the cobblestone streets and spiraled down the maze-like sewer floors. The end destination was the fourth sewer floor. There, all the sewage was screened through many traps set in place to catch unwanted debris.

Finally, the mostly bio-degradable water and waste would flow through a set of pipes and exit into the ocean. Those who chose to do the sewer mission could expect to travel to the fourth floor and then dislodge and remove any debris too big from the traps. This included tree branches, rocks, and waste that wouldn't decay over-time. Even the occasional body sometimes ended up stuck there, but that was very rare.

We circled around the city wall and then took a set of stairs that led a floor down. At the base of the stairs was a pathway blocked by what looked like a jail cell door. It was rusted red with little flakes of metal falling off.

The leading guard pulled out a key and unlocked it. The door squeaked and squealed as he jerked it open. We all walked inside and waited while he pulled the doorway closed and then relocked it.

My eyes were almost adjusted to the change in lighting when the guard scooted past us and lit a lamp. "Stay close behind." The pathway was narrow and we were forced to walk one behind the other. Only after walking for a bit over thirty seconds did we leave the narrow hallway and officially enter into the sewers.

The tunnel was wider, and had two walkways on opposite sides. In between that was a flowing stream several feet across filled with murky water. It was impossible to discern the exact color due to the lack of lighting.

"This way." He beckoned us before heading down the left path-way. The extra space allowed us to walk side by side as we traversed the dark corridor. The smell that wasn't quite so bad at first steadily grew in intensity. As we moved further away from the entrance tun-nel, less and less fresh air was blowing through.

The air had become stagnant, but didn't smell like sewage just yet. It simply smelled like old water mixed with a small amount of garbage. It was unpleasant, but not unbearable. The lighting continued to decline until I could only see the bright lamp dangling several feet in front of me.

I held my hand over the murky water and summoned a fireball. The dark tunnel was illuminated, completely solving the question of visibility. The guards leading at the front stopped abruptly and jerked their heads back. Only after they saw it was me did they breathe a sigh of relief and continue moving forward. It was obvious the stress they were under was considerably higher than ours.

As we moved through the tunnel and the range of my light flickered and extended, the darkness just outside its reach looked menacing, like the maws of a beast waiting to swallow us up. The fireball in my hand never allowed that darkness to engulf us.

By now, I could tell we were moving downward ever so slightly, and the curvature of the walls told me we were moving in a spiral motion. We came across several openings, but the officer never strayed from our original route.

I was curious as to why, and he satiated that curiosity. "The only way to not get lost is to follow the outer path the entire way down." It made sense. There were pathways constantly opening up to us on the opposite side. Entering into there would lead us into a maze that would be hard to get out of.

I could see the murky water below much more clearly, a mixture of brown and green. There were particles of food and other waste floating at varying depths within. "Shouldn't this be flowing?" I asked. The water looked almost stagnant.

The guards stopped and looked at the water more closely. It was true, the water was barely flowing. "I've never seen it so bad," he mumbled.

"There must be a considerable blockage," another agreed.

"How far down are we?" Aaron asked. We had been walking for around a half-hour.

"We're about to enter the second level."

It wasn't long until we could see it: the entrance to level two. The route was blocked by a stone wall with doorways for both sides of the path. Without a key you couldn't continue, unless of course you were fine taking a dip in sewage and swam under the barrier.

The guard unlocked our side and we passed through. The other side was more of the same. I finally couldn't take the stench anymore and pulled out my mask and covered my face. The airflow was almost non-existent now.

A bead of sweat slid down the nape of my neck and decided to peel my damp shirt from my back. This was what hell was like, I was sure of it. The guards in front seem unfazed by the change in temperature and smell. They walked on without complaint.

The one person I expected to protest and complain was completely silent. Isabelle was fully gloved and masked up behind me. She pinched her nose hard but didn't say a peep.

She noticed me staring back at her, "Ghwat?" I turned around without a word before smiling quietly to myself.

We were half-way down the second level when we came across the first truly out-of-place occurrence. There were bits of trash spread along both pathways. Swarms of roaches and flies hovered around a mostly barren chicken carcass.

The pathway became a shade darker, and there was a clear waterline on the wall. It was obvious the water had overflowed here, leaving debris and even trash residue on the wall and floor.

Pockets of gnats assaulted our faces as we had no choice but to walk through them. I put my hands over my mask for extra protection, but still felt a strong urge to pull it off and sneeze.

The waterline on the wall continued to rise until the entire tunnel was a shade darker. Trash was still strewn about along the pathway floors as little critters shuffled away from the light of my fireball.

"Was the entire tunnel filled with water?"

"There was heavy rain two days ago." It was the only explanation, and also told us we weren't on a rescue mission. Without a doubt we were looking for bodies.

We had our first encounter on the third floor.

We had just passed the threshold between the second and third floor when we heard a skittering. There was a bug, an abnormally large sized cockroach in our path. It was easily the size of a two-liter of soda. The guards' abrupt stop and subsequent action made it apparent this was abnormal.

The entire group came to a halt as we watched the disgusting little creature 'look' in our direction. The two antennae on its head swiveled back and forth before rubbing along the floor. Its head had two beady little eyes and a pair of pincers as big as a man's fist.

The antennae stopped their swiveling and then went between the big pincers where a tongue came out and began licking them clean. Almost immediately after that it let out a hiss and then scurried towards us.

I always thought the little cockroaches were quick, but this thing was like a freakin' jet. There was just barely enough time for the front guard to remove his spear and stab out. He accurately pierced the backside of the roach and pinned it to the ground below.

I broke out of my stupor and moved forward to cast *Inspect*.

THIEF BUG LEVEL: 7 INSECT EARTH

HP: 675   MP: 0

STR: 7

AGI: 20

DEX: 4

VIT: 5

INT: 1

AN INSECT KNOWN FOR ITS IMPRESSIVE ABILITY TO PLUNDER AND STEAL.

The Thief Bug was in its dying throes. Its legs scurried along the floor while its head twisted and turned in every which direction. Despite its efforts, the spear tip kept it firmly pressed onto the ground.

The monster's mandibles constantly opened and closed as if trying to bite everything and pull apart anything it could grasp. Eventually, the twisting and turning of its head allowed its mandibles to grasp a part of the spear shaft.

We witnessed an impressive display of strength once the creature latched onto the spear. Its mandibles squeezed the metal spear tip with enough pressure and force to leave several indents. If left long enough it would be able to snap the tip right off.

Aaron couldn't watch any longer and nocked an arrow. There was a whistle as the arrow pierced directly through the Thief Bug's head and it ceased its struggling.

"What was that?" Isabelle asked. The guards didn't have an answer. It was obvious they had never seen or heard of anything like it.

We waited in place for what felt like an eternity. It was glaringly obvious the guards didn't want to continue forward any longer. While the Thief Bug was small, there was no doubt about the destructive power its mandibles could unleash.

The shaft of the spear tip sported several new gashes as well as three large indents. It looked as if someone pushed their thumb into a bit of clay. That was also only after a few seconds of gnawing. The Thief Bug could make quick work of an arm or leg if allowed the chance.

Aaron finally walked forward to break this awkward stalemate, "We'll lead the front now."

"Alright, just continue following this path."

Aaron and I led the front side by side. He was in charge of dispatching Thief Bugs while I was the walking nightlight. After walking just a dozen feet we ran into another.

There was no awkward pause between the two parties this time. As soon as Aaron could see the critter, he nocked an arrow and blasted right through its ganglion. It didn't even have the time to react before it was too late.

If fighting the small creatures was always this straightforward, they would be no problem. Unfortunately, it wasn't. As we continued to descend, more and more Thief Bugs filled the tunnel. The skittering and hissing we could hear in the distance made my hair stand on end.

They became so numerous that my light illuminated more with every step we took. Aaron continued to nock arrow after arrow and kill Thief Bug after Thief Bug. We were now moving at a snail's pace.

The only solace we could salvage from this situation was that they were easily spooked. Almost immediately after blasting apart one, the rest would scurry as a group deeper into the darkness.

Aaron nocked his arrow and swiftly blasted apart two cockroaches that were fighting over a decaying pig's foot, only to witness a third scurry from the darkness. It swiftly pinched the pig's foot between its mandibles and zipped away.

If they were giving decent EXP for the effort then none of us would have been dissatisfied with this endless supply of monsters. Unfortunately, each Thief Bug gave 10 EXP: a completely negligible amount.

We were nearing the fourth floor when we found our first real clue to what had happened here. There was a guard's breastplate lying on the path. It was in bad shape with gashes and dents all over it. There were dark splotches strewn about its surface. I couldn't tell whether these were blood or sewage.

As we approached closer to the breastplate we spotted a metal object shining through the murky water. There was a pair of greaves as well as half a spear resting on the bottom. There were no signs of any bodies.

We continued moving forward despite the discovery. Matters weren't at a point where we felt we couldn't handle the situation just yet.

"We're almost there," a guard called from the back. The tunnel's winding corridor had tapered off into something more straight and my light now granted a dozen or so extra feet of visibility. The air at this level was absolutely putrid and smelled of mold. There was another smell mixed in as well, which was familiar but I couldn't identify.

We didn't have to walk more than two-minutes before we noticed an overflow. The sewage water had risen up and onto the pathways. At first it was only just a light puddle and soon it covered up to our ankles.

At this point, the ground was no longer slanted and descending down. We were walking on flat ground.

"That's the final corner." We came to the last twist in the tunnel and turned it carefully.

There was a huge open area in front of us many meters in size. It seemed like this was just one compartment of many that made up the sewer's fourth floor. Columns reaching to the ceiling were spread about unevenly all over the area doing their best to support the ceiling above.

Visibility had dropped to an all time low. The space was too open and my light didn't travel far enough to give us much information as to what awaited us. Not only that, sewage water rested just above our ankles.

It was a challenge just to see a few feet ahead of us. The murky water was once again completely black.

"How far to the traps?" Aaron looked back.

"About a thirty-minute walk," a guard replied.

"Why so far?" I asked.

"The traps are located on the opposite side. We're basically walking from one side of the city to the other. If it wasn't so open down here it would take even longer." I nodded in understanding.

We were all waiting for Aaron to make a decision. It was clear that the workers and guards were all dead, but it was unclear why.

"We've yet to find a body." He paused. "I'm not convinced these little roaches are the reason."

He was right, we didn't have enough information to go back and claim our reward yet. We hadn't truly been in any danger, and yet we were so close to our destination. We had thoroughly taken advantage of Glasses' predicament during our negotiation. I wouldn't feel right if we left without doing our best; I was sure Aaron and Isabelle felt the same.

"Are there any more doors we need to unlock?" Isabelle asked the guards.

"No, it's a straight shot through."

"Then I think you five should return and pass on what we've learned so far." Isabelle made them that offer: it was clear from their demeanor that the guards were not willing to move on.

The guard who had originally led the way pulled a key from his pouch and handed it to a subordinate, "You four head back. Leave the doors unlocked on your way out, just in case." He then turned towards Aaron, "I will stay with you all."

Aaron nodded in approval and then turned to me, "Can you make that any brighter?"

"I can." I started to push more Mana into my hand as the fireball started to burn hotter. It slowly illuminated a bit more of the room.

We were just about to start moving forward, when Isabelle called out. "Wait!"

She closed her eyes and cupped her hands together as if in prayer. Her lips began to move and a mystical language came out, whatever it was, it wasn't human. She was chanting a spell.

Her hands began to glow as a blinding light did it's best to escape from between her fingers. She opened her eyes and then pushed her hands outward, almost as if throwing a dove into the sky.

A glowing fairy flew out from her palms and into the center of the room. It was bright enough to completely illuminate our surroundings, even casting dark shadows behind the columns.

The Thief Bugs that were hidden on the ceilings and walls hissed before scurrying into the small patches of remaining darkness. No doubt my face was sour as I stared at Isabelle.

She looked back at me, her fingers once again pinching her nose, "What?"

"Why...didn't you use this earlier?"

"Weeeel... you looked so proud summoning your little fireball earlier. I didn't want to embarrass you."

I was at a loss for words.

"Forget it," Aaron said. His eyes scanned the room carefully for any danger before slowly walking forward. We walked in a loose single-file line. I was behind Aaron, Isabelle was behind me, and behind her was Mr. Guard.

The Thief Bugs seemed to instinctively want to avoid the light from Isabelle's fairy and did their best to stay in the columns shadow as we moved. It wasn't until we traveled through three rooms that we saw the remains from a guard's armor, and then another.

It was also then we saw the creature who could have been the real culprit for this mess. I cast *Inspect*.

```
┌─────────────────────────────────────────────────┐
│  MALE THIEF BUG    LEVEL: 18      INSECT  EARTH   │
│              HP: 7645        MP: 5                 │
│                    STR: 35                         │
│                    AGI: 10                         │
│                    DEX: 10                         │
│                    VIT: 20                         │
│                    INT: 1                          │
│  A LARGER AND CLUMSIER VERSION OF THIEF BUG. IT DOESN'T │
│         LOOK VERY PROFICIENT AT STEALING.         │
│                                                    │
└─────────────────────────────────────────────────┘
```

If a Thief Bug was as big as a 2-liter of soda, this was as big as a dog. Its legs kept it clearly suspended above the ankle-high water. Its increased size also gifted it a larger head and mandibles. There was no doubt the mandibles could snap a man in half.

Aaron knew about my ability to inspect, "How's it look?" He asked.

"Honestly… not good. This thing has stats similar to the High Orc we encountered on our way to the safe-zone. We were lower level then, but we had a tank. Not only that, we also had advantageous terrain."

Without a tank, and nothing between us and this goliath of a bug, I wasn't excited. "Do you think *Heal* can re-attach limbs?" I asked jokingly. There was zero chance anything grasped by those mandibles wasn't getting cut in half.

Isabelle didn't seem to appreciate my attempt at humor. "Let's test it right now." She nudged me from behind.

The Male Thief Bug in front of us still had yet to move towards us with any intention of fighting. The fairy's bright light reflected off its bead like eyes. I raised my staff and threw the first punch: *Shackle!*

Spikes quickly rose around the bug and enclosed it, before golden-purplish chains wrapped around them, cleanly trapping it inside. A hiss escaped from the monster's mouth as it bit down on a chain, gripping it tightly.

The monster didn't have an impressive AGI stat and I fully expected *Shackle* to give us plenty of time to work with. I was wrong. The mandibles gripping the golden chain closed with ungodly strength. There was a pop that echoed throughout the chamber.

The chain between the mandibles snapped like a twig and split apart. Its burly body struggled to squeeze through the gap as half of its body already rested outside my shackle. I started to channel *Arcane Missiles* while Aaron readied a *Power Shot*.

This was the first time *Shackle* felt so useless. The idea in my head that it was an absolute cheat-like skill now faded. We couldn't even get to the 900-damage threshold before the Thief Bug had plowed his way out.

By the time my third *Arcane Missile* had connected with its frame, the Male Thief Bug had escaped the enclosure. *Shackle* had only bought us three seconds of time. It was also at this moment that Aaron's *Power Shot* left his bow.

A green arrow whistled through the air causing the water directly below the creature to ripple. A breeze brushed past my face. I was hopeful for its power.

The fourth void bolt from *Arcane Missiles* had just left my hand when Power Shot connected. The green light slashed right into the back of the Thief Bug before sliding across its carapace and disappearing into the next chamber.

"Oh," I groaned aloud.

357

A shot with so much power only managed to leave an indentation along the Thief Bug's back. It was like a walking fortress. The Thief Bug let out an ear piercing hiss that let us know it was truly upset.

It tilted its head downward and rushed forward like a charging rhino. It was at this moment that Mr. Guard slipped through the three of us and rushed forward with his spear held out. His move was so sudden I couldn't even tell him to wait.

The guard was a veteran, and his use of the spear showed that clearly. In the short distance he traveled, he accurately located the most vulnerable opening and stabbed out. The spear tip pierced one or two inches into the front leg joint, just beside the Thief Bug's neck.

This was a testament to just how sturdy this bug's body was. The guard and Thief Bug smashed into each other like two trucks, and yet the spear tip barely scratched the surface. The guard leaned in and put all his body weight against the spear shaft. It was all he could do to keep himself from being run over.

The Thief Bug's mandibles constantly opened and closed as it moved forward like a tank. The guard's heavy boots skid along the slimy floor inch by inch as he was pushed backwards. We mustn't miss this chance.

I started to channel a *Fireball* while Aaron sent arrow after arrow into any non-armored joints he could. Burns and open wounds started to accumulate near its legs and from its neck leaked a thick brown goop. It became more frantic.

Finally, the monster's mandibles gripped down on the spear still embedded in its front leg. It didn't snap the spear but instead grasped it firmly before jerking its head to the side. Spear and guard went flying before landing with a splash ten feet away.

Although the bug was now free of any restraints, the damage to its front legs slowed it considerably. It huddled like a fat linebacker in our direction with no indication it was going to stop. We started to move backwards at a steady pace while continuously throwing out attacks.

It just didn't want to die no matter what we threw at it. I was of the mind to cast *Shackle* once more when Mr. Guard rushed in from the side and slammed directly into the monster. The Thief Bug was caught by surprise and offered little resistance to his charge.

While it was a durable tank, it wasn't so heavy it couldn't be pushed over. Pairing the force of his charge with its damaged and unsteady legs, the Thief Bug plopped over onto its side and continued on to roll fully onto its back.

Its legs flailed in the air as it tried to rock its body side to side. It was a pleasant surprise to see a soft abdomen and underbelly. There was none of the dark and hard armor that covered its back.

The guard quickly scurried away and grabbed his spear after flipping the Thief Bug while Aaron and I prepared our next attacks. A *Fireball* and *Power Shot* flew out and connected with that soft abdomen.

The Thief Bug wailed like a banshee for a few moments before becoming still. It was finally over. I opened my stats and checked the EXP we gained.

```
CURRENT EXP: 23345/46000        LEVEL: 19
           MAGE           FORMIDABLE
        HP: 1282/1282    MP: 400/472
                   STR: 11
                   AGI: 11
                   DEX: 20
                  VIT: 15 +2
                  INT: 27 +14
                 AVAILABLE: 0
```

The Male Thief Bug had granted 1200 EXP to each of us. I had gained around 200 EXP earlier from the Thief Bugs Aaron had dispatched on the way, for a total of 1400 EXP since my last check. I couldn't help but breathe out a sigh of relief.

The body of the Thief Bug remained there for a dozen seconds before slowly vanishing. I was curious how the guard would react to such a phenomenon. In fact, he was unfazed, as if it was normal.

A piece of its outer shell floated in place where its corpse once was. I rushed over to pick it up.

```
               CHITIN ARMGUARD*: VIT +7
        AN INCREDIBLY DURABLE PIECE OF EXOSKELETON.
```

I immediately thought of Mark, it was such a fine item for a tank. "Does anyone need it?" Aaron and Isabelle both shook their head. I put it away regretfully.

We huddled together as a group of four while we caught our breath. I couldn't help but look to the Guard and praise him, "We at least know their weakness thanks to you." The Male Thief Bug had a weakness: being flipped over onto its back. We would have to use their thick bodies and inflexible legs against them.

The guard held up his spear with a grim look on his face. The metal tip was bent to almost ninety degrees. It was obvious just how much force the Male Thief Bug put into that toss. Isabelle quickly realized her mistake and cast *Heal*, just in case he had suffered any injuries.

"Thank you," he replied.

"We still don't know your name," I said. It had gone past the point of awkward. He was risking his himself alongside us. I wanted to know his name at the very least.

"Lance," he responded coolly. We each took a turn introducing ourselves. I didn't expect Lance to fight without a spear, but he could at least help protect us. I pulled out the Stone Buckler from my inventory and passed it to him.

He took it with both hands and knew full well his job without needing an explanation. We continued deeper into the fourth floor of the sewer.

Our next encounter with a Male Thief Bug went infinitely better than the first. I cast *Shackle* to start the encounter and Lance rushed around to the backside of the Male Thief Bug. The shackles weren't meant to hinder it, but to give Lance an opportunity, and he grasped that opportunity flawlessly.

Lance charged the Male Thief Bug when it was half-way out of the shackle. He grasped the Stone Buckler with two-hands and held it fully in front of him. Despite noticing his charge, the Male Thief Bug had no way to intercept him. Half of its body remained trapped inside Shackle, fully stripping its ability to turn its burly body.

The Stone Buckler connecting with its left shoulder caused its pincered body to spin like a barrel. The Male Thief Bug was now laying flat on its back, tightly squished between *Shackle's* metal spikes. I looked on nervously as its legs flailed and kicked.

Thankfully, my fear dispersed soon after. Despite kicking and struggling against the spikes, it wasn't able to free itself, nor flip itself back over. Aaron and I made quick work of it. Its soft abdomen exploded a dozen seconds later before its body vanished.

We now had a solid strategy, and a relatively safe one at that. The previous anxiety abated ever so slightly as we moved room to room executing our foes with relative ease.

The stench continued to grow stronger and stronger as we neared closer to our final destination: the traps. We were just minutes away from our goal when we encountered something new.

We stepped over the boundary separating one chamber from another and found ourselves in a horror film. Every crevice of every wall, even the area where the column met the roof, was absolutely covered by egg sacs.

There must have been hundreds of eggs in this room alone, all of them still unhatched. An ominous feeling washed over me, and a reality that I should have realized ages ago came along with it.

We had yet to see a Female Thief Bug on our entire journey, and yet these egg caked walls were all I needed to see to know she existed.

"This… is disgusting." Isabelle started to dry heave through her mask.

"Yeah…" Even Aaron seemed revolted at the sight. It wouldn't have been so bad if the eggs weren't squirming and pulsating on the walls. There was a mushy sound that accompanied every movement.

"More than one insect usually hatches out of an egg… right?" I asked. The thought of hundreds of little baby Thief Bugs bursting from an egg caused me to shudder.

Isabelle grabbed her arms at my comment and shivered while making weird noises with her mouth. I felt the same way as she did.

"We should get rid of these." If we allowed them to hatch, there would be thousands more of these menaces running around. I prepared a fireball in my hand while waiting for Aaron's decision.

"Do it."

I launched the fireball like a firework to the top right corner of the chamber where it landed in the middle of a batch of writhing eggs sacs. Only seconds passed until there was a small combustion and the entire bunch of egg sacs lit fire and started to burn.

The underdeveloped Thief Bugs inside began to shriek and squeal while helplessly burning alive. They didn't have the power to burst from these eggs just yet, which was absolutely vital news for us.

Fire made quick work of them, and I continued to throw fireball after fireball. The smell of sewage faded until the entire chamber smelled like burning hair. Without anywhere for the smoke to go, it simply floated towards the ceiling where it lingered. The smoke entered through my mask and left a stench on the back of my throat that swallowing just wouldn't take away. I pulled out my water pouch and took several big chugs before replacing my mask.

Around five minutes passed before all the egg sacs were burnt beyond recognition. A large majority had slipped off the wall and fell into the sewage water where they floated, like little rafts of fire.

We waded forward and into the next room where the same sight greeted us. Every corner and every crevice was packed with more eggs. I quickly got to work.

Just as I had reached the halfway mark, a bug rushed through the entrance way from one room ahead and hissed at us. It was not a Thief Bug and also not a Male Thief Bug, the differences were glaringly obvious.

Lance didn't wait for any command and simply positioned himself in front of us. He held the Stone Buckler steadily.

Inspect!

FEMALE THIEF BUG* LEVEL: 24   **INSECT SHADOW**
HP: 17645   **MP: 15**

STR: 30

AGI: 20

DEX: 20

VIT: 30

INT: 3

THE MOST DANGEROUS FORM OF A THIEF BUG——HER SMALL AND NIMBLE BODY CONTAINS EXPLOSIVE POWER.

Its body was somewhere in size between a Thief Bug and Male Thief Bug. Its carapace was completely green.

"Really… really not good." I told them. I had never described a situation in this way before.

"That bad?"

"It's an Elite." Both Isabelle and Aaron knew what that meant: our *Shackle* and flip tactic would not work.

"How much HP?"

"…seventeen thousand." I mumbled out. The situation couldn't get much worse. We didn't have *Shackle* to retreat with if it came to that.

There was also the added problem that our strategy wouldn't even work. Her upper body was more compact and lower to the ground. As a side effect of that, her legs stuck out further from her body and would definitely provide more balance.

"This...maybe we should retreat." Isabelle suggested. It was looking like the best solution currently.

Before we could even make that decision the Female Thief Bug was upon us. Lance was the only one prepared for the sonic-like speed. He leaned forward awkwardly to compensate for her small size and the two collided like raging bucks.

The Stone Buckler held strong despite her onslaught, but I could see Lance's bulging forearms quivering. Retreat was impossible, and we all knew it after witnessing her speed.

We moved to encircle her, as well as distance ourselves as much as possible. Once in position, Aaron and I went on the offensive. Just after launching our first volley of attacks, Lance fell to one knee. The Stone Buckler slammed into his chest as he could no longer bear the weight.

This entire scenario played out in just seconds. Lance was by no means small. Even putting all of his weight as well as the assistance of gravity, he could not overpower this bug the size of a poodle.

Off balance and out of strength, Lance tipped backwards with the Stone Buckler on top of him. The Female Thief Bugs mandibles were just inches away from his extended leg. There was no doubt her strength would allow her to cut it clean off.

It was then that a green arrow whistled through the air and pierced directly into the monster's exposed abdomen. The arrow burrowed inside with no resistance, like a hot knife cutting through butter. That wasn't the end of it.

Immediately after Aaron's *Power Shot*, a spike of ice jutted from beneath the Female Thief Bug and pierced her. The icy tip dug in several inches and locked her in place. Ice started to spread from the wound and creep along the underside of her body. I had cast *Glacial Spike* on a whim, hoping it would do something to help salvage the situation.

This was my first time using the spell, as I deemed it inferior to *Fireball*. It cost more MP to cast and also had a longer cast time. But I was glad I gave it a chance here, the fact that the damage came from below was crucial.

The Female Thief Bug let out an eardrum-shattering screech and tilted its head directly at the sky. All of its focus immediately left Lance as it forcefully turned its body around. The glacier embedded in its abdomen broke off with a crack and then quickly dissolved.

The Female Thief Bug looked directly at me. She spread her mandibles wide and a sound like gargling water came out.

"Move!" Aaron yelled at me. When I understood what was happening, it was already too late.

A greenish liquid sprayed from her mouth and towards my direction. The only reaction I could manage was covering my face with my hands. I felt the liquid collide with my open palms and arms while a good portion of it was caught by *Energy Shield* and floated in the air.

I nearly fainted from the intense pain. My melting skin was sending electrical shocks to my brain causing me to scream out in agony. *Energy Shield* flickered and sizzled as my Mana drained rapidly.

> ### You have been afflicted with *Deadly Poison*

The initial damage wasn't high, but my health was dropping at an alarming rate. A third of my health was gone within one second and my decision-making was being hindered by the mind-numbing pain.

It took everything I had to simply keep myself from falling over. I started to vomit. Another second passed and I had a moment of clarity. *Am I going to die?* It was the only clear thought that came through my fogged brain.

My vision started to black as if curtains were closing around my eyes. The only sound I could hear was a constant ringing. Death was coming.

Then there was a moment of relief, a familiar feeling washed over me. I was healed. Isabelle had healed me just before my health hit zero. That moment of relief allowed me to hear the tail end of what Aaron was yelling.

"—*nacea!*"

…*nacea? Panacea?* A bolt of lightning struck my brain. I thought the word and a *Panacea* entered my hand. I didn't hesitate to use it.

> ### Curing Abnormal Status Effects.
> ### You are no longer afflicted with Deadly Poison.

Instant relief. My brain could finally think clearly again. I checked my status.

```
CURRENT EXP: 37945/46000        LEVEL: 19
            MAGE          FORMIDABLE
        HP: 145/1282     MP: 0/472
                    STR: 11
                    AGI: 11
                    DEX: 20
                    VIT: 15 +2
                    INT: 27 +14
                AVAILABLE: 0
```

The next tick of poison would have killed me despite Isabelle's heal. I pulled a White potion and Blue potion from my inventory before chugging them down. The White potion provided an immediate buffer. The second *Heal* came a moment later, fully capping my HP.

It felt like an eternity to me, but less than five seconds had actually passed. I couldn't help but thank whatever entity allowed me and Isabelle to meet. Her thoughtfulness to precast heal on me had saved my life. I could never repay her, but I was sure as hell not going to tell her that.

The Female Thief Bug was still at the spot from which she had spit out *Deadly Poison*. It was obvious from her lack of movement the amount of pain she was in. Aaron's arrow remained embedded in her abdomen with only the feathered end sticking out. The gash from *Glacial Spike* had fully thawed and a white goop was leaking into the murky water.

My nerves were high as we didn't know how many more times she could cast *Deadly Poison*. I didn't want to feel such an excruciating pain ever again.

"It's shadow property." I hollered at Isabelle. This was an important detail I should have disclosed to her earlier. She nodded with a serious expression and began chanting.

By now, Lance had climbed to his feet and positioned himself behind the Female Thief Bug. He had fully witnessed my endeavor with *Deadly Poison*. If inflicted, he would die without a doubt.

The four of us were fully committed to this fight, we would hold nothing back, it was win or die for us all. I cast *Glacial Spike* while Aaron nocked back a *Power Shot*. Time seemed to slow down as we cast in unison.

The soundless ice spike pierced through the murky water and into the Female Thief Bug's abdomen. It entered her open wound and dug several inches deeper than the previous one had. A frost began to spread to her underbelly.

The Female Thief Bug reacted with a scream, and Aaron was prepared for it. Almost the exact time she raised her head and screeched in pain his *Power Shot* pierced her exposed neck. The arrow disappeared inside and even continued into her chest.

It was then that the Female Thief Bug focused on Aaron. That gurgling sound began to surface from her spread mandibles. She was preparing another *Deadly Poison*.

Unfortunately for her, Lance would have nothing to do with it. The flat side of the Stone Buckler came down hard on her backside. Her already unsteady legs buckled as she dropped completely to her stomach. The *Glacial Spike* still embedded in her abdomen pushed all the way through and out the other side.

Even this was not enough to kill her. Her legs scurried under the murky water as she frantically tried to raise her mouth above water level. Try as she might, she could not shoot the *Deadly Poison* prepared in her throat.

The room was forcibly silenced in the next moment. Isabelle finally released her cupped hands and raised them to the sky. A transcendent voice escaped her lips. "*Magnus Exorcism!*"

A blindingly white light illuminated the entire room and engulfed the Female Thief Bug. It didn't even have time to react before it caught fire. To my surprise, *Glacial Spike* didn't melt in reaction. The blinding white fire was a type of Holy Fire. It didn't burn hot at all.

Under the intense holy fire, the Female Thief Bugs originally green carapace turned white as snow. Its body smoldered as the screeching from its throat grew quieter and quieter. It stopped flailing and struggling just as the ground effect from Magnus Exorcism ended. Its bleached corpse started to fade away.

> CONGRATULATIONS! YOU HAVE REACHED LEVEL 20. AS A REWARD FOR LEVELING UP, YOU HAVE BEEN GRANTED THREE STAT POINTS!

I opened my stats. I had gained thirty HP for leveling up, as well as 8 MP. I hesitated before adding another three points to INT. It was something I had been planning even before coming to Eastrath. The immediate damage boost was nothing to scoff at either.

```
         CURRENT EXP: 545/49000 LEVEL: 20
              MAGE            FORMIDABLE
         HP: 1312/1312    MP: 120/480
                     STR: 11
                     AGI: 11
                     DEX: 20
                     VIT: 15 +2
                     INT: 30 +14
```

```
                    AVAILABLE: 0
```

The amount of EXP the single Female Thief Bug provided was mind boggling, each of us receiving 8,600 EXP. I was once again reminded why they were called Elites. I turned my focus to the fading corpse just in time to see the spoils of victory. Aaron and Isabelle were waiting for me there.

```
   BOOK OF ADVANCED INSPECT***: ONLY USABLE IF INSPECT LV.
                    1 HAS BEEN LEARNED.
   CASTING INSPECT NOW BROADCASTS RECEIVED INFORMATION TO
                    ALL PARTY MEMBERS.
```

I clawed at the air like a fiend before snatching it up and gripping it tightly to my chest. *This... this is what I'm talking about...* I learned it straight away.

```
┌─────────────────────────────────────────────────────┐
│                                                       │
│   CRUDE VENOM GLAND*: POISON RESISTANCE +10%          │
│   WEARING THIS NEAR YOUR HEART SEEMS TO MAKE YOUR BLOOD│
│                  FLOW SMOOTHLY.                       │
│                                                       │
└─────────────────────────────────────────────────────┘
```

To be honest... it looked disgusting. But after experiencing a deadly poison first hand, I couldn't help but want it.

Aaron and Isabelle noticed my shivering before Isabelle passed it in my direction.

"Are you sure?" I asked.

Isabelle pretended to vomit, "the texture... SO GROSS." She didn't want anything to do with it.

Aaron had just as much use for it as me, which would hopefully be never. The last item floating there was a ring.

```
┌─────────────────────────────────────────────────────┐
│                                                       │
│   SKULL RING**: HOLY SPELL AFFECTS +5%; REDUCED DAMAGE│
│          RECEIVED FROM SHADOW PROPERTY BY 5%.         │
│   A RING OF CRUDE CRAFTSMANSHIP. THE PURIFIED SKULL ATOP│
│                ITS BAND LOOKS MENACING.               │
│                                                       │
└─────────────────────────────────────────────────────┘
```

"Yes? Yes? Yes? Yes?" Isabelle started to chant, before snatching it and slipping it on her finger. All the loot had been cleanly distributed.

The high of receiving two new items faded quickly. I didn't want to eat a meal down here, but my brush with death earlier left me famished. Before I could do that though, I had something to take care of.

Chapter 17: Lady Briele

I resumed blasting fireballs at the remaining egg sacs hanging around the room. Once they were dispatched, I found the nearest clean column and leaned against it before receiving my food pouch.

I was happy that I hadn't fallen over earlier, else everything inside would have been coated with a layer of sewage. My hand fumbled inside before pulling out an apple, which I happily munched on.

The others saw me eating and joined in. Even Lance looked at us expectantly. With our current situation, we had more than enough food to spare, and I happily shared what was available.

Despite the circumstances, it was the tastiest apple I'd ever eaten. Maybe it was because my mouth and nose had grown accustom to the constant sewage air. I chose to believe the apple was just that good.

We scarfed down our food without delay and assessed the situation.

"The traps are located in the next chamber," Lance said. Just through the next opening was a chamber many times larger than any we walked through previously, and with good reason.

The traps were a series of underwater grates with several layers. All of the sewage water collected here and passed through them. I was hesitant to move on, but our destination was just in the next room. We had to at least assess the situation.

We walked forward in a tight group, Isabelle's fairy floating just above us to light the way. I poked my head through and took note of the terrain. The area was completely open with no walls, only innumerable columns reached from the floor to the ceiling.

The wall across from us was the same distance away as if we traveled three rooms. I looked left and then right, I couldn't see a wall in either direction. The traps in question were on our left, somewhere around two-hundred feet away.

The darkness made it impossible to accurately judge the danger level. I beckoned to Isabelle and her fairy slowly flew into the room. I couldn't see anything out of the ordinary at all. We stepped through as a group.

Only after entering inside did we realize the gravity of the situation. An uncountable number of beady little eyes stared at us. The roof above us for as far as I could see was caked with layer upon layer of Thief Bugs.

There were so many in fact, that they were crawling over each other.

"Guys…" I was scared, rooted to the spot, but still managed to nudge my head towards the ceiling. Aaron, Lance, and Isabelle looked up with me. I felt Aaron's hand grip my shoulder and then pull backwards slightly. It was time to leave.

I lifted my foot and began to back away when a screech rang out. It was one at first, and then it was hundreds, and then thousands. The silent room came alive. The sound of hissing was nearly buried by the sound of their little legs scurrying over each other.

My head instantly became tingly as if ten thousand ants were crawling through my hair. That was when I saw it. The sudden commotion having attracted its attention, its burly body skittered from behind a column.

It was a Thief Bug a head taller than a Male. Originally, it would have been hard to make it out in this darkness. But its entire carapace was coated in gold, causing the fairy's light to reflect off it perfectly. It basically glowed in the dark.

That alone wouldn't have been enough to make me panic. No, it was the red skull resting above its head. "R-rrrun…" My voice was quavering. I'm sure that Aaron could feel my body shaking through the hand on my shoulder.

I completely threw away the thought of retreating slowly. We turned as a group and ran as fast as we could in this ankle-high water.

It sounded like a storm forming behind us as every Thief Bug began to move. They scurried down the ceiling and through the opening before spreading out along the walls and roof. All I could hear was the droning of their movements.

Isabelle and Lance were confused by my visceral reaction, but they probably hadn't seen the boss. Aaron might not have seen it either, but he had felt the trembling of my body in that moment. It was serious shit.

We managed to stay ahead of the swarm of Thief Bugs only due to the fact that we needed to cover less ground. While we could drive through the water in a straight line, they had to crawl along the entire length of the wall and roof. This essentially doubled the distance they needed to travel.

Despite this big advantage, the droning sound following us was only a room back and showed no signs of stopping its assault. A distance we originally spent thirty minutes traveling took us only five. That's just how fast we were moving.

"I really hope your subordinate left the door unlocked." Our lives depended on it, literally. My lungs were burning and the soles of my feet were blistering and tearing. We had been walking in sewage water for so long that the skin up to my ankle was thoroughly pruned.

We finally saw it, the last twist in the tunnel that we exited from. In just a few moments we would be traveling on dry ground. That alone would boost our speed tremendously.

We rounded the corner like professional athletes and rushed upwards. The level of the water quickly dropped until we were merely trotting through a puddle. Our feet splashed harder than before as droplets of water assaulted my chest and face.

The sound of our splashed feet drowned out the sound of our pursuers. We turned the final bend and could see the open door to floor three. We only needed to get through there and the nightmare was over. At least for the moment.

We rushed up to the gate and quickly passed through the doorway. All four of us were breathing hard, we were on our last legs. While most of the Thief Bugs would be stopped here, a good portion would squeeze through the gateway to chase us.

Even worse, there was no way to lock it and I worried the sheer amount would force the unlocked door open. Lance closed the door and started to wrap the chain around it, but there was no way to lock it in place.

I suddenly had a bright idea as I rushed to his side. "Hold the chain for me." I looked in my inventory and pulled out two items that I had carried with me from the beginning.

Broken Short Sword.
A useless scrap of metal.

As well as:

Dagger of Ghoul: Poisons target.
A dagger made from the humerus bone of a Ghoul. You can feel your life draining by just holding it. HP -1 for every 10 seconds it's equipped.

Lance aligned the two chain ends for me and I slid the broken short sword inside. I did the same for the Dagger of Ghoul. "This should keep it from opening, at least."

My idea didn't end there. I pulled out my water pouch and started to pour water on the chain. "Move back," I said. Lance stepped away from the door as I began to chant *Glacial Spike*. They looked at me with curiosity. The droning sound of Thief Bugs was coming closer. There was probably less than ten seconds before they would reach us.

A *Glacial Spike* appeared out of thin air and pressed into the dangling chain. Within seconds, the water that I had poured froze solid, locking the Dagger and Short Sword in place.

"Add some more water to it!" I urged them. By now, they understood what I was doing. They uncorked their pouches and began to pour water onto the chain. As soon as the water touched the growing block of ice it added to the effect of the spell.

When their pouches were empty, a reasonably thick column of ice reached all the way to the floor completely encased the chain and door frame. Even without the chain, the sheer amount of ice should keep the door from opening.

The droning was now just on the other side of this concrete barrier. The Thief Bugs were so numerous that even the walls and floors started to vibrate. I looked at the singular route to our side: the exit for the barely flowing sewage water.

I would leave nothing to chance. I cast another *Glacial Spike*. A four foot section of murky liquid completely froze over, there was absolutely no way for them to reach our side.

"Phew." I wiped my hand with my brow. "Let's get out of here." We turned and walked briskly away.

Fresh air had never tasted so good. I felt like I had aged ten years during that mission, and yet only four hours passed since we originally walked through this rusted gate.

We were finally out of danger, but our mission was not over. The traps were still clogged and an even bigger problem lurked beneath Egestor.

"What caused you to react that way back there?" Aaron asked. Isabelle also looked at me intently.

"There was a boss down there," I said.

"Are you sure it was a boss?" Isabelle asked.

"Do you remember the red skulls during the welcoming party?"

"Yeah." They both responded in unison.

"It had a red skull above its head. I saw it, for sure. Absolutely. One-hundred percentoo," I mumbled.

Aaron put his hand on his chin, it was textbook 'say no more I'm thinking'.

Isabelle was still interested though, "What did it look like?"

"It was a big golden-looking bug."

"Was it big?"

378

"Yep."

"How big?"

"Big."

"Like this big?" She held out her hands.

"Bigger."

"How about THIIIIIS big?" She stretched them even further.

I was starting to get a headache. "Bit more." Despite a slight sense I was being pestered, her irreverent attitude made me feel as if things were back to normal.

Glasses was waiting for us when we arrived at the mission hall. He couldn't even wait for us to get inside before asking questions, "Is it taken care of?"

"Let's talk inside." We sat down in a far off corner where no one would bother us and carefully explained the situation.

"There's a boss below Egestor? Ahhhhh" He gripped the bridge of his nose and furiously began to rub it. "And you're sure?" he double-checked.

"Absolutely." We gave him all the information we had. The levels of each mob we encountered, their stats and hp, the egg sacs.

"This is serious then." He paused. "Since you accomplished what I asked, you'll all be receiving the B rank as promised."

"What of the boss?" I asked; we all wanted to know the answer to that question.

"From what you've explained, this would be an A rank mission even without the boss. With the boss...I'm not sure exactly how we quantify this level of difficulty. I have to take this information back to my superiors: expect something big in the coming days."

We nodded in understanding. Glasses couldn't make the sole decision on how to solve this problem. He would need to pass this information along. From there they would speak to Egestor royalty and decide on a course of action.

All we could do was wait and find out what the resulting mission might be. Glasses told us it might be as little as three days or as long as a week.

With that we stood up to leave, making sure to shake hands with Lance, who had made all the difference and earned our respect. He remained in the mission hall with Glasses.

As we left, I felt like a massive weight had been lifted off my shoulders. We took our time walking back to the inn.

My mind was now free to wander, and that wandering was pre-occupied by this incredibly uncomfortable feeling in my feet. My footwear was drenched and squishing. I was aching.

We sneaked up the inn stairs on Aaron's orders and regrouped in his room. Once inside I stripped off my shoes and looked at my pruned feet. They were white and had bits of pieces scraped off completely. There was a bit of blood mixed in.

I couldn't help myself and turned to Isabelle. "Hey," I said.

"What?"

"Mind casting a *Heal* on my feet?"

"What?"

"Please."

"Oh." She could see my point.

The feeling was wonderful, like a massage. While my feet remained pale, the open wounds on them closed up. I was no longer in fear of an infection. Isabelle took off her own boots and did the same, and then treated Aaron's feet as well.

We were ahead of schedule by quite a margin. In less than a week we climbed from F rank to B rank. The three of us, however, agreed not to take on any new missions until we heard the verdict on the sewer situation.

I missed having a tank. In convincing myself we three could progress in the game without one, I underestimated the value a good tank brought to the party. It was a weird thing to say: you don't know you need a tank until you really need a tank. We were too used to dispatching monsters quickly, or relying on *Shackle* to carry us.

It became apparent that monsters would keep getting stronger, tankier, faster, and more deadly. The list of problems went on and on. It all pointed to fights that would one day wipe us all out. Even though the Female Thief Bug fight had lasted less than thirty seconds, I nearly died in that time frame.

I was lying on Aaron's bed looking straight up at the ceiling, "Hey. I've been thinking. Let's beg Jason and Mark to come back." Our five-man team was what I wanted again.

"Jason left two days ago," Isabelle said. "He came to see me and say goodbye."

"What about Mark?"

"He's been drinking himself into a stupor every night."

"Will you ask him?" I looked expectantly at Isabelle.

"Do you think I didn't try already? He's always been this stubborn, if he says no then he really means it."

I crawled out of bed and made for the door. "Well, I'll see you both in a few days." I tried my best to hide it, but I was still shaken from that near death experience. I stood out in the hall for a minute and tried to calm my unsteady hand. I hoped the tremor would stop soon.

When I returned to my room I opened my skill book and looked at *Glacial Spike*.

```
GLACIAL SPIKE
CAST TIME: 2 SECONDS
MP COST: 7
DISTANCE: 7 METERS
SUMMON A SHARD OF ICE TO PIERCE YOUR ENEMIES FROM BE-
LOW.
LV. 1 20/100
```

I had obtained both *Arcane Missiles* and *Glacial Spike* at the same time. In my stupidity I decided to compare the two just by their MP to damage value without really thinking of the pros and cons of each skill.

My ranking put *Arcane Missiles* as my number one single target spell, followed by *Fireball*, and then *Glacial Spike*. For AOE I had *Meteor Storm*. Not only had I not encountered a fire monster, I had been too stubborn to consider using *Glacial Spike*.

I neglected the existence of Status effects. While its cast time was longer, it had utility that *Fireball* did not. Then too, there was the existence of elemental affinities, which meant some mobs would be especially vulnerable to cold.

This was the first and only time I would forgive myself for such a slip up. I blamed the cheat-like ability *Shackle*. I hadn't needed any extra utility because of it. This mission had taught me *Shackle* was not infallible.

I spent the next four days doing my best to clear my mind of the negative thoughts I was having. It was incredibly hard to forget that feeling, that moment of clarity just before death. I spent the majority of my time in bed.

Not because I was depressed, but because I was truly enjoying the stress-free time I had left. I had experienced enough stress for a lifetime in just four hours. I deserved a break. There was good news to be had as well.

Glasses had gotten in touch, we were to meet him tonight just after dark. It seemed a consensus had been made about the boss. Not only that, it hadn't rained in the last four days. Pair that with the rising temperature: the sewer should be mostly dried out by now.

I couldn't say for sure if that was good or bad for us. But not having to stand in ankle high water for hours was definitely a morale booster. I decided to enjoy my last few free remaining hours with a nap.

I woke to the sound of knocking. It was Aaron and Isabelle waiting outside my door. I rubbed the crust from my eyes and had them wait while I dressed. We were out the inn door and on our way after.

The tremor in my hand had subsided over these four days. I spent a lot of time thinking about my mistakes. It was a wakeup call: I wasn't nearly as safe here as I believed myself to be. Even Veronica's death hadn't shaken me from my conviction that this was what I was good at. That this world was meant for me. But the poison attack proved that I couldn't afford to be complacent.

We walked side by side to the mission hall without a clue as to what the verdict would be.

There was no doubt the mission rank would be A. The question was, would they make an exception for us? If not, there was nothing we could do about it.

As we approached the mission hall, we noticed the security was tight. There were four guards standing atop the stairs completely blocking the entrance. A man was in front of them arguing, "The Mission Hall shouldn't be closed just yet, let me in!" He barked.

"It's closed." They gave him a curt reply but that didn't seem to be enough for him. He continued to bark and nip at their heels.

One of the guards was fed up with his yapping and suddenly gripped the man's shoulder hard, "There are several important figures inside, shall we go in together and ask them what your punishment should be?"

The expression on the man's face fell. "No, no that's fine. I'll just come back tomorrow." He lifted both hands in forfeit. The guard squeezed a bit harder on his shoulder before pushing him away. The man yelped in pain as he staggered down.

The same man noticed us ascending the stairs just as he was leaving. It seemed he felt like watching a show at our expense as I noticed his grin out of the corner of my eyes. He crossed his arms in expectation. If he was looking forward to our being forced back, he was in for a disappointment.

The guards merely split apart and allowed us entry inside. They were expecting our arrival. I looked back at the man and our eyes locked. He snorted in anger before disappearing into the night.

I was surprised at the sheer amount of people gathered inside the mission hall. Judging from their clothing, there was royalty and Adventurers mixed in together. The lively atmosphere suggested we were late to the party.

Glasses spotted us before making his way through the crowd, "These are the three I told you about." He introduced us to various people.

I felt like an animal being showed off. The Adventurers and royals alike looked in our direction with curiosity. Some didn't bother looking for more than a moment before turning away.

My eyes traced the group that had now spread out in front of me, as if we were supposed to put on a grand spectacle for them to enjoy. I was taken aback momentarily. The man and woman from the Naga invasion were among the people here.

Glasses interrupted the viewing gallery, "As I've said before. These are the three who originally discovered the boss. They are currently Rank B. Since the mission is rank A, the mission hall will leave the decision of their participation up to the Adventurer group."

I understood what was happening now. This was our tryout so to speak. Glasses looked at me as if to say 'go along with it'.

"What levels are you? Classes too?" One of the adventurers asked.

We went one at a time explaining our level and class. There was a bit of discussion afterwards.

"I say we leave them."

"Me as well." More and more people continued to express their desire to go without us. It looked like we were going to be sitting it out.

"I think we should take them." It was a female voice. It was the woman from the beach who spoke up for us.

"What's the point? They're too low level."

"I just think it couldn't hurt to have three more people." It seemed she had considerable sway in the group. People who were disinterested before changed their tunes. "What do you think Bryan?"

"If Lady Briele is fine with it, I have no objection." Bryan said. Soon it was clear that she alone had managed to secure our positions into the raid.

In my excitement I couldn't help but speak out, "Thank you everyone. We won't let you down." I could see a few of the adventurers' chuckle before going back to ignoring our existence.

Lady Briele spoke to me through telepathy. *Don't misunderstand... I didn't suggest taking you because I think you'll be of significant help. I just thought it would be a good experience for you. Underestimating a boss will get you killed.*

The 'meeting' had doubled as a party and most of the Adventurers were doing their best to network with the royalty located here. Egestor was a goliath on the continent of Eastrath. Getting on their good side would provide many benefits. The party only wrapped up around midnight.

It was only after the party that I understood what Lady Briele meant. We joined the fifteen man group and could finally see their levels. Almost every single party member had a level in the 40s, the only exception to that was a level 38 healer.

I felt my cheeks flush with embarrassment on thinking back to my 'we won't let you down' exclamation.

The raid planned to set out first thing tomorrow morning and attempt to reclaim the sewers in a single day. The logistics had all been taken care of, and the party was well balanced between support and damage. The two highest levels were the tank and Lady Briele.

Given the lack of information on the boss, a simple strategy was developed. The tank would engage the boss supported by healers. Everyone else would keep their distance while the boss's abilities were discovered. Only after that would the group move in as a whole with a real attempt to defeat it.

It was a good plan, but absolutely not a fail proof one. Many of the most dangerous boss mechanics only activated after the boss fell below a certain HP threshold. Valkyrie Geirdriful was one such example. She *enraged* at low health increasing her killing power several times over.

"We should take tomorrow as a learning experience," I said. Isabelle and Aaron looked at me as if to say 'where did that come from?' "Lady Briele said that to me."

"Telepathy?" asked Aaron.

"Yep."

I slept well and arrived fully awake at the mission hall. I wasn't the first to arrive, and also wasn't the last. We waited as a group for around fifteen minutes before everyone assembled.

Just before we left I got to see a bit into the Adventurers' culture. The main tank did a gear check and required everyone to make sure they were bringing everything required to successfully defeat the boss and complete the raid.

Once the gear check was completed, a consumable check was called. All in all we spent around ten minutes double checking to make sure everything was in order.

There would be no guards coming with us this time, and we found the gate to the sewer still open when we arrived. After four days of no rain and high temperatures, the murky river was nowhere to be seen.

The smell was mild with no sewage water present. The only difference was how much hotter the tunnels were.

Aaron, Isabelle and I made sure to stay well out of the main groups' way. We followed about five feet back so as to not cause any confrontation. It was smooth sailing all the way down.

We were at the threshold to the fourth floor when I heard a voice from the front, "Take a look at this." I could see he was fiddling with the chain lock. Specifically, the one I hammered the dagger and broken sword into.

"Was this your doing?" Bryan looked back.

"Yes, we didn't have much of a choice."

He pulled the items out. "Do you want them?"

"It's alright." I didn't really care for them. One was literally a piece of scrap metal and the other slowly drained your life force. If a regular person decided to use it they would fall ill.

When we reached the final twist of the route and officially rested on the fourth floor, Bryan called us up to the front. "Is it alright if I ask you to guide us there?" With no guards, we three were the only ones who had been here before.

Our previous experience left us hesitant. Aaron beckoned to Isabelle to summon her fairy. She sent it flying out into the room and only after I could see the walls and ceiling were free of Thief Bugs did I agree to move forward.

The chambers took on a completely new appearance despite being exactly the same. The difference between being filled with water and not was like night and day.

"Ohh, what's that called? I've never seen it before." The level 38 healer looked at Isabelle. Apparently, her fairy was something out of the ordinary.

"Uhm, it's called Hierophant's Helper."

"Do you mind if I see its details?"

"How do I do that?"

I continued to walk forward while Isabelle stayed with the level 38 healer. From their conversation it seemed possible to let other people see your abilities in detail. I managed to zone out of the talking behind me and focused only on what was in front.

I purposely walked at a slow pace. The pain from *Deadly Poison* was fresh in my mind and I refused to be ambushed by anything. It took about twenty minutes before we came across the room that we first encountered egg sacs in.

When Hierophant's Helper entered the room I shivered in disgust. There were now egg sacs completely covering the floor. There was no more water, and therefore nothing stopping the females from laying them everywhere.

"You should see this." We called Bryan and let him look for himself.

He looked over the room in contemplation, "How much further?"

"It's just four more rooms ahead."

"Alright, good job. We'll take it from here." I quite liked him as a person. He spoke to us as equals and didn't push his authority as a leader. We moved to the back. I made sure to grab Isabelle on our way.

Only so many people could fit in the chamber doorway so I couldn't see their preferred method of destroying the eggs. I could smell it though. They chose to burn them as well.

Whatever spell they used burned much more intensely than my *Fireball*. Black smoke billowed through the room and entered my lungs. For a while, the only thing I could smell and taste was char.

When it was our turn to walk through I saw the blacked floor caked with soot. There wasn't even a fragment of egg sac remaining. All of it had been scorched to nothingness.

Hierophant's Helper stayed at the front and continued to assist the raid while we settled for the light of a fireball in the back. They made quick work of the remaining three rooms and soon we were all huddled just outside the final chamber.

"I will enter first and assess the situation. If the boss isn't anywhere in sight then we will clear an area and slowly search." Bryan said. He was the first to walk through and into the trap area. He was the main tank of this raid.

Just like we experienced, his presence alerted the thousands upon thousands of Thief Bugs sitting on the ceiling and column corners. The scurrying and writhing caused my hair to stand on end.

Unlike us, he didn't show any sign of fear or hesitation. He looked all around the chamber carefully in search of the boss. He continued to walk further towards the opposite wall, only stopping mid way. In that position there were no blind spots. Only the areas just outside the light range of Hierophant's Helper remained unsearchable.

I was confused where his confidence came from. I refused to believe his skin was more resilient than metal. Even if it was, how long could he hold up if he was engulfed by Thief Bugs?

It wouldn't be long before I found out. There was a screech, and like an exploding dam, Thief Bugs rushed from all directions and towards him. They came down the columns and even a few flew through the air in his direction.

I was expecting to see him fight for his life or run in our direction for assistance, but he didn't. Instead, he raised both of his arms to his side and then shouted. It was a deep bellow that shook the very foundation of the sewers.

Every Thief Bug even remotely close to him was sent flying backwards. They smacked into walls, columns, and even each other before lying completely motionless. Their innards started to seep through their cracked joints in a liquefied mess.

The sheer vibration from his shout had turned their insides to mush. Those that were far enough away to not instantly die scurried deeper into the darkness. The only problem now was the floor was covered with an endless number of corpses.

"Briele, will you come in here and blow these away please?" Bryan asked.

"Can't Luther do it?" she complained.

"I asked you nicely didn't I? Please?"

"Fine."

"Thank you." As she stepped over the boundary and began chanting, I could see in his eyes that Bryan was infatuated with her. Moments later a strong breeze that came from seemingly nowhere rushed down the hall.

I could hear the Thief Bug corpses being blown away like leaves as the wind traveled onwards into the distance. "All done." She wiped her hands together.

"Alright, everyone in." We made our way through the barrier and regrouped inside. "Where did you see it?" Bryan asked me.

I looked to the left, "About five Columns that way."

He nodded, "Stay loose everyone." We spread out to minimize any AoE attack and started to move. We didn't have to walk long before encountering our first Male Thief Bug, and then our first Female Thief Bug. They were swatted away like flies by this raid.

"You guys did pretty good to deal with these without a tank." Bryan complimented us from the front. The bugs started to show up more frequently and I realized we had only seen the tip of the iceberg.

A Female Thief Bug managed to spray *Deadly Poison* onto Bryan. The scene I was expecting didn't come at all. "Ouch, this actually really stings. I heard you got sprayed by this too? It must have hurt like a sonuva bitch."

I still didn't quite understand why he was being so friendly with me. But I knew that Lance had gone into much greater detail about the previous mission with Glasses than we did. Somehow I had won over his favor, or maybe it was something Briele had said to him.

We continued to explore but didn't manage to find the boss. There was nothing saying it couldn't move around freely in this entire floor. If that was the case, we could spend hours looking for it. I worked up the courage to make a suggestion.

"Maybe you should torture one of the Females?" I asked. They were killing them so quickly that they didn't have a chance to screech. From the bugs perspective we were silent assassins infiltrating their lair. "I saw the boss just after we killed a Female Thief Bug. She called out multiple times before dying."

Bryan seemed to accept my idea without much resistance.

When we encountered the next Female Thief Bug, he put my idea to the test. She came in confident but found herself skewered on his sword. He pierced her directly through the underside of her chest and kept her there.

She started to gurgle up *Deadly Poison*, which he promptly blocked with his shield. "So you don't wanna cry for me, eh?" He started to saw his arm back and forth, tearing and twisting the sword into her guts.

I was deriving pleasure from this inhumane torture. *Was I a bad person? No way, these things nearly killed me.* The bugs had sub-human intelligence stat. They were dumber than even goblins.

He continued to 'play' with her on his sword until she finally let out her dying cries. A mucus filled screech echoed down the pathway and into the darkness. The Female Thief Bug died and then disappeared from his blade.

The only negative emotion I had while watching that entire sequence was that I received no EXP. The difference in our levels was too much. The Female Thief Bug dropped only one item that Bryan pocketed away.

I didn't have any qualms with the raid leader taking the loot. He had disposed of her all by himself. And maybe there was a system for sharing it out in the end. There was probably a great market for good low level gear, especially on Eastrath.

"Eh?" He stopped wiping the guts from his blade and hands before looking up with great concentration. "Get ready," he said. I couldn't see anything, and from the looks of their faces, most people couldn't.

This must have been another benefit of having a good tank. His battle sense alone detected an enemy. And within moments a glowing bug appeared from the darkness, the red skull still above its head.

The raid boss continued to walk towards our tank. Its antennae brushed and swept along the sewer floor. I finally got a better look at it as fully entered the range of Hierophant's Helper.

The monster was larger than a Male Thief Bug, but its body was more proportioned and balanced, similar to the Female. The back of its carapace was as high off the ground as a grown man's waist.

The carapace was not actually glowing, but was instead coated in a metallic gold color. Even its pincers shined golden in the light. We backed away as a group, all focused on observing its movement. Even just watching the boss walking towards us could provide information on its mobility, speed, and attack range.

We continued to back away as the golden bug advanced in our direction. It never took its attention off the sewer floor below as the antennae made a meticulous sweep. It came to an abrupt stop when it reached the tank's previous position. The floor there was splattered with the goopy insides of the dead female.

Remaining stationary there for several moments, the golden bug finally raised its head. Its antennae left the floor and swayed in the air. Eyes that seemed completely black suddenly turned a bright red. Whatever was originally covering them had simply peeled back.

The enemy boss raised its head and let out a screech that continued to rise in intensity and pitch. Despite seeing the vibrations of its throat, the sound became so high that I couldn't hear it anymore. There was a scurrying from behind it as four more Thief Bugs joined its side.

Their carapaces were purple in color and they had what looked to be antlers coming from atop their head.

"Stick to the plan. I'll take the boss and you guys can deal with the rest. Nothing's changed."

To my mind, the only issue was that the raid had only designated a single back-up tank.

"Jericho, can you handle the two on the right?" Lady Briele yelled out.

"Can do!" The second tank moved into a forward position, he was ready to intercept two of the mini-bosses.

Lady Briele continued to shout orders, "The rest of us will focus our fire power on the left two. Pull them back so Bryan has enough space to control the boss." With a basic plan set in motion, we were ready to start the raid.

Bryan moved forward as the Thief Bugs came towards us. He cleanly intercepted the boss while Jericho caught the two rushing from the right. The two on the left were about to dog pile Bryan when Lady Briele pulled the both of them in our direction.

"Get ready!"

I cast *Inspect*, knowing that with the advanced upgrade the rest of my group would get to share the result.

```
ROYAL THIEF BUG** LEVEL: 36       INSECT  EARTH
            HP: 55221             MP: 115
                    STR: 50
                    AGI: 20
                    DEX: 30
                    VIT: 55
                    INT: 25
A ROYAL GUARD AMONG THIEF BUGS. TRUSTED AID AND PRO-
            TECTOR OF THE TRUE KING.
```

Reading the monsters stats made me so incredibly happy that we didn't run into one of these monstrosities on our first trip. Hopefully, the information they could now see was valuable to everyone, especially the affinity of Earth and the relatively weak AGI score.

With no tanks available to hold the two left royals down, the most agile damage dealers were forced to tangle with them. Regardless of the almost ten level differences, these monsters were two-star elites. Their attacks were nothing to scoff at.

Every time their pincers chomped down in an attempt to latch onto an arm or leg, it sounded as if a hydraulic press was smashing down. Even standing twenty feet away in relative safety, each snap caused my heart to skip. I was nervous for the three members in close combat.

Arrows, spells, daggers and swords bashed and battered into their purple carapace. Even their impressive defense and high vitality wasn't enough to stop our gradual chipping. A gold-green blood was now seeping through the cracks of their carapaces. A clear goopy substance poured from their battered leg joints.

I was throwing out fireball after fireball in an attempt to be somewhat useful while Aaron was nocking arrows. Even if we weren't all that much help, at least in this way we could raise our skill level, if nothing else.

Isabelle remained the farthest back, grouped together with the raids other three healers. The majority of healing power was being focused towards Jericho, who was fighting off two of these Royal Thief Bugs by himself.

Bryan was still facing off against the boss, but up to this point was in a complete standstill. The Golden Thief Bug had yet to make an earnest effort to attack. This was an acceptable and fortunate outcome. If he could avoid engaging it too heavily until all four Royal Guards were defeated, he would have the full support of the party, as well as a back-up tank.

Seeing their earth property and high HP, I was itching to cast *Meteor Storm*. Something I had appreciated, however, even from the first cast was that the Meteors materialized high in the sky. I didn't and couldn't test it here. If I cast it in this underground sewer, the Meteors might materialize above Egestor and pelt random civilians. How could I explain that accident? I couldn't.

A part of my focus shifted over the rest of the raid. We weren't held in high-regard, and because of this, I didn't have a great idea of the party makeup. No one had bothered to explain it to me. I had only managed to pick up a few names from their conversations. Looking now I could tell it was balanced.

Including me, there were three magic users, the other two being Lady Briele and a man named Luther. Bryan and Jericho were our two tanks. There were four healers total including Isabelle. Aaron made up one of three archers, and the final three party members were melee. All in all, a fifteen-man raid.

My attention was pulled back to the front. There was a shriek as one entire side of a Royal Thief Bug's legs were cut clean off, causing it to plop to the ground unevenly. Its throat began to gurgle as a viscous liquid sprayed out indiscriminately. With no real way to maneuver and position itself, the poison landed on the sewer floor in front of it.

The ground began to sizzle and smoke as the liquid melted a few inches into the surface. The royal guard was defenseless, its neck completely exposed. A greatsword came plummeting down onto it, lopping the head clean off.

The legs of the decapitated guard continued to flail and twitch in response for several moments before ceasing their movement. There was only one guard remaining on my side.

While it seemed like this series of events took a long time, in reality only about fifteen seconds of time had passed from the start of battle to the beheading. It was a quick and overpowering kill.

The pressure on the second guard rose exponentially as his movements became more erratic and desperate. The death of the royal guard had triggered the golden bug, who had now started engaging with Bryan. His shield let off sparks as the golden pincers brushed past it.

We were making quick work of the second guard when something peculiar happened. The royal guard crouched onto the ground and curled up, similar to what a roly-poly would do. It retracted every limb before its carapace began to morph and change. It looked like a last-ditch defensive effort.

Physical attacks couldn't even leave a dent in this new armor. Spells were deflected away and did no damage.

"What a pain in the ass." One of the melee whined. Everyone was of the same idea, it was just trying to stay alive, a natural instinct.

"Get back! NOW," one of the healers yelled out.

Something was happening inside that locked-down bug's armor, considerable energy was building. It began to tremble ever so slightly on the floor and even cracks started to form. Two of the melee had immediately retreated on the healer's command.

The third seemed to have a shitty attitude, and didn't like being bossed around. He hadn't taken the call seriously and was retreating at his own pace. The lump on the sewer floor went off like a bomb.

"*Holy Barrier!*" One of the healers yelled out from behind. His reaction was incredibly fast, and thankfully so. The armor disintegrated into shrapnel. The pressure of the explosion was so high that every piece shot out like a bullet.

I could see the near-invisible barrier in front of me morph and retract several times from the constant impacts. I could also hear a thunder-like cracking all around me, as pieces of debris shot off into the walls, columns, and ceiling.

The strength of the shrapnel was mind boggling. Each impact created a fresh new crack, or simply knocked off a large chunk of material from the walls. The columns directly surrounding the explosion were riddled with scars.

The man who had not heeded the warning had been flung twenty feet away and into a column, his back caked with wounds several inches deep. The rest of us stared in astonishment. A healer rushed over to him and began to provide treatment, "He's alive!" the healer yelled. Despite that, our melee comrade was unconscious and completely out of the fight.

Chapter 18: A Pleasant Windfall

Bryan and Jericho were both startled by the explosion. They were completely in the dark as to what occurred. "Someone tell me what's going on?" Bryan called back.

"We're okay! Stick to the plan," Lady Briele said. We moved as a group to the opposite side and were finally able to assist Jericho with the two remaining guards. We were prepared for the explosion this time. When one of the guards curled into a ball in an attempt to explode, we all rushed dozens of feet back and positioned ourselves behind any Column available.

His companion in battle was not so lucky. The second Royal Thief Bug had perished as a result of the self-destruction of the first. There were clear holes all the way through his carapace, a testament to the sheer power the explosion contained.

"Phew." Jericho wiped his sweaty brow. He took the time to assess his shield and scowled at the sight. There were indents and thick gashes. One gash forcefully tore into his shield and through the other side. "This was brand new too…" He pouted.

"When did you upgrade your *Inspect*?" Luther looked towards Lady Briele.

"Wasn't me." She glanced in my direction. From the look on both of their faces, it seemed the advanced version of *Inspect* was rare. At least rare enough to the extent that neither level 40+ caster had it.

It was now that we took the time to assess the overall situation. "How is Bryan doing?"

"We haven't had to heal him much. When we did, the damage was acceptable. It seems the boss is somewhere between high thirties and low forties in level. However, there is one problem…"

"Yes?"

"That was our only *Barrier*. We desperately wanted to save it in case of an emergency in the boss fight."

This news was worse for us than for the boss bug. While it might take a certain amount of damage from a long-range attack or AOE ability, there was a very low possibility of it dying from such attacks without a serious misjudgment or mistake.

On the other hand, Aaron, Isabelle and I could not say the same. Depending what ranged attacks or effects the boss had, we could easily die, and at the very least we were likely to be on death's door. Whether a healer could bring us back from that was uncertain.

The group started to fan out around Bryan as it was time to take on the boss. The two remaining melee classes approached carefully, waiting for Bryan's instruction. "Stay behind him and you should be okay. He's not very fast but he packs a hell of a bite." That this was true could be seen by the pincer holes on our tank's shield.

Try to Inspect *it.*

I looked towards Lady Briele and realized she was watching me with an expectant look. My previous experience told me *Inspect* didn't work on bosses. This was advanced *Inspect*, however and might be worth the attempt. I got close enough to try.

> **SKILL HAS FAILED. INSUFFICIENT LEVEL.**

I was not discouraged in the slightest. The first time I attempted to inspect a boss was inside the safe-zone. It was Necromancer Sezhul, The Blightcaller. There was also Feroce, but he didn't have the red skull above his head.

I still wasn't sure if he was a boss. Maybe he was considered a quest boss? Regardless, both casts had returned a simple "Invalid target," suggesting Inspect didn't work on bosses.

Advanced *Inspect* had returned a different response. I couldn't be sure if the level referred to my *Inspect* skill or my own level. Only time would be able to tell. I shook my head towards Lady Briele.

I'll talk to you after. She left me with one final message before turning away.

The two melee classes were in position behind the boss. One held an impressive looking double-axe and the other sported two daggers. They both went in to attack together. There were two clinking noises as the daggers struck the golden carapace. Its defense stat was so high that not even a scratch was left on the surface of its back.

"My turn!" The axe wielder raised it high before smashing it down with all his might. It came down like a jackhammer and landed blade first. The impact caused the air to crack and a sound wave rushed past us and into the darkness. It was so intense that it traveled and echoed all the way back to us. The echo of the blow repeatedly sounded out around us.

Besides causing the Golden Thief Bug to lower his body from the strength of the blow, there was no visible damage. The golden carapace remained unscratched, and the blow only managed to enrage it.

Unfortunately, the same could not be said for the axe wielder. "Fuck, that's hard." There was no more curve to his blade, it had thoroughly flattened on impact. It might as well be a hammer now instead.

This wouldn't be so bad if that was all. The webs of both of the fighter's hands had ripped open, especially the web of his thumb. His hands were covered in blood that dripped down the handle of his axe, making it slippery to hold. He backed away in a hurry and let go of the handle, doing his best to stop the shaking of hands.

One of the features of this boss Thief Bug that was different to the others was that its abdomen was not exposed in anyway. The carapace on its back went all the way across the top and even curved below a bit. Unless you were directly under it you couldn't see its abdomen.

The carapace that mostly enclosed this abdomen slowly opened like the walls of a fortress. Just a small portion of the tip was exposed. This minute movement was barely visible but I was studying the boss closely. Neither Bryan nor his dagger-wielding comrade were responding to it.

"Watch out!" I cried.

The axe wielder had broken an unspoken rule. Never take your eyes off the boss. This became especially true with how close he was to it. Yet, he was standing five or six feet away staring at his hands.

The abdomen silently pulsated before what looked like a stinger launched out. By the time he realized something was even moving in his direction it was too late for him to react. He looked down just in time to see this 'stinger' like object retract. It disappeared back into the abdomen and the fortress doors closed.

There wasn't enough time for the warrior to even scream in pain. He collapsed as if he didn't have a single bone in his body. The blood coming from his wound ceased being red and quickly turned black. The veins under his skin were turning black as the poison made its way up his neck.

The dagger-wielding man was quick to react and grabbed his companion beneath his armpits before dragging him away. He pulled out a *Panacea* and forcefully fed it to the poisoned raid member. Multiple *Heals* rained down on the wounded man. His life was saved, but he was out of the fight.

The dagger wielding man didn't return to battle either. Not out of fear, but because he was thoroughly useless. It was best for him to remain out of danger and to avoid wasting healer mana.

The golden armor seemed impenetrable. I felt there was now a lot of pressure on Lady Briele and Luther to perform. It was at this moment that Lady Briele's hands shone a deep shade of red. She slowly raised them from waist level and upwards towards the ceiling.

In response, a pillar of fire fully engulfed the golden Thief Bug. There was no expected reaction, no screech or even movement. The boss marinated in the fire as if unaffected, it almost seemed as if the fire was enjoyable to it.

Lady Briele looked surprised by the outcome. Not only were most insects earth property and thus weak to fire, it seemed the body of this boss was mostly gold. The pillar of fire burning beneath it was definitely hot enough to melt gold.

There were only two possible explanations for this phenomenon. One, the boss was so magic resistant the pillar had no effect, or two, the boss was fire property.

With a glance between them, Luther and Lady Briele began another round of magic spells. The temperature immediately dropped by several degrees.

There was suddenly a cool breeze in this stagnant chamber. I felt a chill up my back and neck. The sweat that was originally doing its best to keep me cool was now freezing cold. I couldn't help but shiver.

A storm materialized in the area just surrounding the golden Thief Bug. At first it was a strong gust of wind followed by a trickle of rain. That rain became hail and started to pelt the bosses' body. Finally, that wind and hail became a fully-fledged blizzard. The spell evolved into something incredible. Snow began to build up and coat the body of the boss.

For the first time we saw a reaction from the boss. It had taken every spell, every arrow and every slash without much effect. There was clear discomfort evident now though as it tried to force its way out of the storm. Bryan stood steadfast in front of it, refusing to budge an inch.

Luther added his spell into the mix. Giant shards of ice formed in the air before piercing downwards. They weren't hard enough to penetrate, but the weight and power behind them hammered into the Golden Thief Bug.

The sturdy body was quickly smashed into the sewer floor and gold-green blood started spurting from between its mandibles. Its legs were fighting against the weight of the onslaught until it could no longer hold out. Its legs slid outward on the now ice-covered floor. It was doing a split.

The snow continued to cover it until we could no longer see its body. Instead, there was a mound of white fluff where its body used to be. Both spells were soon coming to an end. In grand finale fashion, an icicle started to form in the air. It was dozens of times bigger than any that had previously appeared. A giant stalactite several feet in diameter came crashing down with great force. The impact shook the entire sewer.

I was thoroughly impressed by the destructive ability of these two spells, although when all was said and done, there was a block of ice and snow several feet tall and wide just in front of Bryan. I couldn't help but feel the ending to be anticlimactic.

As if my mind had been read, there came a cracking noise. The sound was intense and deep, like the snap of thunder. A sudden explosion of energy sent shards of ice, as well as Bryan, flying from the mound. He had not let his guard down and kept his shield well in front of his body. Despite that, he was sent flying over ten feet and smashed into a pillar before sliding down.

The tomb of ice that was encasing the golden Thief Bug had shattered like glass and flew in every which direction. My energy shield flickered to block part of a shard of ice. The rest continued onward and slid across my cheek directly under my left eye. I reached up and felt the gash that now had blood flowing out if it. It hurt like hell.

I was positioned very far in the back and had only been spectating. There was really no place for me to involve myself with a boss twice my level. Despite the distance I had put myself at, I could have easily lost an eye.

Some of the people in front of me were not so lucky. Shards of ice had peppered their face and arms leaving skin deep gashes and holes. The wounds were by no means deadly, but they must hurt like hell.

The golden Thief Bug did not give us the time to assess the damage. It was now free from its restraints and a faint red glow surrounded it. There were visible gaps in its armor all over its body.

A purple carapace could be seen below. It was the same color as the Royal Thief Bugs.

Bryan had been blasted into the main group and was nowhere near in range to intercept the boss. This was exactly why tanks in general were so important, and why they had prepared a back-up. Jericho rushed forward to buy precious time.

Standing in front of the boss, Jericho smashed out with his shield. A simple blunt attack aimed at delaying an opponent. The boss seemed to want nothing to do with him. It's now golden-purple pincers grasped his shield, which crumpled like aluminum can as the pincers closed around it.

The shield was nearly cut all the way through when the golden Thief Bug jerked its head. Jericho went flying like a tossed doll, before smacking into the wall. He had gained us just three seconds of time.

Fortunately, three seconds was all the time Bryan needed to stand and get in front of the party once more. He rushed with shield and sword in hand before stabbing out. Aiming clearly for the purple carapace beneath the golden coloring, his guess did not let him down.

The purple carapace below did not have nearly as much resistance to attacks. The tip of his sword managed to pierce half an inch deep before it would go no further. "Aim for the purple!" He yelled back.

The Golden Thief Bug tried to throw him off in an attempt to make it to the main party. Bryan would have nothing to do with it. He used his sword like an expert, counter-attacking at every possible moment. Arrows continued to find their way into every crack and crevice. The bug started to panic.

As a familiar gurgle came from the Golden Thief Bugs throat, Bryan crouched and covered his entire body. A liquid as dark as night and goopy like tar sprayed out and coated the front of his shield. It started to melt instantly, like pouring boiling water onto a stick of butter. Bryan was left with no choice but to throw it aside.

Bryan didn't let that faze him. He pulled a new shield from his inventory, albeit a lower quality one, and continued to hinder and harass the boss. In particular, he seemed determined to not let the boss get past him.

The golden armor continued to be chipped away by the ongoing assault. The purplish carapace was revealed piece by piece, until most of the golden armor had been blown off. Our enemy was looking more and more like a Royal Thief Bug.

The boss's movements became sluggish. It stopped dodging attacks as arrow and spell alike bombarded it. The purple carapace was beaten and worn, not offering nearly as much resistance as before. Screeches of sorrow occasionally left its throat.

The situation was dire for the golden Thief Bug. It was putting in a mighty effort just to stay standing, which wasn't enough. Arrows littered its back and the area around its neck. Its originally majestic body was riddled with wounds. It looked like a porcupine.

Gold-green blood dripped down its barely holding legs and pooled below it. Finally, came the killing blow: a shard of ice dropped from above and pierced directly through its back, nearly splitting it in half. It let out one last cry before its red eyes rolled back. It ceased moving.

Everyone watched with bated breath. Not daring to let their guard down for a moment. Relief came as soon as the boss started to despawn. It was finally over.

Bryan wiped the sweat from his brow before falling to his ass. "Phewwww."

"Yahhoooooo."

Everyone quickly gathered around the corpse in anticipation of the loot. Knowing that I wasn't going to receive anything put a damper on my excitement. I would rather not know what dropped than see something amazing and be unable to grasp it.

Although I said that, seeing the shining light from between the bodies of the raid participants made me incredibly curious. Something they were standing around was glowing gold. As far as I'd ever seen, items glowed white. Even the Advanced Inspect skill book was glowing white.

Hey, come over here.

I made my way over filled with anticipation. A little path opened up for me and I managed to slip in between Bryan and Lady Briele. I finally got to see what the golden glow was.

It was a gemstone the size of a fist rotating in the air. There was a golden glow around it, while the gem itself changed colors depending on the angle I viewed it from. It was like a rainbow had been trapped inside. Adjacent to the stunning gem was a spell book.

"Would you stop drooling and take the book?" Lady Briele nudged me in the arm.

"Huh?" I came to my senses only to be shocked by the words coming out of her mouth. "But why? I didn't do anything." I really didn't contribute much. After witnessing the Royal guard's explosion, I didn't dare go near in the second scuffle.

"Just stop complaining and take it." I looked around for confirmation and noticed a lot of unhappy faces. It seemed it took considerable convincing on her part to get them to allow me to have it.

"It's fine, take it," Bryan repeated.

"Thank you." I scooped it up and quickly backed away.

BOOK OF BALL LIGHTNING LV. 1
CAST TIME: 3 SECONDS
MP COST: 12
DISTANCE: 10 METERS
THROWS OUT A BALL OF LIGHTNING THAT REPEATEDLY STRIKES ENEMIES IN AND AROUND ITS PATH

I read the description as I made my way to Aaron and Isabelle. The two of them were off to the side, also excluded from loot discussions.

"What was that about?" Aaron asked.

"I got a skill book."

"You-you got an item? For what?"

"Dunno," I pulled out the glowing white book and hugged it tightly. "But it's sweeeeeeet."

I learned it in front of the two of them. It was the first lightning spell I had obtained. The fact that it was practically free somehow made it that much sweeter.

Reading the ability gave me a realization. It sounded incredibly similar in description to the ball of lightning Lady Briele had used during the Naga invasion. This might explain why I was allowed to have the book. Both spell casters probably owned the spell already.

"Let's see it cast," Isabelle asked.

I held out my hand and started channeling *Ball Lightning*. The hairs of my right arm began to stand and a tingling sensation filled the air around us. Isabelle couldn't help herself and poked Aaron.

"Ouch," he exclaimed. The two of them had received a little shock.

A ball of lightning formed in my hand about the size of an apple. Electrical snakes raced over the surface and all around my hand. I watched it floating above my hand before 'throwing' it out like a baseball. Contrary to what I expected to happen, it didn't fly out with the speed and force at which I threw it.

The *Ball Lightning* seemed to have a predetermined speed. It started off fast and then slowed considerably, shrinking and disappearing after reaching the ten Meter distance. That suggested there was a 'sweet spot': the spot between my casting point and the ending point, where it would deal the most efficient damage.

I summoned another *Ball Lightning* and then threw it out as well. I studied the distance to the best of my ability. It seemed like the ball traveled fast up until about four meters away. Once at four meters, it slowed considerably and then diminished as it maintained that speed until disappearing at ten meters.

Four meters was the closest I would want an enemy to be to me if I planned to use this efficiently. I also couldn't be sure how far the leaps of lightning would reach when leaping across to enemies.

These observations confirmed to me that this was the spell cast by Lady Briele during the Naga invasion. I had absolutely no complaints about the distance and destructive power of each bolt hers had produced. The only issue was that if my *Ball Lightning* was an apple, hers was a watermelon. It would be foolish to guess at my destructive power based on her mastery of the spell.

I was so entranced that I didn't realize the discussion had concluded. The sparkling gem had been assigned to someone, I didn't know to whom though.

Defeating the boss was only the first objective in this mission, albeit the only difficult one. The second was to assess the traps and determine the reason for such poor water flow. The traps were not far from our battle, about a thirty second walk. We made our way over.

The reason was appalling. The base of the trap was stacked high with decaying bodies. The smell was tame and almost unnoticeable, but only because most of the bodies were picked clean. A few still had bits of bloated flesh on their bones.

The missing guards' armor and weapons lay scattered about the ground as well. The evidence of how gruesome their deaths had been was readily apparent. There were hands inside gloves, feet inside greaves, and even entire ribcages inside their armor.

Thief Bugs seemed to have an instinctual dislike for water, at least enough to avoid falling into it. It was most likely that these bodies were picked clean recently, probably in the last day or two. It would've had to happen after the water level dropped. It was a valid hypothesis: their king was fire property after all.

A disgusting thought entered my brain that made me even more depressed. What if some of them hadn't died instantly? What if they had discovered the Thief Bugs' fear of water and had knowingly jumped into the trap? How long did they sit in this sewage water hoping for rescue?

A priest walked forward and started to pray, "Dear lord, accept these souls unto your mercy. The journey is treacherous. I beg you to guide, protect, and accept them into your care. Amen."

"We'll report this when we get back." Bryan said.

"We're done?" I was curious. I thought we would go on exterminating everything.

"A secondary team will come down to clean up. That includes checking for any remaining egg sacs and bugs, though I doubt they'll find any." I could only accept his answer.

You shouldn't worry about it so much. It was Lady Briele getting into my head again. *Usually with colonies like this, killing the king or queen is a death sentence for all its members.* She was too far away for me to respond so I simply nodded my head in understanding.

It was time to leave this wretched place. I allowed the main force to go in front and stayed towards the back with Aaron and Isabelle. The two injured members were still unconscious and needed to be carried out. *Could this really be a success?*

We had clearly succeeded, but was that good enough? The occasional cheer and excited chattering at the front confirmed that the rest of the raid felt so. We made it halfway to the surface when Lady Briele squeezed through the front crowd and walked with us.

"Am I intruding?" she asked.

"Well… no, but you could have used telepathy." Her walking beside me and talking to me for some reason brought me several annoyed stares. She was too popular for her own good.

"Then how will I hear your response?" She had me there. "Do you two think I'm intruding?" She looked towards Aaron and Isabelle.

"Not at all." Despite saying this, Aaron grabbed Isabelle and quickened his steps.

Lady Briele slowed her steps in response and soon there was a large distance between us and the main group. "What's gotten into them all the sudden?" she smiled. I looked at her face and eyes, highly suspicious that she just used telepathy. "I wanted to ask you about *Inspect.* Do you remember?"

"Uh-huh."

"Good. So tell me, where did you get it?" I told her about the battle with the Female Thief Bug in detail.

"So the little bug dropped it?"

"Right." I couldn't help but look at the spell description again, taking note of the three stars next to its name. Those stars and Lady Briele's interest showed that it was very rare.

"So when you cast it on the boss, what did it say?"

"Skill has failed. Insufficient level."

"Do you know the most valuable thing when fighting a boss?"

"Uhh…." I racked my brain, but there were so many answers I could throw out.

"It's information." She tapped my head. "If you haven't already noticed, *Inspect* can't be used on bosses, super-rares, and three-star uniques." I nodded my head to follow along. I'd never heard of a super-rare, and I'd never seen a three-star unique before. "It's not a matter of your level, or skill level. *Inspect* will never work on those three mob types."

"So you're saying that I will eventually be able to see the stats of those monsters?"

"Yep, and while it isn't so important on Eastrath, it's incredibly important in North Maledith."

"Why's that?"

"Well… It's because a boss spawning in Eastrath is a rare occurrence, but not so much in North Maledith."

"I don't understand." Aaron had told me the difference in the two continents was simply level range of monsters.

"Monsters appear much more frequently in North Maledith, dozens of times more." She continued. "In Eastrath you can leave Egestor and travel by foot to the nearest city or town. You might

414

encounter a monster here or there, but your journey will mostly be peaceful. You can't do that in North Maledith."

"It's that bad?"

"Yep, many people arrive thinking they can handle it, only to decide they want nothing to do with it. Most of those people end up stuck, but the ones who can afford the trip back return to Eastrath."

I was wondering what the point of her telling me all of this was, "Is that what you did?"

She forced a laugh, but I could hear a bit of anger behind it. "You seem to be mistaking me as a coward that runs away?"

"I… I wouldn't dare."

"Good. We're here for business." She noticed me staring in the direction of the crowd ahead. "I'm speaking for me, Bryan, dagger boy, the nasty, snarling archer, and the healer who said the prayer. The rest just happened to be available for this raid."

The nasty, snarling archer… It was an apt description I had to admit. "So can you tell me why I got the skill book?"

There was a bit of hesitation before some flowery words came out, "I think you deserved it."

"So… it isn't because you have a skill just like it?"

"No… no not at all," she fumbled out.

"A similar skill that you used during the Naga invasion, perhaps?" I hit the nail on the head.

She coughed. "Okay. Luther and I both have it. The others wanted to sell it and I didn't think that was right. Best to have someone using it. Happy?"

I actually did feel happy. "So why do monsters spawn more frequently in North Maledith?"

"No one knows the specific reason why. But as you move more west the monster spawns increase and so does their strength."

"West of the continent?"

"No, the western part of Yetera."

"So what about West Abithos then?"

"Uninhabited hellhole. You're liable to die a hundred times just trying to get over there, let alone stepping on the shore."

"Has anyone tried?"

"Of course they've tried. Some have even succeeded. However, none ever stay for long. Those that try to stay too long end up staying forever, if you catch my drift." How ominous.

It was time to ask the question that was bothering me the most. "So why are you telling me all this?"

She countered my question with one of her own, "After hearing all of this, do you still want to go to North Maledith?"

I could have just thrown out a 'hell yeah!', but I really wanted to think about my answer. We walked in silence for a few minutes before I was ready. "Yeah, I want to go." In the end, I thought about the excitement I had when playing with *Ball Lightning*. That was just one such example. There was a hunger inside of me that didn't exist before.

She suddenly had the most beautiful smile on her face. "Okay. You should pack up soon 'cause we leave in three days."

"Wai... huh?"

"My party is leaving in three days on a Zeppelin. Oh, I guess Luther is coming along as well. He's gonna help with the wind magic. It won't be as fast as the association's Zeppelin, but a month isn't so bad, right?" She rambled on. "Three days from now at the mission hall, tell your friends!" She didn't even give me a chance to respond before rushing away. Just before she passed through the crowd our eyes met. *Don't be late!*

Aaron and Isabelle kept looking back at me curiously. Even after she left I had maintained my slow pace and didn't bother trying to catch up with them. They were left with no choice but to fall back to my distance.

"So what did the pretty sister want?" Isabelle asked.

"Are you two absolutely certain you want to go to North Maledith?" They both looked confused at my sudden question.

"Yes. But where did that come from?" Aaron asked.

"They leave in three days. She offered us a spot on their Zeppelin." Offer didn't seem to be right word. It was almost as if I had no choice but to accept.

"That's...FUCKING GREAT!" Isabelle shouted. It echoed down the tunnel and attracted everyone's attention. "Oh, oops." She covered her mouth.

"Let's do it," Aaron said. His response was calm but he was jittery with excitement. I nodded at both of them.

I had to be honest with myself. A part of me had scoffed at the idea of coming on this raid for 'experience.' I felt much better after receiving the skill book. The biggest reward, however, was definitely this free airfare.

A feeling of disappointment and uncertainty when looking at those two injured members vanished like the wind. In just about a month I would be standing on continent of North Maledith.

Everyone on the raid was treated like royalty immediately upon return. The mission hall had been completely closed off and guards lined the pathway leading up its stairs. They stood statue still and saluted us. It was all so surreal.

Don't get used to it. Lady Briele winked at me.

The top brass of the mission hall, as well as royalty, were waiting inside for us. I felt so out of place. They crowded around Bryan as he theatrically described the battle. He made sure to embellish the story for a bit more excitement. They ate it up.

Lance was one of the guards stationed inside. Not that we needed protection, or that the guards could even keep the royals safe from the Adventurers, it was all formality. It was all for show. I walked over to him.

"Been a few days," I said.

"It has." His answer was curt, almost rude. I noticed his eyes glancing towards a certain mission hall representative. It seemed he would get in trouble for doing anything other than quietly watching.

"Well, I wanted to thank you." He seemed genuinely confused. Not for why I was thanking him, but that an Adventurer would bother to go out of their way to thank him, a regular person. He didn't respond so I kept talking. "I think it was probably your doing. You put in a good word to Glasses for us. I doubt he would have even considered giving us a chance if not."

I continued to ramble on and on and he seemed genuinely relieved that I wasn't pushing him to respond. He stood there like a statue quietly absorbing every word. "There's a chance we'll never see each other again after this. It was nice knowing you."

The three of us left the mission hall well before the party ended. The quiet walk back to the inn made me realize I didn't have any real attachment to this place. Leaving would be easy.

The three days flew by.

I made sure we weren't late on the third morning. Lady Briele was waiting and waved us over.

"This is Frederick, our priest."

"Nice to meet you," Frederick said.

"This is Cid." It was the nasty snarling archer.

"Hmmph." He only grunted. His nickname was well deserved. "And this is…"

"Venom, I like being called Venom so call me that." The fighter with the daggers interrupted Lady Briele. "Nice to meet you."

I could see Bryan and Luther standing in the back. I had already met the both of them. "Everyone's here so let's get going." Bryan said. We walked as a group to the royal compound. We didn't go inside. Instead, we walked around the beautiful castle to a garden behind.

What might have once been a garden was more accurately called a field. The Zeppelin was waiting above an open patch of grass. I had an image of a Zeppelin in my mind, and somehow the picture in front of me was almost identical.

It was a moderately sized boat with a long balloon hovering above it. There were sails – currently kept out of the way – for controlling and gathering the breeze. It was gently hovering just above the grass below.

We took turns climbing a ladder on the side before standing atop the deck. It was a lot cleaner that I had expected. The floors were smooth and shiny, as if waxed. The boards didn't creak at all either. I expected something more worn and rugged.

There was a crew already atop waiting for us. They started to take our luggage and showed us to our room. I was honestly surprised, but I didn't know what gave me the idea we would be flying it ourselves. Everything about this was above expectation.

The rooms were small but had a cozy feeling. The beds were nice and especially clean. There was actually nothing I could find fault with. After I thoroughly inspected my room I returned to top deck.

The crew had just finished pulling up the anchor that kept us from floating off slowly. Aaron and Isabelle seemed just as surprised and delighted as I.

"I can see why the charge of seventy-five," Aaron said. We all both nodded our heads in agreement.

It seemed that Bryan had overheard this comment. "Actually, those association airships are pretty junk. They pack you in like rats on those. This is private."

I decided to take the time to understand the airship better and worked my way around the deck. Without bothering the crew, of course.

I couldn't help but move from person to person and peek over their shoulder to see what they were doing. One guy controlled the mast and steered the craft carefully. There was another crewmember below deck feeding a furnace with coal. The hot air pumped into the balloon and kept us afloat. Another could be found below deck working strictly on navigation. The others that were around either acted as chaperone's and made sure our needs were met.

For the first hour or so we simply floated into the sky. There was serious balance involved to keep us level. Too low and we risked crashing, too high and other problems arrived: mainly breathing ones.

A horn blew to symbolize things were good to go and Luther and Lady Briele got to work. Their job was to simply blow the sails, and blow the sails they did. We moved above the ground at a decent pace. It looked slow from our perspective, but it was only because we were so high up.

Unfortunately, the marvel of it faded pretty quickly and boredom set in. There wasn't much to do, wasn't anywhere to go. I wasn't allowed to haphazardly cast spells either, just in case I ended up destroying something.

The first week was spent twiddling my thumbs and passing the time any way possible. A bit of the excitement came back once we started passing over the ocean. The saltiness in the air was a nice change of smell.

I was standing on the deck with Lady Briele beside me. "Why don't they attack us?" There were monsters flying around in the air. They looked menacing enough, but always kept their distance. I was actually itching for some action.

These flying monsters hadn't started appearing till we were two days out to sea and there was an assorted variety. Some I recognized – the wyverns and the harpies – others were completely foreign to me.

"Instinct," she said. "Take that monster over there for example. It's only level twenty-seven. If you were level twenty-seven would you want to fight a Zeppelin full of forties?"

The monster in question was so far out. It seemed to sense her attention and bolted into the distance. "You cast *Inspect* from this range?" I asked.

"Are you jealous? The one with Advanced *Inspect*? THE super-duper-rare Advanced *Inspect*? Stop whining." She flicked my forehead. In the past few days I had gotten used to such behavior. Flicking or poking, my head was absolutely not off-limits to her. I had stopped complaining about it at all.

I felt spoiled. The journey was going too smoothly. I actually wanted something challenging to happen for the excitement.

Unfortunately, nothing did. We were about a day out when the North Maledith continent came into view.

"We're gonna drop you three off at the coastal town Cape Tou."

"We're not going with you?"

"Did you wanna die, idiot?" She flicked my head again. "You have to progress on your own."

"Okay."

My curt response seemed to worry her. "Don't worry. It's a noobie town. You'll be fine."

"Alright, thanks."

"If you wanna get there faster then don't distract me, these sails aren't gonna blow themselves."

We arrived early next morning.

Aaron, Isabelle and I huddled together right on the edge of the Zeppelin. We were coming down just above the water. There was a manmade dock that stretched from the coast of Cape Tou about a hundred feet into the ocean.

"I'm sure you'll catch up to us soon." Bryan looked over our group. We had all grown fond of him during the trip. He was like the big brother you didn't have but definitely wanted. No question ever seemed to get on his nerves, and he was always ready to help.

"Alright, this is as low as we go," said Lady Briele.

It was time for us to get off. We made for the side ladder when a gust of wind blew the three of us off the Zeppelin and placed us safely on the dock below. I couldn't help but look back in astonishment.

"Why didn't you do this when we needed to get on?" I yelled up.

"You-you little brat! I do something nice and this is how you respond?" Lady Briele was giving me a scolding from the edge of the deck. I was definitely too far for her to flick me in the head now. I couldn't help but chuckle

"I think I can speak for all three of us when I say we can't thank you enough." Aaron started to bow. Isabelle and I followed his lead.

The Zeppelin started to rise once again into the sky. Luther and Cid were nowhere to be found, but the other four were standing at the edge wishing us well. They each said goodbye in their own way.

Frederick closed his hands as if in prayer and gave us a bow in return. Bryan started to slap his sword into his shield over and over. The metal crashing into wood sounded like loud clapping. Venom was perched on the side of the ship with both daggers in his hand. He swirled them between his fingers with a smile on his face. I thought he was going to fall at any time.

Lady Briele was basically hanging off the ship like a lunatic. She kept waving her hands back and forth, "Good luck! Don't forget me when you're famous!" She yelled down. We happily waved back.

Very soon the shouting and clapping faded out. The Zeppelin became a blip in the sky above us. All we could hear was the sound of the wind and waves. We walked forward completely unsure of what we were getting ourselves into it.

The scenery after stepping off the pier was nothing I expected. The ground was like a hard sand, and the buildings around were not advanced in the slightest: like beach huts on a tropical island.

What shocked me the most though, were the people. There were crowds of people everywhere.

"Looking for a level twenty plus tank! You must know the skill *Shield Crash*!"

"Party of four seeking priest, prefer beautiful females but all may apply!"

"I'm looking for a party for crusty cove! I'm a level twenty-three Assassin!"

"Hey you! Come check out my wares here, I got tons of good stuff!"

"Is anyone here a blacksmith? I need a blacksmith to repair my sword!"

The entire area was bustling with requests and offers. I was blown away. I looked at Aaron and Isabelle with a smile. "It's time to level."

Level Up publishing specializes in LitRPG and GameLit books. If you have enjoyed *The RPG Apocalypse* you might be interested in our other titles, which can be found at www.levelup.pub/books

To join our mailing list for news about forthcoming books and opportunities to be an ARC reader, just fill in the form on that page.

You can also find us on:
Facebook @LUPublishing
Twitter @LevelUpPub
And by searching for Level Up WhatsApp group

www.ingramcontent.com/pod-product-compliance
Lightning Source LLC
Chambersburg PA
CBHW030913050726
47498CB00003BA/717